# Praise for

### TWILIGHT EMPRESS (Theodosian Women #1)

"A fun, fast…addictive read, as Justice chooses her key moments wisely, weaving a decades-long narrative about Placidia's layered life as she rises to eventual leadership." — *Kirkus Reviews*

"Solid historical fiction, with full marks for a little-used time period and setting. It totally gets extra points for giving us a female lead character who's not written about to death." — *Historical Novel Society Reviews*

"A fast-paced historical novel that is filled with romance, political and courtly intrigue, and drama that will keep you turning the pages. I can't wait to read the next book about Empress Pulcheria. — *History from a Woman's Perspective*

### DAWN EMPRESS (Theodosian Women #2)

"Justice chronicles, with a skillful blend of historical rigor and dramatic action…a gripping tale of a royal sister's fraught political machinations. The prose is razor sharp, and the tale is as impressively unsentimental as it is genuinely moving." — *Kirkus Reviews*

"A deftly written and impressively entertaining historical novel in which the author pays due attention to detail while ably crafting memorable characters and riveting plot twists and turns." — *Midwest Book Reviews*

"Justice has penned another outstanding novel…Highly recommended." — *Historical Novel Society Reviews* Critics' Choice

### SELENE OF ALEXANDRIA

"Readers will be captivated…and find a promising new historical novelist [with] the gift for wonderfully researched, vividly evoked, good old-fashioned storytelling." — *Historical Novel Society Reviews*

"*Selene of Alexandria* is pure fiction magic…I couldn't put this book down… [It] made me laugh and cry, hope and despair." — *Story Circle Book Reviews*

"This book is outstanding, not just for a first novel, but for any novel. Once you've read it, I'm sure you'll join me in waiting impatiently to read Justice's next project!" — *Lacuna: Journal of Historical Fiction*

## BOOKS BY FAITH L. JUSTICE

### Novels

*Selene of Alexandria*
*Sword of the Gladiatrix (Gladiatrix #1)*
*Becoming the Twilight Empress (Theodosian Women Novella)*
*Twilight Empress (Theodosian Women #1)*
*Dawn Empress (Theodosian Women #2)*
*Rebel Empress (Theodosian Women #3)*

### Short Story Collections

*The Reluctant Groom and Other Historical Stories*
*Time Again and Other Fantastic Stories*
*Slow Death and Other Dark Tales*

### Non-fiction

*Hypatia, Her Life and Times*

### Children's Books

*Tokoyo, the Samurai's Daughter (Adventurous Girls #1)*

# Dawn Empress

## Faith L. Justice

Raggedy Moon Books

**DAWN EMPRESS: A NOVEL OF IMPERIAL ROME**

*(Theodosian Women Book Two)*


*Copyright © 2020 Faith L. Justice*
*All rights reserved.*


*2020*
*Raggedy Moon Books*
*Brooklyn, New York, USA*
*raggedymoonbooks.com*


*Cover design by Jennifer Quinlan*
*historicaleditorial.com*


*Paperback ISBN: 978-0917053269*
*Hardback ISBN: 978-0917053238*
*Epub ISBN: 978-0917053177*
*AudioBook: 978-0917053252*
*Library of Congress Control Number: 2019914538*

*To my bright, creative daughter Hannah Justice Rothman,
without whom I wouldn't be a novelist.*

*"The Byzantines did not call themselves Byzantines,
but* Romaioi--Romans.*"*

Robert Browning, *The Byzantine Empire*

# CONTENTS

# Theodosian Genealogy

Emperors shown in SMALL CAPS.

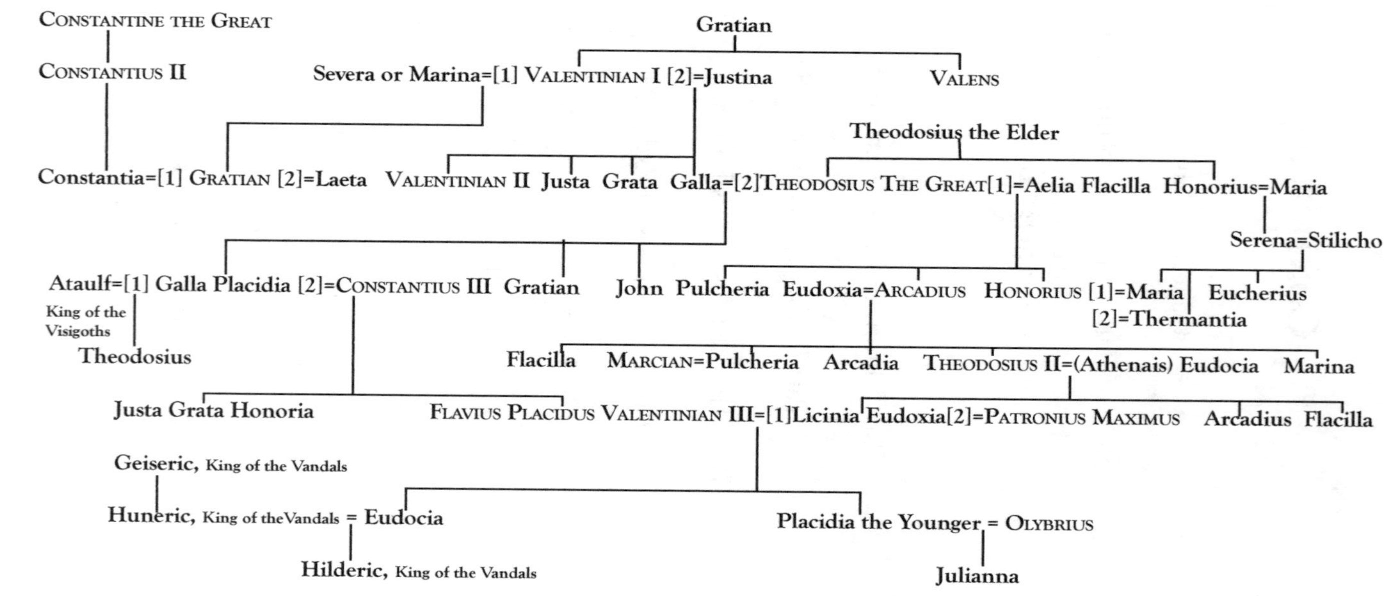

# Note on Imperial Titles and Place Names

IMPERIAL ROMAN TITLES EVOLVED OVER TIME. The title AUGUSTUS (Latin for "majestic," "the increaser," or "venerable") is the equivalent of the modern "Emperor," and was conferred on the first emperor, Octavian (great-nephew and adopted son of Julius Caesar), by the senate in 27 BC. Every emperor after held the title of Augustus, which always followed the family name. The first emperor conferred the title AUGUSTA on his wife, Livia, in his will. Other imperial wives (but not all) earned this supreme title. By the fifth century, sisters and daughters also could be elevated to this status, but only by a sitting Augustus. I use Emperor/Empress and Augustus/Augusta interchangeably throughout the text.

Octavian took his adoptive father's name, Gaius Julius Caesar, but later dropped the Gaius Julius. CAESAR became the imperial family name and was passed on by adoption. When the Julio-Claudian line died out, subsequent emperors took the name as a sign of status on their accession, adoption, or nomination as heir apparent. By the fifth century, it was the title given to any official heir to the Augustus (it's also the root of the modern titles Kaiser and Czar).

Children of imperial families were usually given the title NOBILISSIMUS/NOBILISSIMA ("Most Noble" boy/girl). This is the closest equivalent to the modern Prince/Princess, though not an exact match. The title was usually conferred some years after birth, in anticipation that the child would take on higher office (Caesar or Augustus for a boy, Augusta for a girl). I generally use the modern title Princess instead of Nobilissima throughout the text.

There is no direct Roman equivalent for the title Regent—someone who legally rules during the absence, incapacity, or minority of a country's monarch. In Imperial Rome, only males could wield magisterial power. An underage Augustus was still ruler in his own name. He must sign all laws and declarations for them to be legal. In reality, adults stepped into the role and administered the empire for minors. Placidia Augusta filled that role for her son Valentinian Augustus III (*Twilight Empress*). Anthemius does that for Theodosius II in *Dawn Empress*. The legal Roman term for that person is *tutela* meaning "guardian" or "tutor" for an adult (usually a man) who handled the affairs of someone (usually women and children) who would ordinarily be under the legal protection and control of the *pater familias* (male head of the family), but who were legally emancipated. I chose to use the more familiar term Regent throughout this book.

With one exception (Constantinople for modern Istanbul), I chose to use the modern names of cities and the anglicized rather than Latin names of provinces.

# CHARACTERS (*fictional in italics*)

## EASTERN ROME

### The Imperial Family: Constantinople Court

FLAVIUS ARCADIUS AUGUSTUS married to AELIA EUDOXIA AUGUSTA
**Daughters:**
AELIA PULCHERIA AUGUSTA
Arcadia
Marina
**Son:**
FLAVIUS THEODOSIUS AUGUSTUS II married to AELIA EUDOCIA (ATHENAIS) AUGUSTA
**Their daughters:**
LICINIA EUDOXIA AUGUSTA (married to Valentinian Augustus below)
Flacilla

### Imperial Servants:

*Nana/Elpida*, nurse
Antiochus, Chief Eunuch and head of household for Arcadius
*Father Marcus*, priest assigned to the nursery, and tutor to Pulcheria
Chrysaphius, Chief Eunuch and head of household for Theodosius II

### Nobles and Government Officials:

Anthemius "The Great", Patrician and Praetorian Prefect of the East
Isidorus, son of Anthemius, and Praetorian Prefect of the City of Constantinople
Flavius Anthemius Isidorus Theophilus, son of Isidorus and grandson of Anthemius
Paulinus, Theodosius' childhood companion, best friend, and Master of Offices
Placitus, Theodosius' childhood companion
Aurelian, former trusted advisor to Eudoxia Augusta, Patrician to Theodosius II
Olympiodorus of Thebes, pagan poet, diplomat, and historian
Leontius of Antioch, Athenais' father, philosopher and chair of rhetoric at Athens
Asclepiodotus, Athenais' maternal uncle, Praetorian Prefect of the East
*Doria*, wife of Asclepiodotus
Valerius, Athenais' brother, Prefect of Illyricum
Gesius, Athenais' brother, Prefect of Illyricum
Candidian, Count and imperial envoy to Ephesus
Cyrus of Panopolis, Praetorian Prefect of the East
Constantinus, Praetorian Prefect of the East

**Military:**
General Lucius, Master of Soldiers
General Plinta, Master of Soldiers in the Emperor's Presence, Consul
General Ardaburius, Master of Soldiers in the Emperor's Presence
General Aspar, Master of Soldiers in the Emperor's Presence
Tribune Marcian, later General

**The Church of Constantinople:**
Archbishop Atticus (406-425)
Archbishop Sissinius (426-427)
Archbishop Nestorius (428-431)
Bishop Proclus (434-446)
*Basil*, envoy from Proclus to Pulcheria
Archbishop Flavian (446-449)
Archbishop Anatolius (449-458)
Dalmatius, Archimandrite
Eutyches, Archimandrite

**Other Church officials/Holy Persons:**
Passarion of Jerusalem
Bishop Cyril of Alexandria (412-444)
*Archdeacon Paul* of Alexandria
Bishop Memnon of Ephesus
Melania the Younger
*Geilar*, Arian priest and envoy from King Gaeseric of the Vandals
Bishop Dioscorus of Alexandria (444-454)
Bishop Juvenal of Jerusalem (422-458)
Pope Leo I "The Great" of Rome (440-461)

**WESTERN ROME: RAVENNA COURT**

**Imperial Family:**
Flavius Honorius Augustus (co-ruler with Arcadius and Theodosius II above)
Galla Placidia Augusta (half-sister to Honorius and Arcadius)
married to Flavius Constantius Augustus III
**Their children:**
Justa Grata Honoria Augusta
Flavius Placidius Valentinian Augustus III married to Licinia Eudoxia (above)
**Their daughters:**
Eudocia "The Younger"
Placidia "The Younger"

# Dawn Empress

# Part I

# Princess to Empress

# October 404 - November 415

# Chapter 1

*Imperial Palace, Constantinople, October 6, 404*

PULCHERIA WINCED AS HER FATHER'S HAND GROUND HER FINGERS together. She stepped on the hem of her night shift and stumbled. Father jerked her upright.

"Come, girl, when did you become so clumsy?" His voice was rough with wine, anger, and pain. Pulcheria had never seen him so distraught in her five short years of life. For the first time her father Arcadius, the Emperor of Eastern Rome, frightened her.

When he had awakened her moments before, her head muzzy with dreams, she knew something was wrong. Father never came to her chambers. The palace nursery, where she and her siblings Arcadia, Theodosius, and baby Marina lived, was the province of nurses and tutors. She only saw him on those rare occasions he ordered the children to accompany him on some outing. Her mother, Empress Eudoxia, inspected the nursery and questioned the servants about her children's health and well-being when it suited her—which was not often. Now her father dragged her down the echoing marble halls toward a part of the palace to which she had never been.

They entered a sumptuous but disordered receiving room. A half-eaten meal of beef doused with fishy smelling garum sauce sat on a silver tray, the Persian carpet lay askew, and several cloaks lay carelessly on a gilt chair. The disarray only added to her chaotic feelings of fear and bewilderment. She tried to lag behind, but her father dragged her forward, nearly pulling her off her feet. Pulcheria whimpered at the pain in her hand and shoulder but refused to cry out.

Antiochus, the Chief Eunuch and head of the imperial household, sat near the door to another chamber. He rose, approached her father, and bowed low. "I'm so very sorry, Augustus, but your blessed wife is dead. She passed on to God's good grace but moments ago."

"More likely she passed on to the devil. She will make him a good whore." Arcadius' face went purple as he spat the words at the eunuch. "The child?"

Antiochus glanced at Pulcheria and lowered his voice. "He came much too early to save."

"Better dead than another set of horns on my head," her father muttered.

Pulcheria struggled to find meaning in the words of the adults. Her mother was dead? What child? Her father grew horns? She looked at his forehead with muddled curiosity but saw no bumps.

Father started forward, pushing at the eunuch's chest. "Out of my way."

Antiochus stepped back, but still blocked their path. His voice quavered. "Most Kind Augustus, is this really the place for the princess? Let us at least ready the body before she views it."

Pulcheria tugged on her captive hand and cried, "Please, Father, let me go back."

Father's hand tightened on hers, but he turned and dropped to one knee to look into her face. "This is important, Pulcheria. You will be first lady of the land now. Show me how an Augusta behaves."

Pulcheria steadied under his gaze. She wanted to make him proud. "Yes, Father, I will do as you wish."

"That's my girl. You've got a backbone, unlike your sniveling brother."

A small flame of anger at this attack on her baby brother warmed Pulcheria's chilled body. Theo was not quite three, and still a child. As the oldest, everyone demanded more from her, and she was proud to give it. It wasn't fair for Father to compare Theo to her!

One look at her father's angry face doused that flame. She had no way to fight for herself, much less her brother. Helplessness clove her tongue to the roof of her mouth. She nodded. Father's lips curved into a smile, but he didn't look happy; his eyes were red with tears and his breath stank of wine.

Antiochus stepped aside, sparing a pitying look for Pulcheria. Arcadius straightened and led the girl into the bedroom. Antiochus' words came rushing back. Her mother was dead. What did it mean? What would she see? A sense of dread knotted her stomach and again slowed her steps, so that Father had to, again, tug on her arm.

As her father opened the door, she heard the soft chanting of priests and the shriller murmurs of female servants. Burning musky incense failed to mask an odor that left a coppery taste in her mouth.

Blood.

She remembered the smell and taste from scraped knees and split lips. Blood usually meant stinging pain. This room reeked of it. Pulcheria's heart raced. She took shallow breaths through her mouth, trying to avoid the stench.

Olive oil lamps shone steady, illuminating the brilliantly painted scenes on the walls. Pulcheria noticed fleetingly that most of the images were of naked people entwined in awkward positions. Servants and priests bowed their heads as they passed. Her gaze fixed on the wide bed dominating the room. Her mother's court ladies screened the bed from her sight, but she couldn't miss the blood-soaked rags piled in a bronze bowl. At the sight of her father, the women parted, darting horrified glances at Pulcheria.

More gently this time, Arcadius pulled her to the foot of the bed and stood behind her, his hands on her shoulders. "Here are the wages of sin, Pulcheria. Blood and death."

Pulcheria held her breath as she gazed upon the still body. Her mother's face looked angelic, eyes closed and face pale. People always praised her mother's beauty. The height and comeliness Eudoxia inherited from her father's Frankish ancestors had captured the heart of the teenage Emperor Arcadius nine years before. Those same people lamented that Pulcheria seemed the only one of their four children with the stamp of her dour-faced father.

Except for the sweat-soaked blond hair tangled about her face, Eudoxia looked asleep. A peaceful look, unlike the impatience her mother's face usually bore with her children. The last time Eudoxia visited the nursery, she spent most of her time complaining about ink spots on Pulcheria's robes and the disordered state of her hair. Mother would not be happy, knowing others now saw her own hair in such disarray.

Pulcheria's gaze strayed lower. She gasped at the fine linen sheets sodden with red gore. The stench caused her stomach to heave. An acid taste flooded her mouth. She took a deep breath.

"F-Father, must I stay longer?"

Arcadius squeezed her shoulder. "No, my good girl, you have seen enough."

A midwife approached Arcadius with a still bundle, no bigger than one of Pulcheria's dolls "What should I do with the babe, Augustus?"

"Give it to the dogs!" Arcadius snarled.

The woman gasped and backed away quickly. Pulcheria shrank from her father's renewed anger, but his left hand held her shoulder fast. Antiochus approached the woman and whispered in her ear.

"Antiochus!" Arcadius pointed at the eunuch. "You will see that my daughter does not grow up to be like her twice-damned mother. Teach her the Gospels, train her to be a good Christian woman, modest and obedient."

"As you will, Augustus."

Her father's hand began to tremble on her shoulder. In a choked voice, he cried, "All of you out." Servants, priests, and court ladies filed out a back door, silent, but with frightened looks at the Emperor standing over the body of his wife.

Antiochus came forward to take Pulcheria's hand. "Shall I take the princess back to the nursery?"

"Yes. Go."

As they exited, Pulcheria glanced over her shoulder. Her father knelt at the foot of the bed, narrow shoulders shaking with sobs as he buried his face in the bloody sheets.

"Your father is distraught, Princess. Pay no heed to his words." The eunuch led her through the receiving room and back to the marble hall.

She shivered, suddenly aware of her bare feet on cold stone. No braziers chased the icy fall air from the corridor.

"Are you chilled, princess?" The eunuch bent to look at her face.

"Y-y-yes." Her teeth chattered uncontrollably. From the chill? The blood? Her thoughts and feelings reeled from the sights in the bedroom. What would happen to her and her brother and sisters?

Antiochus gathered her up in his arms and held her close. Warmth radiating from his soft plump body helped dispel some of the chill. "Poor child," he muttered. "Poor, poor child."

Pulcheria lay quietly in his arms, listening to his heart beat steadily in his chest, as he carried her slight weight back to the nursery. The regular double-thump settled her nerves. As they grew closer, his breathing grew more labored. A question nagged at her thoughts. "Is Mother in Heaven?"

He hesitated. "I don't know, child. Only God knows."

"Father said not."

"Even the powerful Emperor of Rome does not command God. The Good Lord in his mercy will judge your mother's soul. Hush now. Think no more of it."

But Pulcheria could think of nothing else. Her father never took an interest in the nursery. If her mother were not on earth or in Heaven to look out for them, would the servants bring them food or help them bathe? Pulcheria thought she could care for herself, Arcadia, and possibly her brother, but baby Marina needed a wet nurse. Would Nana leave? The thought of losing Nana, her nurse since she was a baby, brought on a new wave of shudders. Surely Nana would never leave me!

The eunuch grunted as he shifted her weight to one arm and opened the door to the nursery. The outer room filled with murmurs from servants as they clustered around low-burning lamps. Pulcheria spied her nurse and struggled to escape the eunuch's arms. He set her down.

"Nana!" she cried, speeding to the comforting arms of the heavy-set woman whose plain features lit up Pulcheria's world.

Antiochus followed her. "The Empress is dead." He cut off the ritual wails with an upraised hand. "The Emperor is understandably distraught. He will not be pleased when his grief has passed if he finds his children neglected."

Pulcheria noted a few raised eyebrows and pursed lips at this declaration.

"Attend them with good will. I will return in the morning to see to their affairs."

Nana rose, Pulcheria clinging tightly to her leg. "Forgive me, Antiochus, but should not the Emperor appoint a court woman to oversee the children's daily welfare? You are tasked with the entire household and have many duties to perform."

"Daily care will proceed as before. The Emperor asked that I see to their religious instruction in the future." He shrugged. "I don't think the Emperor wants any of his wife's women to influence the children. Perhaps I could appoint you to oversee the nursery. We will decide when this sad time is over."

Nana offered the eunuch a slight bow. "Thank you." She put her hand on Pulcheria's back. "Come, dumpling, let's get you into a nice warm bed."

Comforted by the eunuch's words and Nana's presence, Pulcheria suppressed a deep yawn, nodded, and followed her nurse to bed. She struggled against sleep, her mind still awhirl with the changes to come. Her worry gave way as lethargy crept up her limbs and sleep quieted her mind.

*****

TWO DAYS LATER, NANA DRESSED PULCHERIA IN HER FINEST PURPLE ROBES, with gold thread that scratched her neck and arms. Her sister Arcadia tugged at her own robes, whining. Theodosius ran around the rooms shouting about a wagon ride.

"Quiet, all of you!" Nana chided. "Can't you be more like your sister?" The nurse grabbed Theodosius as he careened past her and wiped a streak of dust from his face.

"Are they ready?" Antiochus stood in the door, dressed in his finest court robes—white silk tunic embroidered in purple and gold, with a short purple cloak draped over his shoulders. He cradled a gold staff of office in his left arm.

"All but the baby. Marina is too young for such a long ceremony. I'm not sure Theo can tolerate it."

"The boy has to learn court decorum some time." His eyes lighted on Pulcheria. "How is the princess?"

"Doing as well as might be expected."

Pulcheria, annoyed at being talked about as if she were not present in the room, spoke up. "Antiochus, what will happen today?"

"A procession through the city to the Church of the Apostles, prayers for your mother's soul, and a feast for the dead. I will be with you, your sister, and brother."

"Honey cake?" Theodosius piped up.

A sad smile crossed the eunuch's face. "I'm sure there will be honey cake, young Caesar."

Pulcheria straightened her shoulders and took her brother's hand. "Come, Theo, let's go on our wagon ride."

Antiochus' eyes glinted with approval as he escorted the three children to the enclosed imperial wagon that her late mother once used for trips around the city. The outside glittered with gilded wood. Two black horses in silver harness pulled the carriage. Theo forgot himself, tugged on her hand, and exclaimed, "Horsies, Ria! I want to see the horsies!"

"Not today, Theo." He stuck his middle two fingers in his mouth to suck on—a sure sign he was upset.

A guard stepped forward to lift them into the spacious interior, decorated with purple silk drapes and cushions. The middle dropped so passengers could sit with their feet in the well rather than be forced to recline.

The short trip started with wails and lamentations just outside the palace walls. The loudly mourning crowd frightened the younger children. Four-year-old Arcadia whimpered, pulled her knees up, and wrapped her arms around her little legs, rocking back and forth. Theo's eyes grew wide and bright with tears. Pulcheria looked to Antiochus. He ignored the children's distress.

She remembered how Nana soothed them and comforted her brother and sister with physical pats, murmurs, and nonsense words.

"Thank you, Princess." Antiochus frowned at the children sitting across from him. "I hope they are better behaved at the church."

"Apologies, Antiochus. I'll see to it."

He sighed and peeked out the window from behind the curtains.

Curious about a world she had never seen, Pulcheria tried to push the heavy purple cloth aside. "What do you see?"

"No, Princess!" Antiochus shouted. He slapped the curtains back in place, but not before she caught a glimpse of sorrowful faces covered in tears and ashes.

Startled, Pulcheria shrank back onto her cushions, her momentary sense of confidence shattered.

Antiochus told her, more softly, "It is not permitted for the common people to look upon the sacred faces of the imperial family."

She wanted to ask why, but the deep frown on the eunuch's face deterred her. *Everyone in the palace can see our faces. Aren't we just as sacred inside the palace as outside?* Arcadia began to sniffle at the eunuch's sharp tone. Pulcheria put her arms around her sister and filed her question away for another time.

They soon arrived at the Church of the Apostles. Antiochus led them through a thick corridor of Imperial Scholae—the Emperor's personal guards—who kept the crying, mourning people at bay. Pulcheria gasped as they entered the cool orderliness of the church. She was used to the much smaller scale of their nursery chapel. Here, the ceilings soared high above, held up by multi-colored marble columns. The walls glinted with colored frescoes of the Apostles' lives, lit by hundreds of candles and gold chandeliers. Gold glittered on the altar, the robes of the bishop, and the people gathered in the nave.

It was beautiful! Pulcheria stared in awe, soaking in the majesty. This was truly God's house! The sweet woody smell of incense wafted on the air from the gold censers on the altar. She pulled the soothing scent deep into her lungs—so different from the piney smell tinged with blood she remembered from her mother's room.

"This way, children." Antiochus broke her concentration. He escorted them up marble stairs to a screened balcony overlooking the altar. They could look out, but the people standing in the packed church couldn't see them.

Theo ran to the carved wooden screen and pointed to a dark red stone box lying before the altar. "What's that?" The sides were carved with several scenes. From this distance, Pulcheria couldn't tell what story they told.

"That's a sarcophagus," Antiochus answered. "It holds your mother's earthly remains."

"What's a sar-sar…" Arcadia struggled.

Theo asked, "What's 'mains?"

"The sarcophagus is the red stone box. Her body is inside."

Theo's eyes went wide. Arcadia's face paled. "Is it dark in there? Won't Mama be scared?"

"No child, she isn't scared." Antiochus patted their heads. "Her soul is with God. Now it's time to be quiet."

"I'll explain later," Pulcheria whispered to them. "Let's sit." She helped Arcadia onto a low padded bench and sat down herself.

Theo still looked puzzled, but one of the first things they learned in the nursery was to be quiet when an adult asked them to. Antiochus picked him up and sat him on the bench next to Pulcheria. His short legs swung over the edge.

Pulcheria took his hand. He smiled up at her and leaned against her shoulder. Arcadia curled up with her head in Pulcheria's lap. Their trust tugged at her heart, making her sense of helplessness all the more hurtful. Her stomach roiled and throat began to close. She couldn't keep them safe. She wasn't Nana! An unsettling thought nibbled at the edge of her mind: *even Nana could be sent away by Antiochus…and Antiochus could be dismissed by…*

Her father and several richly dressed men entered the nave from the side to take seats in another screened area to the right of the altar. Her heart beat slower and her stomach calmed. Father was Emperor. No one could send him away, and he would never let anything happen to his children, especially his son and heir. Pulcheria pulled Theo tighter, praying that their father lived a long life.

The next morning, in the nursery playroom, Pulcheria looked up from her primer on Greek letters. She found the chaos here, among comfortable cushions, the clutter of toys, and the low gossipy chatter of the nurses and servants, distracting. She much preferred the quiet calm of the classroom or—even better—the prayerful drone of the nursery chapel.

Delighted cries from one corner attracted her attention. Baby Marina took some tottering first steps, to the loud acclaim of her wet-nurse. Arcadia sang a rhyme and played a simple hand-patting game with Nana, while Theo kicked a stuffed leather ball from one side of the room to the other. Their lives had quickly settled back into a comfortable routine, but Pulcheria felt uneasy. Her mother was dead. What other changes lurked in the future?

The pleasant noise faded to silence a few minutes later when Antiochus came through the door with a stern-faced priest in tow. Nana stood, smoothed her wrinkled stola, and approached the two men. She bowed.

"Antiochus, Father, what can I do for you?"

Antiochus indicated the priest. "Elpida, this is Father Marcus. He will be overseeing the children's religious instruction."

Pulcheria was momentarily confused. *Elpida?* She had assumed *Nana* was the name of the woman who raised her.

The eunuch frowned at the playroom chaos. "Father Marcus will also oversee the children's chapel and lead the nursery staff in observing canonical hours with prayers."

Pulcheria couldn't see Nana's face, but her back stiffened and shoulders straightened. "Not all the offices, surely! This is a nursery, not a monastery. The children's health will suffer if you wake them during the night every couple of hours for prayer."

Father Marcus smiled, softening the stern lines in his thin bearded face. "Only those offices during the day and before bed—Prime through Vespers. I had a child of my own before Christ took her to heaven and called me to the church, Nurse Elpida. I am here to ensure the health of their immortal souls, not to endanger their physical bodies. Do the children know their prayers? Can they read the Gospels?"

"Not the younger ones, Father." Pulcheria noted the red blush spread up the back of Nana's neck. "But Princess Pulcheria is very bright and her tutor says she is making remarkable progress with her Greek and Latin letters. She should be able to read the Gospels."

"Then I will start with her and instruct the other children as they are able." Father Marcus looked around the room, caught Pulcheria staring at him, and nodded.

He seemed pleasant enough, with intelligent black eyes and an olive complexion. His gray-streaked beard contrasted with his dark curly hair. Something about his erect stance and precise voice told her he led a disciplined life, but laugh lines framing his eyes hinted at a sense of humor.

"Do as you must." Antiochus nodded to the priest. "Come see me when you're through and I'll show you to your quarters."

Nana led the priest over to Pulcheria. "Princess, this is Father Marcus—"

"I heard, Nana." Pulcheria closed her codex and stood. "This way to the classroom, Father."

Nana snapped her gaping jaws shut and nodded. Pulcheria led the priest to an adjoining room, smaller than the playroom and much more severe. Except for an embroidery basket, no fabric, cushion, or carpet softened the austerity. Bookshelves covered one wall, containing bound volumes on history, geography, philosophy, plays and poetry. Maps of the Empire covered another. A standing work desk of light maple stood in one corner. In the middle of the room, a short chair sat at a low table containing stacks of wax-covered tablets and a stylus to incise the wax or scrape away mistakes. A couple of folded backless camp chairs leaned against a third wall. No windows offered distractions, but an ornate brass chandelier held a dozen olive oil lamps, casting a warm glow over the room.

Marcus opened a camp chair and sat. "Please stand here, Princess." He pointed to a spot directly in front of him. When she had positioned herself, with shoulders and back straight, he asked, "What have you studied so far?"

"I'm learning to read and write Greek and Latin. Tutor has started me on sums and differences and geography. I'm also learning comportment and embroidery. Would you like to see?"

The stern set to his face softened slightly. His sharp black eyes held a hint of laughter. "Yes, Princess, I would like to see your work."

She went to her small table and brought back her practice tablets and embroidery basket. "Tutor praised my hand. It is much better than last year." She showed him her writing samples. It still wasn't perfect; she frowned at some of the awkward letters. Her embroidery was more of an embarrassment. She tried and tried, but could not master Nana's small, neat stitches.

"Very nice work, especially for a child of your age." He took a small codex of scripture from a pocket tied to his belt. "Do you read the Sacred Word, child?"

There was that word again: sacred. She shook her head. "No, Father, but I read some poetry." Pride echoed in her voice. Four-year-old Arcadia was just starting on letters, and Tutor didn't even try to get three-year-old Theo to sit for lessons. "I have a question for you."

"Yes?" He leaned back, looking at her sharply.

"You describe the Gospels as 'the Sacred Word.' Yesterday, Antiochus said it was wrong for the common people to see my and my sisters' 'sacred faces.' What does 'sacred' mean? The common people can see and hear the Gospels. Why can't they see and hear us?"

"That, Child, is a very grown-up question. Sacred means holy—of God. The Gospels are the Word of God. Your father, the Emperor of Rome, was chosen and anointed by God to be His viceroy on earth, to rule in the way of Caesars. Thus, emperors and their families are accounted sacred. That's why you live in seclusion and common people are not allowed to see your faces."

"But Nana and the servants see our faces. They are common people." She frowned.

"Good thinking, Princess!" His face split into a large smile. "You've put your finger on the complexity of the matter. Nowhere in the Gospels does it say an Emperor and his family may not be seen. That is a rule—like many—made up by men for their own purposes. Your father's mother, Aelia Flacilla Augusta, used to go out among the people and care for the sick and the poor with her own hands. She obeyed a rule from the Gospels, 'Care for the least of these.' It is good to know what rules are made by God and what are rules made by man. You should never break God's rules."

"But I can break man's?" Pulcheria was confused. "I can go out among the people without covering my face?"

"Sometimes. If all men obeyed God's rules, there would be no need for additional ones, but that is not the world we live in." Father Marcus sighed. "I can see you are going to be an apt pupil. We will work through these questions and many more in our studies. Be patient, Princess. As you grow older, more will be revealed."

Annoyed at the constant admonition by adults to "wait until you're older," Pulcheria was inclined to demand an answer now, but her native caution took over. "Yes, Father. I look forward to learning the answers with you."

His smile disappeared; the stern look of a teacher returned. "Do you know any stories from the Gospels?"

"I know about Christ's birth and His re-re—resurrection?" She looked down in embarrassment over the stumbled word.

"That's good, but there are older parts to the Bible, many stories that have lessons for us." Marcus flipped through pages until he found the passage he wanted. "Do you know the story of Queen Jezebel?"

Pulcheria shook her head.

The priest closed the book and leaned forward. "King Ahab and Queen Jezebel of Israel were bad leaders and wicked people. They worshiped false gods, made war on their neighbors, and did murder. You might hear some say your mother was a modern Jezebel. She *did* do some wicked things, but nothing like the Jewish Queen. It's my job to make sure you stay true to the Christian path, that your soul pleases God, and you get to sit at His right hand after the Second Coming."

"Do you think Mother is in heaven?" That question haunted her. Despite her mother's indifference, Pulcheria did not want to imagine her in torment.

"I don't know, Princess." Marcus thought a moment, hand tugging at his graying beard. "Your mother's sins were those of pride and of the flesh. If she truly repented her sins, God forgave her. If she didn't repent…" He shrugged expressive shoulders.

He handed the codex to Pulcheria. She turned the chunky volume over in her hands. Its fine leather was worn with much use. What did her mother do that was so wicked? Would she find the answers in this book? Father Marcus counselled patience. She hoped, with time, all her questions would be answered. For now, she would do her best to learn his lessons.

"Your Father commands that you receive instruction in the scriptures, so you do not stray from the path of righteousness. Today we will begin with the creation and Eve's fall from grace. Stand straight and declaim in a strong voice."

She straightened her shoulders, opened the holy book to the first page, and read, "In the beginning God created the heavens and the earth…"

# Chapter 2



*Imperial Palace, May 408*

ANTHEMIUS, PATRICIAN, PRAETORIAN PREFECT AND SECOND MOST powerful man in the eastern parts of the Roman Empire, left Emperor Arcadius' bedroom to confront the anxious crowd in the anteroom. He was followed by the handful of councilors and priests who had shared his vigil through the night and acted as witnesses to the passing of power. No one had expected Arcadius to die at the young age of thirty-one, but a sudden fever carried him off, leaving Anthemius with a succession crisis. As prefect, he had been running the government for his dull-witted Emperor the last eight years and saw no reason he shouldn't continue. *The boy is only seven, for God's sake! It will be years before he can take the reins.*

Silence descended on the courtiers and foreign ambassadors as Anthemius schooled his lined face and made the expected announcement. "The Augustus is dead. God rest his soul."

The crowd echoed, "God rest his soul. Blessings be upon him."

Anthemius ran a hand through his impressive head of curly silver hair, then stilled his unexpected fidgeting. *I must be more tired than I thought. When did I lose the ability to work through the night and greet the dawn with vigor?*

He took a deep breath and addressed the crowd. "Our beloved emperor, Flavius Arcadius Augustus, named his son, Flavius Theodosius, as Caesar and heir some years ago. The Imperial line continues. Theodosius is the next Emperor, the Second of that Name." *It never hurts to remind people of illustrious ancestors!*

He scanned the crowd for hints of dissatisfaction. This was a dangerous time for the boy emperor and Anthemius was on the lookout for any sign of rebellion. Most of the men wore grave or sorrowful faces. He made note of those few showing a blank or calculating mien. He paid little attention to the women ritually crying and praying.

"The city prefect will arrange the funeral. I will continue to serve as Patrician to the emperor and praetorian prefect of the East. The senate will appoint a regent for Theodosius Caesar, soon to be Augustus." Anthemius waved his hands toward the door. "You are dismissed." He turned to several young pages and gave them instructions on whom to notify.

"Patrician?" Antiochus bowed before him as the last of the youngsters left. "May I have a word?"

While Anthemius ran the empire, Antiochus ran the palace and had physical custody of the emperor's young children. The two had worked well together over the years. Antiochus had had a calming influence over the moody Arcadius and didn't try to exercise power beyond the palace. The prefect hoped to enlist the eunuch in his plans for the children.

"Certainly." Anthemius nodded to his son. "Isidorus, join us." He had been grooming his son for high honors since boyhood. He hoped to leave the empire in his capable hands—someday—in the future.

The three men stood at an ebony sideboard laden with food left over from the night's vigil. Anthemius ignored the wilted lettuces, crumbs of cheese, and picked-over meats in their congealed fat. He signaled a servant to pour chilled pomegranate juice over crushed cherries in silver goblets.

Antiochus declined, but Isidorus took a large drink. Anthemius frowned at the tart taste as he sipped his own.

"Your Sublimity, this sudden and tragic death leaves us a dilemma." The eunuch shuffled his feet and looked longingly at a padded chair.

"Only one?" Anthemius gave a sour smile.

"What is to be done with the children?"

"They are to be cared for, as always."

"I hesitate to bring this up, Noble Prefect, but I fear for their safety." The eunuch put up his hands as if in defense. "Not that I suspect any specific person of plotting rebellion…uh…or wishing them harm. But they are young and without champions. It is an easy thing to shove aside a seven-year-old boy in favor of a mature man. Perhaps they should be housed in a more secure location?

I could take the children to the palace in Hebdomon, away from the public eye."

Anthemius was pleased at the eunuch's concern. "Rest assured, Antiochus, I know of no one who wants to put aside the new emperor. The palace is the safest place for the children, especially with such a vigilant person as yourself in charge. The senate will soon appoint a regent. That should settle the matter until the boy reaches his majority."

"Theodosius' Uncle Honorius is now senior Emperor and might want some say in that appointment."

"More likely his General Stilicho will claim some influence, since he acted as regent in the West during Honorius' minority. I'm sure the eastern senate will be unanimous in its will to have one of their own in the position."

Antiochus raised a questioning brow but did not comment on Anthemius' bold assertion of independence in the East. "I still fear some disaffection in this court. Luckily, Emperor Arcadius—blessed be his soul!—provided a safeguard."

"What's the nature of this safeguard?" Alarm quickened Anthemius' blood. *What the devil has the eunuch been up to? Will he oppose my regency?*

"At my urging, the late Emperor—may he be honored in heaven!—named the Persian King guardian of his son." Antiochus flashed a satisfied smile, handing Anthemius a sealed packet. "This letter from Yazdgard, First of his Name, declares that he will wage war if the boy comes to harm. Please make it known to others of the court and the council."

Anthemius broke the seal and scanned it quickly. He had not suspected the eunuch of being under foreign obligation. Antiochus had not tried to influence foreign policy, so was likely just taking a small pension from the Persian king for general information about the court, a common practice. *I need to strengthen my network of informers inside the palace to confirm Antiochus is not more ambitious. We have a history of eunuchs getting above their station.*

Anthemius handed the letter to his son. "There is no need for such foreign protection. I give you my word, no harm will come to our new emperor."

"Your word is good with me, Patrician, but you do not command all. There are many ambitious men about. I'll leave you two to your deliberations. I must inform the children of their loss." Antiochus bowed and left.

With the eunuch gone, the prefect waved his son over to the chairs and took a deep swallow of his own drink.

Isidorus looked at his father over the brim of his goblet. "Well, Father?"

"Well, what?" he answered with a touch of asperity.

"Are you one of those 'ambitious men'? You have managed the empire successfully for the last eight years while our 'Blessed Emperor'"— he rolled his eyes—"drank himself to death. Many would rally to your cause."

"I have sworn before God and the people of Constantinople to protect this empire. I will not break that oath by instigating a civil war." Anthemius frowned at his son. "That means protecting the young emperor and running his empire to the best of my ability."

Blood flooded his son's face at the mild rebuke. "I meant no disrespect, Father. I do not doubt your loyalty, but many are dissatisfied after the disastrous rule of Arcadius and are looking for change. General Procopius claims descent from the Great Constantine. He could make a bid for the diadem."

"The good general has never expressed an interest in ruling. Besides, I have plans for Procopius. I believe he would be much happier with a connection to our family, where he could accumulate wealth and influence without the headaches of wearing the diadem." Anthemius smiled. "I've been looking for a good match for your sister."

Isidorus looked startled, then nodded. "A very good move. Best to bring him into our faction and avoid civil war."

"The senate is sure to name me regent." Anthemius stared into his goblet for a moment. "I'll replace Arcadius' corrupt friends with men of good repute throughout the government. People will see a change and our young emperor should reap the benefit. If he proves as malleable as his father, we continue as now. If the boy shows strength of character and good judgment, he will keep us close. Either way, we benefit and avoid a civil war."

"What if he grows strong-willed and foolish?"

"It is our job to surround the boy with good tutors and amiable friends who will have his ear for many years. By education and example, that is how we form a sensible man and competent ruler."

"And keep him away from the wine." Isidorus grinned.

"Yes, moderation in all things is the Hellene way." Anthemius rose and stretched. "It was a long vigil last night, and I have more work to do. I best get to it."


A month later, Pulcheria prepared her brother for one of the most important days of his life. "Stand still, Theo, or we'll never get you ready for your acclamation. You do want to be the emperor of Rome, don't you?" The cherubic toddler had grown into a weedy seven-year-old, missing his front teeth, and usually stinking of horses and dogs. One of his favorite hounds paced the carpet by his side, whining at the commotion.

Pulcheria inspected her brother with reserved approval. His attendants had arranged the boy's dark blond hair in glistening curls and dressed him in new robes of purple silk encrusted with gold thread, seed pearls, and amethysts. He positively glittered! Theo was a handsome boy even with his gap-toothed smile. He reached down to sooth his hound, mumbling, "I am emperor. Nobody can take that away from me."

She raised one eyebrow, an affectation she practiced in a mirror and used to devastating effect on servants. She needed Theo to know the precariousness of his position, but didn't want to needlessly frighten him. It was enough that her stomach clenched with apprehension.

Pulcheria tried again, "One would think you have not studied your histories. Many an emperor has lost his throne and his life because the army or the senate did not want him."

"But the people love me!" Theo whined.

She sighed, resisting the urge to tousle his carefully coifed curls. Pulcheria worked hard to keep up with the outside world, isolated as they were in the palace. Instinctively, she knew knowledge was power, even if she had no way of wielding that power as a child. It infuriated her that the adults in her life tried to deny her this one safeguard. Nana patted her on the head and suggested she not worry about such things. Antiochus deliberately kept disturbing news from the nursery, so her tutors deflected her questions on current events.

Only Father Marcus kept her apprised of the current state of the empire. For a priest, he seemed well informed and had the bonus of respecting Pulcheria's questions. But he had no access to the thinking of powerful men and that was the knowledge she sought. Luckily there were no restrictions on history, so she concentrated on learning as much as she could about past imperial rulers— what traits made them successes, and which made them vulnerable.

The one history lesson she learned over and over again was that the emperor was always in danger. That knowledge was a curse. As she had after her mother's death, Pulcheria struggled with a sense of helplessness. She was a young girl with an impossible task. What could she do against an entire court of adults to keep her family safe? What could she do if the army revolted?

Little to nothing, except pray.

If the worst threatened, Pulcheria planned to ask Father Marcus for asylum for the children in the church. Whereas the people of the court were all too vulnerable to bribes and promises of power, Father Marcus taught her God granted his grace to innocent children and would protect them.

Pulcheria blinked tears from her eyes. How to get through to Theo? Should she? If they can do nothing, shouldn't she let him enjoy his innocence? No. Through God's grace, and good luck, her brother would become emperor. He needed to know how to rule. If the tutors wouldn't do it, she would.

"Brother, we live in perilous times. Father Marcus tells me the Huns have invaded from the north, the Goths muster under Alaric, and General Stilicho returns to the West by our Uncle Honorius' order, leaving the East vulnerable. In the past, people have turned quickly against any emperor who cannot protect them. We must have the support of the eastern armies, as well as the people, or our lives are forfeit."

Theo's face turned somber. "How did you become so wise, Ria?"

"I had to. No one else looks after us except Nana and Father Marcus. What can one old woman and a priest do to protect us?" Pulcheria thought bitterly of her drunken father. Could he not have lived another five or six years, until she was of age? She had little affection for him, but alive he kept the vultures of the Court from his children, and Pulcheria knew some peace. Now all was chaos and uncertainty. With a boy on the throne and she only nine years old, their fate fell to whoever the senate declared regent.

"When I come into my majority, Sister, you will be my foremost advisor." Theodosius gave her a lop-sided grin. "For I know you love me and have my best interests at heart."

Pulcheria swept her brother into a hug, just as Antiochus appeared at the door. "Children, it's time to go."

Pulcheria straightened her robes and her brother's, bowed low, and pointed to the door with an outstretched arm. "Emperor Theodosius, your people await you."

A fearful expression flitted over the boy's face.

"You'll do well, Brother. Show the people you are worthy of our grandfather's name."

Theo's face settled into the mask of genial good humor all imperial children learn at an early age. He offered his arm. They walked out the door side-by-side.

A chaotic crowd milled about the entrance to the imperial palace. June sun scorched the plaza inside the Chalke Gate. Heat waves rose from the paving stones. Sweat dampened Pulcheria's hair, trickling down her back, making her heavy embroidered robes even more uncomfortable. She surreptitiously wiped her damp palms on her outer cloak and glanced at Theo. He seemed unaffected by the heat, smiling expectantly at the people bowing before him.

Guards, senators, servants: all made way for the imperial children with deep bows. Anthemius, the praetorian prefect of the East, came forward to greet Theodosius. As the highest official in the eastern parts, it was his responsibility to raise funds for and oversee the celebration. "Caesar, you will take the chariot. Your sisters will follow in the women's imperial wagon."

Theodosius looked with approval on the gilded chariot decorated with the imperial eagle, symbol of the Roman Empire, drawn by four perfectly matched white horses. Pulcheria whispered in his ear. He turned to Anthemius. "My sisters find the arrangement unacceptable. They wish to ride in an open chariot as well, the better to see the crowd and be seen by them."

Anthemius' studied smile disappeared. "It is unseemly for the princesses to ride in a chariot. The people should not look upon their sacred faces."

Theodosius glanced at Pulcheria. She gave the barest negative shake of her head. A frown clouded Theodosius' face. "It is my wish as well. Am I not the Emperor?"

Anthemius, not wishing to provoke an imperial tantrum, countered with, "Perhaps the drapes to the wagon can be drawn back somewhat so the princesses can look out, but they are shielded from the gaze of the people."

"That will be acceptable," Pulcheria answered for herself. Anthemius gave her a calculating look. She gazed back with an innocent smile. She had only proposed the chariot knowing it would not be approved, hoping to force Anthemius into an acceptable compromise. Over the past several years, she had finely honed the art of bargaining while wheedling concessions from Nana and Antiochus. Father Marcus seemed immune to her strategies.

Theodosius entered the commodious ceremonial chariot with Anthemius and the driver. Imperial guards in striking white tunics and purple cloaks surrounded them, polished helmets and steel-tipped spears glittering in the sunlight. Pulcheria's heart raced when separated from her brother. Many usurpers demonstrated their power with a public assassination and drive for immediate acclamation. Before Theo took power from the hands of his army would be a good time to strike.

With a sense of resignation and a prayer to God for protection, Pulcheria entered the imperial wagon with her sisters. Pulcheria directed Arcadia and

Marina to the seat with their backs to the front of the carriage. They settled in, arranging their miniature royal robes to be comfortable, and looked to Pulcheria for approval. She leaned forward to tuck a brown curl behind Arcadia's ear. "Good girls. Now, Marina, remember not to suck your thumb. Sit on your hands, if you need to. When we leave the wagon, smile at the people."

"Like this, Ria?" Her littlest sister screwed up her face in an exaggerated smile, making Pulcheria laugh.

"No, Sweetling, if you smile like that you will scare the people. Think of something you like and let your face do what it wants."

"I like flowers and puppies and honey cakes and…" Pulcheria let her baby sister babble on while she surveyed the entourage through a partially drawn curtain. Guards formed up around the wagon, and they joined the procession out of the palace gates.

Despite her apprehension, Pulcheria felt a thrill. This was only the third time she'd left the palace, and those had been short trips to the Church of the Apostles for her parent's funeral services. She eagerly anticipated this trip to the outer suburbs through her city, which she had studied on maps but barely saw.

The procession moved from the Chalke Gate, in the southeastern palace precincts on the First Hill, into the Augusteum, named after Constantine's mother Helena. Every child knew the story of how Helena went on a pilgrimage to Jerusalem and discovered the cross upon which Christ had been crucified. She returned to Rome with pieces of the holy relic, convinced her son to become Christian, and converted the Empire to a Christian State. Pulcheria said a silent prayer for the great woman.

Marina peeked out at an impressive statue dominating the square that was the center of political life in the city. "Who's that, Ria?"

"Helena Augusta, the Great Constantine's mother." Gazing on the calm, beautiful face, Pulcheria drew strength. Here was a woman of power and piety. She could be one too.

They proceeded around the square, past the imposing basilica of the Senate house on the east and the ruins of Hagia Sophia, the Church of Holy Wisdom, on the north. It had burned down many years ago, shortly before her mother's death. "That's a shame!" Pulcheria murmured to herself. "Why hasn't someone rebuilt that church? When I'm old enough…"

She sighed. There was so much she wanted to do and couldn't, because she was a child.

Pulcheria put aside thoughts of tomorrow to gaze upon the crowd. The people dressed in their best to receive their emperor, smiling and eager to glimpse the boy. Their grandfather Theodosius had been a formidable general and popular emperor. After the disappointing reign of their father, the hopeful crowd wanted to believe the grandson of Theodosius the Great had the qualities of his namesake. Pulcheria cared not why they loved the lad; she was just grateful they did. Popular support made a public attack far less likely. As he passed, she heard their formal shouts of acclamation led by strategically placed imperial agents, "Theodosius Augustus, chosen and anointed by God and the Roman people! Blessed is Theodosius, Second of his Name!"

They headed west out of the Augusteum, and entered the central thoroughfare of the city, the Mese—Middle Street. The wagon hit an uneven patch; the girls were tossed about, Arcadia whooping in delight, Marina's face screwing up to cry. Pulcheria pulled the little girl onto her lap. "I'll keep you safe, Rina. It's just a little bump in the road." She pulled back the curtain a bit and pointed. "Look! It's the monument to the Great Constantine!" Pulcheria gazed at the huge column of porphyry drums exquisitely carved with scenes from his life and triumphs, topped by a massive statue of Constantine as Apollo. The statue was ancient, done by a Greek master, the head replaced with a modern rendition of Constantine crowned by a halo of seven rays, facing the rising sun. In a monumental city, Constantine's column was among the most impressive. "In the next forum we'll see Grandfather Theodosius' column. When you're older, we'll climb the stairs inside and spy on the city."

The little girls' eyes widened with anticipation. Arcadia asked, "When we grow up can we build columns and have statues?"

Pulcheria shook her head solemnly. "No. Men build columns, women build churches. We'll build beautiful churches all over the city." Struck with inspiration, she silently prayed, *Dear God, keep us safe and deliver us to power over your most holy kingdom on earth and I will keep my promise. Constantinople will be a city of churches dedicated to doing your good work.*

The prayer calmed her, filling her with peace. Pulcheria took this as a sign from God of His favor and brightened considerably.

She continued an animated commentary about sites of the city as they continued past new construction of houses, shops, baths, and tenement buildings to the coastal plain where the army drilled and emperors were traditionally acclaimed.

The wagon jittered to a halt. Pulcheria sat quietly. Her younger sisters took their cue from her. Soon Anthemius came to escort them to a wooden reviewing stand covered in more purple cloth. They ascended the stairs to sit under a welcome awning. Servants plied them with grape juice and cucumber water.

Pulcheria sipped her juice while examining rank after rank of soldiers in their polished armor flowing across the plain, their standards boldly announcing their designation. Pulcheria saw archers dressed in leopard skins, cohorts of Gothic cavalry, and the mainstay of the Roman army—foot soldiers. The officers sat astride their finest horses at the front of the columns near the reviewing stand. Sunlight bounced and flickered off helmets, shields, and tack. *They must be sweltering. I can barely stand it in the shade!*

Theo's chariot made an entrance. Anthemius descended. Then the driver raced the chariot back and forth in front of the assembled soldiers, who beat their swords on their shields in a rhythmic din. Pulcheria's heart swelled. Maybe the army did love their new emperor. Maybe they were safe for the moment.

The chariot made its way to the reviewing stand. Anthemius escorted her brother up the stairs. Theo, flushed and smiling from the exhilarating ride, winked at Pulcheria as he passed. After several moments, Anthemius raised his hands and the roar died down. "Soldiers of Rome!" Criers echoed down the ranks so all could hear the words. "I give you Flavius Theodosius Augustus, son of Flavius Arcadius Augustus, grandson of the Great Flavius Theodosius Augustus!"

This time the soldiers raised their voices to chant for over ten minutes, "Blessed is Emperor Theodosius, Second of that Name, beloved of God and the Roman people. May his reign be long, wise, and good."

At the end of the acclamation, Anthemius draped the *paludamentum*— the purple military cloak used only by emperors and empresses to signify their control of the military—about Theo's shoulders. Next, he fastened the magisterial belt around the boy's waist, giving him supreme judicial power in the East. Finally, Anthemius tied an imperial diadem of pearls and gems around her brother's hair, signifying Theo as supreme ruler and head of the government. The silk ribbons of the diadem draped down Theo's neck onto his small shoulders. The three pillars of the empire—the army, the law, and the government—embodied in one person.

Thus, with permission of his people and his army, her brother Theodosius became Co-Emperor of the Roman Empire. According to the Church, he was chosen by God to be His viceroy on earth, tasked with protecting and ruling the eastern provinces.

The enormity of the responsibility made Pulcheria gasp. *He's just a little boy! How will he be able to do it? How can anyone?* She calmed a bit as Anthemius spoke to the army. The praetorian prefect ruled and ruled well according to Father Marcus. The priest felt Anthemius would likely be regent, and that he was an honorable man. She would watch and learn from Anthemius how to govern so she could guide and teach Theo. *Merciful God, I pray Father Marcus is right. Please give me the strength and knowledge to keep my brother and sisters safe.*

Yet the closer Theo came to his majority and sole rule, she felt, the more dangerous it would become. *We have a few years. I can learn more. I can grow. For now, we disappear into the nursery and allow Anthemius to rule in our stead—but our time will come. Good God watch over and keep us from harm and all we do will be in your name!*

# Chapter 3

*Imperial Palace, June 410*

PULCHERIA SUFFERED NANA'S MINISTRATIONS AS THE NURSE CLUCKED and complained. "Dumpling, let me do something with your hair today. You are eleven and a young woman. Pulling your hair back into a tight bun is for matrons, not maidens."

Pulcheria perched on a silk-covered stool while Nana brushed her hair. Pulcheria observed herself in the polished silver mirror. Her hair was beautiful—long, lustrous, a dark chestnut with red and gold highlights and a natural wave. It almost made her plain face pretty. When she realized her thoughts, her face paled and her lips pinched together.

"Nana, get the shears."

Her nurse looked puzzled, continuing to brush out her hair. "But why, Dumpling?"

"You must cut my hair. It feeds my vanity and Father Marcus teaches that vanity is a sin."

"No, child. You are too young to sin. No one will fault you for keeping your hair."

"The shears, Nana, or I will do it myself."

Nana turned to a chest and rummaged through the contents, the stiffness of her back signaling her disapproval. She withdrew a pair of bronze shears and held them loosely in her hands, as if hoping they would fall away and Pulcheria would forget this latest fancy.

When Pulcheria met her eyes in the mirror, the nurse's mouth set in a firm line. She raised the first silken tress from the back of Pulcheria's neck. The shears cut through the hair with a decided "snip." Tears came to Nana's eyes, but Pulcheria sat still as her nurse continued to shear strand after strand, laying each carefully aside. When Nana had finished, barely two inches of hair waved on Pulcheria's skull. She ran her hands through the remaining hair, nodding in satisfaction. "I will cover my head as the holy women do. Nana, make it so."

Nana, hurt and anger warring on her face, muttered, "What will the people think when you show up in procession with no hair."

"I shall be a good example to them. My mother was beautiful and what good did she do? She warred with the church and caused my father pain." Pulcheria's face set in a frown. Servants still gossiped about her wanton mother after all these years. "The priests are right. Beauty should come from within, through a chaste and holy spirit. Physical beauty is prone to corruption and lasts not beyond youth, whereas beauty of the soul lasts beyond the grave."

Nana continued muttering about Father Marcus and his effect on Pulcheria as she dressed her charge in a plain blue woolen stola and a white linen veil.

Pulcheria ignored her.

Nana had lost the battle on clothing suitable for a princess the year before. She would add this latest act to the store of indignities she felt she suffered trying to raise an imperial child to her high station. Pulcheria preferred the simplicity of the religious life, although she regretted the aggravation it caused her servants when she dispensed with the ritual involved with imperial dress and toilet. She heard them worrying about their places in the palace if they had no purpose.

Nana finally finished, a look of extreme disapproval on her face. "Come to breakfast then and be prepared for the other children to stare and laugh."

"They will not dare laugh." Her brother and sisters looked to her for nearly all things. She sometimes felt more mother than sister to them. Her brother's friends, Paulinus and Placitus—installed by Regent Anthemius two years ago to share Theo's education and provide him male companionship—would not cross their emperor. "I would not be surprised if my sisters ask to have their hair cut."

Nana gave a suitably horrified snort.

"And I will not attend breakfast. It's Wednesday. I'm fasting."

"But it's not a holy day, and children are not required to fast even then!"

"I intend to fast on Wednesdays and Fridays. Father Marcus does it, and says it is good for the soul to deny the flesh."

"The Good Father says that, does he?" Nana's eyes flashed. "Well, Father Marcus is a man, well grown, and can afford to miss a meal or two." She surveyed Pulcheria with a critical eye. "You, on the other hand, are a child."

Pulcheria winced. "A moment ago, you said I was a young woman. Which am I to you, a child or a maiden?"

"I will always see the child I nursed in your face, no matter how old you grow." Nana's eyes glistened with unshed tears. Her breath caught in a swallowed sob. She turned Pulcheria to face the mirror and stood with her hands protectively on her shoulders. "You are a remarkable child. You've had to grow up fast with no father or mother to guide you. You soak up knowledge like a sponge does water. If I close my eyes while talking to you, most days I would think you were an adult. But my eyes are open, Dumpling, and what I see is a child's body—no matter how quick the mind. A child's body needs good food and lots of it." Nana's tone sharpened. "Remember the bad cold you had last winter? That comes from being too thin. The vapors penetrated your chest and your body had no way to fight them off."

"But Father Marcus—"

"I grant Father Marcus may know best for your soul, but I know best for your body. And it doesn't include starving a child who is already too thin. Besides," Nana said, hugging her close, "what will Theo do if a fever carries you off, as it did your father?"

"He can be happy for me that I am in Heaven," Pulcheria snapped, knowing defeat. Nana knew her few soft spots, but thankfully used her knowledge infrequently. The fact that Nana pulled out her most powerful weapon—Pulcheria's need to protect and guide her brother—indicated how much it meant to her nurse. Pulcheria sighed, turned and embraced her nurse in a brief hug. "You're right, Nana. I need to protect my health, for Theo's sake as well as mine. I will attend breakfast with the others. But make sure Cook knows I want plain meals from now on. No fancy spice or sauce; no sweets or honey."

"Of course, Dumpling. You are the imperial princess and can have your food however you wish."

Pulcheria caught the barely muttered, "as long as you *do* have food," and smiled to herself.

*****

Later that day, Pulcheria toiled over the passage of scripture Father Marcus daily set her when Regent Anthemius entered her study. "News from Rome?" she asked.

Pulcheria had slowly come to trust the Regent over the last two years. He seemed a man genuinely dedicated to the welfare of the empire and his charge, the emperor. He also seemed to harbor no ambitions for himself, but then he was effectively the most powerful man in the East. The danger to her brother lay in any ambitions he might have for a relative. Pulcheria prayed every day for his good health—remembering the real danger after her father's sudden death.

Anthemius, to Pulcheria's delight, also recognized her precocious nature and provided her with the best tutors in rhetoric, history, natural science, and mathematics. When time allowed, he answered her questions about the state of the Empire. The fact that he came at this time, when the council usually met, meant something important had happened.

Anthemius' face was drawn with worry. Dark circles under his eyes indicated he had had little sleep the night before. "Where is the emperor? He should hear this as well."

"Theo is with Father Marcus, learning his scriptures."

"Fetch the emperor," Anthemius snapped at a loitering servant. "And be quick about it."

They waited but a few moments before the boy came bounding through the entryway, his tunic spotted with ink from his exertions. "Are the barbarians at our gates?" He conducted a mock sword fight with his goose quill pen. "If so, let them beware! The mighty Emperor Theodosius will vanquish all before him!"

"Theo!" Pulcheria put all the gravity of her eleven years into the rebuke. "Sit. Regent Anthemius has important news for us. This is serious."

Only somewhat chastened, Theodosius settled on a silk cushioned chair, his foot tapping to an irregular rhythm. "What's this important news, Anthemius?"

"King Alaric of the Goths has stripped his pet emperor Attalus of the diadem."

Pulcheria let out a breath. The barbarian Goths had pillaged Gaul and Italy with near impunity since her Uncle Honorius, in a fit of fear, executed Stilicho, the only general capable of holding them in check. Twice in two years they threatened Rome, heart of the western part of the empire. The first time the city beggared itself, providing a bribe. The second time, with nothing left to give, City Prefect Attalus convinced the barbarian king to anoint him emperor, effectively declaring a civil war on their Uncle Honorius in the West.

"But that's good news!" Theo bounced off his chair. "Has he been executed yet?"

"His fate is unknown. But you can claim the victory, Augustus. If not for our sending forty thousand troops to your uncle's aid in Ravenna, he would be deposed."

"So, it comes down to whose army is greatest, and we have the best in the world!" Theo boasted in little boy fashion.

"It's not that simple, Theo." Pulcheria sometimes despaired of her brother. "Attalus was unwise in his choice of ministers. The man he sent to Africa to ensure supplies was easily dispatched by Uncle's man. Without African grain, Rome and Alaric's army starve. Starving people always turn on their leaders. Luckily for Alaric, he can put the blame on the false emperor and retain his power." Pulcheria turned back to Anthemius. "Where is Alaric now?"

"He marches on Rome for the third time. I don't believe he will negotiate with the western senate again. This time he will put the city to the torch."

Pulcheria loved her own city and shuddered at the thought of Rome going up in flames. "What of our Aunt Placidia? Is she safe and well?"

"She sent personal word to your uncle. She has survived. She spent most of her portable wealth feeding and caring for the people of Rome during the siege and now stands with her people. She will not return to the Ravenna court. I fear she is in great danger."

"May I go now?" Theo said, a faint whine in his voice.

"Of course." Pulcheria watched him scamper off. Better he be gone than leave a bad impression on the Regent. *I must spend more time on his comportment. It does not do for such important men as Anthemius to think Theo incapable.*

She turned back to the regent. "I'm concerned Aunt Placidia refuses to return to her brother and the safety of Ravenna. Do you think she is unaware of the danger?"

"She is aware but, like a good ruler, refuses to leave her people."

Anthemius' gaze slipped away from hers, making her suspicious. Growing up in the imperial household, Pulcheria had a keen sense of when people withheld information or outright lied to her. She suspected there was more to the story.

"Did my Uncle Honorius not order her back to Ravenna?" Pulcheria leaned back in her chair, watching the regent closely. "Why doesn't she obey her brother and emperor?"

"There is a good deal of history between your uncle and aunt that you are not aware of, Princess." He squared his shoulders, looking directly at her. "For that matter, there is history between your aunt and your late father."

*More secrets! How am I to learn if people keep things from me?* She took a deep breath and asked, in as reasonable a tone as she could muster, "Regent, don't you think it's important I know about my own family? My brother is co-emperor with our uncle. We must work together for the good of the empire."

"Yes, Princess." Anthemius ran a hand through his hair—a rare gesture Pulcheria noticed he used when he seemed uncertain. "Not all brothers and sister are as fortunate as you and the emperor in loving and supporting one another. Placidia is half-sister to your father and uncle. Her mother Galla married the Great Theodosius after his wife—your grandmother—died."

"That is not enough reason for disobedience. Half brothers and sisters can get along." Surely Anthemius was aware Theo might not be her father's child. For years the court gossiped behind closed doors about her brother's paternity—which later shed light on her father's rant when he dragged her to her mother's deathbed. After her father's death, the whispers abated, probably because no one wanted the chaos of a civil war. Even if Pulcheria was Arcadius' sole surviving child, women were banned by Roman law from ruling in their own right. In her mind Theo's paternity was a moot point. He was her beloved brother, acknowledged by her father as his heir, chosen by God and acclaimed by his people to be Emperor of Rome.

"What bad blood existed between my father and aunt?"

"Your father resented the new marriage and the new baby girl, both of whom your grandfather loved and lavished with honors and gifts. Your father refused to let them live here in the imperial palace when Galla came to Constantinople while your grandfather campaigned."

"I see." Pulcheria thought a moment. "But that doesn't explain Placidia's reluctance to return to Ravenna."

"When Placidia was orphaned at age seven, she went to live with General Stilicho and his wife Lady Serena. They raised her with their children. Since your uncle Honorius executed General Stilicho and his son—Placidia's intended husband—I'm sure your aunt has no wish to return to his court."

"Of course! I had no idea the relationships were so complicated between East and West. Why were we kept in the dark about this?"

Anthemius shrugged. "People are reluctant to gossip, Princess."

The absurd idea that people didn't want to gossip tickled something in Pulcheria. An inappropriate bubble of laughter started in her chest. She tried to stifle it. It came out as a loud snorting sound, then continued as a cascade of giggles. She gasped, trying to regain her dignity. "Regent! I thought you an honest man!"

"My apologies, Princess." Anthemius grinned, then joined in with a hearty laugh. "That was a terrible lie." Which led to another round of giggles.

When they both settled down, he continued. "It is good to see you can laugh, Princess. I worry about you being so serious all the time. You are a bright child with a surprising grasp of complicated issues. You should take some time to be frivolous while you can. Soon you will be of marriageable age and have your own little empire to run."

*Marriage? 'Own little empire'?* His words sobered her. Pulcheria had never considered that possibility. In her own mind, she always sat next to her brother, helping him rule. The thought of leaving Theo on his own, marriage to a strange man, giving birth…images of gory sheets and the coppery smell of blood invaded her senses. Her vision grayed for a moment. She grasped the arms of her chair to hold herself up.

"Princess?" The regent's concerned face came into focus. "Are you all right?"

"I'm fine. The laughter weakened me." Pulcheria covered her lapse with a diversion. "Regent, send agents to see to our Aunt Placidia's safety. Extend her an invitation to our court. I believe we should know her better. This rift between the Eastern and Western parts of the empire is dangerous. Any other news?"

"The new city walls are going according to plan." Anthemius seemed genuinely excited, as he did about most construction projects—and he had many planned. Constantine had built his city in a hurry and some of the shoddy construction showed nearly ninety years later. "They will hold off any army and should stand a thousand years."

"Excellent. I look forward to touring the site. And I am most pleased with the results of your delegation to Persia on the emperor's behalf. I prayed that King Yazdgard would allow our co-religionists to worship as they pleased, and you attained that privilege for them. God sees your good work, Regent."

"Thank you, Princess. That is all for now." Anthemius rose, ducked his head in a slight bow, and left.

Pulcheria stared at the bible verse she had been studying, without seeing it. She had much to think about. Her aunt's safety, the legacy of discord between East and West, her brother's need for more maturity, and—most frightening of all—the regent's plan to marry her off. Did he also have plans for Theo? Did

Anthemius reassess his worth and position? After all, he had just appointed his son to the important post of city prefect and married his daughter to General Procopius, who claimed descent from the Great Constantine—normal actions for a man in the position to help his family, but they could also be signs of something more.

She shook her head. No. Anthemius was an honorable man. She didn't believe he wanted the diadem for himself or another of his clan, but she and he obviously didn't agree on what was best for the emperor and empire. She had been so focused on the danger to Theo, she hadn't thought about possible danger to herself. Anthemius wouldn't move until she was of age.

*I still have time to chart my own course. But how can I thwart his plans for me?*

# Chapter 4



*Constantinople, September 410*

PRINCESS PULCHERIA, MAY I PRESENT FLAVIUS ANTHEMIUS ISIDORUS Theophilus?" Anthemius bowed, indicating his grandson. Even to his biased eyes, the boy looked awkward and embarrassed—the legacy of being fourteen and not much around girls. He did show some promise of height and had dark wavy hair and laughing brown eyes. "I thought you might enjoy company on our tour of the walls."

Pulcheria gave the regent a sharp look at this last-minute addition to their party, then smiled at the boy. "I always enjoy sorties into the city and talking with anyone knowledgeable. Is there one of your four names you prefer over the others?"

"My friends call me Theo." The boy blushed to the roots of his hair.

"I'm afraid I can have only one Theo in my life." The princess frowned. "I'll call you Izzy to distinguish you from your father Isidorus."

Anthemius shepherded the two young people to the palace courtyard where the imperial wagon waited. Pulcheria shot question after question at his grandson; he answered in monosyllables. *This is not going as planned,* Anthemius thought, *but I should have known the princess would not act like a normal girl.*

"You two will take the wagon, with Antiochus as chaperone." He waved at the mounted guards chatting with his son. "I'll ride with the guards. Servants will follow with food and drink. I thought a picnic on the wall might be entertaining."

"Thank you for your kindness, Regent." The princess' smile didn't reach her eyes. "I'm sure your grandson will be great company and can answer all my questions about the construction."

A panicked look crossed the boy's face.

"I can answer all your questions at the site, Princess." Anthemius helped her into the wagon where Antiochus waited, then whispered in his grandson's ear. "Talk to her!"

He strode over to Isidorus, scowled, mounted a block and swung his leg over a spirited bay. He settled in the four-horned military-style saddle and clasped the horse tightly with his legs. After settling the restless animal, he turned to his son. "Didn't you prepare the boy?"

"As best I could." Isidorus frowned. "He's at an awkward age. Too old to companion the emperor and too young to interest a budding female. Luckily, we have a few more years for them both to mature. Let them become friends before we propose the marriage."

"The Princess might not agree to the marriage. She has considerable influence over her brother." Anthemius looked thoughtfully at the wagon exiting the Chalke gate. "She's precocious for her age and sex. She believes she has the right to rule at her brother's side and daily prepares for that role. I've never seen such will in one so young. She has even taken over the emperor's comportment training, showing him how to dress, what to say, when to smile and how to moderate anger." He shook his head. "I fear her increasing religiosity. Even today, for an outing, she dresses like a holy woman, not like a princess, much less a girl of eleven. She could be a disaster for the empire, if her brother follows her lead. It is past time we pried his sister from his side. He'll be a much better ruler and happier man under our more moderate influence."

"Can Antiochus help with our plans? The eunuch is close to the emperor." Isidorus held his black gelding to a sedate walk behind the carriage.

Anthemius nodded. "We've worked quite well together. He's happy with the proposition of marriage between the princess and our house."

"And the gifts we've provided?" Isidorus' mouth quirked into a lopsided smile.

"Yes, he's quite happy with our donations. Antiochus whispers in the emperor's ear about what a fine match it would be. The boy already trusts me with the empire. I don't see that he'll object to trusting me with his sister. As soon as she starts to bleed, we'll make our proposal."

Anthemius sighed. *I just hope my grandson is up to the task of wooing the girl.*

*Perhaps I should find an older man, one with more experience, who could better handle our precocious princess.*

PULCHERIA SAT QUIETLY IN THE CONSISTORY, EMBROIDERING A CASULA—A poncho-like garment Father Marcus used in celebrating the Eucharist. Her stitches had improved in six years; even Nana said so. But she did not embroider in the council meetings just for the glory of the Lord. Anthemius reluctantly let her attend and only did so after recent pressure from Theo and solemn promises that she would be unobtrusive. Pulcheria found that sitting in the corner with eyes downcast at her stitching made her nearly invisible. The council members soon forgot her presence as she listened attentively.

Anthemius, with his various honors as regent, patrician and prefect of the East, ran the council and set the agenda. Pulcheria could tell what the major topics would be by the attendance. Today was a war council with the emperor's Master of Offices, most senior legal and money advisor, the two generals heading the armies in the emperor's presence, and a couple of other notable citizens including Anthemius' son Isidorus as the city prefect.

"The news from Rome is not good." Anthemius put down the papyrus sheets from which he had read a brief report. "Alaric's horde is on the march south. Our agents report he holds the Princess Placidia hostage and intends to invade North Africa."

There was little muttering around the table; most, if not all, had already heard the news. The palace was equipped with a very efficient means of transmitting gossip.

Pulcheria continued stitching as Isidorus asked the inevitable question. "What are we to do? Alaric will devastate the Italian peninsula as he did the Greek but fifteen years ago!"

"We do nothing." Anthemius retorted. "We've sent forty thousand troops to Ravenna at Emperor Honorius' request. If they are needed in Africa, the Augustus can transport them at his own expense. Rome is already ravaged. It is up to the western emperor to rule his portion of the empire."

"And the imperial princess?" the Master of Offices asked.

"Again, it is up to Honorius to recover his sister. Let us turn our attention to matters closer to home."

Pulcheria stitched away.

When the meeting concluded and all the others packed up their reports, she questioned Anthemius. Why did he recommend moving this army unit to that posting? Why appoint this man to an office when a more suitable candidate seemed available? How goes the dredging in the harbor? What of the most recent embassy from Persia? He answered all her questions fully and in as much detail as she wished until she finally asked, "Is there nothing we can do for our aunt?"

"No, Princess."

"Can we not send agents to her rescue?"

"The barbarian camp is heavily guarded, and, as I said, it is up to Honorius to free his sister. We should not interfere in the affairs of the West."

"I do not like this kidnapping of royal personages." She frowned, stirred by a vague uneasiness that popped up at inconvenient times. "What if some barbarian snatched me or Theo off the streets of Constantinople while we progress?"

"It is my personal responsibility to ensure the safety of you, your brother, and your sisters. I will double the guard when you progress and make certain our agents are alert for any abduction plots. I understand you are to visit the bread steps tomorrow. Do you wish me to accompany you personally? Or I could send my grandson with you."

"No, Regent." *He proposes another meeting only days after that boring outing with his ignorant spotty grandson?* She knew the regent's motives in throwing the two of them together and vowed to resist him any way she could. She placed her hand on his wrist. "I am more at ease. Please forgive my fancies."

"It's been my experience that a healthy sense of caution makes for a longer life, Princess. I do not want you to fear unreasonably, but you should always be aware of who your enemies are and what their likely next move will be."

*Including you, Regent?* she thought, but asked, "And Alaric's next move?"

"I believe you have nothing to fear from Alaric. He passed by our strong walls in favor of sacking the weaker Rome. But he can't eat gold and silver. His people will starve and his hold on them will weaken. He will be busy dealing with his own problems and not have resources nor inclination to hatch a plot against your person."

"And the Huns?"

"You've been studying your brother's maps and reports of troop deployments. What is your assessment?"

"The Huns seem contained by the forts on the Danube. Reports from the borders indicate they do minimal raiding across the river. I assume they are busy integrating the Gothic peoples and other barbarians they have subjugated in the past years. They must take time to digest what they have swallowed before turning their attention to us." She rarely surprised Anthemius these days and was pleased when her grasp of the subject met with a calculating smile.

"And your recommendation?"

She considered a moment. "Send a diplomatic delegation to explore trade, make gifts to their leaders, and gather information about the Huns and their capabilities."

"Have you been reading my mind, Princess? I intend to send a delegation headed by the historian Olympiodorus next spring, when it is safe to travel again."

"Olympiodorus?" She frowned. "I don't know of him."

"He's from Egypt—Thebes to be exact." Anthemius shuffled his papers and glanced at the door, as if gauging when it would be circumspect to leave.

Pulcheria sensed a reluctance in the regent to speak more about this Olympiodorus. Why? "Is he a capable agent?"

"He's a renowned traveler, speaks several languages—including Greek and Latin—and chronicles his adventures in verse and prose. I doubt your tutors would have you study him."

"Is he a pagan?" Pulcheria frowned. "If so, I'm not sure he would be the best person to represent our Christian emperor."

"The Huns are pagans, Princess. Olympiodorus has much experience dealing with barbarian peoples." Anthemius spoke in clipped tones. "He is the perfect diplomat for this mission."

"I bow to your superior knowledge of this situation, Regent." Pulcheria knew she would not win this argument.

Anthemius surprised her by saying, in a soft and respectful tone, "You have a grasp of events uncommon to most who are twice and more your age, Princess." Anthemius' smile grew sad. "Your grandfather, the Great Theodosius, would be proud of you. But you still have much to learn."

"Thank you, Regent." Pulcheria felt the blood rushing to her cheeks. She looked him in the eye. "I intend to advise my brother and strive to make myself fit for that task. You have been most helpful. I pray you will continue to support me." She knew she took a risk stating her position so boldly, but perhaps it would spur Anthemius to be more open about his own intentions.

His smile disappeared, replaced by a sober look. Anthemius bowed deeply. "I have pledged my life to protecting the glory that is Rome. I will uphold Theodosius' rule and his right to choose his advisers."

*But not me specifically.* Pulcheria noted the omission and knew to be on her guard. This man, first among the citizens of Eastern Rome, bowed to her and acknowledged her brother's rights. She felt sure he would honor his word, but he made no promises as to her own role. She knew what place he had in mind: firmly in the net of his own family. A prospect that frightened her, but he didn't have to know that. She would rule at her brother's side. She just had to figure out how to avoid the trap Anthemius set for her. *Good Lord show me the way.*

# Chapter 5



*Imperial progress through Constantinople, September 410*

PULCHERIA'S CONFIDENCE IN HER ABILITIES TO RULE LASTED UNTIL HER progress with Father Marcus the next morning. The abstractions of hypothetical future battles with Huns and Goths in distant lands were replaced with the reality of a city teeming with people struggling to feed and clothe themselves.

Pulcheria's heavily guarded entourage progressed to the small harbor named for her grandfather on the southern Propontis Sea. She and Father Marcus traveled in a smaller covered litter rather than the conspicuous imperial wagon. However, the palace guards, in their white uniforms and purple cloaks, made it evident a personage of note was about in the streets. People gathered in knots, speculating on who might be behind the closed curtains.

Pulcheria peeked into the street. Her stomach fluttered. Was this venture a mistake? She turned to her companion. "Father, I need your advice."

"Of course, Princess. How may I help?" Father Marcus leaned forward; hands clasped in his lap.

"I know how to comport myself at court, but I've been isolated from the people of Constantinople. Anthemius and Antiochus keep us immured in the palace. I don't know how to act with the people of the city."

"You are an imperial princess. Why is it important to you?" Marcus' tone was reminiscent of the classroom.

"I'm curious. If we are to rule the people, we should know them and their needs. That's why I wanted to inspect the bread distribution." She paused. "Also, the Lord commands that we care for the poor and the hungry, the sick and lame, but I don't know how."

"If you wish the people to like you, be your active curious self. Ask questions. Show interest in their lives. If you wish the people to love you, make their lives easier."

"The first is easy, the second harder. I can do little on my own. You've spoken frequently of my grandmother Aelia Flacilla and her ministry to the people. I want to do that. I want to honor God with my service."

"Remember the verse in the old part of the Bible? 'To everything there is a season, and a time to every purpose under the heaven.' In time, Princess, you will come into your own. Trust in God to lead you down the right path."

"Thank you, Father. You are a comfort to me as well as a teacher." She learned back and considered when her time might come.

At their destination, Pulcheria alighted behind a dense screen of guards.

The Master of Harbors, a thin dapper man of middle years, approached with a worried frown. He bowed low. "Welcome, Princess. May I escort you to my offices for refreshments?"

"I did not come here to eat, but to inspect your operations, Harbormaster. Those ships," Pulcheria indicated a small fleet moored at the docks, "are they from Africa?" She strode toward the docks, surprised adults scrambling to catch up with her.

"Princess!" the Harbormaster puffed, "The docks are no place for a ch–uh– for a person of your rank. Let me take you inside for a repast."

Pulcheria stopped abruptly, causing a comic pile up of retainers as they tried to avoid her and each other. The Harbormaster's face wore an expression of disappointment and anxiety. What was wrong? She was being her curious self, asking questions.

"Give some consideration to the Harbormaster, Princess," Father Marcus whispered in her ear. "No doubt he has several family members and a number of clients in his office who wait to meet you. For many, even a glimpse of a member of the imperial family gives them status for the rest of their lives."

"Really?" Pulcheria muttered.

Father Marcus nodded. She turned to the Harbormaster with a warm smile, favoring him by touching his arm. "Forgive my enthusiasm, Sir. I do not often escape the palace. I look forward to sharing food with you…after you have shown me the ships."

The Harbormaster's face relaxed. He smiled back. Father Marcus gave her an approving nod. So small a gesture to reap such cooperation. She turned toward her goal once more as the entourage untangled itself.

They approached a line of men, bowed down with heavy sacks of grain on their shoulders, trudging from the ships. They filled waiting carts, then moved more slowly back to the dock for their next load. Pulcheria once observed a line of ants carrying food back to their nest in much the same way. "Would it not be faster for the men to form a line and pass the sacks from one to another, as the fire *vigiles* do buckets?"

"Likely not, Princess." The Harbormaster wiped sweat from his brow with a limp rag.

"It would be less work, since the men would stand in one place. They could move the bags faster."

The Harbormaster stood slack-jawed at the suggested innovation, then replied, "This is the way it has always been done, Princess."

Only a few of the dull-eyed, scrawny men mustered the curiosity to look up at the girl dressed as a holy woman, accompanied by palace guards. All sported a brand on their cheeks, indicating they were imperial slaves who worked in public factories. "Who are these men? Where do they come from?"

"Captives, debtors, criminals." The Harbormaster shrugged. "No one you need be concerned about. We use them to unload the ships and grind the grain to flour."

"They seem malnourished. Would they not work harder if they were better fed?"

"They would indeed have more vigor, but that would make them more difficult to control. We would need to employ many more guards if they were less docile."

Pulcheria frowned. What the Harbormaster said made sense, but it didn't seem right. Except for violent criminals, most slaves were freed after some time in servitude. Men shouldn't die of starvation for a debt or petty theft. Everyone was redeemable in the Lord's eyes. She would discuss this with Father Marcus later.

The Harbormaster motioned to one of the men. "You there, bring your sack here, and be quick about it." A youngish man with dark eyes and missing front teeth, shuffled to the group and put down his burden with a sigh. The Harbormaster untied the neck of the sack and lifted a fistful of fat brown seeds, letting them trickle through his fingers. He said, with a touch of pride, "We have barley from Alexandria today, enough to feed a whole district for a month.

Grain is the lifeblood of the empire and it all comes through my harbors."

"Where is it stored?" Father Marcus broke in.

"We have five stone cornstores up the hill." The Harbormaster indicated behind them with a vague headshake. "Inspectors certify the grain's purity and volume. From there, it is issued to the mills, which supply the bakeries. We also store a surplus in case of emergencies."

"How much surplus do we have on hand?" Pulcheria asked.

"Enough for six months."

"You could feed nearly a million souls for six months?" She looked at the dulled-eyed man with his ribs prominently showing. It must be torturous to carry grain day in and day out, knowing others would benefit by having the bread he was denied. Pulcheria remained silent as the Harbormaster pointed out the construction of the stone docks.

A light breeze blew from the northeast, freshening the usual harbor smells of rotting seaweed and dead fish. "The deep harbors are on the Golden Horn side, Princess, but the consistent northeast wind makes rounding the peninsula difficult, so we established these small harbors just to handle the grain ships from Africa."

After they met briefly with a ship captain, the Harbormaster escorted her back to his offices where, indeed, a small crowd waited. She had a cup of watered wine with the Harbormaster's portly wife and nibbled the delicacies on which the good woman evidently spent enormous effort. She chatted with several merchants about their businesses, noting the looks of surprise many were unable to conceal at her more discerning questions. After observing the required courtesies, she caught Father Marcus's attention, raising an eyebrow.

"It is time we moved on," he said, fanning himself. "The Princess wishes to see the bakeries. We should be there before the sun gets too warm in the heavens."

The Harbormaster started to protest.

"Thank you, but we must go," Pulcheria cut in.

His wife approached a final time to bow low. "Bless you, Princess. Not since your sainted grandmother, Aelia Flacilla Augusta, has anyone from the palace honored us with their presence. Please know that you may call on us at any time for any reason."

Pulcheria took the woman's hands in her own. "Bless you and your family for the important work you do here. I return the favor. If you have any needs, send word and I will look into it."

In the litter, bumping their way to one of the twenty bakeries that provided government bread to the citizens of Constantinople, Father Marcus gave her a thoughtful smile. "Well done, Princess."

"In what way, Father?"

"Your respect for the people and their work. People saw your genuine interest and concern and love you for it. You may not be able to pass laws or lead armies, but the love of the people is no small thing. That power, used wisely," he shrugged, "can be just as effective in ruling."

Father Marcus' words jolted Pulcheria. She had thought of her curiosity as an aid to ruling, and her service a gift to God. She hadn't considered the power it could bring. Power had always been the ability to get your way through station—you had command over others through birth or position—or brute force. "The abstract has become concrete," she muttered.

"What?" Father Marcus looked puzzled.

"I counsel Theo frequently about keeping the love and consent of his people and the army. But those are just words. What do they mean? How does a ruler *act*? History shows, without the support of the people and the army, an emperor will fail—sometimes forfeiting his life." She shuddered. "I now have a more concrete idea of how to protect my brother and sisters. You have given me much to ponder, Father."

The smell of baking bread permeated their litter, masking the usual smells of sweaty bodies and horse dung. Pulcheria's mouth watered despite her recent meal.

They halted. Her captain opened the curtains to help her alight.

A pair, the opposite of the Harbormaster and his wife, greeted Pulcheria with low bows and elaborate greetings. The baker was a rotund man; his wife whip thin. Both faces flushed red from the ovens and streaked with flour, which they had vainly attempted to brush off.

"Welcome, Princess!" The Masterbaker ushered Pulcheria, Father Marcus and a contingent of guards into an enormous rectangular space, blazing with the heat of dozens of dome-shaped ovens. Boys stoked the fires under the ovens, taking wood from stacks covering one long side of the enclosure. Men and women shoveled large round loaves in and out of the ovens on flat paddles, transferring the finished loaves to baskets. The men wore only brief loincloths, the women short sleeveless tunics. All glistened with sweat.

"These people have no brands. Are they not slaves like the dockhands?" Pulcheria asked the Masterbaker.

"No, Princess. These are members of my family and others of the bakers' guild. Bakers maintain their own craft. Those born to it stay with it."

*Like a princess born to the purple, birth is destiny among the craft guilds,* Pulcheria realized. "What are they doing now?" She indicated a boy lugging a full basket away from the ovens.

"When a basket is full, the underbaker signals one of the boys, who carries the basket to a back gate. An imperial inspector counts the loaves and checks for uniformity of weight. Then the boy deposits his basket in a cart which takes the bread away for distribution."

Sweat popped out on Pulcheria's forehead, soaking through her head covering. Trickles started down her ribs. She felt a bit faint. "How do they stand the heat?"

"We are just finishing the day's bake. We try to do most of it in the cool of the morning, before the sun rises and reaches its zenith. They also drink plenty of water and eat salt fish for breakfast." The Masterbaker indicated the short end of the courtyard, covered by a peristyle. "Let us watch from there, where it is cooler."

It was much cooler out of the sun and away from the immediate vicinity of the ovens. A dozen women worked there, mixing the bread and shaping the loaves. The Masterbaker's wife evidently supervised this area. She stepped forward to explain. "Every loaf must be the same weight and quality. We are at the end of the process for the day. This batch of dough is done and we will make our final loaves. My daughter Marcia can demonstrate, if the Princess has time?"

"Oh, yes!" Pulcheria watched a girl, not much older than herself, pull a portion of dough from a glazed bowl. With deft strokes of floured hands, she pulled and patted the dark dough into a round loaf shape on a flat stone. Her mother tied twine around the circumference of the loaf to check for size, then cut shallow grooves in the top to make eight perfect wedges.

"I should like to try shaping the dough." Sheltered from the mundane details of everyday living, Pulcheria had an abiding curiosity about how things worked. How was bread baked, a wall built, fish caught? How did water get from the cisterns to her bath? With these and thousands more questions she pestered her tutors and attendants, so was surprised at the shocked look on Marcia's face.

"Oh, no! The Princess mustn't—" The girl clamped her mouth shut, with a frightened look, realizing she spoke her thoughts out loud.

"My daughter didn't mean to offend." The Masterbaker's wife bowed low.

"She only meant the Princess shouldn't soil her hands with such work."

"I hope my hands won't soil your good bread." Pulcheria smiled, raising her hands for inspection. "They are usually covered in ink. You do such a fine job shaping the dough. I only wished to see how it feels."

"By all means, the Princess shall do as she wishes. Marcia, show her how it is done."

The girl said, with a shy smile, "The Princess might want to roll up her sleeves." Pulcheria did as bidden. "Now cover your hands in flour, so the dough won't stick." Marcia picked up a handful of dark flour from a small bowl on her right and rubbed her hands together. Pulcheria followed suit. "Now take your dough from the bowl and pat it into shape."

Marcia slowed her motions for Pulcheria to see, but the princess still struggled to produce a specimen as fine as the baker girl's. Dough stuck to her fingers and her loaf remained stubbornly lumpy, but the sheer joy of doing something ordinary lightened her mood. Her days were filled with study and planning. The opportunity to pound yielding bread dough and get covered in flour was a luxury.

The Masterbaker's wife appraised her effort with a critical eye. "Not bad for a first try. After you have been making loaves for a few days, you'll be as skilled as Marcia. We produce four thousand loaves a day here. She has lots of practice." Marcia continued to make more loaves while they talked; there were now nine perfect loaves and Pulcheria's misshapen one waiting for the ovens. "Does the Princess wish her loaf to be fired? She could take it with her."

Pulcheria looked at the lumpy loaf with regret. "I am afraid we cannot wait for it to bake, and I would not have it wasted. I am sure it would not pass the sharp eyes of the inspector. Please, Marcia, make it perfect, like yours." The girl added more dough and straightened the loaf in a few seconds. Pulcheria could not tell which was hers except from its position on the stone. "Thank you again for the opportunity to try your trade." She dipped her hands in the bowl of water used by the bread girl and wiped them on a coarse cloth. "It's been an education." She left amid shouts and acclamations from the workers for her good health.

"That was fun!" Pulcheria crowed back in the litter.

"And another success, Princess. The people were impressed."

"But I didn't do it to impress them!"

"All the better. Your natural impulses are good. The people respect that. Most people will spot false actions."

They next traveled to one of the bread steps, where a portion of the eighty thousand government loaves was distributed each day. The head of her guards brought the litter to a halt and opened the door to say, "I'm sorry Princess, but we should not stop here."

"What is the problem?" Pulcheria asked impatiently.

"There seems to be some disorder at this step, Princess." The captain dipped his head. "I believe we should go to another or preferably back to the palace."

"What is the nature of the disorder?"

"The bread seems to be delayed. The crowd is restive. If it does not arrive soon, I fear they may grow violent."

"Then I must address their concerns."

"You must not, Princess!" The captain's horrified look was echoed in his tone. "It is not safe. Regent Anthemius would have my head if any harm came to you."

"As he should." Pulcheria's spine stiffened. "Send a soldier to find out where their bread is." Her blood rose as he hesitated. "Now, Captain! I will feed these people from the palace kitchens, if I have to."

To her surprise, the captain bowed and turned to his troops, dispatching a couple on the bread-finding mission. She used that commanding voice with her servants but feared the captain might balk and override her wishes.

"Are you sure about this, Princess?" Father Marcus asked with concern. "You've had two successful encounters. Going back to the palace seems the safest course."

"These are my people. They are not yet violent. If I can prevent injury and death through my actions, I must act. Besides— " she smiled, "—did you not tell me just hours ago to trust God to show me the right path? Perhaps this is the season I can care for the people."

They proceeded to the bread step where the captain announced her presence. Pulcheria stepped down from the litter. Her guards surrounded her. "Captain! Let me be seen!"

He reluctantly ordered his men to her side and back. Pulcheria made a note to praise the captain to Antiochus. After this trip, she planned many more. Having a compliant man in charge of her guards would come in handy.

She turned to the hungry crowd. The people prostrated themselves before her, shouting her name. Most wore rags and were barely better nourished than the dock slaves. This bread might be their main meal for the day. Her heart hurt at the sight. These were her people. They needed food.

She addressed them in her best rhetorical voice. "My people, I understand you have no bread today."

A jumble of shouts arose from the crowd.

"Yes."

"No bread."

"My children starve."

She put up her hands for quiet. The volume lowered to an occasional mutter. "The Good Lord and the Emperor Theodosius will provide. I have sent officers to investigate and will stay here myself until you receive your share. You will not go home without!"

Cheers from the crowd were interrupted by angry shouts from a rat-faced man, holding the hands of two dirty urchins. "What will you do about Felix? He's the reason the bread ain't here more days 'n not."

"Who is this Felix?" Father Marcus asked.

"He's the agent that runs this step." The angry mutters increased. "And he's crookeder than a dog's hind leg. He steals the government bread and sells it in the market for profit. I seen him."

"I will not tolerate theft of my people's portion. Be assured I will look into this. If your accusations are true, Felix will be punished most harshly." *And anyone else engaged in this corruption. Does Prefect Isidorus know?* Anger rising, Pulcheria turned to her captain. "Find this Felix person and bring him to me."

Within moments, a guard dragged a cowering man from the step offices. He wore fine clothes and flashy jewels, but the look on his smooth face at being confronted by an imperial princess was of blind terror. He prostrated himself gibbering before she could even ask a question. "It's the carters, Your Highness. They're the thieves. Half the bread doesn't make it from the bakeries, and the people blame me."

The rat-faced man shouted again, "Who splits the take with the carters? Where'd you get yer rings?"

"My wife has money of her own. These are gifts." Felix pleaded, "Please, Princess. I did no wrong!"

"Guards, take him into custody. We will sort it out later. For now, the priority is to get these people their bread."

Even as she spoke, hooves clattered on the paved street. Cheers broke out at the back of the crowd. "It's here. The bread's here. God bless Princess Pulcheria!"

"Father Marcus, please join me." With her guards, they passed out bread to the hungry crowd. Pulcheria silently thanked the Lord for the speedy recovery of the bread and the favor of her people. Up close, Pulcheria saw the rheumy eyes of the aged, touched the boney hands of starved children, smelled the unwashed bodies of street beggars. Not a one snatched at the loaves. All blessed the hands of the giver.

When the last loaf was given to a widow with three small children, Pulcheria blessed the woman and gave her a few copper coins. She was tired but elated. The afternoon's tasks left her with a feeling of euphoria at having served her people well.

That feeling didn't last.

On the way back to the palace, Pulcheria scowled.

"What is it, Princess?"

"Isidorus will hear of this." She huffed. "As city prefect, he should have been aware of this corruption and taken steps to see the guilty parties punished. Did he get some gift for looking the other way?"

Father Marcus shrugged his shoulders. "Many government officials grow rich from such graft, but you have no reason to believe Isidorus is one of them."

"You're right, Father. Something about the man sets my teeth on edge. I have no cause to believe he is stealing from the poor, but I will watch to see he does his duty to stop it." She sighed, leaned back, and gave in to the soothing swing of the litter. She had been so excited about the procession, she'd gotten little sleep the night before. "Thank you, Father," Pulcheria said, with a barely concealed yawn.

"What for, Princess?"

"Your wise counsel. Without it, I would have embarrassed the Harbormaster, disrupted the bakers, and not had the righteous courage to help the mob at the bread step." Her head nodded, eyes closing as she murmured, "I think I know now…how to help…brother…people…."

She didn't notice Father Marcus pull a cloak around her shoulders and smooth the hair back from her forehead.

# Chapter 6



*Imperial Palace, September 412*

Patrician, are you well?" Pulcheria put aside Olympiodorus' report on his mission to the Huns. Despite her misgivings, she had to admit the pagan poet served the empire well as an excellent ambassador and spy. He also wrote witty, entertaining reports.

Anthemius wiped sweat from his pale face. "A recurring fever, Princess. Nothing for you to worry about."

But she did worry. Her brother had barely turned eleven, and she was only thirteen. If the regent's health failed, she could not count on a similarly accommodating and honorable man for his replacement. Although Anthemius plotted her marriage to his grandson, at least it was a traditional and acceptable plan, one that left Theo in nominal control. A new regent could bring radical changes. Perhaps a forced marriage for her and the convenient disappearance of her brother.

"You must see our court physician when you leave." Pulcheria pointed to a padded chair. "Please sit and have a cool drink." One of the ever-present servants approached with a goblet of lemon water.

"Your concern does you great credit, Princess." He waved the servant away. "I do wish to discuss this report with you but feel I should retire."

Pulcheria rose and accompanied Anthemius to the door of her work room. She clasped his hand in hers. "I will pray for your returning health."

"Bless you, Princess." The old man's eyes glittered. With fever? Tears?

"Antiochus waits on your pleasure. Should I send him in?"

"Tell him ten minutes." The older she got, the more the chief eunuch tried to assert his power over her, as if he sensed her growing abilities to function without him and grasped for lost influence. When Theo talked to Pulcheria of a possible match between her and Anthemius' spotty grandson, she knew who whispered in his ear. She had called for Antiochus and kept him waiting deliberately. He had informants among her servants and tutors. Pulcheria was sure he read her correspondence. He was well-intentioned, but she needed to come up with a permanent solution to the eunuch's meddling.

Pulcheria tidied her worktable, running her hand over the smooth black lacquer finish and relishing the tidy piles of papers and precise placement of ink, quill, and wax seal. The plain workroom held no extraneous items. Each served a function. Even her one indulgence—a bronze bowl burning cedar incense— calmed her nerves and raised the moods of her visitors.

"Most Noble Princess!" Antiochus bowed in the doorway. His stomach flowed over the ornate chain that belted his saffron silk robes; his chins wobbled.

To Pulcheria, excess flesh signaled sinful physical appetites, but she schooled her face into a bland smile.

"Come." Pulcheria moved to a divan and indicated an uncomfortable carved wooden chair opposite. "Have some refreshments with me."

She waved a hand, and a serving girl poured the chief eunuch watered wine and offered honeyed dates stuffed with pistachio paste. She herself took a goblet of water.

Antiochus balanced his bulk on the small chair, declining the sticky dates with a mournful headshake. "Princess, how may I be of service?"

"I wish to speak to you of the emperor's education and companions."

Antiochus' face gave nothing away, but a slight hesitation sipping his wine indicated his wariness. "The emperor does well in his studies and seems content with his companions. Has he some complaint he is hesitant to express directly to me?"

"He masters the traditional courses in Latin, Greek, rhetoric, and composition. I review his work every evening, as you know."

Nothing happened in the royal household that Antiochus did not know.

"I find the boys able companions," she continued. "Paulinus, with his intelligence and drive, pushes my brother to excel. Placitus offers congenial companionship and the opportunity to show charity when my brother helps him with his studies. The emperor has no complaints. My concerns come from a different…uh…more spiritual place."

Antiochus pursed his mouth in an unspoken question.

"Father Marcus is a dear friend, but we have outgrown his basic instruction in the scriptures." Pulcheria put down her goblet. "I want to invite holy men to come and instruct us. Our government must have a thorough grounding in church teachings. The emperor agrees. We need to be seen in the churches of the city, participating in the services. The people need to know we have God's blessing and, through us, they are blessed."

Actually, the people just needed to see them. It was far too easy to forget about the young emperor and princesses immured in their palace, while the great men of the city conducted business—for good or ill. Two years had passed since her adventure at the bread step. She had sent a servant with gifts to the Harbormaster and the Masterbaker but found it difficult to get additional information. For all she knew, that corrupt Felix paid off Isidorus and continued pocketing his ill-gotten gains.

She had had little opportunity to get out of the palace since then. Even Theo sided with Antiochus and Anthemius once the report of her performance at the bread step became common knowledge. Her brother alternately sobbed in her arms and stamped his foot in anger that she might have been murdered by the mob. All her assurances that she had been perfectly safe with the people and her guards were quickly shoved aside. She—again!—became a prisoner in her own home.

The regent's poor health reinforced Pulcheria's plan to grasp more freedom. She gave up wheedling for more visits to the city, but appealing to her brother on religious grounds won his enthusiastic support. That her schemes also satisfied her religious cravings and made Theo more known and loved by the people was a double bonus.

"As the princess wishes." Antiochus lowered his eyes. "Perhaps next month."

"Tomorrow."

"So soon? There are many arrangements to be made and the emperor's safety to be considered."

"Sunday, then. Surely you are competent enough to arrange an outing within three days?" Pulcheria sipped her water, observing the eunuch through lowered lashes. "I was thinking of a service at the Church of the Apostles and a visit to our parents' tombs."

He nodded in acknowledgement. "Yes, Princess. That would be appropriate."

"That is all for now."

Antiochus rose and bowed. "God bless and keep you, Princess."

*Good! I wish I'd thought of this two years ago.*


Pulcheria stared at her thin face in the polished silver mirror. She cherished these moments of peace when, freshly returned from church services, the grace of the Lord still dwelt within her. After her talk with Antiochus, three months earlier, she and Theo were much more out in the city. Pulcheria more than Theo, but it still helped. The people shouted her name whenever her wagon appeared on the streets. An almoner always accompanied her to provide money for the poor. Visiting the sacred spaces in the city nourished her, gave her the strength to carry on when she had doubts. But the peace did not last. Even in the privy, she had attendants. Any words to the servants went immediately to Antiochus.

"Princess? They wait for you." A matron from her entourage stood in the doorway, slightly disapproving. Prominent families gained prestige when their women served as companions to the royal princesses, but none were true friends. Due to her young age, all tried to dominate her. When that failed, they flattered and cajoled, hoping she would wield what power she had to favor their families. Pulcheria knew it was the nature of the world. Did she not push for and protect her own family at the expense of others? Yet it was wearying, not having someone of similar rank and birth to confide in. She sighed. Her sister Arcadia was only a year younger and could be her confidant, but she was such a sweet and innocent child. Pulcheria hesitated to share her burdens with her. Time enough when Arcadia and Marina were older.

Pulcheria rose, smoothing her blue woolen robe and white hair covering. She glided past the older woman. Several more joined her train. Marble corridors echoed the slap of their leather slippers and murmur of soft voices as they progressed to the audience chamber in the Daphne—the oldest part of the palace. Since it neared winter solstice and the celebration of Our Savior's birth, braziers lent heat to the cold corridors. The sweet smell of jasmine incense, warmed by the flames, reminded her of the morning's services. She took a deep breath and relaxed.

"You may go." Pulcheria dismissed her women as she entered the audience hall. Except for a few servants, she was the only female in attendance. Men bowed, murmuring greetings as she passed.

Theo, resplendent in purple and gold, chatted with Paulinus at one end of the audience chamber. Her brother wore a thin gold diadem, which held a single large pearl to indicate his rank. Anthemius and several councilors clustered near a column, talking. The ubiquitous guards stood by the door and the carved padded chair raised on a carpeted dais at the far end of the chamber. Various petitioners lurked in the corners. Servants bustled among the elite, serving sweet and savory pastries, and fine Falerian wine in silver goblets.

One man caught her attention. General Lucius stood alone, surveying the hall. His eyes slid from hers when they made contact. Odd for the magister militum. Pulcheria had heard that soldiers, especially if fresh from the battlefield, sometimes expressed nervous behavior in crowds. She shrugged, continuing down the hall.

Theo caught sight of her and waved her to him. "Sister!" He pulled her close, kissed her cheeks, and whispered, "My savior! Please get me out of this boring audience."

She stepped back with a half-smile. "Boring or not, you are the emperor. You must be seen by your subjects on occasion and entertain their petitions."

"I know." Theo pouted. "But promise me you'll faint or have some female vapor if it goes on too long."

A sudden disturbance thwarted Pulcheria's reply. She turned to see General Lucius rushing toward their small party, a grim smile on his lips. Guards by the doors and at the back of the room moved forward but were too far away to help.

Cold dread gripped Pulcheria's bowels. She stepped in front of her brother and raised her hand. "General Lucius! Halt! What is your business with the emperor?"

The general put his hand on his sword.

"Help! To the emperor!" Pulcheria shouted.

Theo, behind her, give a small whimper.

She spread her arms, wide sleeves making her seem larger, and stepped forward, shouting, "Stay away from my brother!"

The roar of the audience chamber and confused movement faded as Pulcheria stalked toward the astonished soldier swaying before her. She heard only her own heart, beating fast and loud.

Lucius tugged at the hilt of his sword. It stuck in the scabbard. He tried a second and third time. Then his hand fell nerveless to his side.

"Forgive me!" he cried, falling to his knees, tears streaming.

Noise and movement crashed down on Pulcheria as guards hauled Lucius away. Anthemius grabbed her elbow.

"Drink this." The Regent put a goblet to her lips.

She choked on the strong wine; the fumes went to her head. She pushed the goblet away. "Theo?"

"The emperor's safe. He's being escorted to his rooms. You should follow."

Pulcheria nodded. Her knees suddenly gave way. Only the Regent's gentle hand kept her upright. She mumbled, "What just happened?"

"You saved your brother's life, Child." Anthemius guided her to a seat. "It was bravely done."

After a moment, Pulcheria's senses returned. "General Lucius?"

"The guards took him to the holding cells below the palace. I will interrogate him myself."

"Good." Pulcheria's strength came back. Rising, she hissed between her teeth, "I want to know anyone connected with this. Then I want Lucius dead."

"It will be done, Princess," Anthemius replied in an equally resolute voice.

# Chapter 7

*Imperial Palace, December 412*

WHY DID YOU TRY TO KILL THE EMPEROR?" ANTHEMIUS, IN HIS ROLE as chief magistrate, questioned Lucius in the holding cells of the palace guard. The chief of the guards, along with several beefy underlings, stood by, trying to menace a man who seemed unaware they existed. A palace scribe sat in a corner with a lap desk, taking down the testimony.

"The voices. They told me to." The general seemed a husk of his former vigorous self; thin and wild-eyed.

"The voices? Your co-conspirators?"

"No one, Regent. I acted alone." The General's eyes drifted to the shadows in the dark corner. He drew himself in, shivering.

"Then whose voices?" Anthemius was bewildered.

"What?" The would-be assassin looked up, dazed.

"The voices!" Anthemius lost patience. He shouted, "Who told you to kill the emperor?"

"I don't know! I thought they were the gods, but then…" He put both palms to his temples and pushed as if trying to squeeze something out of his brain. He moaned.

The Regent exchanged a glance with the Chief.

"Then what?" Anthemius asked in a gentler tone.

"The woman. A large woman. Taller than any man I've ever seen. The goddess Fortuna?" The man's eyes drifted upwards. He began to slump.

A guard shook his shoulder, bringing him back. Lucius looked around the room as if seeing it for the first time.

"This woman told you to kill the emperor?" Anthemius tried again.

"No. She saved him. I was going to kill him. I tried, but she enveloped him, turned her face toward me. Her face. I couldn't see it. The light." He shielded his eyes. "Demons. The voices must have been demons." His voice trailed off into incoherent mumbles.

Anthemius reached across the table and grabbed the man's jaw, wrenching his face around to stare into his eyes. "One last chance, Lucius. You were a well-regarded man and loyal soldier. Tell the truth. Why did you try to kill the emperor? Who helped you?"

"The demons told me to. I acted alone."

Anthemius released his grip, stood, and took the chief a side. "I'm afraid his wits are disordered."

"It doesn't matter. Only priests, children, and pregnant women are exempt from questioning under torture in cases of treason."

Anthemius nodded. He turned to the guards. "Bring him." He indicated the scribe. "You, too."

They trooped to a large room at the end of the corridor, past a couple of empty cells. Most criminals received swift and severe justice from the city magistrates. These cells were built to hold the occasional problem slave or guard found drunk on duty.

They entered a dark room. One guard lit torches set in standards along the wall. Anthemius noted the full array of knives and hooks to tear flesh. An unlit brazier, used to heat rods for burning skin, or melt lead to pour down a throat, stood in one corner. Whips with knotted rope, and flogs with iron tips, stood at attention in a rack along the wall. In the middle of the room, a broad wheel, taller than a man, sat in a frame with a crank in the axle.

"Put him on the wheel," the chief ordered his men.

They bound the assassin's feet to iron hooks fitted in the floor, stood him back against the wheel, and bound his hands overhead to a crossbar on the rim. Two men manned the axle crank.

Anthemius stood before Lucius and asked again, "Why did you try to kill the emperor? Who are you working with?"

"I swear to all the gods! The voices! I acted alone."

The chief nodded. The guards began to crank the wheel, pulling Lucius up and backwards. He screamed. The chief raised a hand to halt the wheel, letting the screams turn to whimpers. At his nod, the guards released the wheel a fraction, allowing the prisoner some relief.

"Tell me, Lucius, and end this," Anthemius said in a soothing tone. "You are of a noble family, entitled to a swift death by beheading. Tell me why you tried to kill the emperor and who helped you?"

Lucius mumbled incoherently, tossing his head from side to side.

"Again." Anthemius nodded to the chief. This time the prefect heard an audible pop as the assassin's shoulders dislocated.

Lucius screamed until his voice gave out. He fainted. They released the pressure. One guard threw water on the prisoner to revive him.

The regent's stomach gave a lurch. Bile crept up the back of his throat. He swallowed convulsively, wiping cold sweat from his brow when the guards turned their eyes away. This was a waste of time, but by law he had to do his duty.

"Why did you try to kill the emperor? Who worked with you?"

Lucius lasted several hours before fainting beyond their ability to revive. He never admitted to any co-conspirators.

Anthemius left the room, pale and coughing.

Rage, mixed with a heady dose of fear, flowed through Pulcheria's veins like molten lead. She paced across the length of her workroom. *I almost lost my brother! What if…* the appalling thought circled her brain and she could not banish it. She took a deep breath to steady her voice and faced Anthemius, Antiochus, and the chief of the palace guards. "How did this happen?"

They stood shamefaced before her. The chief obviously had taken time to dress in his most elaborate court uniform: a white silk tunic decorated with gold thread at the neck, cuffs and hem, and a short purple cloak thrown back over his shoulders. He stood with soldierly calm but sweat popping out on his forehead betrayed his nervousness.

*He should be nervous. I should have his head, or at least dismiss him for this incompetence.*

Anthemius, on the other hand, wore the same clothes as the day before, rumpled and stained from the damp cellars. Dark circles ringed his eyes; his jowls drooped in a grimace of weariness and pain.

Her anger cooled somewhat. She sat, patting the divan. "Regent, you look tired. Please sit."

Anthemius straightened sagging shoulders. "Thank you, Princess, but this report is best delivered standing. We questioned Lucius all through the night. He insisted he acted alone. There were no conspirators."

"Questioned under torture?"

The regent nodded.

"Is he dead?"

"Yes, Princess."

"Do you believe him? That no one helped him?"

The chief stepped forward. "We're questioning his friends. They know nothing. A few said General Lucius changed since coming back from the border. He lost a childhood friend in the fighting and mourned excessively."

"That's no excuse for trying to kill my brother!" she shouted.

"He didn't pull his sword," Anthemius soothed.

"He tried! I saw him. He pulled three times and seemed astonished it didn't come free."

"It's a miracle!" Antiochus raised his eyes to the ceiling. "Lucius claimed a large woman enveloped the emperor in her arms and prevented his sword from leaving the scabbard. Surely the Virgin Mary kept your brother from harm."

"Where did you hear that tall tale?" Anthemius threw him an annoyed look.

"One of the guards told me." The eunuch looked pleased.

"What?" Pulcheria leaned forward, stunned. *Had the Holy Virgin appeared to save my brother?*

"Lucius' mind was disordered." The regent gave Antiochus a sharp look. "He identified the specter as the Roman goddess Fortuna."

"The general was a pagan?" Pulcheria fumed. "This is what happens when you allow unbelievers in positions of power!" *When I rule, one of my first acts will be to expel all pagans and Jews from the army and the administration. This will never happen again!*

"He likely mistook your own brave and protecting presence for that of the goddess." The chief ran a hand through his thinning hair. "We examined the sword and scabbard. It appears a loop of leather around the hilt kept it in place. It is a common precaution for ceremonial swords, so they don't come loose while riding. Lucius must have forgotten to remove it in his nervousness or haste."

Pulcheria leaned back, disappointed, filing the story away for the future. It wouldn't be a bad thing if people thought the Holy Virgin personally protected the imperial family. "Was the sword his?"

"He claimed so." The chief nodded.

"But he didn't know to release the restraining loop?" She cupped her chin in her hand, staring into the middle distance. "This seems suspicious to me. I'm not convinced Lucius acted alone."

Pulcheria saw the men glance at one another and guessed their thoughts. *Silly girl. What does she know of swords and conspiracies?*

"We will follow up with all due diligence and apprehend any additional conspirators, if they exist." Anthemius went down on one knee, head bowed. "I promise, Princess, on my honor, I will do all in my power to ensure this doesn't happen again."

Pulcheria placed a hand on his shoulder. "I know you will, Regent. You have ever been a friend and protector of our family."

"It will be easier to protect you and the emperor if you curtail your travels in the city, Princess. Perhaps you should be more…retiring?" Antiochus offered a brief, pleading smile.

"This happened in our home!" Pulcheria's rage returned. She stood. "I sometimes think we would be better protected by our good people in the streets than by the incompetents in charge of the palace. You two—" she pointed at the eunuch and the chief. "—are dismissed from my presence. I wish to confer further with the Regent."

Antiochus and the chief paled, expressing apologies as they bowed out her door.

*Good! A little fear for their positions might spur them to better efforts.*

Pulcheria turned to Anthemius. She caught the ghost of a smile flee his face.

"Princess, for such a young woman, you have a remarkable way of putting people in their place."

"Antiochus irks me to no end. He treats me like an idiot child."

"I believe he thinks better of you."

"He can't resist ordering our lives. You may be regent, but that means you govern the empire. Inside these walls, Antiochus rules, and his will is law. As long as we are children, he wields power over our persons like no other. I can suggest and order, but things happen at his will and in his time."

"May I make a suggestion?"

"You know I value your advice." She took his hand in hers, noting the age spots and wrinkles that signaled his advancing years.

"You are nearing womanhood."

Pulcheria blushed, nodding. Her breasts were budding, her hips taking on more curves. She had yet to bleed, but Nana assured her it could be any month now.

"It is time to think of marriage. In a year or two, you could be betrothed to a suitable man. In three, married, with a child of your own on the way. Betrothal shifts the balance of power. You could dismiss Antiochus."

Marriage and childbirth, her twin dreads. The first because of its threat to Theo; the second because of its threat to herself. Just the mention triggered feelings of fear and helplessness. She pushed those feelings away, schooling her face.

"My brother could dismiss Antiochus today, but he has an odd fondness for the man." And she lacked any evidence of outright animosity to sway her brother to her side. The eunuch accepted gifts from people wanting favors, but that was to be expected.

The regent's eyes widened.

Pulcheria pursed her lips. She hadn't meant to comment on Theo's great weakness, his malleability. He was only a boy. She hoped he would grow out of the habit of bowing to others' whims as he got older and wiser.

"I will think on your proposal." She released his hand.

"Good. All men's days are numbered on this earth. I would see you and the emperor in safe hands before I depart."

Into whose hands did he want to consign their fate? She trusted Anthemius to act honorably, but not his son. Isidorus showed more ambition and less patience. He would likely become the dominant force in the government after his father died.

"God keep you safe and grant you long life, my friend, so we don't have to face those challenges." She escorted him to her door. "Now go home and rest."

# Chapter 8



*Imperial Palace, January 413*

PULCHERIA WOKE IN THE MIDDLE OF THE NIGHT. A HEAVY CRAMPING sensation roiled her lower abdomen. *Sweet Jesus and Holy Mother Mary, what affliction is this?* She curled around a knife-like pain. *Am I poisoned?* Another pain stabbed her through the belly. She moaned.

"Mistress, are you ill?" The servant that slept at the foot of her bed stared round-eyed at her, raising an oil lamp.

"I fear I'm dying." Sour bile rose into her throat. She leaned over the bed to vomit on the floor.

The servant jumped back with a cry. The oil lamp flickered.

"What's this?" A soothing voice floated from the darkness.

"Nana! I'm poisoned! Send for a priest." Pulcheria heaved again. The smell of vomit pervaded the room.

The nurse's bulk crowded the paralyzed servant out of the way. She snatched the oil lamp and ordered the girl to light more lamps and candles.

Pulcheria felt a cool hand on her forehead.

"You've no fever, Sweetling." Nana pulled soiled covers off her shivering form. "Ah, that's the problem. You've got your courses."

Suddenly, Pulcheria noticed the wet sticky sensation between her thighs. She wasn't dying. A different kind of cramp gripped her belly. "The chamber pot! Quickly!" She voided her bowels and moaned. "Are you sure I'm not poisoned?" The stench in the room brought on another bout of retching. "It hurts, Nana!"

"I know, Sweetling. Some women have a hard time with it." Nana held her shaking form as Pulcheria threw up again, this time bringing up little more than bile. "I know some remedies, as do the midwives. We'll have you right in no time."

"You." Nana indicated the frightened servant. "Rouse the rest of the servants from their beds to clean up this mess. Send for willow bark tea. Bring a hot brick wrapped in a cloth."

Nana set to work cleaning her charge with warm water, tying a linen cloth padded with rags between her legs and dressing her in a fresh night gown. The servants stripped the bed, aired the room, and lit cedar incense. Pulcheria settled on a couch with a hot brick on her stomach and a warm blanket around her shoulders while the others worked.

"Drink this." Nana thrust a cup of willow bark tea, sweetened with honey to mask the bitter taste, into her hands. Nana fussed over her, smoothing her hair. "That should help some. If you need stronger, I'll ask the doctor for some poppy juice."

"That won't be necessary, Nana." The pain lessened to a dull throb as Pulcheria sipped the tea. *So, this is Eve's curse. How could childbirth be any worse?* She shuddered. *A woman's burden. Why didn't God make me a man? Life would be so much simpler.*

She immediately felt a wave of guilt, and prayed, head bowed, "Good Lord, forgive me for questioning your ways. I will suffer this test and more in your name. Amen"

*The Walls of Constantinople, January 413*

ANTHEMIUS ALLOWED HIMSELF A FEELING OF PRIDE AND SATISFACTION. WORKERS set a small statue of Theodosius II on its pedestal over the Third Military Gate in the new wall surrounding Constantinople. The emperor would dedicate the statue later in the week. Anthemius wanted to ensure all was perfect.

His son joined him on the wall. "You've done good work, Father." Isidorus looked out from the massive four-story wall connecting ninety-six defensive towers strung from the Golden Horn to the Propontis Sea. "You've earned the title the people shout at the hippodrome."

"'The Great?' I believe that title is reserved for emperors and generals, not city builders." Anthemius shook his head. "The walls are almost done. No barbarians will ever threaten us again. Well, threaten, maybe, but they will never breach these walls."

He clapped his son on the shoulder. "That's not why I asked you here."

"The Princess?"

"I believe she's at the root of the matter." The regent ran a hand through his silver hair. "I had word she started her courses and formally approached the emperor about a possible match with your boy. He seemed hesitant."

"I thought Antiochus said Theo would sanction the match."

"Pulcheria, as I've noted, is strong-willed and clever. She counters the eunuch's advice with a compelling argument—the truth. A new man in the palace threatens Theo's position."

"We mean the boy no harm! He is much more valuable as a figurehead— the grandson of the Great Theodosius. Unlike the tumultuous West, the East has had no wars, our people rest secure behind strong walls, Constantinople is respected, and our merchants bring prosperity. That is all your doing, Father."

"I agree, and had hoped to govern many more years, but my health fails." A fit of coughing underscored his statement. "I will soon have to pass the reins to you and your younger compatriots."

Isidorus opened his mouth as if to contradict his father, then closed it. Anthemius read acceptance of truth in his face. His son shook his head, as if trying to rid it of unwanted thoughts.

"What are we to do about the emperor's objection to the marriage? As regent, could you not make this marriage happen, whether he wanted it or not?"

"Not without some deception. The emperor is the emperor, no matter his age. I might propose the laws, but they are not legal until he signs them. If I tricked him into approving this marriage, I'd lose all his trust. When he came of age, he'd dismiss me and all he felt served me. For a short-term gain, we'd lose all. No." Anthemius shook his head. "This is a delicate matter and must be done with the emperor's blessing."

Isidorus looked out over the walls, watching builders carry bricks and mortar stone. In a low voice that carried only to his father's ears, he said, "Would it not be better if an older man took the diadem? It galls me to see this boy playing the tunes and you dancing. You're ten times the man—and the ruler!—he is."

"We've had this discussion before," Anthemius replied in irritation. "I am the Patrician and Regent. I gave my oath to Arcadius to protect his family. I renewed that vow in public and before God when I took on the regency. You will not speak such treason to me again!"

"Yes, Father." His son cast his eyes down, while blood crept up his neck to stain his cheeks.

Anthemius hoped it was shame, but feared it was anger.

Looking up, Isidorus asked, in a mild tone, "How do we change the boy's mind and win this marriage?"

"I've been giving that some thought." Anthemius chewed his lip a moment. "Antiochus and I will renew our suggestions, but in a milder tone. Give the boy time to reflect on what is best for him and the empire."

"You should make a case for his sister's happiness and duty to the empire. After all, a woman is only fulfilled as wife and mother. He wouldn't want to deprive his sister of that satisfaction."

Anthemius laughed. "You have not spent much time in the Princess' company. She is the last girl to yearn for wifely duties and dream of motherhood."

"Then we point out how she is disobedient and undeserving of his affection and protection. He, as the male, is the head of the household. She is only a girl and should do as her brother—and emperor—wishes."

"That might work. I'll have Antiochus school the emperor's companions. Nothing spurs a boy's vanity more than the encouragement and taunts of his peers. Paulinus is a bright boy, and his father a friend. I'm sure he'll follow our lead."

Anthemius looked down on his creation and sighed. If only he could leave a government as strong as these walls, he could die in peace.

*Imperial Palace, January 413*

"I wish to speak to my brother privately." Pulcheria waved at the ever-present servants and bodyguards in Theo's private anteroom. "Out, all of you."

The guards looked to Theo, only leaving when he nodded his assent.

"You look tired, Ria. Have you been getting enough rest?" Theo poured her a goblet of mint tisane with honey—one of her favorite drinks. She didn't understand people who were fond of strong wine. It clouded the senses and roiled the stomach.

"A walk in the garden would do me good, but it's cold and raining." Pulcheria shivered, savoring the warming liquid.

Theo nodded. A walk in the garden was their code for a private conversation away from prying eyes and ears. Pulcheria had discovered several false walls where spies could listen or watch their rooms. She found the first by accident when she noticed a flicker of light through a carved screen. The rest she searched for by tapping on walls. They found one in nearly every private room. Secret corridors riddled the palace. Luckily, they found only spy holes—no entrances to their rooms that could allow assassins access—so she kept her knowledge secret from all but Theo. Knowing someone watched her did not disturb her—Pulcheria was rarely alone. It was that she didn't know to whom these spies reported. Most likely Antiochus, but she couldn't be sure.

"Come sit by me." He patted the cushions on the divan.

She dropped beside him with a sigh, lowering her voice so it carried to his ears only. "It is time to dismiss Antiochus and Anthemius."

"Antiochus I understand, but why the regent? He has served our family and the empire well and honorably."

"He plots to marry me to his grandson, Isidorus Theophilus."

"What plots?" Theo laughed. "He's been honest in urging the match." He turned sober. "It's not a bad match, Ria. The family is much admired in the city. You could fulfill your God-appointed role as wife and mother. What's your objection?"

"If God wanted me to be a wife and mother, he would not have made me your sister." Pulcheria snorted. "Use your head, Theo. Anthemius is ill. He thinks this marriage will protect us and secure the empire, but his son is a different man. I don't trust Isidorus. He might be tempted to raise his own son to the purple, or even his sister's husband, General Procopius. The general claims descent from Constantine the Great. You will not attain your majority for four more years. Plenty of time to convince the people of Constantinople you are of little use compared to a vigorous mature man—especially one married to an imperial princess."

Theo's forehead wrinkled in consternation. "Do you have proof?"

"No." She closed her eyes, rubbing her temples. "But it is a possibility we cannot ignore. It means your life."

She hugged her brother close to whisper in his ear. "I could not bear to lose you, Brother. Please trust me in this."

He nodded. "I do trust you, Ria, but how can we forestall Isidorus when he comes to power?"

"Isidorus is a problem. I have no solutions—yet—except prayer for his father's health. We can act on Antiochus. Dismiss the eunuch immediately.

Give him an estate and retire him far from the city. I'm nearly fourteen and will take over the household. As to Anthemius and the marriage? Only you can stall the regent." She stroked his arm. "Please, brother? Do this for me?"

He patted her hand. "Of course, dear sister."

## *March 413*

Bishop Atticus, Patriarch of Constantinople, wended his way through the labyrinthine complex to the Daphne, the heart of the imperial palace. Here, the emperor held his audiences and entertained embassies in his glittering audience hall. Today the bishop met with the young princesses on "a matter of some urgency."

His guard guided him to the door of a large room filled with sunlight from an external garden just starting to bloom with the first spring flowers. Lilacs scented the air. Strategically lit oil lamps brightened dark corners; braziers chased the spring chill away. Several women, young and old, worked on various domestic tasks: some spinning thread with a drop spindle, some weaving at a standing loom, others sewing garments or decorating cloth with close stitching. The industrious women duplicated the work of holy women across the city and pleased him in this imperial setting.

He nodded to Father Marcus, who sat in a corner, reading scriptures aloud to the women as they silently worked. Good man, Marcus! He did well in teaching the young emperor and princesses the ways of the church.

He spied Pulcheria, dressed in modest robes and covered hair, sewing with a group of women, and approached. "Princess, I believe you requested my attendance at my convenience. This beautiful spring day seemed to fit that requirement."

Pulcheria looked up from her sewing and smiled. She put down her work to stand with outstretched hands. "Bishop Atticus! Holy Father, thank you for attending us."

He nodded, accepted her hands, and gave her the kiss of peace on both cheeks. "Daughter, how may I be of service?"

"I have lately been thinking on your treatise, *On Faith and Virginity*, and have some questions."

His eyebrows rose. "I'm flattered you read my words and contemplate their meaning. I'll be happy to answer any questions you have."

She ushered him toward a small seating arrangement in one corner. "Do you mind if my sisters join us?"

"Of course not, Princess." He occupied a padded divan. The three princesses arranged themselves on chairs in front of him. Pulcheria's severe dress and stern expression made her seem much older than her fourteen years. The younger princesses tried to emulate their elder but seemed lesser copies. Where Pulcheria wore her asceticism as armor, the younger sisters wore theirs as a burden; their youth and beauty blighted by the strict requirements of their older sister. The bishop felt a twinge of pity. The ascetic life should be chosen, not imposed.

A servant approached with food and drink. He waved her away.

The sisters did the same.

"What questions do you have, Daughter?"

Pulcheria leaned forward, clasping her hands in her lap. "I understand Mary Theotokos—Mary Mother of God—and I understand the miracle of the virgin birth. Mary remained a virgin after giving birth to Christ, thus confirming his godhood and releasing women from Eve's curse. But you write, 'by emulating Theotokos a woman will receive the King of the Universe in her womb.' How is that possible?"

Bishop Atticus was impressed. Few, other than a handful of philosophically minded churchman, cared to get into the finer points of church doctrine. He answered with the same level of seriousness. "My dearest princess, it is part of the mystery of God. The Lord cursed women after Eve's disobedience, but through Christ and Mary Theotokos women are redeemed."

"So, through my obedience to God, I might give birth to Christ as well?"

"Not physically as Holy Mary, but mystically. A woman who casts off every sin, who makes her body worthy of the kingdom, will bring the Christ into her bride-chamber."

"Not physical birth, but spiritual birth." Pulcheria leaned back with a smile. Arcadia, the middle princess, seemed bewildered by the discussion; Marina, the youngest, bored.

"Such women live as Mary Theotokos and therefore partake of her holiness." the bishop explained. "They hold a special place in the people's hearts, as they make sacrifices others can't. A pledged virgin is revered by the people."

A calculating look passed over Pulcheria's face. "In the same way the archimandrites, who dedicate their lives to prayer, and the stylites, who live on top of pillars, are loved? People believe their holiness is reflected on them?"

"Yes, the people honor their sacrifices. A pledged virgin gives up the traditional protections and advantages of marriage and childbearing for the more glorious mystical function of receiving the Divine Word in her own body." The bishop looked from one girl to the next. "But this state is not to be entered into lightly."

"Of course, Bishop." Pulcheria startled him with a new tack. "Are there any churches dedicated to Mary Theotokos in the city?"

"No, Princess."

"I wish to build one, here in the palace district. Mary Theotokos, First Founded of Constantinople. I will have the imperial architect draw up plans. Will you help me oversee construction and bless the church?"

He bowed his head slightly. "My pleasure, Princess."

"Of course, it will take many years to complete." Pulcheria sat silent a moment, tapping her index finger on the carved arm of her chair. "Would you object to dedicating a chapel of the Great Church to Mary Theotokos? My sisters and I will pay all expenses of decoration and dedication. I would like the people to be able to visit such an inspiring place."

"That's a novel idea, Princess. What do you have in mind?"

"New frescoes showing the life of Holy Mary, an altar with a dedication from me and my sisters, and an appropriate cross and candlesticks." She smiled. "I hope to have it finished and dedicated by this summer. Such a project will require frequent meetings, I'm afraid. Can you spare the time to meet next week?"

"As you wish, Daughter." He smiled. "I always have time for such dedicated patrons as yourself and your imperial sisters. Send word to my secretary and we will establish a time. Is there anything else I can do for you?"

"I wish to avoid heresy in my thinking and advice to my brother. I know you were instrumental in expelling Bishop Chrysostom during my father's reign. Could you explain how he erred in orthodoxy?"

"Of course, Princess." He settled on his divan and signaled the servant for a goblet. This was going to be a long session.

Bishop Atticus left the palace, hours later, vastly impressed with Princess Pulcheria. She seemed to have a genuine vocation, a sharp and subtle mind.

She listened closely to his arguments and asked pointed questions. Too bad she was born to the purple. Pulcheria would have made a great holy woman, but an imperial marriage and childbearing was her lot. Something about their earlier conversation about Mary Theotokos nagged at him. Then a smile broke across his face. He muttered under his breath, "Clever princess! It will be interesting to see how you pull this off."

# Chapter 9

*The Great Church, Constantinople, June 413*

PULCHERIA PRAYED AT HER PRIVATE ALTAR IN HER QUARTERS BEFORE THE ceremony. "Holy Mother of God, Mary save me. Guide me in the right path, so I may preserve my brother, my sisters, and myself. Send me wisdom and confound my enemies. And thank you for the friendship and wisdom of Bishop Atticus. Amen."

She rose to seek out her younger sisters, being dressed for church.

"Is this all right, Ria?" Ten-year-old Marina slowly turned so Pulcheria could inspect the dresser's work.

"Lovely!" All three sisters were dressed in plain white silk, unbelted gowns, topped with enveloping purple silk cloaks, encrusted with seed pearls and gold embroidery; hair cut short and unbound. "You must remember to walk straight and slow. Glide, as if you balanced a codex on your head and didn't want it to fall off."

Marina practiced gliding with a concentrated frown. A pretty child, she would grow into an attractive woman. Would she forgive her sister for the step they were about to take? *At ten, I shouldered adult duties, but I've sheltered my sisters. Was that a mistake? If my plan works, Marina would not have to follow my path. I could protect her.* She shook her head. *No. They needed to present a united front, or their enemies would take advantage.*

Pulcheria turned to Arcadia, who had been harder to persuade. "You understand why we're doing this?"

"I understand, but I don't like it." Arcadia screwed her mouth into an unattractive pout. "Since I was a small girl, I dreamed of marriage and children."

"While you played with dolls, I learned to govern. The dangers to Theo and all of us are real. You lack by one year my age and have started your courses. The regent could marry you off to some noble to cement an alliance or send you away from your family to a foreign land where you know no one."

Fear and doubt clouded Arcadia's eyes. Pulcheria enfolded her sister in her arms, kissed her forehead, and added, softly, "That's the value of an imperial woman—a commodity to be traded for money or security. My way, we stay together, protect our brother, and lead independent lives. I need you, Sister. You will be my right hand. Believe me, I do this not just for me, but for you, Marina, and Theo."

Arcadia pushed out of Pulcheria's arms and sniffed. "You have always seen clearer on these matters than I, Sister." She wiped a tear from her cheek and regained her composure. "I will be guided by your wisdom."

The sisters donned knee-length veils and trooped out to their imperial wagon, accompanied by their female entourage. Pulcheria smiled behind her veil. The women dressed in their finest and gossiped like fishwives, thinking this an ordinary service to dedicate an altar in the Great Church. They would follow the wagon on foot.

As they proceeded through the streets of Constantinople, the people cheered their princesses, shouted their names, called blessings. It was good luck to see the royal wagon, even if they couldn't see the sacred persons inside.

Bishop Atticus met the entourage at the top steps of the Great Church and escorted the princesses to the front of a newly refurbished chapel. Passing through the nave, Pulcheria looked approvingly on the murals showing the life of Mary from her birth, through marriage, the birth and death of Jesus, her death and ascension to heaven. Soft flickering candlelight gave movement to the scenes rendered in brilliant colors.

The princesses took their positions at the front of the congregation. Their female companions and city notables filled the rest of the space. Normally they sat behind screens, out of public view, but it was vital they be front and center for this ceremony. Pulcheria, feeling her brother's eyes on her, spared a glance at his screened balcony. She could not have done this without his help and blessing. Anthemius did not attend. His health failed him; he could not stand for a lengthy service. Pulcheria spotted his son, Isidorus, and smiled behind her veil, anticipating his consternation.

The musky scent of incense and chants of the priests soothed her. Her soul filled with peace. Her mind cast out the last hints of doubt. This was right. This was good for her and her sisters.

She turned her attention to the marble altar, covered with an elaborately embroidered cloth. She and her sisters had spent many months covering the purple silk with gold and silver crosses. The crowning glory, a massive gold cross decorated with precious gems, sat in the center of the altar, flanked by gold candlesticks.

Bishop Atticus, in full regalia glittering with gold and gems, stood before the altar. "May the Good Lord bless us all, as we pray for peace, wisdom, and special blessings for our generous imperial princesses who gave their personal wealth to beautify this chapel and provide a fitting altar." The Bishop led the congregation in prayer and a dedicatory service. He consecrated the altar and cross.

At the agreed-upon place in the ceremony, Pulcheria and her sisters approached, dropped their veils and elaborate cloaks, and prostrated themselves before the altar. The Bishop recited a prayer. They rose. Pulcheria took the cross and held it in her arms, straining against the weight of the gold. Maybe she and her sisters shouldn't have been so generous! Arcadia and Marina each took a candlestick.

They turned to the congregation.

Pulcheria stood before the assembled court, bare faced, holding the cross before her with trembling arms. It was important all the witnesses know it was she and her sisters, not imposters, who took these next steps.

She spoke in her best declamatory voice. "On this day, taking my subjects, the priesthood, and God Himself to witness, I dedicate this altar on behalf of my own virginity and my brother's rule." She paused to allow the gasps and murmurs to die down. "I will take no husband but Christ and have no children other than my people. I have set these words in stone on the face of this altar for all to see."

Bishop Atticus held the cross while she reverently removed the altar cloth. Underneath, her holy vow was carved in blazing white marble and picked out with gold letters for all to see—a permanent symbol of her vow. The bishop returned the cross to its position atop the altar, and her sisters returned the candlesticks.

Arcadia stepped forward. Pulcheria searched her sister's face for any sign of doubt or rebellion. There was none. Arcadia declaimed, in a strong voice, "I join my sister in her vow. I dedicate my virginity to the Church and my brother's rule. I will take no husband but Christ and have no children other than my people."

Marina stepped forward to echo her sisters' actions and words in her childish voice.

The three knelt before the bishop. He laid his hand on Pulcheria's head. "In this sacred place, your subjects, the priesthood, and God Himself witness your vows. Go in peace, Sisters in Christ, and may your holiness reflect on and protect our emperor and the people."

The sisters recovered their cloaks and veils and proceeded through the nave to their waiting carriage. A rising tide of voices accompanied them, as the congregation realized what they had witnessed. Pulcheria glided, head high, heart beating fast in exaltation.

She had done it! She had found a way to protect her brother and thwart her enemies!

Imperial agents planted by her brother along the return route led a rousing chorus of shouts.

"God bless our Virgin Princesses!"

"Long may Emperor Theodosius rule!"

"God bless and save Pulcheria, the Pious One!"

At the Chalke gate to the palace, Pulcheria finally relaxed against her seat. They were safe from the regent's machinations. Only one more surprise remained for Isidorus and the council.


Isidorus stormed into his father's room but calmed immediately upon seeing the slack face on the pillow. Pine needles steamed in a pot by the bedside; the sharp scent couldn't mask the stench of illness—a combination of stale urine and bodily decay.

"How is he?" he asked the physician at his father's side.

"Better. He breathes easier with the hot mist and took some strengthening broth." The physician shook his head. "But it is the nature of this disease that he might recover for a while, then relapse."

His father's eyes flickered open. "You shouldn't talk about me as if I weren't here."

"I thought you asleep." Isidorus approached the bed to take his father's hand. He nodded to the physician. "Leave us a moment."

The man rose. "Don't stay too long. He needs his rest."

Anthemius snorted. "I'll rest in the grave. For now, I have business to conduct."

The physician exited, frowning.

Isidorus tried to suppress a smile. His father wasn't in the grave yet!

"Given your entrance, Son, I take it you are agitated. What happened at the church?"

The memory of the princesses vowing virginity wiped the smile from his face. His voice grated with anger. "Pulcheria has neatly blocked our plans, Father."

Anthemius raised his brows.

"She and her sisters have publicly dedicated their virginity to their brother's rule. They pledge not to marry and vow their holy acts to protect their people. Bishop Atticus accepted their vows, and the people acclaimed them."

"Clever girl." Anthemius closed his eyes. "I should have seen that move coming. Pulcheria has been much in the company of Bishop Atticus since she started her Mary First Founded Church. I'm sure they colluded. She could not have done this without him."

"What are we to do, Father?"

"Nothing, for now." Anthemius opened his eyes. "Any action we take to force the princess would meet with severe approbation from the Church and the people."

"I never thought the boy would be so susceptible to his sister's blandishments." Isidorus rubbed his jaw. "He had to agree to this, as well."

"We underestimated the familial attachments. Pulcheria has been more mother than sister to the lad for the last ten years." His father sighed. "I thought, as he matured, he might take more masculine advice, but she is still first in his affections and trust."

"Will that last? All boys chafe under their mother's rule at some point and leave them for the men's world. Given another couple of years and his majority, Theodosius might set his sister aside."

"We must be ready, my son." Anthemius gripped his hand with surprising strength. "Pulcheria has removed herself and her sisters from the playing board but left the most powerful piece. The emperor cannot pledge himself to celibacy. He needs heirs. We must switch places. While Pulcheria busies herself advising her brother, we shall dabble in matchmaking. Be on the lookout for a suitable candidate for our boy emperor. We will fight a woman with another woman."

A slow smile crossed Isidorus' face. "Yes, Father. That we can do."

*Imperial Palace, June 414*

A trumpet blast silenced the packed audience chamber. Isidorus surveyed the empire's top officials, generals in residence, and senators speculating on the boy-emperor's announcement. Theodosius, Second of that Name, stood in full imperial regalia. He was a handsome lad with light wavy hair and regular features. Somewhat slight, but he could fill out with some martial training. Isidorus vacillated on the wisdom of keeping the boy in the palace or initiating him in his grandfather's trade.

A year had passed since the princesses made their vow of virginity. During that time his father had recovered from his illness and relapsed twice, finally giving up his battle for life last week. The emperor honored his father with an elaborate funeral. Isidorus' heart throbbed with grief at the memory of the people clogging the streets expressing their sorrow, but now he must carry on his father's work.

His emperor motioned to the trumpeter for a second blast. The crowd quieted. His thirteen-year old voice cracked with the first signs of manhood.

"The death of Anthemius, our beloved Patrician, regent, and prefect of the East, grieves us deeply." Theo put a hand to his forehead, bowing in silent prayer.

Isidorus did likewise, fighting back tears. *Rest in peace, Father.* Despite his grief, Isidorus looked forward to coming into his own. His tenure as city prefect would shortly end. He looked forward to his next promotion. Surely the emperor would name him to his father's old position as prefect in the East and—possibly—regent. He had been doing his father's work, as the latter grew increasingly ill.

Theodosius looked up. "As we mourn Anthemius' passing and rejoice in the knowledge he sits with God in heaven, we must continue our work here on earth. Our wise prefect must be replaced. After much thought and consultation, I name Aurelian to the post and, by means of this writ, award him the additional title of Patrician—Father to the Emperor."

Isidorus arrested a step forward in shock. A small wave of sound, signaling more surprise than approval, circled the room. Aurelian, a staunch ally of the former Augusta Eudoxia, the emperor's mother, retired from public service long ago. He would be but a figurehead for that most important post. *Was the council even consulted on this? Why wasn't I told?*

A frail old man, wearing red robes and walking with a gold-headed stick, approached the dais and bowed his head. Theodosius moved quickly to prevent Aurelian from prostrating himself. "I would not have obeisance from my mother's dearest friend and trusted advisor. You have my permission to sit in my presence."

A servant fetched a padded chair for the old man.

"Thank you, Most Generous Augustus. You do me too much honor." Aurelian accepted the writ formalizing his new titles, bowed, and took the seat.

Another trumpet blast, and the doors at the far end of the chamber opened to reveal Princess Pulcheria garbed in a white silk robe, glittering with silver thread and purple amethysts. She walked down the center of the room, head held high, wearing an elaborate wig arranged in the latest court style with layers of curls and braids. Quite a contrast from her usual ascetic style. *What's the bitch up to? Now that she is of age, is she going to go back on her vow of virginity?*

Pulcheria kept her eyes fixed on her brother. At the bottom of the steps leading up to the dais, she knelt.

The boy descended the steps and placed his hands on her head. "It is with love, and confidence in God's plan, that I name my beloved sister Aelia Pulcheria Augusta, Empress of Rome!" A servant brought a richly embroidered purple paludamentum—matching his own—which Theodosius put around his sister's shoulders.

Isidorus ground his teeth at this newest affront. Most imperial woman must give birth before being named Augusta. *She's fifteen, for Christ's sake—fit for a marriage bed, not a throne room!*

Theodosius raised his sister—and now co-Augusti—from her knees. The chamber broke into wild cheers of acclamation as Theodosius tied a pearl and amethyst diadem, the final symbol of imperial power, around Pulcheria's elaborate wig.

Isidorus clapped his hands and mimed the words, but they were ashes in his mouth. He grudgingly admitted the emperor had the right to declare his sister Augusta, even in his minority. Imperial actions by the emperor were legal and binding, no matter how young the ruler.

Holding his sister's hand, Theodosius announced, "It is also by my will that

I appoint my sister regent for my minority. All she does, she does in my name."
He whispered in Pulcheria's ear. They both smiled.

*The council could not have sanctioned this!* Isidorus put a stiff smile on his face
as his emotions roiled. His father warned him not to underestimate Pulcheria,
but he never imagined so sweeping a victory. Mere days after achieving her
majority, she had taken total control of the Eastern Roman government and the
most powerful military in the known world. *All my plans dashed; all my plotting
undone by a wisp of a girl!*

His father's final words offered a sliver of hope. "Find the boy a wife!"

*Pulcheria may have won the battle,* Isidorus vowed, *but the war continues.*


THE NEXT DAY, PULCHERIA SAT AT THE HEAD OF THE TABLE IN THE CONSISTORY,
trying not to fidget as the scribe read her first imperial constitution—approved
law—to a room full of men designated to guide her with their advice. The
design and decoration of the room reflected the majesty and importance of
decisions made there. Decorated with treasures from across the empire, it gave
her confidence. *God would not have chosen me and Theo to rule, if we were not
capable.*

She ran a hand over a table made from the most expensive materials
from Africa, ebony and ivory inlaid in a geometric pattern. Matching chairs
sported cushions of red silk and gold tassels from the far east. Niches in the
walls held antique marble and bronze Greek statues. Frescoes showed Emperor
Constantine at battle with his foes, protected by the sign of the cross.

Pulcheria straightened her back and stilled her hands. Being the center of
attention at the council meeting rather than stitching away in the corner felt
odd, but her four years of apprenticeship stood her in good stead. She looked
around the table. *I know you all—your strengths and weaknesses—and will be
making changes, some sooner than later.*

"Esteemed Augusta, I beg you be guided by older heads on this law." Isidorus'
voice was reasonable, but his rigid face and stiff shoulders told her he held
back considerable rage. "By tradition, Jewish synagogues are private property
entitled to protection. If you ban new construction and allow destruction of
existing ones, you give permission for people to attack their Jewish neighbors.

The Jews are a far-flung people and important citizens in many large cities. There might be violence in Alexandria, Antioch, even here in Constantinople."

"The imperial constitution reads 'destruction of synagogues *in desert places*,' Prefect. The holy fathers and mothers of the desert sanctuaries feel their sacrifice for the people is polluted by the presence of Jewish institutions and wish them gone. The Augustus and I agree. The Jews will still have their places of worship and the freedom to do so in the cities." Pulcheria looked around the table at carefully schooled faces. Only one or two showed open dissatisfaction.

Isidorus sank into his chair with a scowl. He had more to say, but wisely held his tongue.

"What's next on the agenda, Patrician?"

"We need to appoint generals for the two armies stationed in the emperor's presence," Aurelian wheezed.

"I recommend Generals Procopius and Anatolius," Isidorus said, immediately jumping back into the fray.

*Of course you do.* Pulcheria sighed. *You wish your allies close to the city and in charge of the emperor's safety. That will not happen.* "I will take your recommendation under consideration, Prefect." She settled in for a long contentious council meeting.

Two hours later, she brought the meeting to a close with a prayer. The men gathered their papers and shuffled out with bows and felicitations. She signaled Isidorus to stay behind, dismissing Aurelian and her scribes. There was no need to humiliate the man before a crowd.

He bowed. "Augusta, how may I advise you further?"

"The Augustus and I are agreed that your family has been of considerable service to the empire and we wish to give you the gift of freedom from that burden. Your tenure as city prefect ends soon, but we wish you to vacate the post immediately. Your services on the council are no longer required. You may retire to your estates in the country."

"You're dismissing me?" His jaw hardened and eyes flashed. "You can't—"

She raised a hand. "I can and I do. You and your faction seek power over my brother. I won't allow it. Retire to your country estates and take your incompetent son with you. Be grateful Christian charity prevents me from implementing more harsh measures." She waved to the door. "Be gone!"

A flicker of fear thrilled along her nerves as Isidorus wrestled with his rage. Just as she prepared to call for the guards, he got his emotions under control and stalked out.

Pulcheria watched him go with a niggling of regret. *Anthemius, I wish you had lived longer. I could have worked with you, but your son...*she shook her head...*is not his father.*

# **Chapter 10**



*Imperial Palace, June 415*

Patrician, I want this executed at once." Pulcheria imprinted the warm wax on the imperial constitution with her brother's seal, handed it to Aurelian, and leaned back in her imposing chair. She had moved her reception and workrooms to the Daphne to be closer to the imperial audience hall and foreign embassy delegations. When she finished here, she would join Theo in noon prayers, then hold a joint audience in the afternoon to receive petitioners.

"As you wish, Augusta." Aurelian squinted at the fair copy and read: "'Anyone polluted with the crime of pagan worship will be purged from the army's officer ranks and government administration.' That will ensure a stampede to the baptismal fonts."

"We save the souls of those willing. Those too wrong-headed will suffer the consequences of their beliefs."

Pulcheria was quite pleased at the changes she had implemented in the court in the past year. Early on, she overheard one woman complain about the prayers, plain dress, and fast days; commenting the court was boring compared with her mother's extravagances. Pulcheria dismissed her from her entourage but welcomed the comparison. The last thing she wanted was a reputation like her wanton mother's.

She was also pleased with Aurelian. She suspected her mother had approved of him because he was so malleable. The old man brought a veneer of continuity, yet allowed Pulcheria to wield all the power. A few council members initially balked at her leadership, complaining to Theo, but with his backing, and the example of Isidorus sulking outside the city, bereft of titles and power, they fell into line.

A palace page entered to whisper in Aurelian's ear. Pulcheria raised an eyebrow. The Patrician cleared his throat. "Augusta, there are two delegations from Alexandria wishing to meet with you. They want imperial intervention in a conflict there. The Bishop sends a representative, and the city council a delegation."

"Is this the trouble that our Prefect Orestes was unable to quell?" She rested her chin in the palm of her hand, recalling details from the report by her agent—Timothy?—to the city. "The prefect was badly injured, if I remember right, and a learned woman philosopher murdered. Cyril is Bishop there, isn't he?"

"You have a most acute and accurate memory, Augusta."

She had become used to blatant court flattery and paid it little heed. "The Alexandrines are a quarrelsome bunch. Sometimes I think the hot climate breeds hot heads." Pulcheria frowned at her cluttered worktable. "This is a delicate matter, not suited for the afternoon audience. I'll receive the delegations now. Attend me."

She took Aurelian's arm and walked through an adjoining door, followed by the young page. In this, her formal reception room, her women worked on their various domestic projects and priests read scripture aloud. She sorely missed Father Marcus's deep voice lending drama to his readings. With her elevation, he considered his work done. Pulcheria sent him to his favorite monastery, with tears in her eyes and alms for the poor, to dedicate his life to prayer.

They crossed the multi-colored marble floor to the gilded chair occupying the low carpeted dais at one end. A realistic fresco on her right-hand wall looked as if you could walk into a flower garden even in winter. Pulcheria took her seat, surveying the room with a deep sense of satisfaction. In private life, she preferred plain furnishings, but in public she needed ostentation to signal her rank.

Pulcheria turned to the page. "Send in the church representative first."

He bowed and left. Aurelian took a red silk-cushioned chair to her left, off the dais, where servants plied him with wine and his favorite sweets. Pulcheria smiled at him. Habits she would not tolerate in younger men she forgave in

Aurelian. He could be enjoying his retirement as he wished, but her mother's advisor had answered their call back to duty. She did not begrudge some small compensations.

"Presbyter Paul, representative of Bishop Cyril of Alexandria," her page announced from the doorway. Pulcheria frowned at the churchman's rich embroidered robes and ring-encrusted fingers. He hesitated at the door, taking in the modest dress of the Augusta and her attendants. The long walk from the door to dais would provide him plenty of time to realize his tactical error.

Paul prostrated himself before the Augusta. When Pulcheria gave him permission to rise, he doffed the jewel-encrusted cloak and stripped his hands of rings, leaving him in an elaborate tunic embroidered with gold and silver. "Our most Holy and Virgin Augusta, please accept these small tokens from the Bishop of Alexandria, to be given to the Great Church of Constantinople. I also bring with me several bolts of cloth and donations of silver for the poor of the city."

"We thank you on behalf of the people of Constantinople for your bishop's generosity." She waved for a servant to bring a chair and refreshments. "Please sit and tell me of the troubles in your city. I was most displeased to hear our imperial representative was injured…and by a monk!"

The churchman sipped his wine, letting his face fall into sorrowful lines. "I'm afraid Prefect Anthemius served the emperor poorly in his choice of city governor. Orestes listened to the advice of pagans and Jews, taking their part over your most Christian subjects. He rarely attended church, and openly attacked our bishop in word and deed."

"I understand differently. My dearest friend, Bishop Atticus, personally baptized Prefect Orestes, and vouches for his sincere Christian beliefs." Pulcheria leaned back, spearing him with a direct gaze. "My own agent observed the chaos in your city and advised Bishop Cyril against fomenting riots and murder. This behavior on the part of the bishop is utterly foreign to those who serve in the name of Christ."

"Those acts were in answer to a terrible assault. The Jews murdered Christians and Orestes did nothing. Our Sainted Bishop Cyril could not stand by. He roused the Christian populace and we purged the city of the Christ-killers." He lowered his eyes to his goblet. "We felt we were following your will, after the imperial constitution you ordered that forbade the construction of new synagogues and required the destruction of existing ones."

"Destruction of synagogues in desert places…if that could be accomplished without riots," she snapped. It galled her that Isidorus had been right on the consequences of that constitution. She had thought it a limited law that would protect the desert monasteries. She had not counted on exuberant Christians burning and looting synagogues in the cities, causing major upheavals. Those riots cost her a year delay in purging top levels of the army and government of Jews and pagans. She didn't want to make the same mistake twice and took the year to study the consequences of the earlier law. She was confident in her plan to implement this next phase.

"Saving souls is not always a bloodless process, Most Wise Augusta," Paul said in a soothing tone. "Alexandria is now firmly Christian. Those unhappy with your policies and our bishop's actions can immigrate to pagan Persia and be damned to hell."

"What of the philosopher? Lady Hypatia? I understand she was a learned woman and well beloved by her city." Pulcheria remember the voluminous letters she had received after the Lady Philosopher's murder, asking for redress. "I've scores of petitions from the city fathers and her former students, protesting her murder. Many of those men hold high posts in both the Church and the government."

"Hypatia brought on her own fate, Most Holy One. She studied sorcery, astrology, other pagan arts. She cast a spell on Orestes, held him in thrall. He didn't make a move without consulting that woman!" The presbyter realized his mistake and amended, "Not that taking advice from a woman is wrong but taking advice from a pagan forever put Orestes outside of and at odds with the Christian community."

From her agent, Pulcheria knew Hypatia to be a chaste and learned woman on good terms with the former bishop. Only when Cyril took the bishopric did rumors of sorcery start to swirl. Her brother studied from Hypatia's textbooks on algebra and astronomy. The philosopher's fervent supporters pointed out in their letters that she taught there was only one God, and to know Him one had to live an ascetic life like Christian holy men and women. Pulcheria felt a distant kinship with the ascetic woman, who led her community and ably advised city elders. Given other circumstances, she would have liked to meet the famous Lady Philosopher.

Pulcheria sensed the churchman's great unease and had no wish to alleviate it. "What is it you wish of us?"

"The city fathers are unhappy over the deaths and riots. They blame Bishop Cyril for exciting hot tempers and accuse him of using our private hospital staff of parabalans to incite riot and disorder. They wish the bishop reprimanded, the parabalans disbanded, and Hypatia's murderers held accountable. The parabalans are blameless. They serve in our charity wards, moving the sick, injured, and dead. The bishop had nothing to do with Hypatia's death or the riots that caused it. We wish the matter closed and the name of our good bishop cleared."

"Somebody attacked our prefect and murdered the Lady Philosopher. If not the parabalans, then who?"

"The people were outraged at pagan sorcery and rose up in defense of their faith."

Pulcheria studied the man wiping nervous sweat from his brow. She knew the desert Nitrian monks, called into the city by Bishop Cyril, were responsible for Orestes' injuries. There were rumors a presbyter named Peter led a civilian mob that murdered Hypatia, but those were unconfirmed. What was done, was done. A good woman died, but Alexandria was quiet and Christianity won out.

"I will consider your petition."

Presbyter Paul rose, bowing low. "I'm certain our Most Holy Augusta will see the merits in our case."

After he left, Pulcheria saw the delegation from the Alexandria City Council. The three men told the same story as Cyril's representative, but with a different point of view. In their tale, Bishop Cyril overstepped his bounds and instigated unrest by closing rival Christian churches and calling on the volatile desert monks to riot. The parabalans were a lawless group of thugs arrayed by Cyril to enforce the bishop's will on innocent citizens. The representatives' voices differed little from the Hellene faction she had disbanded in her own court. They advocated tolerance in religious practice and a respect for law based on Greek tradition rather than Christian scripture. After listening carefully and asking a few questions, Pulcheria dismissed them. "What is your inclination, Augusta?" Aurelian had sat listening to arguments of both sides.

"The Great Constantine once said, 'One Emperor, one Empire, one God.' He knew the disorder and disunity of the pagan Empire. People who worship many gods follow false prophets. The only way to hold this empire together is if all worship the One True God and obey His Viceroy on earth, their emperor. Church and Empire must be one; rule and laws based on scripture."

She motioned to a scribe. "Take this down and deliver it to both parties: The emperor denies all requests to remedy the consequences of the actions taken by Bishop Cyril in his capacity as leader of the Christian community, with one exception. The number of parabalans will be limited to five hundred and vacancies will be filled by the city council. The parabalans are also banned from public meetings or spaces."

It was a shame her prefect was harmed and a learned woman murdered, but—as the presbyter pointed out—Alexandria was now firmly in the Christian camp and at peace. She shook her head and focused on the present. "What is next, Aurelian?"

The Patrician smiled. "The portrait bust you ordered is finished, Augusta."

"Excellent!" She still resented the time taken to sit idle for the artist's drawings, but the result would be worth it. "When is the dedication?"

"Next week, I'll unveil it in the Senate House next to your brother's and uncle's. It will be a potent symbol, showing all you are of equal status with your fellow Augusti."

"Thank you, Aurelian." She patted the old man's hand. "You've been a most loyal advisor this past year. I believe the senate has come to terms with my rule but be observant at the ceremony. Report back any senators that seem displeased by my actions."

"It goes without saying, Augusta." He bowed. "My duty is to you and your brother."

Pulcheria scanned her court, satisfied all was going according to her plans. She felt a deep need to give thanks to the Lord. She turned to Aurelian. "Patrician, I believe it more than past time to restore the burned Hagia Sophia to its position of Great Church. I'll speak to the emperor today about funds to rebuild."

*Yes, this has been a hard year, wrenching the government from the Hellenes and their lax ways. But the empire is at peace, the populace is happy and prosperous. It is past time to honor My Lord and care for my people through good works.*

She spotted her sisters embroidering in a corner. *And long past time to give my sisters a purpose.*

# Chapter 11



*Athens, Greece, September 415*

OLYMPIODORUS OF THEBES SALUTED LEONTIUS OF ANTIOCH WITH his wine goblet. "We are a dying breed, my friend, flocking to the Academy of Athens, the last great bastion of free thought. We who dare to deny that ridiculous triple-god of the Christians congregate here in hopes of peace and liberty."

"We've had quite an influx of your native Egyptians, since Cyril became Bishop in Alexandria." Leontius shook his head. "Did you know the Christians have added a Mother Goddess to their pantheon and daily elevate dead men and women to the rank of saint—whatever that is. They will soon worship more gods than our ancestors!"

"Those who do not know philosophy and history are most intolerant. Educated Christians recognize the roots of their resurrection myth in the mysteries of Egypt's Osiris and Greece's Dionysius. They accept the Christian God as another manifestation of the One."

"Then why do those educated ones profess belief in Christ?" A soft voice from the door drew his attention.

Olympiodorus turned to the questioner. His friend's eleven-year-old daughter carried a tray of olives, goat cheese, oil and bread into the solar. The child already showed signs of great beauty: clear pale skin, regular features, golden curls and remarkable blue eyes that in some light looked violet. She set the tray on a low table between the men.

"Athenais, my sweet." Leontius smiled at his daughter and patted a cushion next to him. "An excellent question, which I'm sure our guest will answer in full."

Olympiodorus, eyes shining, smiled at the girl. He had known Leontius for many years and dandled Athenais on his knee when she was but an infant. The girl had a good head for learning and her father indulged her. "Let me ask you a question in the way of the Great Socrates. Why do you think people believe and profess *any* religion?"

Athenais sat next to her father, mouth pursed in thought. "They have a calling? A true belief in the teachings of that religion?"

"Very good." He nodded. "I have met true believers of many faiths in my lifetime: priests of Serapis, Delphic oracles, Zoroastrian fire worshipers, Jewish rabbis, Christian archimandrites—all dedicate their lives to their gods and live strictly according to those precepts. They would gladly die for their faiths. But they are few, and followers of these religions are many. What calls these others?"

"Tradition, the religion of their ancestors, and community," Athenais said with conviction.

"That is most people. As your father follows the tenets of the great philosophers, so he teaches you and your brothers. It is easy to believe what your family and tribe believe. That is why it is against the religious practices of many to allow marriage outside the tribe. Outside beliefs bring strife and disharmony."

"Then why do so many people convert to Christianity and leave the religion of their fathers?" The girl's forehead puckered in a frown.

"Ah, that is an astute question and gets at the heart of my discussion with your father."

She turned a questioning eye on Leontius.

"Olympiodorus and I were discussing the latest law from Constantinople. It seems our emperor, under the advice of his most pious sister, has banished all non-Christians from his administration and leadership of the army."

"Oh, Father!" Her eyes went wide. "Does that mean you won't get your chair at the Academy?"

"No, my pet." He patted her hand. "Olympiodorus still has some influence with the Athenian council and they make the appointment. The Augusta's prohibition will not go so far down as a lowly chair of rhetoric. But your brothers...?" He shrugged. "They have greater ambitions. If they want to get ahead in government, I'm afraid they will have to convert."

Athenais looked at Olympiodorus with wide eyes. "So, the reason many convert is to gain power and prestige?"

"Some. Most convert just to get along, to avoid persecution. It has ever been the way of people to follow their leaders, if it requires little effort. Some few will object on principle, but the majority will do as told to live their lives in peace. Many people take on the new beliefs while clinging to the rituals of the old, thus making a hybrid. What's the difference between the stories of the resurrected Osiris from my land and resurrected Christ of Palestine? A matter of detail. The new religion is only a few centuries old and has already absorbed many holy days, rituals and mysteries of its predecessors. Easter service is taken from the Jewish Passover and celebration of Christ's birth is at the same time many people mark the longest night of the year and the return of the sun."

"That is why religion is for the masses and philosophy is for the few, my dear." Leontius smiled. "Most people are incapable of the thought and dedication necessary to attain knowledge of the One. They are content with ritual and mysteries, while we philosophers ever search for the Truth."

"I see."

"Then off with you, child. Go study, while I continue to discuss business with my guest."

Athenais hopped off the divan and gave Olympiodorus a decorous curtsey before exiting.

"A brilliant child, my friend. And only two years younger than the Emperor?"

Leontius nodded.

"Anthemius, my patron at court, is gone, but a few men in the capital still heed my words. I will soon be engaged to write a history of our young emperor and will be much about the court." Olympiodorus gazed thoughtfully at the door. Isidorus had spread the word among the Hellenes that he was looking for an appropriate maid for a very advantageous match. "In a few years, Athenais will be a grown woman. It might be in her best interest to live with her relatives in Constantinople. You have some there, I believe?"

"Yes, my wife's brother and his wife. Asclepiodotus is already installed in a position of importance in the palace."

"Excellent! I will seek him out when I go back to Constantinople."

"My sons can accompany you. They plan to move to the capital and seek their fortunes in government. Of course, that means they will have to be baptized." Leontius looked sorrowful. "Your discussion with Athenais touched a sore spot in my heart. It's a sad thing when your sons forsake you and your chosen beliefs.

I had thought at least one would show some interest in philosophy, but I am left only with a daughter who cannot follow in my footsteps."

"Leontius, I thought better of you! How can you forget Sosipatra of Pergamon or Hypatia of Alexandria?" He tutted. "Both famed for their learning and teaching, and only the most recent among a long line of lady philosophers. Why, Plutarch, head of our Academy, teaches both his son Hierius and his daughter Asclepigenia. I understand he favors the daughter and believes her more capable of understanding the more subtle nuances of philosophy than her brother. If Athenais wants to learn and teach philosophy, I say let her do it!"

"No!" Leontius shook his head violently. "You know what happened to Hypatia! We old men can rail against the Christians, but they are the future for our children. I would not have my daughter meet the same grisly fate as the Lady Philosopher of Alexandria. Athenais will find her own fortune, but not as a philosopher."

"As you wish, my friend." Olympiodorus soothed his colleague. "Athenais is young. All will be well in time. I will stay in touch and help your family as much as I can in these dangerous times."

"You were ever a good friend." Leontius reached across to clasp his forearm. "Now, if you can only get me out of this ridiculous initiation rite for the Academy, I'll be forever in your debt. I'm too old to be pushed and pulled at the baths. It offends my dignity!"

Olympiodorus laughed. "If you want the chair, you are the object in the tug of war at the baths! It's tradition." His friend scowled, but Olympiodorus knew he would go through with the ritual. Leontius was nothing if not a traditionalist!


*Imperial Palace, November 415*

"What do you think she wants of us?" General Ardaburius asked his father-in-law as they strode into the palace. They made a sharp physical contrast: Ardaburius' dark countenance and stocky body with Plinta's fair features and tall stature. But they were closely aligned in military philosophy and bound by family ties. They were also close in age, his father-in-law being only a handful of years older. "Does she mean to strip us of our commands?"

"I think not. She could have done that by decree. This meeting feels different. I think she wants to see for herself if we of barbarian heritage have horns and hooves. It's been fifteen years since that idiot Gainas rebelled against Arcadius and occupied Constantinople. He tarred me and all who share his Gothic heritage with treason and rebellion. I believe the Augusta is rethinking that policy. She has reordered the civil government to her satisfaction and I believe she turns her eyes on the military."

Ardaburius nodded. "She would do well to put her best generals in the field with the Huns stirring up dust in the north and the Persians restless in the east. We have sat on the sidelines too long, while those of lesser talent moved ahead."

Arriving at the imperial family's personal quarters, they were relieved of their swords and knives by the guards. Ever since the incident involving General Lucius over seven years ago, no weapons of any kind were allowed in the emperor's or Augusta's presence, except for the imperial guards. Ardaburius understood the restriction but felt naked without his weapons. The guard opened an elaborately carved door onto an odd domestic scene.

The musky scent of incense pervaded the Augusta's antechamber, tickling his nose. Ardaburius stifled a sneeze. He knew of Pulcheria's pious ways but was unprepared for the monastic atmosphere of her personal space. There was little of comfort in the spare room; the only object of beauty, a personal altar and gold cross in a niche. The Augusta herself dressed in modest woolen clothes and wore the diadem over a linen hair covering as proof of her imperial identity. She sat on a plain chair, at a serviceable wooden table, dictating to a scribe. Two other girls, minus the diadem but similarly attired, sat on a divan, sewing and talking quietly. *They must be the younger princesses,* Ardaburius thought, watching them closely. They seemed at peace with their religious vocation, but he was glad his own daughter showed no such inclination. It seemed such a restricted life.

Ardaburius followed Plinta's lead, making his obeisance before the young Augusta. She seemed innocuous, slender to the point of gauntness, plain of features except for the brown eyes, which sparkled with intelligence and something more. Curiosity? Ambition? It was not hard to believe she outmaneuvered Isidorus and his faction at the tender age of fifteen. The military had a tradition of young brilliant leaders going back to Alexander the Great. Had she been the eldest son showing such promise, no one would object. But...

"Generals, you may rise." She nodded to servants who brought two folding camp chairs. "Please sit. You may speak freely in my sisters' presence." She indicated the two girls sewing. "They have little knowledge of war and politics but keep me company."

Ardaburius now looked on the two younger princesses with some interest. It was unlikely they were there as chaperones. Was the Augusta grooming her sisters for a more active role?

The men seated themselves, accepted the offer of well-watered wine, and declined the offer of food. Ardaburius appreciated the light vintage from Southern Thrace but wished for something stronger. He was used to drinking his wine undiluted.

Once the niceties of hospitality were satisfied, Plinta bowed his head slightly and asked. "Augusta, we are honored you asked us to join you. How may we serve?"

"I hope you will serve me well." The Augusta's steady eyes speared each man.

Ardaburius straightened his shoulders. Good! He was anxious to be back in the first ranks after several years under suspicion because of his barbarian Alan heritage.

"You know I'm purging pagans and Jews from my brother's government and the army," Pulcheria continued.

"But only from positions of responsibility?" Plinta gave a sweeping gesture. "If you dismiss the non-Christian soldiers, you will cripple the army. Many worship Mithras. Most who are Christian follow Arius' teachings."

"An army of pagans and Arians. I sometimes curse the day Emperor Constantius sent those heretic priests of Arius to convert the barbarians. A few years delay and you all would be orthodox and save the empire much strife." Pulcheria gave a sour smile. "You are a Goth, are you not? And your son-in-law an Alan? I assume you are Arian Christian, as well?"

"We come from those tribes and follow those beliefs, but we are Romans first. That is where our loyalty and duty lie." Plinta frowned. "We have served the empire honorably…when allowed."

"From what I hear, General, you are the best in the field and wasted in your current administrative duties."

Plinta allowed a small smile. "I'm grateful for the praise and strive to live up to it."

"I believe Anthemius erred in his caution these last several years. Your peoples have lived in the city peaceably for a full generation. I have faith in the civilizing influence of our dynastic city." She raised an eyebrow. "And I am not so foolish as to cut the heart out of the army that protects my people. My Uncle Honorius made that mistake and has battled barbarians that Rome trained for the past eight years. Arians are still Christian, if unorthodox. We both believe Christ died for our sins."

*Smart girl*, Ardaburius thought. *I had feared you too bound to your orthodoxy to act with such pragmatism.*

She turned to Ardaburius, as if reading his thoughts. "And you, General? Can you speak for yourself?"

"I have pledged my honor and my life to emperor and empire." He bowed his head. "I will serve you faithfully in any capacity you command."

"Good. These are your new assignments" She handed each of them a scroll, sealed with the emperor's imprint. "Anatolius will command the Army in the East. You will each be given an army in the emperor's presence. If you serve us well, there will be honors and rewards." She looked directly at Plinta. "Possibly even a consulship."

"There is no higher honor than guarding the city and the emperor." Plinta bowed again.

*Keeping us close! But our presence gives us more opportunities to influence the imperial court.*

"Thank you, Augusta. Your trust is all the honor I wish." Ardaburius flashed a brief smile. "Could I make one small request?"

She nodded assent, frowning slightly.

"Our wives and children reside in the city. They make do with religious services in private homes. I ask that we be allowed to build churches and worship God in peace and freedom."

"Your faith and commitment to your people serve you well. You have my permission." She smiled. "Perhaps, someday, your people will see the error of their ways and those churches will take the orthodox position that Christ is of, and equal to, God, not created by and subordinate to Him."

"Perhaps, Augusta." Ardaburius bowed in acknowledgement of this favor. His personal religious leanings were more toward the martial god Mithras, but his wife was a devout Arian Christian and he followed their tenets for her sake. He loved his wife and was happy he could please her with this news.

"Generals, I look forward to working with you."

Ardaburius and Plinta rose and bowed at the obvious dismissal. "Long life to you, Augusta."

In the corridor, Plinta turned to his son-in-law. "Well?"

"I think our sources on her inflexibility were exaggerated." His white teeth flashed in a feral smile. "I believe we are out of the wilderness. Our enemies at court should be wary."

# PART II

# EMPRESS AT WAR

## FEBRUARY 420 - JUNE 425

# Chapter 12



*Imperial Palace, February 420*

BROTHER, YOU MISSED THE MORNING AUDIENCE AND THE DAY'S PRAYERS." Pulcheria's gaze pinned Theo as he traversed the corridor to his private rooms. The boy emperor had grown into a man during the past five years. Riding, hunting, and sword practice honed his body and gave him an animal grace. He would never be a burly man, but her brother was handsome and healthy.

He turned; a blush crept up his neck to suffuse his face. "My apologies, Sister. Paulinus invited me to spend the day. We rode and dined at his father's estate." His eyes took on a wary cast. "I told the Master of Offices. Did he not inform you?"

"Of course." Little or nothing happened in the palace that she did not know of. When she took over running the household after Antiochus' retirement, she also took over his network of informants among the servants. As government absorbed her time, over the past couple of years she had turned more and more responsibility for running the palace over to Arcadia. Luckily, her younger sister showed an admirable talent for organizing, and took to the tasks willingly. Pulcheria did not want another eunuch meddling in her life.

She took her brother's arm as they walked towards his rooms. At their posts, the ever-present guards stared straight ahead. Servants retreated to the walls to stand with downcast eyes as they passed. "I was disappointed you did not see fit to tell me yourself." She let him squirm during the moments of silence that followed.

His mouth twisted into a sulk. "I never get to leave the palace. I'm emperor and have less freedom than any of my subjects. People attend me constantly. Court ritual and Church obligations mark my hours, night and day."

"God did not make you emperor to constantly carouse and ignore His business on earth. You were chosen and must fulfill your obligations to empire and Church." She patted his arm. "But I'm sure God did not intend you to have no recreation to lighten your burden. You are just shy of nineteen. Exercise and pleasant companionship are good for the soul, as well as the body. What did you and Paulinus speak of?"

"Not much. Hunting. Horses." His voice trailed off.

Pulcheria gave him a sharp look. Theo's boyhood companions were a constant thorn in her side. Her brother had a true and loyal heart. He lavished honors on the boys and their families. Placitus had taken an important position in Moesia and was thankfully gone from the palace, but Paulinus shadowed Theo still. She suspected Isidorus coached the boy to bend Theo to his will. She could almost feel Anthemius' son lurking in the shadows. She needed to keep a closer eye on Paulinus.

They arrived at the brass-bound door marking Theo's suite of private rooms. He dithered, obviously not wanting to invite her in.

She dropped his arm to confront him. "We have important news from Persia. May I come in?"

"What news?"

"Something not to be discussed in the corridors!" She pursed her lips in exasperation. *What's wrong with Theo?*

"Fine. Come in." He opened the door and bowed her in.

His rooms were austere, but not as monastic as her own. The walls of his personal audience chamber sported frescoes of nature and hunting scenes. Niches which normally held statuary contained fragrant pots of flowers grown indoors over the winter. The lavenders teased her with the scent of spring, still a month or two away. Pulcheria passed carved oak chairs sporting purple cushions with gold tassels but chose to sit on a bench devoid of padding.

Inside, Theo relaxed a bit, taking one of the chairs across from her. "Are you sure we shouldn't walk in the garden?"

"In this weather! We'd freeze." She gave a fake shiver and laughed. The use of their childhood code brought a rush of affection, pushing aside her irritation. Busy with the work of running an empire, she did miss her brother! The code also reminded her their days in the nursery were anything but carefree. Pulcheria glanced at the servants. "Warm spiced wine for the emperor."

Her action brought another frown to Theo's face. "I am capable of directing my servants, Ria."

"I know." She waited until the servants left the room. "It was my way of getting us a little private time. The palace will soon be ringing with the news."

"Are you going to tell me before the servants announce it?" His eyebrow rose in imitation of her own when exasperated.

"King Yazdgard executed a Christian bishop and several of his followers."

"What?" Theo leapt to his feet and started pacing—echoing another of her habits. Theo's cheeks turned red again, this time with the hot blood of anger. "How dare he execute Christians? We have a treaty!"

Pulcheria's fears that the Hellenes led her brother to light-mindedness receded. She had been unaware she carried such a burden until it lifted like a weight from her shoulders. She should never have doubted her brother's faith and dedication to the Church, having raised him in piety. His occasional small rebellion was a function of his youth and vigor, to be expected. *I should find him a suitable wife soon, one without the burden of too many family connections. It is time he fulfilled his dynastic obligations and produced an heir.*

"The bishop destroyed a state Zoroastrian fire-altar. He and his followers did not repent. I'm afraid Yazdgard had little choice but to execute them. However, we must be on our guard and object to any further persecution of our co-religionists."

"I don't understand." Theo sat, a frown puckering his brow. "We've been at peace with Persia for years. Prefect Anthemius insured Christian freedom from persecution in exchange for granting the same rights to Persians in our lands. Father even named Yazdgard as my protector in his will."

"A clever ploy to protect you from our more ambitious nobles." Pulcheria snorted. "More likely that scheme was executed by Antiochus than by Father. I always suspected the wily eunuch of taking a Persian pension."

"Really? You never told me."

"You were young and had no need to know." She reached across a low marble table to grab his hand. It was imperative Theo understand her next point. "Brother, it is time your people see their emperor not just as Protector of the Empire, but Protector of the Faith. We will meet with our generals tomorrow to plan our strategy. I hope to avoid further bloodshed, but if Yazdgard pursues

Christians, we must respond. This will not be a normal skirmish about borders or trade. If it comes to it, this will be a holy war."

"I understand, Ria." He squeezed her hand, looking grim. "Now I must repair to bed. Only a few hours until midnight prayers."


General Ardaburius strode into the Consistory with the confidence of a successful man. He spied his father-in-law in conference with Helion, the current Master of Offices, at a sideboard laden with food and drink, and approached. "Helion, Consul."

General Plinta's lips twitched. He was but two months past his consulship and preferred his martial title to the new civil one. "General," he acknowledged. "We were just discussing the Persian—"

"The Augustus and Augusta" a young page announced.

The trio turned as the young emperor and his sister entered the room, linked arm in arm, both cloaked in imperial paludamentums and crowned with matching gold and pearl diadems. Ardaburius always found it a bit shocking to see the Augusta in court regalia and elaborate wig. He had developed a warm relationship with the young woman over the past five years and was more accustomed to her severe religious garb.

The Augusti took their seats at the head of the ebony table. The rest of the small gathering ranged themselves on either side by strict precedence. Aurelian, Helion, Plinta, Ardaburius, and General Anatolius, who now had Plinta's command, along with the court treasurer. *If there is going to be a war, we will need money.*

Servants filled goblets with minted water. An officious middle-aged man stood behind Helion, clutching a sheaf of papers. Ardaburius caught his father-in-law's eye across the table and gave a slight jerk of his head toward the unknown man. Plinta shrugged. *We'll find out soon enough.* Ardaburius angled his body forward as the emperor spoke.

"As you have undoubtably already heard, the Persian King Yazdgard executed a Christian bishop and several of his followers for destroying a state Zoroastrian fire-altar." Heads nodded around the table. "According to our treaty with the Persians, he was within his rights to take this action. However, we have some additional disturbing news from the Persian court." He nodded to his Master of Offices. "Helion."

"Asclepiodotus, my head clerk in the office of *agents en rebus*," Helion introduced the unknown man standing behind him, "will tell you what we know so far."

The man bowed to the head of the table. "Most Esteemed Augustus, Most Holy Augusta, councilors, my people have compiled an extensive report on the number, training, and distribution of the Persian armies." He passed out copies. "I'm here to talk about the mood of the Persian court and our analysis of what we might expect next."

Ardaburius gazed at Asclepiodotus with some curiosity. The *agents en rebus* operated in obscurity, quietly gathering information on various fronts, foreign and domestic. It was rare that you could put a name to one. Helion must be grooming Asclepiodotus for greater responsibilities, to bring him out of the shadows.

"King Yazdgard is ailing," Asclepiodotus continued. That elicited murmurs of concern around the table. "He has been a moderating influence during these past twenty years. His son Vahram is much more hostile towards us, and eager to show his martial prowess. I believe he will move against us after his father dies, if not before."

"What will be the nature of this attack?" The emperor leaned forward, frowning.

"We don't know for sure, Augustus. We think it likely he will attack or expel Christians from his lands. He might test our borders in hopes of acquiring more territory. He might do nothing. We should plan for the worst."

Ardaburius glanced at the curiously quiet Augusta. *Surely, she already knows this. Why has she expressed no opinion? Unless…*he suppressed a smile. *Pulcheria wants her brother to shine on this occasion. She knows the people won't accept a warrior empress.*

Theodosius looked around the table. "And the rest of you? What are your recommendations?"

Aurelian cleared his throat, "Most Wise Augustus, I agree with Helion and Ascplepiodotus. We should watch the situation closely. We have been at peace with Persia for many years. It would not do for us to suddenly attack over this incident, yet we should be vigilant."

*So that's Pulcheria's position,* Ardaburius thought: *wait and see.*

"I believe we should take some precautions." Plinta spoke up. "Strengthen our fortifications on the border; recruit and train additional troops."

Ardaburius and Anatolian agreed.

"Good!" The emperor nodded. "We are agreed on a strategy. We watch Persia carefully and prepare in case of attack. Generals, follow through and report directly to me on the outcomes."

Theodosius and Pulcheria rose and exited as they'd entered, arm-in-arm.

Ardaburius escorted his father-in-law from the room, "Have you ever been in a meeting where the Augusta did not speak?"

"Never." They watched the two imperial siblings exit toward their private residence. "But it is more than past time the young man took up his title and ruled his empire. The Augusta is an able ruler, but in time of war people need a man at the helm."

"The Augusta is a remarkable woman, and I do not see her giving up power, even in a time of war." Ardaburius rubbed his jaw. *And we may be better off if she doesn't.*


*Refugee Hospital, Constantinople, August 420*

"Augusta, please! It is not appropriate that you wash their wounds and feed their children." Helion fussed as Pulcheria tended the Christian refugees from Persia.

"Why? Did not Jesus tend the sick and minister to the dispossessed?" Pulcheria fed another spoonful of broth to an emaciated child. So many families had fled Persian persecutions with little more than the clothes on their backs! With Yazdgard dead, his son Vahram intensified attacks on Christians. *Did I make a colossal mistake in not prosecuting this war earlier? Should I have sent armies to the rescue of these wretched people last spring?* These broken bodies and ruined hopes accused her of timidity, if not outright negligence.

"Jesus was not the Empress of Rome!" Helion fumed. "You've established churches, hospitals, and charities for the poor. The Roman world knows Christian refugees will be honored and cared for in your city. Leave these daily ministrations to the monks and holy women."

"I will not have this argument with you again, Helion. God calls me to this ministry. I answer." She put the spoon down and wiped the child's mouth; a little girl with lank brown hair and green eyes, dulled with hunger. Three years old? Maybe four? The child reached up with stick-thin arms. Pulcheria hugged the fragile body and rested the child's head on her breast. "Hush, child. There is plenty of food here. You will not go hungry again."

A flea hopped from the small form onto her woolen robe. She crushed it between her fingers. The child stank. Pulcheria's nose had become inured to the rank smell in the room: boiled cabbage with a whiff of feces and stale urine.

These people need baths and clean clothes as well as food! Pulcheria looked around for the holy woman running the charity. Seeing Helion still hovering, she said, "If you want to help, fetch me Sister Catherine. I think she's supervising the cooking."

Helion walked stiffly in the direction of the kitchen.

Pulcheria set the girl on her knee. "What's your name, child?"

"Miriam." The girl stuck a thumb in her mouth, looking up with big eyes.

"That's a strong name. Miriam was a prophetess and protected her brother Moses. Is your family here?"

Miriam shook her head.

"Well, then. We'll find you a new family. Have some more soup." The little girl opened her mouth like a fledgling bird, eager to gulp down whatever Pulcheria provided.

Warm nourishment did its job. Soon, the child nodded sleepily. Pulcheria tucked her into a pallet. Helion arrived with Sister Catherine, a round-faced, portly woman in her middle years. She had smile lines at the corner of her eyes and the dark marks of sleeplessness under them.

The holy woman bowed low, trying to muster some energy in her welcome. "Augusta, we are honored by your presence. How may I be of service?"

"It is I who wishes to serve. I've brought my sisters and court ladies to help today."

"God bless you, Augusta!" Tears of relief sprung to the woman's eyes. "We have so much need."

Pulcheria pointed at the sleeping girl. "Do you know this child's story?"

"A wine trader found her along the road, sitting next to the bodies of a woman and a newborn babe. The mother must have gone into labor fleeing the Persians and died in childbirth."

"No sign of the father?"

Sister Catherine shook her head. "The woman and infant had been dead for days, any possessions stolen, and the child starving, when the merchant found them. Yet she protected her dead mother, threatening the merchant with a stick when he came close." Sister Catherine smiled. "A survivor, that one."

"I agree." Pulcheria studied the child's face. She would have no children of her own, but the innocent always tugged her heart, creating a sensation approaching pain in her breasts and womb. "I will establish an orphanage for Miriam and any other Persian orphans that come to you. They will be educated and trained in a profession or trade if they show talent. At the proper time, the girls can marry or enter holy orders. I'll provide a dowry or gift to the church as needed." Watching another flea escape the child's hair, she added, "I'll send over firewood and tubs, so the people can bathe. In the meantime, my almoner will provide you with additional funds to care for the refugees."

Helion opened his mouth and closed it again when he saw her determined face.

"Augusta, you are too generous. Will you pray with me?" The two women dropped to their knees, holding hands. Helion joined them, grimacing as he knelt on the stone floor. "Lord God, Our Father, Jesus the Son, and Holy Mother Mary bless these children. Give them strength to endure their pains and afflictions. Give them Your love and the hope of everlasting life in Your grace."

Pulcheria took up the prayer. "Dear Lord and Mother Mary, give me strength and wisdom, that I may end this persecution of your people, and proclaim your glory throughout this land. Amen."

Pulcheria stood and offered a hand to Helion as he struggled to rise on stiff knees. "I'm sorry, Master Helion. I should have asked for a cushion. I know your joints give you pain."

"Thank you, Augusta." He ran a hand through greying hair. "It is good to be reminded of one's lacks and frailties on occasion. Do you wish me to make arrangements for the child?"

"No. I'll send a servant later. Let her sleep for now." Pulcheria reached to push a stray curl from the girl's forehead. "I'll make things right. It's time to go to war and stop this carnage." She turned to Helion. "We'll need more than armies. We must have a potent symbol of God's grace and approval of a holy war."

"Of course, Augusta. I'll have the mints draw up a design."

"Do that." Pulcheria nodded. "I want something more than the usual communication by coin and statue. I'll give this more thought."

# Chapter 13

*The plain of Hebdomon outside Constantinople, September 420*

THEO BREATHED IN CRISP FALL AIR AS HE SURVEYED HIS TROOPS FROM horseback. He relished these official visits beyond the confining walls of the palace and the city. He was tired of court ritual and public appearances. Pulcheria seemed to order his days to the last minute. At least on the martial field he could escape her attention. Later, he and Paulinus could have some fun.

Generals Plinta and Ardaburius rode at his side. Paulinus trailed behind.

"Are they ready, General?" Theo surveyed the raw recruits lined up in the late September sun. Compared to those armies in the field, this was an uninspiring bunch. Their armor was mismatched and their tunics varied from bright scarlet to pale pink. Not one in ten wore a helmet, and those looked as if inherited from an ancient grandfather. *How did our armies get into such poor shape? Corruption? Three of every four soldi collected in taxes go to defense. One more detail to talk to Pulcheria about.*

"Not yet." Plinta shook his head. "They will be, by spring fighting season. We've several months to whip the new recruits into shape. Our manufactories are working every sunlight hour to provide us with weapons and armor."

"Good." Theo shaded his eyes to look at the angle of the sun. Too late to go hunting. He sighed, signaling Paulinus to join him. "You may return to your duties, generals. I'll be on my way."

"As you wish, Augustus." They bowed from their waists and called up his escort.

Theo set a leisurely pace toward the city walls.

Paulinus grinned. "Bored?'

"Terribly."

"I have a surprise for you in the city, if you wish."

"You know I won't gamble or go to the theater." Theo frowned. Paulinus proposed an endless round of forbidden pleasures. Sometimes he was tempted, but always felt virtuous when he turned them down.

"You'll like this one. Good food, interesting—and quite proper—people. An intellectual salon perfectly suited to your tastes. There will be poets, historians, and diplomats with interesting stories. The host is an administrator in your own government. What's the harm?"

Theo considered the pile of papers Pulcheria probably had waiting for him. "A literary salon? Sounds quite appealing." He kicked his mount into a smooth canter. "Race you to the Golden Gate!" he shouted over his shoulder.

"No fair!" he heard Paulinus yell as his horse leaped forward in a gallop.

His escort milled in surprise, but he soon heard pounding hooves behind him. It felt good to be on his own, riding hard, even for a few seconds.

At the gate, the party reassembled. The captain of his guards scowled but didn't dare complain to him. Pulcheria would hear of it later. For the moment, Theo's blood raced. His spirits rose.

"This way!" Paulinus took the lead as they wended through the streets toward the palace. Most people recognized the palace guard, but because Theo travelled in ordinary nobleman's clothes, surrounded and hidden from their eyes, no one knew their sacred emperor moved among them. The neighborhood just outside the palace district housed mostly high-ranking civil servants. Paulinus reined in at the bronze gate of a moderately large complex. Whitewashed brick walls took up half the block and rose two stories above the street. A gatekeeper let them in; grooms took their horses in a stone-paved outer reception area.

"Whose home are we invading?" Theo looked up at the red inner wall.

"Asclepiodotus', a supervisor in the offices of your *agents en rebus*."

"I've met the man. He works closely with Helion." Theo looked at the imposing force arrayed in the courtyard and turned to the captain. "No need for a full guard here. You will accompany me to the door, but not inside. I don't want to alarm my hosts."

The captain narrowed his eyes. "I have standing orders not to let you out of my sight, Most Gracious Augustus. Your safety is my highest priority."

"I understand, but I am the emperor. This is the private residence of one of my trusted officials." Theo frowned, acknowledging the delicacy of the captain's position, but resenting it all the same. "You may accompany me into the residence but stand guard at the door. That way you fulfill your duty and allow me some pleasure."

"As you command." The captain bowed, then turned to his troop. "Men, at ease, but stand ready."

Paulinus led them further into the complex, sending servants ahead to announce their presence. "Quietly. The emperor is a guest and doesn't want a fuss."

They passed through the atrium into a formal garden complete with fountains and colonnaded sides. Small groups congregated wherever there was seating. Trampled rosemary and mint lightly scented the air. Servants mingled with the guests, carrying trays of small delicacies and flagons of wine.

A short dark man bustled up to them, bowing low.

"Asclepiodotus," Theo acknowledged.

"Your Serenity does my humble home much honor."

A plump woman with improbable red hair followed Asclepiodotus, practically throwing herself to her knees. Their actions drew the attention of other guests. Theo did not wish to be recognized and fawned over. He raised the women with a hand under her elbow. "Please. I'm not here as your emperor. Treat me as you would any other guest."

"Thank you, Augustus." The woman blinked large brown eyes.

"May I present my wife, Doria?" her husband offered. This time she curtsied.

"You have a lovely wife and home, Asclepiodotus." Theo gave both a slight bow.

His host signaled a servant. "Get the emp…my guest a goblet of our best Thracian wine. See to his needs personally for as long as he stays."

Paulinus stifled a cough. "Theo, perhaps I can introduce you to some of the other guests?"

"Of course!" Asclepiodotus backed away. "You'll find quite an interesting mix. May I suggest you start with Olympiodorus? He is holding forth under the grape arbor about his visit to the Hunnic court. I'm sure our guest will find him most amusing. He is also a poet and historian."

Paulinus guided Theo to a small gathering listening to a balding middle-aged man with the robust frame and the deeply tanned face of an outdoorsman. "…the court was in an uproar. I barely arrived and King Donatus dead! Of course his successor, King Charaton, accused me of spying and murder. Only quick talking and the magnificence of the emperor's gifts kept me from the Huns' wrath."

Theo recognized the man as the historian Helion had tasked with documenting his reign. He didn't look like a scholar. That Olympiodorus acted as a diplomat and befriended Asclepiodotus, head of the *agents en rebus*, led Theo to one conclusion. A spy! He never got to talk to the agents in the field. This was, indeed, going to be an interesting party!

Olympiodorus caught Theo's gaze. His eyes widened. Theo shook his head slightly.

"Tell us of your sea adventures." A lovely girl diverted Olympiodorus by grabbing his arm. "I never tire of hearing those stories."

The diplomat continued his tales of wandering and perils at sea. Theo's attention strayed to the girl. She could have modeled for a statue of Venus, her face and form a perfect example of classic beauty: heart-shaped face with large, wide-spaced eyes, small nose and bowed lips. From her golden curls to her neat toes, Theo couldn't avert his gaze.

"Who is she?" he whispered to Paulinus.

"Athenais. Aclepiodotus' niece. Her brothers serve in your provincial governments—Thrace and Illyricum, if I remember right." Paulinus gave Athenais an appraising glance. "Lovely, isn't she?"

"I've never seen such beauty." Theo felt a wave of heat radiate from his groin to his face—an unaccustomed pleasurable pain. He curled his hands into fists, digging his nails into his palms, trying to fight this sinful lust. "She's not like the girls in my sister's court." Theo sometimes thought Pulcheria chose the women who attended her for their plainness, as well as their dedication to God.

"Athenais is not an empty-headed fool, like some women," Paulinus said. "Her father held a chair in rhetoric at the Athens Academy and allowed her to attend lectures in philosophy. She's also an accomplished poet."

"Will you introduce us?" Theo spied his personal servant lurking with a goblet of wine, grabbed it, and gulped. The smooth vintage took the edge off his nervousness.

"Of course." His friend grinned.

Olympiodorus finished his tale as Paulinus approached arm-in-arm with Theo. "Well met, Olympiodorus." He dropped Theo's arm, bowing slightly to the girl. "Athenais, may I present my good friend Theo?"

"My pleasure." Eyes wide, she bowed, but otherwise did not acknowledge his rank. Her deep blue eyes bordered on violet. "Theo, do you like poetry?"

"Yes! Very much," he managed to get out, though his tongue seemed swollen to twice its size.

"Then you've come to the right place. My friend," she nodded to Olympiodorus, "will be reciting some of his work later. It's quite good."

Theo smiled until he thought his face would crack. Paulinus nudged him in the ribs. "I…uh…I understand you write verse as well."

"I only dabble." She lowered her lashes and shrugged delicate shoulders.

"I'd love to hear some." Theo stood tongue-tied, not knowing what to do with his hands and feet.

Paulinus stepped forward, taking both by the elbow. "Perhaps this is too public a place." He led them to an alcove shaded by a fig tree. "Sit here and get acquainted. I'll send the servant."

Theo didn't notice Paulinus' exit. He barely heard Athenais' next remark from the blood roaring in his ears. "Uh, what did you say?"

"I asked where you had been earlier. You're dressed for riding." Athenais' blue eyes sparkled.

"Inspecting the troops. It's my responsibility, you know." Theo wanted to bite off his tongue as the words came out of his mouth. *She'll think you a pompous ass, you fool!*

He caught a whiff of sweat and horses. *Oh, God, I stink!*

He nearly got up to run out, but the servant appeared with goblets. Theo grabbed one to gulp. *Now she thinks you are a drunk, you lackwit!* He set the goblet aside, took a deep breath.

Athenais smiled and his heart nearly stopped. "I've always admired people who learned to ride. I'm afraid my exercise is confined to walking and wielding a pen."

"I enjoy riding, but I find wielding a pen to be more satisfying. Some of my friends call me 'the calligrapher.'"

"How delightful! What do you copy?"

"Mostly ancient texts. Some Holy Fathers, some historians." Theo's breathing slowed as he talked about his favorite hobby.

"I'd love to see your work sometime."

"I'd love to show you." He nearly lost himself again in her blue eyes. A horrible thought surfaced. "Are you visiting your uncle? For how long?"

Her face fell into sorrowful lines. "My father died last year. Uncle Asclepiodotus and Aunt Doria were kind enough to take me in."

Though his heart soared at the news she would not be leaving soon, he recognized the grief of her loss. "I'm so sorry to have invoked painful memories."

"I miss him very much." Tears glistened in her eyes. "My mother died when I was quite young, and he was both father and mother to me."

Theo heard a raucous squawk behind him.

Athenais looked up, startled. Then a smile lit up her face. "Olympiodorus has brought out his pet parrot. He is most amusing and can sing in several languages. I like when he dances."

"Then, by all means, let us go watch this wondrous bird." Theo stood, held out his hand, and accompanied Athenais back to the grape arbor.

Paulinus assured him later the parrot put on quite a show. Theo could only remember Athenais' blue eyes and laughing smiles.

# Chapter 14



*Imperial Palace, October 420*

Sister, the Master of the Privy Purse said you made a significant request of him."

Pulcheria looked up from her correspondence. Her brother lounged in her door. "I told you we need to send donations to the Bishop of Jerusalem."

"The Master claims the amount is excessive." Theo looked troubled.

"Does he?" Her eyes narrowed. She would have to have a talk with the man. "What does he know of prosecuting a war? We need to use our personal funds for the donation to receive the sacred right arm of Saint Stephen Protomartyr to assure our success over the Persians. The Saint's very name means victory. His holy relics need to be under your control so you can claim the victory.

"Do our armies have no part in defeating the Persians?"

"Of course they do." Pulcheria leaned back in her chair. "But the saints' relics will clinch our victory and show the world the strength of God. Unlike our grandfather, you do not lead your armies. It is of the utmost importance that, in the eyes of the people, you contribute to the victory as much as the generals."

"You know I will give you anything you want, Ria. I just need to know what it's for."

"As you should." Pulcheria rose to lead her brother to a divan. She felt guilty for not telling Theo her plans, but he seemed to be gone much of the time. A servant brought food and drink. "This war takes so much of my time; we seem to meet only for prayers lately. I have been remiss in not telling you all I know. Have you time now?"

Theo sipped his wine, glancing at the angle of the sun pouring through the windows. "Some. I'm to meet with Paulinus soon."

Pulcheria masked her disapproval by reaching for a set of drawings on a low table. "Tell me if you approve of these, dear brother. The Master of the Mint sent them over yesterday."

"Doesn't look much like me." Theo squinted at the figures: facing portrait busts on one side, an angel carrying a full-length cross on the other. "Or you, for that matter. Can't the mint come up with a better portrait for the coins?"

"It's not the portrait that's important. It's the message." She pointed to the words running around the rim. "'Master of Victory.' These coins proclaim our intention to protect our people from invaders and heretics."

"As you wish, dear sister." He kissed her on the cheek. "I must go."

A whiff of sandalwood tickled her nose. "Theo, are you wearing scent?"

"Just a trace from the bath oils."

Pulcheria frowned. *I really need to spend more time with Theo. Soon.*

*Home of Asclepiodotus, November 420*

ATHENAIS TOLERATED, WITH SOME AMUSEMENT, HER AUNT'S FUSSING.

"Not the blue stola." Doria sent the serving girl back to the clothes chest. "The white one with the blue embroidery and white silk wrap and veil." She turned back to her niece. "Blue brings out your eyes, but white indicates your purity. You can borrow my lapis lazuli for neck and ears." She produced delicate drop earrings of polished blue stones entwined with gold wire and held them up to her niece's ears, so Athenais could see how they would look in the polished silver mirror. "Yes, they're perfect!"

"Only the lightest makeup." Doria instructed the woman arranging Athenais' hair in a virginal style flowing loose down her back, with ringlets across her forehead. The thin veil would cover her hair but not conceal it. "No kohl, and only a touch of carmine on the lips."

"Aunt, I feel like a doll being dressed." Athenais smiled. "The servants are doing fine."

"You must be perfect!" Doria squinted at a slight imperfection, a tiny crescent-shaped scar on Athenais' chin from a childhood fall. "Cover that," she ordered the make-up servant.

"No, Aunt." Athenais shook her head. "Anyone who has studied philosophy knows that beauty is not in perfection of outward form. Beauty comes from within. Small imperfections make us more interesting."

"Hah! So say all the old ugly philosophers!"

Athenais chuckled, turning back to the mirror. "Theo may be emperor, but he has little experience with women. Paulinus tells me Theo has never lain with a woman. Theo is shy with me. I need to take this slow, not frighten him off."

Her aunt snorted in disbelief. "Still, you must bind him to you. Marriage to the emperor would elevate this family beyond our dreams." Doria pinned the blue-decorated stola at Athenais' shoulders with gold fibulae and belted her waist with a girdle of golden links.

"Romance is a necessity." Athenais' eyes clouded with thought. "I have little to recommend me as an imperial spouse: modest family connections, no wealth. He is attracted to my beauty, but, if he wished, he could have any number of beautiful women in his bed. There must be more or he will slip away." *And I would have more for myself,* Athenais left unsaid.

She knew her duty to her family and had no silly notions about romantic love. She always knew her family would find her a husband. Her father promised she could decline a match, if she had good reason, but no one turned down the emperor. Two months ago, she would not have sought so high, and was a little overwhelmed at the prospect. She was just as sheltered, in her own way, as Theo. *At least we have that in common!*

Her aunt put her arms around her shoulders and squeezed. "Physical attraction is a good place to start."

A servant came to the door. "The emperor awaits you in the receiving room."

Anticipation brought a pretty blush to her cheeks. Her aunt pinned the silk veil to her hair and looked her over. "You're perfect!"


Theo paced in the receiving room, straightening his tunic for the hundredth time.

"You look fine, my friend. Everything is in order." Paulinus slapped him on the back. "It's the girl who's supposed to preen."

"What if she doesn't like me?"

"You're the emperor. She has to like you."

"That's the point!" Theo wailed. "If I were not emperor, would she look at me twice? She's so beautiful and cultured. What if her affection is a ploy? Pulcheria constantly warns that people only want to use me."

"Your sister is right."

Theo looked at Paulinus in surprise.

"There are very few people you can trust in this world. Do you trust me?"

"Of course! With my honor and my life." Theo strode to Paulinus and clasped him in a hug. "You are my best and truest friend."

"Then trust me when I say you could do no better than Athenais. She is sweet, modest, and yours to win. She would never try to dominate you as… uh…others might."

"I do want to win her love, not her compliance."

"Be kind, affectionate. That present is a good start." Paulinus indicated the silk-wrapped parcel on a white marble side table. "But you must also show her you are a man. It is time to take more of the government into your own hands. You're nineteen, well past your majority."

Paulinus struck a chord. Theo's restlessness and boredom might be alleviated if he took over more of the decision-making in his rule and less of the ceremony. Pulcheria did all the work. He pressed his seal to the wax as she bid him. He blurted out his biggest concern. "I worry about the progress with Persia. Did we wait too long?"

"Your sister has served you well—except for the Persian attacks. We should have addressed their insults months ago."

"Pulcheria has plans for receiving the bones of Saint Stephen Protomartyr, which she believes will cinch our victory."

"You don't believe in that…" Paulinus laughed, then turned it to a cough when he realized Theo was serious. "Many pardons, my friend, but armies win wars, not dead saints."

"Paulinus! You studied with me. The Great Constantine won his crown with the cross at the Milvian Bridge. My own grandfather invoked God when he was trapped on the battlefield at Frigidus and the Lord sent a mighty wind to defeat his pagan enemies. The people believe Saint Stephen will hear their prayers and invoke God's help."

"Of course." Paulinus wiped sweat from his forehead with a linen kerchief. Theo thought the room a bit warm himself, but he was nervous. He also knew Paulinus did not share his deepest convictions, but he was a good man. His friend had only his best interests at heart.

Paulinus looked over Theo's shoulder. His smile widened as he whispered, "She comes."

Theo whipped around, tangling his feet, making a clumsy turn. Blood rose to his cheeks. Athenais didn't laugh. She smiled with what looked like true pleasure to see him.

"Augustus." She dropped into a deep curtsy.

"Please, in your uncle's home, call me Theo."

"As you wish."

"*Domina*, have you heard the latest story about Helion?" Paulinus took Doria by the arm and led her to a bench in the furthest corner of the room, giving Theo and Athenais some small measure of privacy.

Theo shot his friend a grateful look.

"Our servants have set out refreshments. Will you allow me to serve you, Aug—uh—Theo?"

He nodded, and they made their way to a table set with an array of fruits, nuts, olives, cheeses, sliced meats and delicate pastries. The sharp fishy scent of garum warred with the aroma of ripe apples and the yeasty smell of warm bread.

He picked up a handful of almonds and nibbled them as she poured him a goblet of wine.

"Is that all you care for?" She looked at him demurely through lowered lashes as she proffered the goblet.

"I'm afraid my appetite deserts me in your presence. I care only for your company."

A delicate blush tinted her cheeks, giving him more confidence.

"Oh! I have a present for you." He raced back to the table, retrieved the package, and handed it to Athenais.

Athenais sat on a padded rosewood divan, the package in her lap. She turned it over, inspecting the wrapping. Theo's heart beat louder in anticipation. What if she didn't like his gift?

She undid the silk cord, letting the fabric drift aside to reveal a small, leather-bound codex. The title stamped in gold on the binding declared it the play Helen by the ancient playwright Euripides.

"It's exquisite!" Athenais brought the book to her nose to sniff appreciatively. "I love the smell of new books—leather and fresh ink!" She opened the codex to inspect the lovely script, then turned to him with shining eyes. "Have you read it?"

"I did the copy work myself."

"It's beautiful work. Some of the best I've seen." Athenais inspected a few pages.

"I chose the story because your beauty outshines Helen's," Theo said softly, immediately regretting his words. How could he be so bold with such a delicate girl?

"I like the play because Euripides shows Helen to be a faithful wife to Menelaus, wrongly used by the gods." She clutched the book to her breasts. "I'll treasure this always. How did you know I value books over jewels?"

"Paulinus told me."

She laughed, patting the seat on the bench beside her. "Of course he did. Paulinus is a good friend to us both."

Theo sat by her side and picked up her hand. He turned it over, running his thumb gently down the lifeline of her palm. A jolt settled in his loins. He breathed faster. Her hand was soft and white, save for a fading ink spot on the inside of her index finger. He studied the spot, trying to control his physical urges. He felt her shiver and released her hand. "I'm sorry. I did not mean to be so forward."

"I do not think you forward, Theo. I find you most considerate." They sat in awkward silence a moment. Athenais tapped the codex. "Do you like the classical writers?"

"I haven't read as widely as I suspect you have. We tended to study the writings of the Church fathers."

"I've read Clement and Origen. They were Christians *and* philosophers." She clasped her hands together. "There seems much to be learned from both schools of thought."

"Are you studying with anyone?"

"Bishop Atticus is tutoring me in the Christian faith. I'm to be baptized soon."

"That's wonderful!" His smile blazed. *I could never marry a pagan.* His heart leaped as he realized he contemplated marriage. Until that moment, Theo thought only of getting to know this beautiful girl better, but his heart had decided without his head. Now he wanted, more than anything in his life, to win her hand...and convince Pulcheria this was a good match.

# Chapter 15



*Imperial Chapel, Palace, Constantinople, January 421*

PULCHERIA STOOD IN CEREMONIAL ROBES AND FORMAL WIG, CRADLING a large wooden cross, trying to still her racing heart. This was the most important day in her life since she dedicated her virginity to her brother's rule. Behind her stood the newly built imperial chapel to house the relics of Saint Stephen; a beautiful marble affair with a richly carved altar and gem-encrusted candlesticks. She had planned the adventus of Saint Stephen's bones down to the last detail with Bishop Atticus. Any error in the ceremony would bring shame on the city in the eyes of the people.

Theo led the procession in full regalia, carrying a large lit candle. He set a stately pace for the dozen top men of the city, who also carried lit tapers. Following them was a lavish wagon drawn by two mules, then representatives from nearly every monastery in and around the city. Bishop Atticus sat in the wagon, holding one end of an elaborately carved box. The other end rested in the arms of Bishop Passarion, a much-beloved ascetic from Jerusalem who accompanied the relics.

Pulcheria watched apprehensively as the procession entered the Chalke gate. The assembled court waved censers and took up the cries from the balcony: "Welcome to Saint Stephen, bringer of victory. Long life and victory to Emperor Theodosius, Second of that Name. Wisdom and blessings on the Virgin Augusta." The entire adventus had marched slowly through the city, to the cries of the people welcoming the saint to his new home. Some older men in the procession looked exhausted. Even Theo looked a bit drawn. Pulcheria tried to keep worry from her face.

Incense wafted across the procession, bringing the piney scent of frankincense with sweet earthy undertones of myrrh, representing the divinity and suffering of Christ. The smell calmed Pulcheria, filling her with lightness.

When Theo arrived before her, Pulcheria handed him the cross, another potent sign of victory: Christ's over death. He briefly nodded, then stood aside with the rest of his entourage. When the wagon carrying the saint's remains arrived, the bishops carried the box to Pulcheria.

Bishop Passarion intoned, "We have brought Saint Stephen to his new home, where he will dwell. His prayers, living and present, will intercede with our Divine Protector to bring victory to the emperor and his armies. He will smite all non-believers and bring fear into the hearts of our enemies."

"We accept this most generous gift from the bishop and people of Jerusalem and have prepared a most fitting home for Saint Stephen's presence, here in the heart of our palace." Pulcheria took the box from the bishops. Heavier than expected, it took all her strength to hold the box chest high and deliver it safely to the altar. The bishops, Theo, and a select few others followed her into the chapel, where they all knelt and prayed.

As she installed the holy relics in a cedar-lined compartment under the altar, Pulcheria felt blood flow through her veins in a rush. She heard a heavenly choir, saw clearly the Great Saint standing before her, smiling, raising his right hand in a sign of blessing. She let her breath out in a slow sigh.

Saint Stephen Protomartyr was pleased with his new home.

She did well. Victory was assured.

*Outside the city of Nisibis, Persia, March 421*

General Ardaburius, heading a column of reinforcements, approached the Roman siege of Nisibis in the late afternoon. It had been a hard march from the province of Mesopotamia, where he had met and defeated the Persian General Narses. He grinned with satisfaction. With General Anatolius backing a rebellion against the Persians in Armenia, the enemy retreated all along the frontier.

"Father, do you plan to inspect the troops immediately at Nisibis?"

His son's voice pulled him from his reverie.

"Yes. Ride ahead and tell them of my arrival." He watched with pride as his son galloped away. Aspar in their language meant "horse-rider" and his son lived up to his name. He was lean, with his father's dark features and mother's lithe grace. *The boy's twenty-two already. Time I gave him a command of his own. Cavalry would be best.*

Arriving at the Roman camp, Ardaburius dismissed his troops to set up their own orderly camps. His infantry marched twenty or more miles a day, with full pack, and set up a secure camp each night. From tribune to foot soldier, each knew his place and his task. He watched with pride as eight-man tents sprung up in rigid rows across the plain. Men dug defensive ditches, put up temporary walls. Cooking fires dotted the darkening plain as soldiers settled in for their dinner of beans, bread, and watered wine. He assigned a watch to patrol the perimeter and guard the gates.

Ardaburius entered the older camp to see how the siege fared. He was tired, dusty, and hungry, but duty demanded he personally review the state of siege before retiring to his command tent for the evening.

Aspar approached with the siege commander and saluted. "General, all is in readiness for your inspection."

Ardaburius strolled from placement to placement, accompanied by Aspar and the commander, inspecting men and weapons. The sun setting in the West bathed the heavily fortified city, sitting on the plain before them, in a bloody light. Were he superstitious, he would take that as a bad omen, but Ardaburius had been in the field long enough to know success depended on preparation and execution.

"Tribune," Ardaburius addressed the commander holding a position on the river that ran next to the city. "How goes the watch?"

The young man snapped to attention. "Well, General. The engineers have blocked the Mygdonius River traffic both north of the city and south. No one will enter or leave by that route."

"Good." He looked at the city, backed by the hulking Masius mountains. "This will be a long, hard campaign. This city is used to sieges. For hundreds of years, Rome and Persia have passed it back and forth as the frontier shifts a few miles each direction. I mean to return it to Roman hands."

"Yes, Sir!"

The enthusiasm in the young man's voice reminded Ardaburius how tired he was. He scratched the sweaty stubble on his chin. *I need a bath and a shave, then food. I don't want to set a slovenly example for the troops.*

A week later, Ardaburius looked up from the reports of disciplinary actions, which increased with each day—one of the disadvantages of siege warfare. Engineers stayed busy, building and maintaining their siege engines. Specialized units pounded the walls with boulders; archers picked off the occasional defender. Most of the troops had little to do except drill, stand watch, and—in the absence of an enemy—fight one another.

His command tent bustled with activity—of the administrative kind. Clerks tallied and recorded all the details that kept a large army in the field: men, horses, and mules incapacitated by illness or injury; jars of oil and wine, sacks of grain and pulse; stores of arrows, javelins and swords. The only clerk that seemed idle was the one who compiled intelligence reports from far-ranging scouts and agents monitoring the merchant lanes. Lack of intelligence worried Ardaburius more than the restlessness of his troops.

The tent was spare, plainly furnished, with planks on boxes for desks and folding camp chairs. Some generals liked to travel in style with all the amenities of home. Not Ardaburius. One of the things he most admired from ancient generals like Caesar was their ability to pack up and move quickly. An army moved only as fast as its baggage train, so he kept his light.

"I spend too much time behind this damned desk!" Ardaburius stood and walked out of his command tent, leaving his clerks gape-mouthed at the sudden exit. The weather held fair for this desert climate in early spring; a perfect temperature, with warm days and cool nights. In a couple of months, the troops would be sweltering in their leather armor. He took a deep breath of fresh morning air, clearing oil smoke from his lungs.

"General!" a young man on a lathered horse shouted, as he raced into the dusty square in front of the command tent.

Ardaburius squinted. "Tribune Marcian?"

The tribune pulled his horse to a heaving stop, dismounted, and strode to the general. "I have important news!"

"About the Persians?"

Marcian nodded, "And the Huns. I have orders from the Augustus."

Ardaburius turned to his guards. "Gather my staff." They went running. The general returned his attention to the tribune. "Come into the tent and refresh yourself. Have you been travelling all night?"

Marcian nodded. "I've been riding several days. I took post horses as soon as I got the word."

No wonder the young man looked pale under the sweaty grime covering his face; eyes red and figure gaunt. Ardaburius had left the tribune prostrate with a fever in Lycia a couple of months ago. He must have a hardy constitution!

"All of you, out!" Ardaburius bellowed at the clerks as he entered the tent. They gathered their papers and left. "There's a basin and water in the corner."

Marcian splashed his face and dried it, leaving streaks of muddy dirt on a linen cloth. "Thanks."

Ardaburius held out a chipped ceramic cup with watered wine. Marcian gulped it down.

"Now, what can you tell me before my staff arrives?"

"The Augusti send their congratulations on—"

"Skip the flowery shit and tell me what's important!"

"Of course, General." Marcian stood at attention. "The Huns, under Ruga, have crossed the Danube, invaded Thrace, and march on Constantinople."

"Most of my army are Thracians. They won't want to stay here while their families are under attack!"

"Additional intelligence has come in from this front. The Persians have regrouped. They have assembled a large army and move to cut you off from the west."

"That's why we haven't heard from our scouts or agents. The Persians must be within striking distance, and my people either captured or cut off." Ardaburius fumed.

Marcian lowered his voice. "You are ordered to abandon the siege of Nisibis and return in all haste to Thrace to take on the Huns."

*Damn it all to hell!* After all his successes, to be so ignominiously pulled from the Persian front! He rubbed his chin, setting aside his disappointment to plan his next steps.

"General!" Aspar entered the tent out of breath, followed by several of his top staff. "What news?"

"We strike the camp and return to Thrace. We'll reinforce the border forts but must move now!"

To their credit, not a single officer offered an objection or asked a question.

They left to rally their troops and execute his orders. The General's chest swelled with pride. He moved to the tent entrance and bellowed at his milling clerks, "Get your papers stored and assemble at your wagons with your kit. The camp moves in two hours."

# Chapter 16



*Imperial Palace, April 421*

SISTER, THE HUNS INVADE OUR THRACIAN BORDERS, PERSIA HAS RAISED THE siege at Nisibis, and their allies strike deep into our territory, threatening Antioch." Theo sat askew on his padded chair, swinging his leg back and forth in a manner calculated to irritate her. Pulcheria had schooled him in appropriate court behavior so he would give nothing away to their enemies through nervousness or habit. *Why did he show such nonchalance during such a serious time?*

"I know, Brother." She looked around the crowded audience chamber, faces studiously turned away, ears sharpened for the least discord between imperial siblings. "Should we not repair to a more private room for this discussion?"

He surveyed the chamber. "I would have Paulinus and Asclepiodotus in council with us."

Pulcheria narrowed her eyes. Paulinus she disliked but understood. Asclepiodotus was a new factor. Some found him a man of middle ability. He had been a fixture at court in lower offices for years, showing competence but little initiative. Helion seemed to be promoting his career. Pulcheria didn't see why. Asclepiodotus' nephew Valerius held the prefecture in Thrace, where the Huns invaded. Maybe that's why Theo wanted him present.

"As the Augustus wishes." Pulcheria bowed and led the way to a small but richly appointed room just outside the audience chamber. Padded chairs clustered around a low table laid out with plates of olives, dates and cheese. A pitcher of wine, and another of water, stood on a carved sideboard, sweating. Pulcheria dismissed the servants.

"Now, Brother, what are your concerns? I recalled General Ardaburius and his army from Nisibis. He has orders to proceed north to deal with the Huns." She tried to ignore the presence of the other two men, but Asclepiodotus cleared his throat.

"Augusta, if I may speak?"

"I assume the emperor asked you here for a reason."

"My nephew Valerius serves the emperor as prefect in Thrace. He sent me word of a most disturbing and…delicate nature."

She nodded for him to continue.

"It seems three silver statues were recently found at the border of Thrace. They appear to be of, uh…" He cleared his throat again. "…uh, pagan origin." He gulped, looking at his feet.

His obvious discomfort pleased her. It was good to inspire some fear in court flunkies. Still, his nervousness seemed excessive for such a small thing. Did the man expect her to throw him in a prison for mentioning the word "pagan"?

"In what way are these pagan statues significant? We come across such frequently. If made of clay or stone, they are destroyed. If of precious metal, they are melted and remade into forms more pleasing to God."

"These are protective statues. When they were taken from the border, the Huns invaded. The troops in Thrace believe they must be returned to their resting places before they can evict the Huns. Valerius requests they be returned to him."

"What nonsense!" Pulcheria snorted. "Common soldiers are notoriously superstitious. Instruct your nephew to provide an example by publicly putting his trust in God, not some ridiculous statues. General Ardaburius will soon see to the Huns." She turned back to Theo. "What else troubles you, Brother?"

"With Ardaburius in Thrace, we have only one army standing against Persia."

"We cannot win against Persia while we fight the Huns." Pulcheria leaned back in her chair, sipping water. "You are right. I've already directed General Anatolius to send envoys to King Vahram to explore the possibility of a peace. We've punished them for their actions towards Christians. It's time for some magnanimity."

Paulinus shot a knowing look at Theo.

Pulcheria knew the Hellenes considered the Persian campaign a disaster.

They were quiet during the early successes, but now that Ardaburius was forced to retreat they howled about wasted lives and treasure. Both concerned her, but the war did one thing she could not do for her brother alone: it elevated Theo to the status of warrior in the people's eyes. If the war ended now, Rome lost no territory, even if they had gained none. They could claim victory.

A slow flush started up her brother's neck. Pulcheria sat still, waiting for him to gather his thoughts.

"Sister, no one appreciates your efforts on my behalf more than I. You have sacrificed your time and happiness to see me and the empire successful." His eyes slid from hers, raising alarms. "It is time I took more responsibility. I am twenty, long past my age of majority. You are no longer regent. It is more than time I took the reins of government from your hands."

"What?" Pulcheria, her mind focused on the war, was taken aback by his announcement. *Theo can't suddenly take over my duties. He's not prepared. He hasn't even been present at most of the council meetings these past several months…* She surveyed Theo's companions. Several clues clicked into place. She tried to calm her suspicions. "Brother, this is a matter of family, and should be discussed between us."

"They are family…to me…as you will see."

She sat up straight, glaring at Paulinus and Asclepiodotus. *What in God's good name were they up to?*

"I wish to make some changes. General Procopius will replace Anatolius as Magister Militum of the East. He will conduct negotiations with King Vahram."

She nodded. Not a bad choice. Procopius was a good general. However, with his marriage to Isidorus' sister, he was firmly in the Hellene's camp. With an army at his command, he could be a rival for the throne. She had no evidence he harbored imperial ambitions but would remain wary.

"I will appoint Asclepiodotus *comes sacrarum largitionum*." Theo continued.

Pulcheria drew in her breath. That position oversaw money collected as taxes and duties, supervised the mints and other imperial workshops, and paid out salaries and donatives to civil servants and troops. Asclepiodotus' previous service did not merit such an appointment. *What the blazes has been going on while I was preoccupied with the war?* She started to reply.

Theo put up his hand to forestall her. "And I wish to marry."

"Marry?" Pulcheria pulled her wits together. "That's a good thing to contemplate. I've always wanted you to marry and secure the succession." *And an imperial wedding will distract the people from other…less joyous news.* "I can start looking for a suitable bride immediately."

Paulinus finally spoke up. "That won't be necessary. I've found Theo a most wonderful bride. A girl of good family…" He nodded toward Asclepiodotus.

"My sister's daughter, sister to Prefect Valerius."

"…and excellent education. Her father held a chair in philosophy in Athens."

Pulcheria turned her sharp gaze on Theo.

"She's beautiful, Sister. Golden curls, creamy skin, rosebud mouth." His face took on the look of one besotted. "And she's learned. She's studied the early church fathers as well as the classics. I'm sure you two will get along famously. You'll have much to discuss."

"I'm sure we will," she muttered. "Does this paragon have a name?"

"Athenais."

"Named after a pagan goddess? Is she even Christian?"

"Bishop Atticus instructs her personally. She'll be baptized before the wedding and take a more suitable Christian name. We discussed a variation on our mother's name, such as Eudocia."

"Meaning 'good reputation'?" Her mouth twisted in an ironic smile. *Especially since Eudoxia's reputation had been anything but good.*

"In honor of our mother. I thought you would be pleased." Theo frowned.

"Of course it's an honor, and I am pleased." She would have words with Bishop Atticus for keeping such a thing from her. Although he might not have known the girl was to become part of the imperial family. "So, you've already proposed. I suppose we can plan for the wedding next year."

"We're looking for an auspicious date in June." Theo's face took on a dreamy look.

Pulcheria's face stiffened. "So soon! That gives us only a few months to prepare." *And for me to convince Theo this is folly.* "When will I meet your intended bride?"

"I've invited her to dine with us, at your pleasure." He leaned in close to take her hand. "You will be such good friends. I know it."

Paulinus smiled over Theo's shoulder. A challenge.

*We'll see.*


Pulcheria didn't see Theo alone until shortly before evening prayers. "Join me in the gardens."

He raised an eyebrow. "Is that really necessary?"

"They are beautiful this spring and calm my heart." She hooked her arm in his. "Come. I wish to take exercise."

They walked in silence among budding roses and date palms. Early herbs, such as lavender, scented the air. Pulcheria brushed a rosemary shrub with her hand and sniffed the soothing fragrance.

As they moved deeper into the garden, the silence grew more tense.

"I know you wish to dissuade me from this marriage, Sister." Theo set his jaw. His gaze wandered over the sea. "It will do you no good."

"Oh, Theo." She reached up to tuck a stray lock of hair behind his ear. "When did you grow so tall? When did you become a man?"

"While you ran the empire for me, dear sister." He clasped her hand in both of his. "Don't you want to give up that burden? Wouldn't you be happy tending your charities and building churches? You have served me well. I want your happiness as well as mine."

"Theo, who put these notions in your head? Who told you I was unhappy in my role at your side? They can't have your best interests at heart, if they wish to sow discord between us."

"It doesn't matter who." He turned his head away. "I'm not a complete naïf. I know men…and women…befriend the emperor for their own gain."

"And who gains from this match?"

"That's the point, Ria. No one. Athenais is an orphan."

"She has a brother and an uncle in government, who will expect favors as part of the family…"

"Two brothers."

"What?"

"Athenais has another brother, Gesius, who is prefect in Illyricum."

"*Two* brothers, then! Men who have wives who have fathers and more brothers. A marriage brings a skein of tangled relationships into the palace that need to be sorted out."

"I can't stay unmarried forever. I did not take a vow of chastity, like you." He dropped her hand and leaned on a low wall. "Besides, I must have a son. Athenais warms my heart and stirs my soul. She will be a fit wife and mother."

"I'm sure she will." Pulcheria sighed. "I just want you to go into this match with your eyes open. There are men in the court who wish to control you. They couldn't control me through marriage, but they might try to control you through a wife."

"Paulinus is my oldest friend. He has never asked anything for himself. I don't believe this marriage is a plot."

"Paulinus asks nothing for himself, because he doesn't have to. You heap honors on him before he can suggest them. You have ever been generous to your friends." Her tone grew bitter.

"Why do you dislike Paulinus so?"

"I don't dislike him." She joined her brother looking at the sea. "His kind is of the past. The Hellenes hark back to old Greek traditions where power is shared among the elite, an oligarchy. We build something new based on God's word and our sacred right to rule. They draw their power from family names, wealth, and tradition. We draw ours from God's anointment and the approval of the people. It will take a people united behind a strong leader to weather the coming storms. The Holy Scripture tells us the End Times are coming, and they are ones of chaos. We must be ready."

"If the End Times are coming, I want a wife at my side who can love and sustain me. Athenais is that woman. I see no plots from Paulinus or Aclepiodotus."

"I hope with all my heart you are right. I pray with all my strength you are happy, content, and safe; but I cannot save you from your own follies. Be aware, Brother."

He turned an angry glare on her. "This marriage is no folly. I love Athenais and will have her as my wife. Be aware yourself, Sister. If you choose to get in my way, I will set you aside."

"Theo, how dare you talk to me in that way! I've sacrificed everything for you." Unaccustomed tears threatened to spill from her eyes, as pain squeezed her heart.

"I didn't ask you to! You *chose* this life. Don't blame me for wanting more." He lowered his voice. "Sometimes I think you love power too much, Pulcheria. You talk of it constantly, judge others by their threat to yours, and don't want to give it up even into my rightful hands."

Shock shuddered through her. "Is that what you think? That I want to keep the throne for myself? Poison," she choked. "Someone has been pouring poison in your ears, while I labored on your behalf."

She turned on her heel, leaving him in shadows, then flung over her shoulder, "Think on it, Theo. Who benefits from our estrangement?"

# Chapter 17



*Imperial Palace, April 421*

ATHENAIS WAS ALL THAT THEO BRAGGED OF AND MORE. PULCHERIA TOOK a drink of diluted pomegranate juice. The sour taste matched her mood. Unable to persuade Theo to give up the girl during the past week, she finally agreed to meet with her. Athenais dressed the part of proposed bride; modest, but in a way that showed off her beauty. She wore no cosmetics but needed none. She wore only plain gold bracelets, and pearls in her ears. She tucked her hair under a thin veil, but several gold curls peeked out around her face. Someone—Paulinus?—had prepared her well for this interview.

"I understand you are an orphan?" Pulcheria put down her plain silver goblet.

Athenais' eyes grew moist. "Yes. My mother died when I was quite young. My father, just two years ago."

"We share that affliction. It's a trial to lose one's parents in youth, but adversity can also give one strength. I understand you have two older brothers who care for you."

"They are both in Theo's...the emperor's, service, stationed away from Constantinople. When Father died, he left the bulk of his fortune to my brothers. For me, there was just enough money to travel here to my aunt and uncle."

"That's particularly harsh, not to provide for a daughter." Pulcheria felt some sympathy for the girl. Widowed or orphan women of lower classes could start businesses or provide services. They were expected to work. Upper class women had few options, other than marriage, if they wanted to retain their status. A dowerless girl was at a disadvantage.

"My father loved me, but always said fortune would favor me," Athenais replied, a touch of defensiveness in her voice.

*So, she does not carry resentment for her father or more fortunate brothers?* Pulcheria prodded, "Sons can go into the civil service or the army. They have the means to make their way in the world. Leaving a daughter without a dowry for a good marriage condemns her to the charity of others. Have your brothers been generous?"

"Enough to provide for my upkeep. Little more." Athenais lowered her lashes. "They have families of their own to provide for and give what they can. My mother's brother is a most generous man and treats me like a daughter. His wife has been a comfort to me."

Pulcheria's chest tightened. As much as she loved Nana, her nurse couldn't guide her in the rough and tumble world of court politics. Would her life have been different with a loving mother or aunt to guide her? She turned her attention back to Athenais. "Have you considered holy orders?"

A blush tinted the girl's cheeks. "I've only recently embraced Christ as my savior. The idea of becoming a holy woman did not occur to me." She turned bright eyes on Pulcheria. "The whole city knows of your devotion, Augusta. Have *you* considered taking holy orders?"

Pulcheria nearly choked on her juice. "I have had more secular concerns to occupy my talents. If I took holy orders, I would be under the command of the bishop. That's not appropriate for Regent or Augusta."

"I see." Athenais smiled, revealing a dimple in her right cheek. "You are Regent no longer, but still Augusta. Please forgive me. I am new to these ways."

Athenais put her own goblet down to look Pulcheria in the eyes. "Augusta, I know this match is not of your choosing. I met Theo...the Emperor..."

"You may call him Theo in my presence."

"I met Theo purely by accident. Paulinus brought him to a salon at my uncle's. We talked and laughed. He treated me with great kindness. When I told him my story, he said he would rectify my father's error. I thought he intended to provide more money to my uncle for my upkeep. I had no idea he intended marriage."

*If that was an accident, I'm no virgin!* Pulcheria had no proof but, given Paulinus' roots deep in the Hellene faction, she did not put it past him to have arranged the "accidental" meeting. "If you find the match offensive or not suitable, you can refuse." She hoped her voice did not reflect the desperation she felt.

"Refuse the Emperor of Rome?" Athenais laughed. "Maybe if he had proposed a sinful alliance, but Theo would never do that. He is honorable and kind. I have grown to love him and wish this match to be successful." A serious look replaced her smile. "I know it will not be successful if we do not have your blessing. Theo loves you too much and respects your opinion. He would be terribly unhappy in a home where his two great loves warred."

That struck a chord with Pulcheria. She didn't want her brother unhappy. *And someone must secure the succession. Better Athenais than me.* She put a hand on the younger woman's arm and said, with resignation, "I have no objections, my dear. Theo and the empire are my first concerns. He is happy with you, so I am content."

"Thank you, Augusta." Athenais bowed. "You do me too much honor."

"You may call me 'Sister' in private."

*The Hippodrome, Constantinople, June 421*

CROWDS ROSE TO THEIR FEET WITH A DEAFENING ROAR WHEN THE IMPERIAL family entered their box at the hippodrome from their private tunnel in the palace. Pulcheria literally felt the wave of sound rush over her and reverberate through her chest. She stood at her brother's left hand, leaving her usual honored right-side place for his radiant bride and his groomsman Paulinus. Arcadia and Marina stood on her left, in the first row of comfortable seats.

A gaggle of Athenais' relatives—for an orphan she had plenty of people claiming kinship!—and members of the council took up the remaining rows of seats to the rear. Marble columns, topped with winged horses, supported a permanent overhang that provided shade from the blazing June sun. Imperial servants offered cushions, wine, and a wide variety of food to the wedding party.

Pulcheria turned her gaze toward the racetrack, admiring the various trophies displayed down the spina—a row of obelisks, statues and art decorating the middle of the hippodrome, around which charioteers raced. She might not approve of lavish living for herself but recognized the need for emperors to show their power by providing public art—particularly when it commemorated their own military conquests. Her grandfather's Egyptian obelisk took pride of place, its base inscribed with the proclamation: "All things yield to Theodosius and to his everlasting descendants." *May it be so,* she prayed.

"How exciting!" one of the aunts—Doria?—shrieked.

That annoying voice interrupted Pulcheria's contemplation. A sharp glance over her shoulder quelled the excitable woman but didn't wipe the triumphant smile from her face. Pulcheria sniffed. *What was she thinking, wearing that ridiculous red wig?* Her own wig of brown curls and braids sat hot and heavy on her head. She felt a trickle of sweat ooze down her back, stifled an instinct to scratch at the gold and silver embroidery covering her stiff purple robes. *I hope there is a special place in hell for the people who thought dressing up their rulers in such uncomfortable clothes was a good idea!*

After a few trumpet blasts, the crowd quieted. A professional announcer shouted out, "Our Most Noble Emperor presents these games in honor of his wedding to his Beloved, Aelia Eudocia Athenais. May their union be blessed with many children. Long life and God's blessings on Theodosius Augustus and his consort Eudocia!" The crowd took up the chant of long life and God's blessings, continuing for several minutes.

*At least he didn't elevate her to the rank of Augusta,* Pulcheria fumed, still smarting over her failure to prevent the match. In the two months since she had given her blessing, she vacillated between irritation at the changes forced on her, anger at her brother for his intransigence, and—after she talked to Bishop Atticus—a measure of resignation and acceptance. With the actual marriage today, her irritation returned.

"Ria." She felt a tap on her left shoulder. Arcadia nearly shouted in her ear, to be heard over the crowd. "Your face has been a thundercloud and body as stiff as a corpse since the wedding. It's done. We have a new sister. Show some enthusiasm—at least in public."

*How dare Arcadia lecture me on public comportment!* A tremor shook her body; anger warred with the truth of the accusation. She looked at the crowd, smiling and shouting their approval. They loved their young emperor and extended their love to his new bride. Pulcheria knew her sister was right. This marriage was a fact. She needed to deal with it. *Let Athenais grow fat with babies and rule over the nursery. Theo knows my worth. Athenais will never rival me in ability to govern or in Theo's affections.*

She pasted a smile on her lips. The people must not suspect any discord in the imperial family.

Theo stood and offered his hand to Athenais, his face glowing with pride. Athenais rose, smiled and nodded. The people stamped their feet, sending tremors through the stone risers of the hippodrome. Pulcheria had to admit the girl looked every inch an imperial consort in white silk and imperial purple amethysts dripping from her neck, wrists, and ears. A double strand of pearls and gems wound through her hair. A gold embroidered purple cloak—but not a palumendum!—covered her shoulders. The largest purple stone Pulcheria had ever seen, set in a gold starburst fibula, clasped the cloak at Athenais' right shoulder.

Theo raised his hands. The crowd quieted. He shouted, "Let the races begin!" The hippodrome erupted again in noisy bursts. Vendors hawked cushions, wine, sweets and other food to people in the regular seats. Despite herself, Pulcheria felt her heart beat faster as excitement rose in the crowd.

The Master of the Games blew a trumpet blast and announced the contestants. The first several races were between junior charioteers; youths younger than seventeen, driving two-horse chariots called bigae. The young men between seventeen and twenty-three, and the most experienced charioteers over twenty-three, would race later in the day, with four-horse rigs known as quadrigae. The most acclaimed champions raced last.

Pulcheria said a prayer for the safety of men and beasts, settled in her chair, and signaled one of the ever-present servants for a cooling drink. The eight youths competing in the first race drove their teams behind the spring-loaded gates at the canted entrance along the flat side of the hippodrome. A monumental bronze statue of a quadriga driven by winged Victory loomed over the gates. The gilded horses looked about to leap off their pedestal and race down the tracks. Pulcheria sighed. No modern artist did such realistic work as the ancient Greeks.

Real horses stamped and snorted as the crowds quieted and tension heightened. The young charioteers pulled on their reins to keep the anxious animals in check. Theo dropped the white signal cloth, and the gates sprang open. The horses leapt into a gallop, with the crowd roaring encouragement for their favorites and curses for their opponents.

The pair of drivers representing the blue faction took the lead, cooperating to block other teams going into the corner. They forced several teams to the outside, making them cover more distance. Because these junior races involved two-horse chariots, and only five laps around the spina instead of the usual seven, they ended quickly. However, the inexperience of the drivers meant the chance of accident and death was more prevalent.

"A *siliqua* on the blues!" Paulinus cried.

Several in the box took up his bet, including the annoying aunt. "I'm for the greens!" she screeched.

"Do you wish to bet, my love?" Theo leaned over to Athenais.

"In the past, I might have risked a coin or two." She gave Pulcheria a cheerful look over Theo's shoulder. "But you and your sisters find the practice distasteful. I follow your rules now."

Pulcheria nodded approval at Athenais' choice to abstain from betting, gave her credit for the love shining in her eyes as she gazed at Theo. The girl may be part of a plot, but it seemed unlikely she was aware of her role. If of a submissive character, she might not be much of a threat.

She shook off her bad mood and pulled her attention back to the contest. In theory, Pulcheria disapproved of the races, but she understood the need for the lower classes to have entertainment. Blood sports, such as gladiator games, were a thing of the past. Chariot racing afforded an opportunity for the masses to gamble and sometimes see a spectacular accident. Pulcheria wished it otherwise but knew converting everyone to her pastimes of prayer and good works an impossible task.

The hippodrome was also the only place regular citizens could confront the emperor directly with their complaints. Frequently, Theo found out about corrupt officials or churchmen while attending the races. It was unlikely anyone would spoil the celebratory nature of this day with complaints, so she settled in for a long afternoon of noise and meaningless chatter.

"I win!" Paulinus cried as one of the blue teams crossed the finish line.

"Not for long," Pulcheria muttered under her breath, already plotting her next move.

# Chapter 18



THEO ENTERED HIS BRIDE'S BEDCHAMBER AS A GAGGLE OF GIGGLING women left. Their significant looks and hushed comments reminded him of his duty, bringing a deep blush to his face. Paulinus had arranged a similar gathering of young men who told rude jokes that embarrassed Theo. He left early, having had only a single goblet of wine, to raucous comments about how he was too eager to make his new wife happy.

He paused in the door to look at his radiant bride, standing at a full-length mirror, golden hair streaming down her back. Athenais wore a plain silk robe, which showed the outline of her lush body as the candles flickered. Theo stared at her in wonderment. *How did I ever win such a beautiful creature?* His manhood swelled, rising under his tunic. Lust warred with guilt. Blood rushed to his cheeks. He turned to leave before he embarrassed himself.

"Theo?" Athenais glimpsed him in her mirror and turned, face glowing with happiness. "Beloved, I've been waiting for you."

Caught, he thought to alleviate his distress the only way he knew how. Theo held out his hand to his wife. "Pray with me?"

Her eyebrows went up even as she lowered her lashes. "Of course, Husband."

They knelt at the private altar nestled in a niche appropriately decorated with the Virgin Mary and her babe. They recited the Lord's prayer together. Theo silently prayed for the courage to do his duty and forgiveness for the sin of lust. When they rose, he took her hand and led her to the bed.

"Do you wish me to undress you, Husband?"

"No! I...uh...I'll do it myself." He snuffed all but one candle, doffed his loincloth and outer robes, leaving only a short linen tunic to cover his nakedness. Athenais slipped into bed wearing only her silk shift.

Theo pulled back the covers and crawled into the bed beside her. He lay still, listening to her breathing.

Her hand crept to his arm. "We do not have to do our duty tonight, my love, if you don't wish it. We can hold each other and sleep. It's been a long and wearing day for us both."

He rolled over to face her. Flickering candlelight played over her features, but he could see nothing distinctly. In a low, trembling voice, he said, "I dreamed of this night and dreaded it both. I come to this marriage as virginal as you."

"That is a great gift to offer God and each other." Athenais stroked his shoulder. Her touch burned. "Take me into your arms and hold me close."

Theo put his arms around her. Her hair smelled of roses, her breath of mint. He felt her breasts push against his chest and thought his member would burst. He suddenly spasmed with pain and pleasure, crying out, "Oh, God!" as he shuddered in release.

Athenais lay still against him. He felt his sticky seed against his belly, soaking through his tunic. He pushed her away, mumbling, "I'm sorry," and fled to a washstand. Theo stood hunched over the bowl, ashamed, thoughts roiling in despair. *Lust is sinful. Spilling your seed is sinful. But I must have an heir! How can I do this?*

ATHENAIS, SHOCKED, LAY QUIETLY IN THE BED. THE DAMP SPOT ON HER SHIFT, where Theo spilled his seed, cooled and stiffened. She had seen animals mate, and her aunt had prepared her for penetration, but not for this. If her husband couldn't perform, what was she to do? How could she help him? Her aunt also warned that she needed to bleed on her wedding night. If she didn't, gossips would say she wasn't a virgin, casting doubt on any children she had.

Stifled sobs from the dark corner tugged at her heart. *Poor Theo!* He was more lost than she.

"Theo, Beloved? Come back to the bed." She heard nothing for several moments. "Please, Husband, I need you."

Athenais heard a rustling sound as he pulled his soiled tunic over his head and came back to her. He crawled under the covers, huddling on the edge of the bed.

She stroked his back. "Dearest. There is nothing to be ashamed of. I've heard this sometimes happens to men. You will grow again, and we can do our duty."

He shuddered under her touch. She took her hand away.

Eventually his breathing evened and deepened. Athenais sought her side of the bed, blaming herself. *What did I do? What did I not do? How can I fix this?* Eventually, she fell asleep, face scrunched in worry.

Athenais woke in the gray early dawn to hear Theo praying at the altar. She peeked at his bowed form, dressed in a coarse woolen robe, which must have itched and abraded his skin. He left shortly after.

She went to her cosmetics table and sought a small knife she used to pare her nails. With a sigh, Athenais cut her thumb and let several drops bleed onto the linen sheets on her bed. She needed to speak to her aunt… soon.

A WEEK LATER, ATHENAIS SWOOPED ON HER AUNT, GATHERING HER INTO HER ARMS. "I'm so glad to see you!"

"My dear! Is anything wrong?" Doria fussed with her red wig, askew after the violent embrace.

Athenais looked around the room of silent women, sewing and listening to a priest reading scripture. "No, Aunt. I just missed your presence these past days." She linked arms with the older woman. "Come keep me company."

They retired to a more private corner where they could speak without being overheard.

"Did the wedding night not go well?" Doria asked, concern in her voice but maintaining a perfectly bland face for the women shooting curious glances her way.

"No." Athenais' eyes strayed. "That is why I asked you to come. All these women are pledged to chastity. I have no one to talk to!"

"Did he hurt you?" Doria put a hand on her niece's knee, leaning forward to inspect her face.

"No. Theo is a kind and gentle man. He would never do such a thing. It's more…intimate." Athenais' eyes filled with tears. "He views coupling as a duty, and any physical pleasure experienced during the act as a *sin*."

"Oh, my dear child." Doria pulled her into a warm hug. "I had no idea. Have you consummated the marriage?"

Athenais nodded. "On the third night, he finally entered me, but released his seed so fast I felt nothing but pain. I didn't tell him of my discomfort, because I knew he would be hurt and even less likely to approach me. He barely touches me now."

Athenais peered over her aunt's shoulder to see her sisters-in-law, Arcadia and Marina, staring at them. She knew little of the younger princesses and had hoped to become friends. They were about her age but seemed completely cowed by their older sister, never expressing views counter to hers or acting independent in any way. They would surely report this visit to Pulcheria, who would want an accounting. Athenais reluctantly pushed her aunt away.

"What am I to do? I am not Pulcheria. I cannot live without physical love." She choked back sobs.

Doria patted her hand. "Your husband needs guidance, and it can't come from you. He'll think you a wanton. Paulinus is his best friend. The Augustus trusts him. I'll have a word with Paulinus and see if we can get this sorted out."

"It might take more than Paulinus. This is rooted in his faith. Perhaps a trusted churchman could talk to Theo. Bishop Atticus seems kind, and knowledgeable about the world." She looked at her hands. "I am not some romantic child, but I had thought I might enjoy a physical as well as spiritual union with my husband."

"I'll see what I can do." Doria gave her a sad smile. "After all, you can't bear children in a chaste marriage."


Bishop Atticus listened to his emperor's embarrassed description of marital congress with growing alarm. He had been warned Theo had some confused beliefs about procreation but had not understood the full extent of the young man's anguish…or his ignorance.

When Theo stuttered to a halt, Atticus put his hands on the boy's bowed head and sighed. "My son, laying with your lawful wife for the purposes of conceiving a child is not a sin in the eyes of the Lord. On the contrary, he orders us to be fruitful and multiply."

"I understand that part, Father. It's the lust I feel for my wife that twists my soul. I look at her and my member swells and stiffens, my thoughts become disordered. I can't see her or touch her without that shameful feeling that I am sinning. I scourge myself by wearing a hair shirt, but that does no good."

"It is not for you to determine penance for sins, my son. God gave that power to his priests, and I see no need for atonement. You have done nothing wrong."

Theo frowned. "Sometimes I spill my seed before entering my wife. When that happened in the past, in my sleep, Father Marcus gave me verses to study and prayers to say as penance for the sin."

"Do you do this with your wife to avoid a pregnancy? *That* would be a sin."

"No!" The young man's face turned scarlet. "I just…uh…lose control. I love her so much and want her so badly…" His voice trailed off. He looked at Atticus with haggard eyes.

The bishop was not an old man. Echoes of youthful lust still pulsed occasionally when faced with a particularly attractive young woman. He remembered the aching loins and the mental anguish of his youth as he sacrificed that part of his life for God.

"You are not a priest, Theodosius. God has not required you to live chastely."

"But chaste living is accounted a great gift to God. That is why the desert fathers and mothers, priests and bishops choose celibacy. That is why my sisters remain virgins."

"The key word is 'choice', my son. Not all priests or bishops choose that life. Synesius of Ptolemais made keeping his beloved wife a condition of accepting his bishopric. And, yes, Melania the Younger and her husband lived in a chaste marriage, but it was agreed to by both parties, not required by God. As to your sisters, there was more than a religious urgency to their choices."

Theo looked puzzled. "What other urgency?"

"That is for you and your sisters to discuss." Atticus leaned forward to take both the young man's hands. "You are the Emperor of Rome. You have a duty to your people to cherish your wife and create a family. You are a man with a lawful wife and have the right to feel attracted to her—but no other! Your soul is in no danger and you need no absolution. As to the …uh…loss of control, that should moderate in time. If it doesn't, consult a physician."

Theo slumped in his seat, lost in thought. When he raised his head, a gentle smile broke across his face. "I am not a sinner?"

"You have not committed fornication." Atticus shook his head. "Go home to your wife, Son, and be content."

"Thank you, Father! You have lightened my soul."

"God's blessings on you, my son." *And may I never have to have this kind of discussion again!*

# Chapter 19



*Imperial Palace, September 421*

IN THE THREE MONTHS SINCE THE WEDDING, PULCHERIA FELT THE COURT settle back into its normal rhythm. Athenais worked hard to fit into the rigorous routines of prayer and fasting, but it was obviously a burden to her rather than a grace. She dressed modestly and participated in the work of the other court women: spinning, sewing and knitting for the Church and the poor. Pulcheria continued to act as chief advisor to Theo but found his mind more influenced by the arguments of the Hellenes than before. Athenais' family continued to rise in honors and offices. Her brother, Gesius, gave up the prefecture of Illyricum to Isidorus—at least that got Anthemius' son away from Constantinople—but now both brothers infested the court, fawned on Theo and expected handouts.

Today, Pulcheria sat at Theo's right side as they received petitions and rendered justice: Theo as magistrate, Pulcheria as his advisor. Athenais insisted on joining them in the receiving room, but had to take a lesser place, one step down on Theo's left, as she had yet to equal Pulcheria in rank. If Pulcheria had her way, Athenais would be confined to the women's work room under the care of her sisters, but Theo indulged his new bride in this.

Master of Offices Helion approached. "Augustus. Augusta. Lady Consort." He bowed. "An embassy just arrived from your co-Emperor Honorius in the Western court. He craves an audience."

"Send him in," Theo said with a frown. He leaned down to tell his wife,

"The last time Uncle Honorius sent an envoy, it was an unmitigated disaster. In February, Honorius elevated his sister Placidia to Augusta, her husband General Constantius to Augustus, and their infant boy Valentinian to Caesar and heir to the West. Without consulting me!"

"How inconsiderate!" Athenais cooed.

Pulcheria struggled not to roll her eyes. "It was more than 'inconsiderate.' Honorius had no right to elevate the General without consulting Theo. And naming that infant his heir! We refused to recognize their elevations and sent back the commemorative statues. I understand Aunt Placidia and General Constantius were not pleased."

"Their elevations were unlawful?" Athenais looked puzzled.

"Not unlawful—a sitting Augustus makes the laws—but Theo is the presumed heir. He should have the prerogative of naming his own colleague in the West or ruling the combined empire, if he wishes, upon our uncle's death. May the Good Lord give Honorius a long life."

Theo echoed, "May the Good Lord bless and keep our uncle."

"What of Placidia? Was he wrong in elevating his sister?" Athenais asked.

"No, my love. An Augustus can elevate a mother, sister, or wife on his own. Your time will come." Her brother looked at his wife with a besotted grin.

*But not for a long time, if I have any say.* Pulcheria eyed her sister-in-law with a tight smile.

Private conversations echoing around the audience chamber quieted as word passed something unusual was happening. The envoy entered, progressing down the length of the room. He was young for such an important post. Pulcheria noted with approval that he presented an elegant, but not ostentatious, figure. He dressed in a dark blue tunic embroidered with silver thread at the neck and hem, his only jewelry a signet ring on his right index finger. His purple-edged, bright white senator's toga draped in perfect folds over his shoulder.

At the foot of the dais, the envoy announced, "I am Senator Bassus Herculanus, special envoy from the Most Noble Emperor Honorius of Ravenna. I bring his warmest greetings to Your Most Gracious Serenities. God grant you long life and health."

Herculanus bowed low and passed on a scroll impressed with the western emperor's seal. A scribe broke the wax and handed it to Theo.

A sigh escaped the emperor. "It is not how I wished it to be resolved, but it takes care of one awkward situation." He handed the missive to Pulcheria

She scanned the page briefly. "General Constantius is dead? Of what?" She pointedly did not use the general's augustal title.

"Pleurisy, Augusta." The envoy looked sorrowfully at his shoes.

"How fares our uncle, without the advice of his Patrician?" Pulcheria knew Honorius was practically a lack-wit, more interested in his chickens than in ruling western Rome. General Constantius had long played the power behind the throne, both before and after his marriage to the emperor's sister.

"As best as one might expect, given this grievous loss. Placidia Augusta is providing solace." The man's eyes darted away.

*Afraid of offending us by using the title we do not acknowledge? Embarrassed that a woman dares to step in? Or is something else going on?* Despite never having met her infamous aunt, Pulcheria sensed a kindred spirit. She hoped their individual ambitions did not come to cross purposes.

"Master Helion, see that our imperial envoy has suitable quarters and hospitality," Theo ordered. They both knew Helion would personally wine and dine the envoy, extracting as much information as he could about the complicated situation at the Ravenna court. Pulcheria already had word through the *agents en rebus* that Constantius had contemplated some military action as a result of their refusing to acknowledge his elevation, but Placidia had talked him out of it. As disastrous as the Persian campaign turned out—they had recently agreed to retreat to pre-war borders—Pulcheria would have been hard pressed to counter a military move from the West. She was grateful to her aunt for that intervention.

After both men bowed and left, Pulcheria said to Theo, in a low voice, "I believe our aunt is making her move. I hope Helion can gain some knowledge of her motives."

Theo watched the two men's retreating backs. "Perhaps Placidia seeks power to expunge the stain of her infamous marriage to that barbarian king."

"More likely she seeks to protect her son and provide for his future." Athenais unconsciously put a protective hand over her stomach. She and Theo shared a tender look.

*Hmm. It looks like we can expect our own heir in a few months. Pulcheria pursed her lips. Good! Perhaps Athenais will spend more time in the nursery and leave the receiving room to me!*

*****

*Birthing Room, Imperial Palace, April 422*

"Push!" One midwife held the groaning Athenais on the birthing stool, while a second knelt to catch the infant through the hole in the seat. While pregnancy had added an inner glow to Athenais' beauty, childbirth contorted her features in pain. Chords in her neck stood out; veins throbbed in her forehead as she moaned and shrieked.

Knowing the pain of her monthly courses, Pulcheria felt sympathy for the laboring woman. Her nose twitched at the smell of blood. Her chest tightened with fear for Athenais' life. Pulcheria shuddered with vague memories of a blood-soaked bed and the still body of her mother. She silently prayed, *Mary, Mother of God, give your grace to your daughter. Guide her safely through these trials. Lift the curse of Eve and give her release from pain.* Her heart slowed. She breathed easier, believing Mary had received her prayer and would not let Athenais suffer much longer.

Next to her, Arcadia and Marina repeated the Lord's prayer, adding, "Blessed Mother Mary, see our sister safely delivered of a healthy son."

All Pulcheria's women attended the birth, as was appropriate to attest to the legitimacy of a child who would wear the imperial diadem. Their bodies produced an almost unbearable heat in the crowded room. Servants fanned the laboring woman with palm fronds.

Athenais grunted and uttered a long, sustained moan.

Pulcheria sensed movement before looking up to see the midwife holding aloft a tiny body, smeared with blood and mucus. The infant wriggled, took a breath, and let out a mewling howl.

"It's a girl!"

*Poor child*, Pulcheria thought. *Forever doomed to serve the whims of men. Unless she follows in my footsteps, rather than her mother's.* She rose from her knees to approach the bowl of warm water where one of the midwives fussed over the baby, washing away the evidence of birth. Pulcheria examined the infant with interest. She had ten toes, ten fingers, and an elongated head.

"Is that normal?" Pulcheria pointed to the misshapen skull. Since all her women were pledged to chastity, she had witnessed no other births.

"Yes, Augusta." The midwife tried to suppress a grin. "The head will take on a more normal shape over the next few days."

The midwife wrapped the babe tight in swaddling clothes and handed her to

Pulcheria. "Beautiful, isn't she?"

Surprised, Pulcheria almost dropped the tiny bundle, but recovered quickly. She pushed a piece of the soft cloth back from the baby's cheek. It turned its head toward her finger, making sucking noises. Pulcheria saw little beauty in the squashed face, but still felt an ache in her breasts. "Yes, she is quite beautiful."

"Push again!"

Pulcheria looked over her shoulder at Athenais, still on the birthing stool.

"Twins?" Pulcheria asked, alarmed. Twins brought ill-luck, frequently in the form of the death of their mother.

"No, My Lady. The afterbirth."

Once Athenais delivered the afterbirth, the midwives packed her vagina with dried moss, washed her body, and put her to bed on clean sheets.

Pulcheria approached and put the swaddled infant into her mother's arms. "You did well, Sister. I'm sure Theo will be happy."

Tears flooded Athenais' eyes. "Thank you." She yawned.

"We'll let you rest now."

Athenais nodded, one hand protecting the small bundle at her side. "Tell Theo—" Her eyes closed.

"I will." Pulcheria pulled the wool cover up over the sleeping woman, stirred by unexpected feelings—empathy and affection.



Theo slurred, "We talked of Licinia Eudoxia."

Pulcheria frowned. She had never seen her brother drunk before and didn't like the look. "Have some water, Brother. I believe the wine has gone to your head."

He refused, pouring himself another goblet. "It's not every day I become a father. You're sure 'Nais is a'right?"

"I left her sleeping, in the care of the midwives. They felt everything went well." She turned to leave, then stopped. "Do you want me to arrange the baptism? It should be in three days."

"Yes." He slumped in a chair.

She studied her brother's sprawling form. "I'll send a servant with food."

"Sure. And send in Paulinus. Time to celebrate!"

"You've celebrated enough for one day."

He frowned. His eyes drooped. The goblet rolled to the floor, spilling bright red wine like blood on the carpet.

Pulcheria rolled her eyes to heaven and prayed he would have a raging headache in the morning. Fitting punishment for the sin of drunkenness.

# Chapter 20

*January 423*

THIS IS YOUR DOING!” PULCHERIA SLAPPED A SHEAF OF PARCHMENT ON the marble table next to a blue silk divan in her sister-in-law's private anteroom. The space was tastefully, if lavishly, decorated in soothing shades of blue and green. Pulcheria sniffed, stifling a sneeze. Her sister-in-law overused a rose scent.

Athenais looked up from her book of poetry by that pagan, Olympiodorus. “Sister. This is an unexpected visit. As you know, it's my habit to retire for two hours after the noon meal. What is so important that you intrude on the only time I can be alone?”

“This latest constitution from your uncle.” Pulcheria stabbed an accusing finger toward the parchment.

Athenais gave a sharp look at the frightened servant hovering in the doorway, then sighed. “Shut the door on your way out, Dorothea.”

The servant fled.

Pulcheria scowled. *Did the girl really think a lowly servant could keep me out of any part of the palace?*

Athenais sat up, retrieved the paper, and scanned it. Since Theo had raised her to Augusta a few weeks ago, Athenais had been more willing to test her power over her husband. It seemed to Pulcheria that whatever relatives and friends whispered into Athenais' ears she whispered into Theo's. More of the Hellenes' agenda became public policy.

145

"You give me more credit than I deserve, Sister. Uncle is prefect in the East, and consul. These are his words, not mine." She looked up from the decree. "And the seal is your brother's."

Of course, Athenais was right. But, if not for her marriage, Asclepiodotus would never have reached the highest offices in the land and polluted her brother's mind with these heretical ideas.

"Then you disagree with reversing imperial policy on Jews and pagans?" Pulcheria probed.

Athenais put the declaration aside. "I don't think this is a reversal. It extends protection to all of our citizens from criminal behavior."

"Criminal behavior?" Pulcheria drew a deep breath. "Six years ago, I and my brother authorized the destruction of synagogues in desert places. This constitution reverses that law." She snatched the parchment and read, "Christians shall refrain from injuring and persecuting Jews and henceforth no person should seize or burn synagogues, nor lay violent hands on Jews or pagans who live quietly and attempt nothing disorderly or contrary to law."

"I see no harm in letting our citizens go about their business. Pagans and Jews contribute to our society through learning and trade. Why persecute them for their beliefs, if they harm no one?"

"But they *do* harm. Their very existence causes discord in our cities. Our people will not tolerate their presence when it is an affront to God and brings His displeasure down on the people."

"Does it?" Athenais looked up with wide eyes.

"What?" Pulcheria huffed, annoyed at this unexpected question. She was unused to people disagreeing with her, especially over matters of law and religion.

"Does the mere presence of pagans and Jews bring God's displeasure down on the people?"

"They believe so."

"Do you?" Athenais waved a languid hand "I've seen no evidence."

"What I believe is not important. Different faiths cause discord and civil disruption. The Great Constantine said, 'One Emperor, One Empire, One God.' He was a wise man."

"But Rome has two emperors and, until recently, we had three. There is no disruption or chaos."

Her sister-in-law's observation gave Pulcheria temporary pause. Diocletian's experiment in dividing the Empire between East and West over a century ago had stabilized the country. Since then, only the rare man of talent and martial temperament, such as the Great Constantine and her grandfather Theodosius, managed to successfully rule as sole emperor. She abandoned that argument for a more vital one.

"The best way to control the Roman Empire is by fusing the emperor and the Church. The emperor is God's Viceroy on earth and rules by His design," Pulcheria explained impatiently. *Was the girl a lack-wit that she couldn't see such an obvious truth?* "If the emperor allows paganism, Judaism, or other non-Christian faiths to flourish within his boundaries, he shows disrespect to God and can be overthrown by the people."

Athenais pursed her lips. "I don't agree with your premise. It seems dangerous to fuse the emperor with the Church. An emperor who rules with tolerance and justice for all people of all faiths seems more likely to achieve harmony and peace. Each faction has a stake in keeping the balance and will cooperate with the ruler for fear they may be the ones out of favor. Outlawing religions drives them underground and promotes rebellion. Did not the Persian War teach us that?"

"I have no time to argue philosophy with you." Blood pounded in Pulcheria's temple. She took a deep breath to calm herself. "Your theories are fancies drawn from books. I've ruled this empire ten years for, and with, my brother. I know what works, and what is right."

"I thought my theories drawn from the Bible. Did not Jesus teach us to love our neighbor as ourselves? And St. Paul taught us, 'there is neither Jew nor Greek, nor slave nor free, nor male nor female.' Are we not all equal in the eyes of the Lord?"

"Jesus also said 'render unto Caesar what is Caesar's.' I'm talking about how to use the power of the Church to support the emperor; how to unite the people against our enemies and bring order to this earthly realm." Pulcheria shook the parchment. "This will bring trouble, I know."

"Perhaps, but it is not our place to challenge the emperor's actions after the fact. It's Theo's name on that law. You should support your brother in his rule or take your objections to him directly." Athenais turned her attention back to her codex.

Jaw firmly clamped at this obvious dismissal, Pulcheria marched out of the room, back stiff and head high. *That ignorant girl and her rabble of a family will bring Theo's reign to ruin!*

She stormed into her women's work room to collapse onto a chair amid stunned silence. The murmuring of women's voices resumed after she shot an angry glare around the room.

"Ria, drink this." Arcadia approached with a steaming cup. "You are obviously upset and need to control your feelings. The women will gossip."

Pulcheria sipped the chamomile tisane sweetened with honey. Her heart slowed. Breathing deepened.

Marina joined them in the secluded nook. "Ria, are you well?"

Pulcheria nodded, setting the cup aside. "That girl will be the death of me!"

Arcadia and Marina exchanged significant glances. Pulcheria's anger returned. "What?"

"Ria." Arcadia sighed. "You must give up this opposition to Athenais. She is our brother's wife. We should treat her as the sister she is."

"It's not just Athenais. It's her relatives and friends. They infest the court, and counsel Theo poorly. They are determined to reverse all the good I've done these past ten years." Pulcheria paused, struck by a revelation. Was that the true reason she detested her sister-in-law? She feared for her legacy? She willed the angry tears from her eyes. She would not show how much that prospect upset her.

Arcadia pursed her lips in disapproval. "Sister, we've talked of this before. You are no longer regent. It is Theo's will we—and the empire—must obey."

Pulcheria shook her head. "But—"

"Ria." Marina interrupted with a gentle hand on her arm. "You are so much wiser than we in many ways, but we feel your…uh…forceful temperament puts our family at odds. If you won't listen to our counsel, perhaps you should talk with Bishop Atticus."

Pulcheria slowly nodded agreement. Her sisters were right; love and concern sometimes led her to overstep her legal authority. Then she recalled her conversation with Athenais and her anger returned threefold. In this, she did not just act out of love, but out of righteousness!


PULCHERIA FELT HER ANGER SUBSIDE AND CALM RETURN AS SHE ENTERED THE Great Church. It was impossible to hold onto any disquiet in the presence of God. She knelt to say a prayer at the altar before seeking Bishop Atticus. When she arose, the Good Bishop approached her. Evidently, some servant or priest had alerted him of her presence, although she had sent no advance warning.

She smiled, holding out her hands.

He smiled back. "What brings you to our presence, Daughter?"

An echo of her anger returned, though not with the same force. "I need your help. My brother is being led astray—again—by those wretched men who control his wife."

"That is a serious accusation." He frowned.

"Let us repair to your offices, Bishop. I would not infect this holy place with secular woes." She turned to her retinue. "Stay and pray. I will return shortly."

Atticus linked arms with her as they walked through the nave to his luxurious receiving room. He dismissed his scribes. She declined food and drink.

"What has you so upset, Daughter?"

"Asclepiodotus—with Theo's concurrence—issued a law reversing our policy on pagans and Jews and imposing severe penalties on Christians who harass them or destroy their property."

"That is serious!" The bishop's eyes went wide with alarm. "Why does Theodosius agree to this?"

All her boiling rage at being outplayed by the Hellenes and replaced by a simpering wife in Theo's affections returned. "Why do you think? His pagan bitch of a wife leads him around by his cock!" Pulcheria's hands flew to her mouth. "Forgive my rude language, Good Father. I didn't realize I was so angry." She stood, blood staining her cheeks, deeply ashamed.

The lines at the corners of his eyes crinkled. His lips trembled, suppressing a smile. "You must indeed be angry."

Pulcheria knelt at the bishop's feet. "Please forgive my unkind thoughts and improper words."

"I forgive you, Daughter. Rise and have a cup of wine. It will calm your nerves."

She rose and took a goblet, relaxing after a couple of sips. Then she lowered herself onto a well-padded divan. "I have better control now."

"Good." Atticus looked at her with concern. "I have to confess, I haven't seen you so distraught since you came to me for advice on avoiding marriage. There seems more at play here than a law. I baptized Eudocia Athenais myself. She is a Christian. This enmity towards your brother's wife cannot be good for the peace of the imperial household, or your soul."

"I've tried to love her as a sister! But her ways irritate me so." Pulcheria slumped on the divan, ticking off Athenais' worst offenses. "She created her own retinue with women from the Hellene faction. They read poetry rather than scripture, spend their time on gossip and music rather than doing God's work."

"Eudocia Athenais is an Augusta now. It is appropriate she have her own retinue of noble women to add distinction to her imperial presence. As you have your virgins and chaste women, she should have matrons with children. What they do neither adds to, nor detracts from, your own imperial dominion. You have your own residences inside and outside the city. Perhaps some distance from your brother's wife would be beneficial."

Pulcheria's hands tightened on the goblet. She wanted to shout, *I can't leave the palace! She steals my brother's love from me!* but knew it sounded childish and petty. Instead, she stated another truth. "Good Father, you know my brother. You've ministered to us since we were children, given us excellent advice. He is a good man with a kind heart that sometimes leads him astray. You know he is vulnerable to the influence of those closest to him. He lacks the will to cross them, gives in when he should be firm." *Another reason I should not leave the palace. At least by staying close I can counteract some of the damage caused by the Hellenes.*

"My daughter, Theo is no longer a child. You should not think of him in that way. He does not need your protection. He is a man of twenty-two, with the responsibilities of an empire on his shoulders. He also has many strengths you seek to deny. Have you not raised him well? Does he not live an authentic devout life? I believe he would surprise you with his strength if you let him."

Perhaps the good bishop did have a point about her view of her brother. She had difficulty thinking of him as anything but a child needing her protection and guidance. Now that he had married, he no longer looked to her for affection. She missed him. Pulcheria sighed. She should encourage her brother to take on more oversight of his officials as emperor; insist he read the papers brought to him to sign. She had raised him right. If he knew in full what his advisors proposed, he would never agree. She needed to retire her role as regent and fully take on the mantle of Chief Advisor.

"You are right, Father. I should moderate my feelings toward my sister-in-law. Our enmity can only cause my brother grief." Pulcheria surveyed Atticus over the rim of her goblet. "The fact remains, this law is a backward step in our governing. The people will be confused. We cannot have good Christians punished for destroying pagan idols and Jewish synagogues."

"Did you come to me for counsel, or action?"

"Both." She set the goblet on a side table. "Please write to the other bishops, encouraging them to protest this law. And I hope you will visit Theo and counsel him. He prizes your advice."

"I'll do what I can, Augusta." He smiled. "You have my full support in this."

*February 423*

Pulcheria hesitated in the doorway, scanning her brother's work room, stuffed with the usual scribes, servants, and a couple of close friends. Paulinus joked with Theo as he signed and sealed various papers. She didn't want a crowd for what was to happen next.

"Augustus, may I have a word in private?" She indicated a sheaf of papers. "There are issues of some delicacy we should discuss."

Theo nodded. "Paulinus, join me in sword practice after the noon meal. The rest of you, out!"

Paulinus gave her a sharp look as he and the others trooped out of the room. Pulcheria sat across the marble-topped table that served as Theo's desk. "Thank you, Brother. These papers need your attention and seal." She put her stack of parchments on the desk.

Theo drew them to him, took out his pen, signed and sealed each. "Is that all, Ria? I thought you had something of urgency to talk to me about."

"I do." She took the papers back, shuffled through a couple and pulled one out. "Did you read this one?"

"You watched me, Ria. I didn't read any. I trust that what you bring me is needed." He snorted. "What is this about?"

"You just sold your beloved wife Aelia Eudocia Athenais to me as slave for this." She handed him a gold solidus. "A bit overpriced, I believe."

"What?" Theo clenched the coin until his knuckles showed white.

Pulcheria gave him the deed of sale. "Read it."

He sat reading, blood draining from his face. "What is the meaning of this, Sister?"

"Of course, I won't enforce this deed, Theo." She shook her head. "Tear it up. Burn it. I'm making a point. You trust too easily. You've installed incompetent and dangerous people to high positions, and they are taking advantage of you. Did you know your consul and prefect of the East had you sign a constitution that punishes Christians for destroying Jewish and pagan property?" She handed him a copy of the law.

Theo skimmed the first page. "This constitution confirmed penalties against heretics: Manichaeans, Novatians, Sabbatians. I discussed it with Asclepiodotus at the time. As to the pagans and Jews, he assured me there were no more pagans. The proscription on burning Jewish synagogues was to rein in the Syrian Barsauma, who was raising havoc in Jerusalem. The Jews of the city appealed to me for relief."

"Look at the second page. Did he discuss the penalties with you?"

Theo read the offending passage. "Any who attack the persons or property of such law-abiding Jews would have to make triple or quadruple restitution, and governors, their staff, and anyone else who connived in such crimes face the same penalty." His jaw clenched. A vein pulsed in his forehead. "The man misled me."

"I thought as much." Pulcheria nodded. "This has wreaked havoc in the lands. Asclepiodotus is enforcing the law. Innocent Christians are being prosecuted. Bishops are preaching against you in the churches. This just arrived from Simeon the Stylite. He addresses you as Flavius Theodosius but does not give you the title of Augustus." She handed him a ragged piece of folded parchment tied with twine. Pulcheria watched as her brother read. Blood drained from his face.

"What does the holy man say?" Pulcheria had a good idea of Simeon's complaint. Bishop Atticus had kept his word and sent letters far and wide. As the Patriarch of Constantinople, he held considerable influence with his fellow bishops.

Theo passed the missive to her with shaking hands. She read:

*Since your heart has grown arrogant and you have forgotten the Lord your God who gave you your diadem and the throne of empire, and since you have become friends, comrade and protector of the faithless Jew, know now that you will soon face the punishment of divine justice, you and all who share your view in this affair. You will raise your hands to heaven and woefully cry: "Truly because I have denied the Lord God has he brought this judgement upon me."*

Her heart thumped with fear. She had expected a rebuke, but this was a serious curse from one of the most revered holy men in the empire. Once the people learned of it, they would riot and denounce their emperor. She needed to mitigate the danger she had unwittingly put her brother in. "Theo, you must take immediate steps to remedy this error." She leaned forward to touch his shaking hand. "Brother, this curse is dangerous, not only in God's eyes, but the people's. Go to church and publicly repent. Revoke this law, dismiss Asclepiodotus, and ask forgiveness from your people."

"I will." He looked at her with some of his old affection. "Thank you, Ria. You always tell me the truth, even when I might be angry with you. You have been, and always will be, my best advisor." He tore up the deed of sale for his wife and handed back the gold coin. "Arrange for my progress to the Great Church. I will send a revocation to all my governors and copies to the bishops."

"And Asclepiodotus?"

Theo hesitated, reluctance showing on his face.

Pulcheria held her breath. Would her brother do the right thing, even if it meant disappointing his wife?

"I will dismiss him."

"Your people and the Church will thank you for it." Pulcheria left, relieved that her appeal to the Church had yielded such valuable results; chastened that it almost led to disaster. If her brother had been less malleable, his reign might be forfeit. His bending to her will also proved her point. He still needed her guidance.

# Chapter 21

*Imperial Palace, March 423*

WHAT DO YOU THINK, RIA?" THEO UNROLLED A SHEAF OF PLANS ACROSS her worktable for the triumphal column she proposed to be erected in Hebdomon. The Persian War may have ended in a stalemate, but her brother needed to be seen as victorious in a holy war. The message of victory on coins wasn't enough. They needed a more tangible and impressive representation of God's favor. She chose the Hebdomon site because troops rallied and trained there. The column would greet them as they assembled and watch over their deployment. "How tall?" She drew her finger along the image.

"The architect has identified a piece of granite which can be carved into a single column over fifty feet high."

"Excellent!" Pulcheria put that page aside to study the drawings for a bronze equestrian statue of her brother to top the column. The raised sword made him look appropriately heroic; however… "May I make a suggestion?"

"Of course." Theo replied.

"Sheath the sword and hold a cross. We want the people to know that God gives us victory."

"I think that is implied in the inscription." His smile broadened. "I'm sure you will be pleased." Theo pulled a sheet from the bottom showing a base carved with angels, the inscription written in the margin:

*Our lord, the gracious and fortunate Theodosius Augustus*
*Commander-in-chief, very mighty, triumphant*
*Over barbarian nations, always and everywhere*
*Victor, through the vows of his sisters, having pacified*
*The Roman world, rejoices on high.*

"Victor through the vows of his sisters." A warm rush of pride and gratitude suffused her body. Pulcheria smiled at her brother—a smile that brightened her plain features to almost make her pretty. "Yes, Brother, I am pleased. When will it be completed? We must plan for the dedication."

They barely started to go over the details when Helion rushed into the room, flustered and out of breath.

"Master Helion, what troubles do you bring us?" Theo raised an eyebrow in imitation of his sister.

"Augustus. Augusta." The Master of Offices bowed to each. "We have urgent dispatches from your co-ruler in Ravenna."

Pulcheria and Theo exchanged startled glances.

"What disaster has befallen our uncle this time?" Theo asked.

"Emperor Honorius has exiled his sister Placidia from Ravenna and remands her into your custody, Augustus. She will be arriving soon with her children."

"What is the nature of her crimes, that she is banished from Ravenna?" Pulcheria asked. "Are we to keep our aunt in close confinement?"

"General Castinus, the Western Emperor's closest advisor, accused her of treason. Specifically of colluding with the Goths to overthrow her brother and put her son on the throne."

"That demands the death penalty!" Theo frowned.

"Your aunt evidently put up a good defense. Her enemies at court were only able to persuade Honorius Augustus to banishment." Blood crept up Helion's neck, staining his cheeks. "There were also rumors of…a…delicate nature."

"There are always rumors." Pulcheria snorted. "Our agents at Ravenna have been reporting for months that the emperor acted inappropriately toward his sister, once her husband died. Her personal guards have been brawling in the streets to quell such scurrilous insults." She sat back, chewing her lower lip. "No. This feels more like Placidia rejected her brother's advances and lost her influence over him as a result." She shook her head. "We'll learn soon enough. Does our aunt travel by land or sea?"

"Sea."

Pulcheria looked out her windows at the gray March skies and roiling waves on the Propontis Sea. "I'll pray for her safe arrival. The captains report bad storms this spring." She turned back to Helion. "Anything else?"

"No, Augusta."

"Then you are dismissed, Master Helion." Theo nodded.

Her aunt would bring another raft of complications to the court. Not least among them, her claim for her son Valentinian as heir and co-ruler of Western Rome upon Honorius' death. *More relatives to deal with.* Pulcheria sighed. *God give me strength.*

*April 423*

PULCHERIA, THEODOSIUS, AND ATHENAIS SAT IN THE FORMAL DAPHNE AUDIENCE hall to receive their western relatives. Placidia and her two children arrived at the court, pale from the sea voyage. A trumpet blast announced their arrival and a herald read out their names and honors for the assembled court.

Her aunt flushed when the title of Augusta was omitted from the various honors given to her, but she had obviously dressed ambiguously, so as not to offend, wearing a dark blue silk gown embroidered with gold thread in swirling leaf patterns, topped with a plain imperial purple cape, faced with red silk and held in place with a gold fibula in the shape of a wolf's head. *A gift from her barbarian first husband?* Pulcheria wondered. Strands of pearls threaded her aunt's upswept dark curly hair in a way that suggested a diadem but didn't quite usurp that prerogative reserved for Augusti.

*What had she expected?* Pulcheria kept a blank face. *We made clear our rejection of her elevation to Augusta.* Theo hadn't consulted with Honorius regarding her own or his wife's titles, but they were women and couldn't rule. Placidia's elevation came with her husband's and son's. Honorius should have consulted with his co-ruler before adding another emperor to the mix or establishing an heir other than her brother.

"Welcome to our court, Aunt," Theodosius offered, as Placidia and her children walked the long room under neutral smiles of the full court.

Pulcheria assessed this woman with the notorious and tragic past: taken from Rome in the barbarian sack thirteen years ago, married to the Gothic King, widowed within two years when an assassin struck him down. Rumors circulated that Placidia personally took her own bloody revenge. Pulcheria did not credit them. Surely, this slender, dignified woman could not have committed vicious murder?

As the family reached the steps to the dais, Pulcheria said, without offering a seat, "I trust you had a felicitous journey?"

"We had one violent storm, but God saw us safely to your shore." Placidia held her head high, returning her niece's gaze with an equally frank stare. "Thank you for your concern."

"I have found, when God is gracious, it is appropriate we honor him in some way." Pulcheria gave her a chilly smile.

"I vowed to build a church when I return to Ravenna," Placidia answered dryly. "And I intend never to tempt His good will with another sea voyage."

"A church is an appropriate recompense." Pulcheria nodded approval.

Of course, Athenais was first to rise and greet her aunt with a kiss. "I am so pleased you and the children landed safely. I'm looking forward to your company." She took Placidia's arm with a genuine smile. "Why don't we retire to a less public place, and have some refreshment? I'm sure you are fatigued after your journey."

Pulcheria frowned. *Already the power shuffle begins.*

"I'll join you when I've finished my audience." Theodosius nodded to Placidia but did not rise. "My sister and wife will take good care of you and your children, Aunt."

Ruffled at being so obviously dismissed, Pulcheria led the way to an austere antechamber. Its multi-colored marble walls bare of paintings; no statues adorned the corners or carpets the floors. Pulcheria positioned herself at the head of the room, on a plain wooden chair.

Athenais sat on a cushioned divan and patted the seat beside her. "Join me, Aunt. You will allow me to call you that, won't you?"

The younger woman's voice and manner exuded the feeling that Placidia's needs and interests were close to her heart. *Yes, Athenais was making her move. Doesn't she have enough allies in the court?*

Placidia removed her purple cape, which a servant immediately whisked away, and accepted Athenais' offer.

Pulcheria waved the children over. "Come, let me look at you."

They approached but did not bow. Pulcheria was torn between admiration in the way they stood up under her scrutiny and annoyance at their disrespect. Four-year-old Valentinian shuffled his feet, stopping when his older sister Honoria pinched him. Both were good-looking children with their mother's dark curly hair and large brown eyes. The girl stared at Pulcheria with frank curiosity and a faint frown.

"Do you have tutors? How advanced are you in your subjects?" Pulcheria queried.

The girl's eyes grew moist. "We had to leave everyone behind." She firmed her quivering chin and reported, "I know my Greek and Latin letters and can read some. I like history best. T-tutor was teaching me sums and differences."

Pulcheria raised her eyebrows at the child's self-control. *That bodes well for her future.*

"And your brother?"

"Val—" she nodded at the little boy, shifting his weight from foot to foot, as if needing to relieve himself "—is just starting to learn his letters. Mother is teaching me to ride. Val is too little."

"Am not!" Valentinian muttered. He kicked at his sister's ankle. "Ouch!" he cried as she pinched him again.

"Children!" Placidia jumped up, grabbing each by the arm. "Apologize to your cousin for your poor behavior."

Both children bowed, mumbling an apology.

"Very good." Pulcheria nodded. "You may go to the nursery."

A servant stepped forward to take their hands. The children looked to their mother. At her nod, they went quietly with the young woman.

Placidia's face transitioned from tight annoyance to affectionate worry as she watched them go. Then she turned back to Pulcheria. "My apologies, as well, Niece. They are fatigued from the journey."

"Understood. We will find them new tutors. Have they started religious instruction?"

"No. They attend private services in our apartments." Placidia frowned. "I think them too young for formal instruction."

"I began my studies when I was Valentinian's age." She thought of Father Marcus with a rush of warmth. Maybe? No, he was content in his monastery. "I will consult with Bishop Atticus for a suitable candidate."

Placidia's jaw tightened, but she did not object.

"Sit, Aunt. Have some refreshment." Athenais drew Placidia back to the divan. "You must be fatigued as well."

Servants brought food and drink—hearty red wine, fruit, and honey cakes. Pulcheria indulged in her usual water. Placidia nibbled at a date stuffed with honey and nuts.

"Aunt, what brings you so precipitously to our shores?" Athenais asked, as trivial conversation about children and the weather wound down.

Pulcheria leaned forward to hear Placidia's side of the story. She had yet to decide whether it would be in Theo's best interest to back Placidia or General Castinus in their bids to influence Honorius.

Placidia looked up from her wine. Dark smudges under the older woman's eyes attested to her trials. "My brother is increasingly prey to suspicions inflamed by those ministers closest to him. Given his current state of mind, I felt it best to remove my children and myself to a safer residence."

Pulcheria's face puckered in a worried frown. "Is your brother's rule stable in the West? Do we need to send troops, or a trusted minister?"

"There is no need for intervention—at this time. My brother's vacillations are of a more personal nature. General Castinus manufactured a plot and lured my retainers into an unwise action in order to discredit me. He convinced Honorius I did not have his interests at heart."

"This breach between brother and sister disturbs me. You have no family but each other. It is not seemly to have this disharmony."

Pulcheria noted Placidia's carefully schooled face. If she was as competent as Pulcheria believed, her aunt knew that all was not as harmonious in the eastern court as they pretended. It remained to be seen if Placidia wished to exploit that fact.

Her aunt set aside her wine. "Our circumstances are somewhat different, Niece. You are older than your brother. You shared many experiences, guided him in his youth, built trust between you. Honorius is my elder by several years, and a half-brother. We lived apart most of our lives. During these last years, we worked closely, but rumors and falsehoods easily lead him astray. It is my understanding my oldest brother—your father—had a similar temperament and was much influenced by your late mother."

Pulcheria gave her a sharp look. "Males of our line do seem to benefit from the gentle guidance of the females." It had been a shock when Pulcheria discovered the contempt in which her late father, the Emperor Arcadius, had been held by his court. From her discreet inquiries, she learned people in power found her father more dull-witted than his younger brother Honorius. His persistent drunkenness after his wife's death did not improve that impression. *Thank God Theo and I take after our mother—at least in intelligence!*

"Pulcheria is modest." Athenais set down a goblet she had barely touched. "She is Theodosius' wisest and closest advisor. Everyone knows, if they wish something done by the Emperor, they must come to Pulcheria."

Pulcheria shot Athenais a glance. *A rather extravagant compliment. What was the girl playing at?*

"It is well known how ably Pulcheria ruled during her brother's minority." Placidia nodded toward her niece. "Your charity to the poor and devotion to God and your brother are admired throughout the empire."

Pulcheria looked towards the heavens—in this case, a ceiling painted dark blue with gold trim. "God put us on earth as His Viceroys. It is through His will that we rule, and we show our devotion through good works and fair governance."

"A most admirable mission, which I would like to duplicate in the West, but sadly must bide my time until my brother can be persuaded to the right course." Placidia suppressed a yawn. "I am fatigued after our journey. My residence is barely fit to live in. I slept poorly last night."

"How thoughtless of me." Athenais put a hand to her mouth. "You must stay with us until your palace is properly furnished and staffed." She waved over a servant. "Tell my chamberlain to prepare the west suite." She turned back to Placidia. "The rooms will be ready shortly. Let's go to the nursery so you can reassure your children."

Placidia rose. "God's grace on you, Pulcheria."

"And you, Aunt."

Placidia followed Athenais out the door, leaving Pulcheria to her thoughts. *Another strong woman in the palace. Will she be ally, foe, or something unknown?*

# Chapter 22

*Imperial Palace, August 423*

THOSE DAMNABLE HUNS ARE RAIDING IN THE NORTH AGAIN." THEO slammed the report down on Pulcheria's worktable.

She looked up with a weary smile. "Asclepiodotus brought down the wrath of the holy men and the ire of our people. Isidorus fails to stop the Huns ravishing our borders in Illyricum. How many of these convenient Christians will fail you before you understand they are not worthy of your trust?"

"'Convenient Christians'?"

"Those who convert or profess greater zeal than they feel in order to curry favor with our court. They don't feel God's grace as we do, in here." Pulcheria placed a hand over her heart. "They look to the ancient philosophers for reason, rather than the Word of God for belief."

"Do you count Athenais among these 'convenient Christians'?"

Theo's scowl warned Pulcheria she was treading on dangerous ground. She shrugged. "She observes the forms but reads more frivolously than I'd like. I caught her and Placidia giggling over those wretched love poems by Ovid last week. Really, both grown women with children! How can they stand that rubbish?"

"Dearest Sister, they have taken no holy vows of chastity." Theo's mood shifted. He leaned to kiss her on the cheek. "I would be most upset if my wife did."

"Placidia is a widow twice over and of sufficient years she should have no

161

interest in the urges of the flesh." Pulcheria turned her attention to the report of Hunnish activity.

"Placidia is only ten years your senior. Hardly a decrepit elder."

Pulcheria looked up in time to catch the tail end of a smile on Theo's face. "Other than the sin of enjoying love poems, how do you feel about our aunt? You've had over four months to observe her and winkle out her secrets."

Pulcheria leaned back. "She and her children attend daily prayers and exhibit modest behavior. She keeps the fast days."

"Is Placidia one of your convenient Christians?"

"No. I sense a genuine religious devotion in her. Placidia is troubled and seeks something. She turns to God for solace." Pulcheria tapped a fingernail on the desk. "Maybe the rumors are true."

"You think our gentle aunt capable of gutting an enemy?" Theo's eyes lighted with interest at this possibility.

"Never underestimate the strength of a woman in a righteous cause."

"Are you speaking of Placidia or yourself?" Theo smiled.

Pulcheria raised an eyebrow, answering with another question. "What do you think of Athenais' proposal that you betroth your Eudoxia to the young Valentinian?"

"It's not a bad idea, but my daughter is still an infant. I don't like to think of her leaving us."

"The idea comes from Placidia. She has not given up her ambition that her son rule in the west. I'm sure she thinks the betrothal will make you look more favorably on her petition."

"Of course the proposal comes from Placidia!" Theo snorted. "Sometimes I feel you treat me as a lack-wit, Sister."

"Never, Brother." *God give me strength! I wish he weren't so prickly on that subject.* She rose to rest a hand on his shoulder. "Your wits are sharp, but your heart is tender. You want to do all in your power for those you love. I understand, but few would do the same for you."

"I know you have only my interest at heart, as does Athenais."

"Of course." Pulcheria withdrew her hand.

A commotion at the door brought their heads around.

"My apologies, Augustus, Augusta." Helion entered, followed by a begrimed messenger. "There is news from Ravenna."

The messenger fell to his knees and extended a letter.

Theo took it, broke the seal and scanned it. "Honorius is dead."

"God save his soul." Pulcheria crossed herself, murmuring an additional prayer.

Theo dismissed the servants. "We must tell Placidia."

"You go. She's in the nursery with Athenais."


Theo surveyed the scene from the nursery door. His wife and aunt chatted on a padded bench. His daughter careened about the room, followed closely by a young servant girl ready to pick her up or offer a helping hand. Walking was a new skill and evidently must be practiced at all times. The older children studied in another room.

Athenais sensed his presence and looked up.

"Speaking of my love…" She rose to greet him with a warm kiss as he entered the nursery.

Placidia picked up Eudoxia and carried her to her parents. "What brings you to the nursery at this time of day, Nephew?"

He took Eudoxia from her and chucked her under the chin before handing her to Athenais. "I'm afraid I bring distressing news."

"What?" Placidia put her hand to her heart.

"Your brother Honorius is dead. We just received the dispatches."

"Oh!" Placidia's eyes widened in shock. "What did he die of?"

"Dropsy."

"My poor brother. The family affliction. Our father died of the same illness." Placidia shook her head. "His health has been fragile for some time."

Theo reached out to his aunt. "It is no small thing to lose a brother, even if you are estranged."

"I would have liked to be with him in the end, to let him know I forgave him." Tears glistened in Placidia's eyes. "I hope he did not die alone and abandoned. I would not put it past Castinus."

"The general is mentioned in the dispatches." Theo shuffled his feet, knowing his aunt would not take the news graciously.

"In what way?" Placidia nearly hissed.

"Honorius knew he was dying and sent several documents, among them a strong recommendation that General Castinus administer the West in my name."

Placidia suppressed a cry of outrage but could not keep the anger from her voice. "Castinus persuaded Honorius to this course, or even substituted his own wishes for those of my brother. By rights, Valentinian should be emperor in the West. Honorius confirmed my son as Caesar and heir three years ago."

"Without my consent." Theo snapped. "As sole emperor, it is my right to designate a co-ruler—or not."

The sympathetic moment between the two shattered like fragile glass. Athenais clutched their daughter to her chest, glancing with alarm at him and his aunt. At her distress, Theo's anger lifted as quickly as it came. Before he could speak, Placidia bowed in acknowledgement.

"Of course it is your decision, Nephew," she continued, her tone softening. "You will choose the colleague you feel best. Now is not the time to discuss this important matter. After the mourning period will be soon enough."

Theo noticed her careful choice of words, assuming he would choose a co-ruler. Valentinian, at five, could not rule in the West. Placidia wished to be named regent, but that would have to wait. His grandfather ruled singly. Perhaps he would do so, as well. He would discuss Castinus' proposal with the council.

Placidia bowed. "I should tell the children. Honoria was particularly fond of her uncle."

October 423

Following the week of mourning, Pulcheria and Theo negotiated with Castinus for two months over the fate of the West. Placidia haunted the palace, upbraiding them by her very presence. Athenais persuaded Theo to approve the betrothal between Valentinian and Eudoxia, with no objection from Pulcheria. It went a little way to assuage her guilt at stealing the boy's birthright. Pulcheria had yet to decide if Theo could rule alone even with her guidance. He wanted to travel to the West to assess the situation for himself, but there always seemed some reason for postponing the journey.

Pulcheria and Theo were holding audience in the Daphne when another messenger from Ravenna arrived. He bowed and extended a packet. "From Emperor John, ruler in Ravenna of the western Roman lands."

"What did you say?" Theo leapt to his feet, blood draining from his face. The audience chamber grew silent.

"The people of Ravenna have seen fit to acclaim John as Emperor in the

West." The man fell to his knees. "He sends his most felicitous regards to his co-Emperor and wishes for your good health."

"Who is this John who usurps the diadem in the West? Where is General Castinus in all this?"

"I only bring the messages, Most Noble One." The man stretched full length on the floor.

Theo snatched the packet. "Detain him until we've had a chance to review these messages."

Two guards escorted the wretched man from the audience chamber.

Theo signed for two pages to attend him. "Find General Ardaburius and have him attend me in the council room," he ordered the first, then turned to the second. "You, find and escort my Aunt Placidia to the council room. She should be in her residence."

They bowed and hurried off.

"The rest of you leave us, except for the council. Attend me." Theo strode off to the Consistory.

Pulcheria hastened to catch up. "What is it? Why do you need the council?"

"When we're all together."

Pulcheria fumed. *Since when am I just one of the council?*

They entered, taking seats at the head of the massive table. Senior administrators sat along the sides in strict order and rank. General Ardaburius came racing into the room a heartbeat after the last sat. Theo banned servants from the room and placed guards on the door.

When everyone settled, he tossed the papers on the table.

"It seems we have rebellion in the West. A man named John has declared himself emperor."

Pulcheria pulled the sheaf of papers towards her, quickly scanning them. "It seems General Castinus became impatient. These read like his words."

"Why would he maneuver such a ploy? He has to know it would displease me."

"In my negotiations with him, he's proved a wily adversary." Pulcheria put the papers down. "The General is too smart to declare himself emperor. He wished to rule in your name in the West. I suspect the betrothal of your daughter to Valentinian panicked him. He read the wrong message in that action, thought you kept him at bay while preparing to replace him with the boy and his mother. Castinus knew Placidia would not tolerate him in her government after his machinations to have her banished, so he raised another he could control."

"This cannot stand, Augustus." Helion looked around the table at everyone's assenting nod. "This John must be overthrown. The only question is whether you do it in your own name or that of Valentinian."

Pulcheria nodded her agreement. *The Master of Offices betrays his preference. Has Placidia been whispering in his ears? Theo could name another—an adult man—to hold the West, but he does not contradict Helion. Is he still thinking of sole rule?*

"How soon could we launch an attack?" Theo turned to Ardaburius.

"A full army?"

Theo nodded.

"Not before spring." The general stroked his chin. "We will need to withdraw some veteran troops from the Persian front and recruit, train and equip reserves. With the Huns active, we cannot leave our northern border undefended."

"You all agree?"

"Yes."

"Then leave us…all but Ardaburius and Helion."

The other officials trooped out.

"Theo!" Athenais cried from the door, a protective hand over her stomach.

Pulcheria started. *Was Athenais with child again? How would that affect Theo's decision—particularly if the child was a boy?*

Athenais hurried inside. "I heard what happened in the audience room."

The guards again shut the door on the much smaller conclave. Theo filled her in on details of the dispatch.

"What are we to do?" Athenais shook her head.

Theo's glance strayed to his wife's still flat stomach. "We have a decision to make. This usurper must be ousted, but who will take his place?"

"Would you rule the West as well as the East?" Athenais asked.

"Sister?" Theo turned to Pulcheria first.

"You are a good emperor, but the West would be a terrible burden. Gaul and Hispania are in constant turmoil. It took General Constantius years to pacify those barbaric tribes and still they fight each other and rebel against Rome whenever the mood takes them. Our grandfather ruled the entire empire from his horse. He led his own armies, ranging over the frontier. He made his sons co-rulers after his death, because he knew neither could hold the empire together on his own." Pulcheria rose. "I will aid you in whatever you decide."

"Athenais?" Theo's gaze softened.

"I will accompany you wherever you travel. If you lead an army yourself, I will be in your tent."

"I won't lead an army, my Sweet. That's why I have good generals." He turned to Ardaburius. "General, what's the military situation in the West? Will they stand with John? Will they be a threat to an invasion force?"

"The armies in the West are weak and disorganized after decades of fighting the barbarians. General Castinus had some slight success in Gaul, which slipped away when the Gothic auxiliaries left the field. I doubt he could put up much of a fight. Felix, in charge of the Italian reserves, is barely competent. Their most able general, Boniface, is in Africa."

"Boniface is a good friend of our aunt's." Athenais said. "He sends funds to Placidia for her upkeep, since Honorius confiscated her western inheritance."

"So Boniface would likely support Placidia if she led an invasion in Valentinian's name." Theo rubbed his smooth-shaven jaw. "We could send fewer troops if Boniface came from Africa. Guard!" Theo shouted. "Bring me a scribe."

A short time later, Placidia hastened into the council chamber.

Pulcheria took her hand. "Dearest Aunt, we have a serious development in the West."

"I heard. A man named John has declared himself emperor. If I remember, he was a supervisor of clerks with no military background or blood claim to the diadem."

"The upstart has the nerve to demand I acknowledge his claim over your son's." Theo's mouth twisted. "I imprisoned his envoy."

"You favor our claim?" Hope lightened her aunt's features.

Pulcheria waved a hand as if dismissing an insignificant problem. "Of course we favor your claim. The empire is too big to rule alone, and Theo and I have all we can handle here in the East, with Ruga and his Huns threatening in the north and the Persians restless on our eastern borders. We leave the rest of the barbarians to you."

A scribe brought Theo several parchment pages. Grinning, he signed each with a flourish, put his seal to the wax, and handed them to Placidia. A smile dawned over her face as she read the imperial confirmation of her elevation to Augusta and Valentinian's to Caesar and heir to Honorius.

"You named me Regent." Placidia put down the decrees. "Thank you, Nephew."

"You are the best one to rule in your son's name. You know the people, the barbarians, and the bureaucracy." Pulcheria arched an eyebrow. "It is always better to have blood protect blood during a minority."

"This one," Theo waved the last sheet, "is an order to General Ardaburius to prepare an army to invade Italy and take back the imperium for Valentinian. I will accompany you myself and crown my young cousin in Rome."

Placidia bowed low. "My sincere thanks to you, my dearest nieces and nephew. God sent me to you for succor in my darkest hour, and you gave freely of your love and wisdom. I and my children have lived with you in amity. We will not forget to whom we owe our future good fortune."

Athenais left her chair and embraced Placidia. "I will miss you, Aunt, and so will little Eudoxia. You are my closest friend. I count the days until we are reunited. God keep you safe."

Theo joined them, putting his arm around his wife's waist. "Fear not, my love. It will take many months to complete our plans and gather the army. Placidia and the children will be with us through the winter. Leave us now. You need your rest." He kissed her cheek. "Placidia, please stay and tell us what you know of this John."

Pulcheria sat back, pleased at the outcome. Her aunt was a shrewd, strong woman. She would fight like a lioness for her children and the empire. She watched with pride as Theo questioned Placidia. Yes, he acted wisely and with decisiveness in this matter. *He is growing into the emperor she wanted him to be.*

# Chapter 23



*Placidia's Palace, Constantinople, February 425*

PULCHERIA ENTERED HER AUNT'S RESIDENCE WITH A TOUCH OF GUILT. Eighteen months since they received word that Honorius had died! Placidia had been more than patient as Theo settled with the Huns in the north—three hundred and fifty pounds of gold a year for that thief Ruga—and dealt with his and Athenais' grief over their stillborn son Arcadius. At last the invasion fleet was ready for the formidable army General Ardaburius had assembled. His son, General Aspar, led the cavalry which would take the overland route.

She followed a servant through the entrance hall, past the audience chamber and dining hall, to her aunt's work room. While Placidia and her children resided in their own palace, they spent most days at the Constantinople court. Pulcheria had never been to Placidia's residence and proceeded with more than a little curiosity. On the eve of Placidia leaving, a flurry of servants packed away paintings, rolled up carpets, covered furniture. The domus, awake for less than two years, was going back to sleep.

She found her aunt busily reviewing lists and giving orders to scribes. Placidia looked up with a genuine smile.

"Niece! I'm pleased to see you. We've had so little time together these past couple of months." She waved over a scribe. "Send for food and drink for the Augusta, to be served in the small triclinium. Then you are all dismissed."

"I did not mean to interrupt your work. Preparing for an invasion takes time and planning."

"No matter." Placidia rose, put a hand to Pulcheria's back, and escorted her down the corridor to a small, finely furnished room decorated in soothing pinks and grays. "I was just about to break from my labors for a bit of food. When I work, I'm afraid I neglect the needs of the body."

"Fasting is good for the soul but I agree, too much can dim the mind." Pulcheria chose a cushioned chair opposite the small divan where Placidia sat. A low marble table, with gilded legs in the shape of lion's paws, separated them.

"Ah, Lucilla!" Placidia looked toward the doorway. "Prompt as ever."

A young serving woman entered, carrying a tray of food, followed by a boy who placed a pitcher of wine on a carved sideboard. Pulcheria had seen the female servant shadowing her mistress about the imperial palace. Her own servants whispered that the young woman was mute. A handy thing in a body servant. When she turned her right side to Pulcheria she looked quite pretty, but on the left hideous scars marred the flesh over a misshapen cheekbone.

Placidia dismissed the boy. Lucilla arranged sliced fowl and boiled beef doused with garum, salad greens dressed with vinegar, pickled eggs, olives, cheese, and a variety of fresh fruits imported from Egypt—a rare treat for this late winter season.

"What brings you to my residence, Niece?" Placidia indicated Pulcheria should help herself to the food, nibbled on a piece of cucumber topped with creamy cheese and crushed walnuts.

"Theo isn't feeling well. His stomach gives him problems. He fears he cannot travel with you to Italy." Pulcheria was not surprised when this illness came upon him. He frequently had stomach problems when the need to travel beyond the suburbs of Constantinople presented itself. Thankfully, that was not often!

Placidia put down her morsel, eyes clouded with concern. "Is he seriously ill? Should we postpone the invasion?"

"The doctors say he is in no danger. His bile is out of balance and they have him on a strict regimen of bland food. I'm not sure which bothers him more, the plain porridge or the stomach pains." Pulcheria tasted the pickled eggs. "We will send our Master Helion to advise you and crown Valentinian in Theo's name in Rome. No need to delay."

"Good. I'm hoping to avoid fighting altogether. The people of the city of

Rome rejected the usurper and minted coins in my and Val's name. They have ever been my champions, since I refused to abandon them during the Gothic sieges. General Boniface halted the African grain shipments to Ravenna, so the hungry people there have no love for the false emperor." Placidia sipped her wine. "Civil war brings nothing but destruction to the people. I pray God grant me the means to avoid it."

Pulcheria lowered her eyes, crossed herself, and added her prayers to her aunt's. "The marshes of Ravenna are formidable. How will you breach them?"

"I'm hoping God will send an Angel to guide me."

Pulcheria raised an eyebrow in question.

"Years ago, a young boy helped me escape from Ravenna through the marshes. If I can find him, he might guide my army back." A smile lightened her features. "Angelus was quite a scamp. His sort are survivors. I'm hoping for the best but planning for the worst."

"Our prayers are with you." Pulcheria looked over her goblet. "I understand you and the children travel by land this time."

"Yes! We accompany General Aspar and his cavalry." Placidia shivered. "I will never travel by sea again. The Good Lord saw us safely to your shores after much trial and prayer and I made Him a promise. My first act upon gaining the throne is to build a church in fulfillment of my vow."

"A most appropriate endeavor."

"How is Athenais faring?" Placidia looked up with genuine concern. "I wanted to be a better friend during the past few months, but with all the final preparations…" She shrugged.

"She is understandably anxious about the upcoming birth, given her previous loss, but the midwives and doctors assure us she and the baby are healthy. We pray for a strapping boy."

"As do we all!" Placidia raised her goblet. "To a healthy son, and long life to his mother and father."

Pulcheria raised her own goblet of water to acknowledge the toast, watching her aunt's face closely for any sign of disappointed ambition. A boy could be a rival in the East if Placidia had ambitions for her son beyond the troubled West. Fortunately, Placidia seemed genuine in her affection for Athenais and her hopes for the unborn child.

They chatted companionably the rest of the meal about Athenais' advancing pregnancy, the health and education of the children, and Pulcheria's recent charity work. Lucilla cleared the remains of the food and poured each a hot brew of mint and honey.

"Aunt…" Pulcheria hesitated, finally coming to the reason for her visit. "I have some concerns about your venture. I don't want to insult you, but a good number of our court feel you are not suited to be Regent."

"Are you one of them?" Placidia leaned forward, jaw clenched. "You seemed to take my part during all these months."

"I have reservations but have not stated them publicly."

"To Theo?"

"Yes, but he rejected them. Athenais pleads your case most eloquently."

"Theo has given his blessing. The venture is launched. Why tell me your reservations now? They serve only to undermine my confidence and incite my enmity."

"That was not my intention." Pulcheria leaned back, staring at her hands. "Unlike the others, it is not your abilities I question. I know a woman can rule as wisely and well as a man. It is your soul, your lust for power that I fear."

"You accuse me of wanting power?" Placidia spluttered. "Look in the mirror, Niece!"

Pulcheria shook her head. Her words came out badly. She tried again. "I sense a darkness in you, Placidia, a hardness that might bring you to ruin."

"You, of all people, know what it takes to keep a young boy alive and on the throne: hardness to do what it takes and power to make sure it sticks. Darkness?" Placidia stood, shaking. "What do you know of my soul? I saw my beloved Uncle and Aunt, the people who raised me, murdered by order of my brother. I cradled two dying husbands in my arms, one covered in assassin's wounds." Her voice grew husky with unshed tears. She clasped her arms across her stomach. "I buried a child of my womb, dead from disease, and four step-children butchered by a usurper. I rode through cities ravaged by war as captive and conqueror. Don't talk to me about darkness until you've lived my life!"

"I do not accuse you! I know you've lived through extraordinary travails." Pulcheria looked up at her aunt. "Please believe me when I say I care for you, Aunt. I sense in you a kindred soul, but you seem in much pain. I want to help. The only way to take the pain away is to offer it to God. In his light and his love, you will be healed. Pray with me?" She dropped to her knees; hand extended to Placidia.

Her aunt knelt, placing her arm around Pulcheria's shoulders. In a low, wavering voice, Placidia said, "I can't pray for that pain to go away just yet. I need it to keep me strong, to remind me what happens when I let down my guard. Val is still a little boy. He will need me sharp and hard for many years." She sighed. "The day will come, Pulcheria, when I can lay down that burden. I will kneel with you then. Come."

They rose. Pulcheria wiped away a tear on the sleeve of her gown. "Until you can pray for yourself, I will pray for you."

"Your prayers are most welcome, Niece. Now I must get back to work."

Pulcheria left with mixed feelings: pride in her aunt's strength and self-sacrifice, sorrow for her past pain and future trials, hope for the future.

*When she is ready, I will help her save her soul.*


*Imperial Palace, May 425*

THEO FINISHED READING THE REPORTS WITH A SENSE OF ELATION. PLACIDIA had taken Ravenna in a bloodless coup. There was a rumor God had aided her by sending an Angel to lead her troops through the dangerous marshes. *I must ask Pulcheria about that!* His aunt seemed in firm control of the West, having executed the usurper and quashed a rebellion led by the soldier Aetius and a band of mercenary Huns. Helion reported they would travel to Rome to acclaim young Valentinian Augustus. *Yes, a most satisfactory ending to this adventure.*

He set aside his reports and surveyed the intimate family setting in this, his favorite room of the palace—a place filled with warm carpets, cushioned chairs, and children's toys. A soft spring breeze wafted the scent of orange blossoms from the garden beyond the open doors. The late afternoon sun faded from the sky. A servant lit oil lamps to chase away the shadows.

His pregnant wife played with their three-year-old daughter, rolling a ball back and forth on the floor. His aunt-by-marriage sat embroidering some trifle for the coming child while she chatted with Athenais. His brother-in-law seemed to be beating Paulinus at a game of *latrones*, judging from the pile of white stones Valerius had accumulated on the side of the board. Athenais only yesterday had urged him to appoint her brother *comes rerum privatarum*—the minister in charge of the private estates and revenues of the emperor. *It would be good to have family in charge of such a sensitive position. How did Pulcheria put it? Blood to protect blood!*

Athenais seemed to struggle to stand. Theo scrambled to give her a hand.

"Thank you, my love." His wife's eyes shone with affection. "I shouldn't get down on the floor when I can't get up!"

"Do what you want, Dearest. I'll always be there to offer a helping hand." Athenais glowed with health, but he worried about her upcoming trial. The midwives assured him third births were easier and safer than first labors, but he couldn't shake his doubts. His own mother died giving birth after several successful pregnancies. He said a silent prayer to ward off the evil those thoughts brought with them.

"Nana?" Athenais turned to the watchful nurse in the corner. "It's time for Eudoxia to go to bed."

"No!" His small daughter, a miniature of her beautiful mother, clutched his leg. "Story first, Papa!"

He lifted her into his arms. "What do you want the story to be about?"

"Lions!" She gave a miniature roar.

"Lions? They're too scary for bedtime stories. You'll have nightmares."

"Won't!" Her little face screwed up in concentration. She roared again.

He pretended to be frightened. "See, lions are scary."

Her lower lip trembled; tears sparkled in her eyes. His heart melted. "All right, my little princess. Lions it is." He took her to a comfy couch and settled her on his lap. Her head rested on his breast where she could hear his heartbeat. "I'll tell you the story of Daniel in the lion's den and how the Lord saved him."

He was barely halfway through the story when her eyes began to droop. Before he reached the scary lions, she was fast asleep. He carried her to the nurse and kissed her forehead as he handed over her limp, vulnerable body. He thought his heart would burst with love for his child. Tears came to his eyes. He wiped them away before turning back to the domestic scene.

Before he could say anything, Pulcheria, Arcadia, and Marina entered the room dressed, as usual, in the modest robes of holy women, and accompanied by a priest. The easy chatter and laughter stilled. A distinct chill filled the room that had nothing to do with the open doors. He looked to the water clock. It was time for evening prayers. His wife and her family felt keeping church hours excessive, but his own heart lightened when communing with God.

"Sisters." He held out his hands and smiled. Arcadia and Marina smiled back. Pulcheria kept that pinched sour look that marked her face more often of late. He worried about her. She spent too much time contending with his other councilors. Theo wanted harmony on the council. Often his sister sowed discord. He knew her heart was in her charity work and regretted she felt so obligated to her role of advisor. *I should give some thought to how I can make her life easier.*

*Imperial Palace, June 425*

"Congratulations on your second daughter, Theo." Pulcheria found her brother properly sober after Flacilla's birth and nodded in approval.

"She's as beautiful as her mother." A broad smile lit his face. "Athenais asked a favor as a birth present."

Pulcheria shielded her alarm. Athenais' brother Valerius had recently been made master of the privy purse, which gave him tremendous opportunity for corruption. Not that Pulcheria had caught him with his fingers in the pie, but given time… "What does your lovely wife wish of you this time?"

"She wishes to endow chairs for thirty professors of grammar, rhetoric, philosophy, and law here in the city."

"Of course she does. Has she built one church? Endowed one charity? What happened to tending to 'the least of these'?" Pulcheria fumed.

"That's unfair, Sister! Athenais attends you when you visit your charities and monasteries. She sees what you do and wishes to emulate you in a sphere in which you've shown little interest."

"Grammar, rhetoric, philosophy, and law—the secular sphere!"

"Which a well-functioning government needs." Theo snapped. "These teachers train our civil servants and offer a path to prosperity for those endowed with intelligence and talent, but little wealth or connection. Why are you so set against that?"

"I'm not! I…it's just…not seemly for an Augusta." She stammered to a close trying to sort through her tangled feelings. "Women should engage in the Church, not the government."

Theo initially looked puzzled, then laughed. "Ria, you do hear how that sounds coming from your mouth."

"I've done what was necessary." Pulcheria turned with a stiff back to stare out the window at the sun sparkling on the Propontis Sea. The harbor bustled with

175

grain boats and merchant ships bringing treasures from the far corners of the empire. The sight soothed her. She took a deep breath of the fresh air. *Why do I let Athenais upset me so! Her request is not an unreasonable one.* She turned to her brother. He surprised her before she could utter an apology.

"I have a gift for you, as well, Ria."

"I need nothing." She frowned. "As you well know."

"This is something you will enjoy…freedom!"

Alarms tingled along her nerves. "Freedom? From what?" *What new scheme has his wife cooked up now!*

"This palace. I know you and our sisters crave a more quiet existence, one more suited to contemplation and reflection." Theo handed her a sheaf of papers with the wax seal of deeds. "You may have the palaces in Hebdomon and the Rufinianai, as well as those you already hold in your own name from our father. As an Augusta, you may have a chief eunuch to run your household. Choose your own man: a eunuch from the palace or someone else. I will also provide a detail of the scholae to guard you and escort you about the city…"

As Theo continued, Pulcheria grew stiffer. He finally stumbled to a halt as he noticed her anger.

Blood suffused her face. She mastered her tongue. "Are you sure this is a gift for me, and not your wife? This is Athenais' idea, isn't it? She wishes me out of the palace, thinking, with me gone, she and her brother can control you and the empire."

"You think so little of my abilities?" Theo dropped his hand, hurt pinching his mouth. "Maybe it's good that you not only move out of the palace, but also give up your councilor duties. Given some distance, you might see I can govern without you and take pride in that."

Her heart sank as she realized her error and the pain she caused her brother. "Theo, no…I didn't…"

He put up a hand to forestall her. "It is done. Please leave with our sisters and your women as soon as you can arrange it."

Theo stalked to the door. There he hesitated to look over his shoulder. "It was not Athenais who proposed this move. It was me. I thought you'd be happier without the discord of the court. I did this for love of you."

"I'm sorry, Brother." Pulcheria bowed low as he left.

*What have I done?*

# PART III

# THE MOST PIOUS EMPRESS

## DECEMBER 427 – JULY 431

# Chapter 24

*Hebdomon Palace and The Great Church, Constantinople, December 427*

WHAT ARE THE TALLIES, SIMON?" PULCHERIA QUIZZED HER CHAMBERLAIN. "Have we enough to build the Mary Theotokos Church in the Blachernai district?"

"Nearly, Your Serenity." He tapped an ink-stained finger against his nose as he studied the accounts. "The bakeries, workshops, and rents are fine. Fees from the docks seem light. I'll look into it."

Pulcheria's life had settled into a routine over the two years since Theo banished her from the council. She and her women still kept fast days and church hours for prayers, but she threw her considerable wealth and energies into church building and supporting the holy men and women who worked among the poor. To Theo's credit, the empire seemed peaceful and prosperous. Maybe she had been guilty of the sin of pride, thinking only she could keep the empire safe.

Arcadia stopped by the door. "Nearly ready, Sister? Bishop Sisinnius delays his sermon for no one, not even you!"

"Coming." Pulcheria dismissed Simon and gathered her things. She and the Good Bishop planned a surprise for this celebration of Mary's Feast.

She, her sisters, and their attendants traveled to the Great Church, accompanied by her guards. As usual, people lined the street to watch their curtained wagons pass and cry blessings on them. The people knew the virgin princesses spent their vast fortunes and time making others' lives better.

At the Great Church, they took their seats in the women's section, behind an elaborately carved screen, separate from the male congregants. Segregation of the sexes irritated Pulcheria, but she couldn't change the world in a heartbeat and so accepted this temporary exile. After the service, she and her women would mingle freely with the bishop and his priests. Theo frequently joined them for communion and Sunday meal with the bishop. He was always cordial, but, despite her efforts, she had not been able to mend the breach between them. The wound to his pride had gone deep.

The familiar service began with chanting and prayers. Pulcheria stood and knelt on cue, breathing incense, letting the rhythms of the routine soothe her nerves and infuse her with peace. Little sunlight filtered through the high narrow windows, so the interior shone with the soft light of candles and oil lamps. When Bishop Sisinnius approached the pulpit, Pulcheria's heart beat faster. When her dear friend Bishop Atticus died two years ago, Sisinnius—an ancient, gentle man—took the bishopric as a compromise candidate. She had backed Proclus, Atticus' secretary and a good friend, but lost. Still, Sisinnius was a holy man, engaging and worthy of his See.

He raised his arms, dropped his head, and offered up a prayer asking for God's blessing on the imperial family, referring to Pulcheria and her sisters as "Brides of Christ." Then he settled into his sermon.

"Today we celebrate the feast of Mary Theotokos—Mary, Mother of God. She who, through faith and goodness, cooperated in the redemption of the universe. From the beginning of time, the sins of Eve dogged our sisters. Women were cursed to bring forth children in pain and tears. God did not intend this punishment to last forever. Mary is the New Eve. As sin entered the world through the disobedience of Eve, so the Divine Word took flesh through the faith of Mary. As Eve set creation at odds with its Lord, so Mary opened herself to the Divine. As Eve brought women under a curse, so the New Eve embodied the glory and rank of her sex.

"Through Mary, all women are blessed. The female can no longer be held accursed, because the rank of this sex surpasses even the angels in glory. Now Eve is healed. Behold the catalogue of admirable women: All praise Sarah, the fertile field of the people. Rebekah is honored, a capable provider of benedictions. Leah, too, admired as mother of the ancestor in the flesh. Deborah wins praise because she led in battle despite her sex. Elizabeth is also called happy for she carried the precursor in her body, and he leapt in delight at the approach of grace.

"I would enroll another name among those great women; a name familiar to you all; a woman of great wisdom, piety and generosity: Aelia Pulcheria Augusta, our Most Pious Empress."

The bishop stepped behind the altar to remove a cloth, revealing a portrait of Pulcheria in the aspect of the Virgin Mary. The congregants shouted acclamations. Pulcheria rose to exit the women's section, proceeding toward the altar with head bowed, holding a bundle before her. She knelt at the bishop's feet and held out her gift, a length of purple silk, encrusted with gold thread, seed pearls, and flashing gems. "Father, I humbly offer this silk robe, which has lain next to my body, as an altar cloth."

"In the Good Lord's name, I accept this gift. Rise, Daughter." He put a hand under her elbow to help her stand. Together they faced the cheering crowd. "Well done, Augusta," he said in an aside for her ears only. "You are much beloved by the people."

"They are my children." Pulcheria said with pride.

*Imperial Palace, February 428*

"HOW GOES THE SEARCH FOR OUR NEW BISHOP?" PULCHERIA ASKED HER BROTHER in one of her rare visits to the palace. It spoke volumes that Theo chose to greet her in his work room and not a more intimate family setting. A month earlier, the gentle Bishop Sisinnius died quietly in his sleep. Pulcheria mourned his passing with prayers and additional gifts to the poor.

"Have you heard of Nestorius of Antioch?" Theo asked. Pulcheria had fretted as her brother floundered in choosing a replacement patriarch. First, he approached Dalmatius, a most holy ascetic who had not left his monk's cell for over forty years. He—rightfully—refused. Next, Theo approached another holy man in the suburbs of Constantinople. He refused, as well. People were getting restive at the delay. Finally, Theo called on her to help with the matter. It was Church rather than government business but gave Pulcheria an opportunity to show she could still be of assistance to her brother.

"Vaguely." Pulcheria frowned. "He's an ascetic from the Euprepius monastery, is he not? Syrian? Why not choose Proclus, well-known and well-loved by our people?"

"I want an outsider, to avoid the Church politics that marred my last appointment. There are factions in the Constantinople See. Putting one above

181

the other will excite jealousies. Bishop Sisinnius was a good and holy man, but he was a compromise—one that only postponed the decision because of his advanced age." Theo paused. "Nestorius is very well regarded."

*By your advisors, I assume*, Pulcheria thought. "Your wife's father came from Antioch. Did she suggest this Nestorius?"

"Athenais has no thoughts on this appointment." Theo rolled his eyes. "Please, Sister, I refuse to discuss my wife with you. It brings discord between us. The reason I invited you today is to discuss Nestorius and his godliness."

"I'm sorry, Brother." Pulcheria put a hand on his arm and a curb on her tongue. *God give me strength. What is the matter with me that I cannot keep my own counsel when it comes to that woman?* "I was wrong to suspect any such influence."

Theo gave a stiff nod of acceptance.

She continued. "There is another factor you should consider when making your decision. You might avoid local discord by asking an Antiochene to take the See, only to inflame more distant animosities. The Alexandrines of Egypt and the Antiochenes of Syria have feuded for centuries over dogma and the primacy of their Sees. Bishop Cyril of Alexandria is a learned man, but ambitious and jealous of his prerogatives. I had dealings with him early in my regency. He might take this appointment as a slight."

"This appointment has no affect on the Alexandria See. Why should he object? If he does, let the Bishop of Rome settle those differences."

"As God's Viceroy on earth—"

Theo stopped her with a raised hand. "I know your opinions on this, Ria. Help me select a bishop for our city or leave."

Why did her brother not understand that the Church was a human institution, prone to human frailties and egos? The Church needed a strong leader and arbiter, just as the empire did. When the Church could not settle its disputes, the emperor needed to step in and impose his will. Pulcheria tamped down her irritation. "What else is in Nestorius' favor?"

"He is comely and has a wonderful voice."

"Another Chrysostom?" Pulcheria asked. "The people still talk of the 'Golden Mouth' after twenty years."

"He has a classical education, with the usual literary and rhetorical training, and puts them to use in his preaching. We would not have heard of him otherwise."

"An ascetic for the monks, rhetorical style for the people, and a classical background for the Hellenes. His origins and personal appearance could recall the popular Chrysostom." Pulcheria ticked off the candidate's advantages on her fingers. "It sounds like you have your bishop."

"You have no objections?" Theo looked pleased.

"None. I'm sure the new bishop and I will build a cordial relationship."

"Good. I'll send General Dionysius to escort him to the capital."

"The *magister militum*? A good signal to the people, that the emperor makes this choice." *At least he got that right!*

"Excellent! Will you join us for evening meal?"

"I would be honored." She took his arm as they walked down the hall. "Now, what is this I hear about the Goths rebelling in the West? I thought Placidia had them under control…"

*The Great Church, April 428*

Pulcheria dressed in full imperial regalia for the Easter Service. Bishop Nestorius had been confirmed only five days before. She looked forward to his sermon on this most holy of days as she took her seat with her sisters and women.

"Ria!" Arcadia hissed. "Look above the altar."

A cloth obscured her portrait.

"I'm sure the attendants forgot to remove it before the service."

"Your altar cloth is missing, as well." Marina pointed out.

"What?" Pulcheria squinted. Her gift was indeed missing from the altar. "Hmm. I'm sure this is an oversight. I'll have a word with the bishop after the services."

Nestorius approached the altar. The congregants quieted. After preliminary chants and prayers, Nestorius took the pulpit to preach a rousing sermon on the resurrection. Pulcheria was quite satisfied with his style and substance.

He finished with the traditional prayers for the imperial family but failed to call Pulcheria and her sisters Brides of Christ in listing their honors. She prickled at the absence. There was a small wave of murmurs as others noted the omission. Another point to bring up with the Good Bishop. He was new and did not know the ways of her city.

After the service, Pulcheria and her retinue approached the grille separating the nave from the sanctuary, to find the gate shut against them.

She spotted a young man hurrying past. "You, priest. What is your name?"

"Most Honored Augusta." He bowed deeply. "I'm the archdeacon Peter."

"Peter, go tell the Good Bishop Nestorius, that Aelia Pulcheria Augusta waits at the sanctuary door for entrance to take communion with her brother the Emperor, His Worship the Bishop, and the holy priests of the Great Church, as has been her wont."

"Of course, Your Serenity."

Peter hurried off. Pulcheria fumed at the delay. Her women exchanged uneasy glances and quiet comments.

Bishop Nestorius came to the grille, followed by several burly monks.

Pulcheria gave a stiff nod. "Sir, the gate is barred against me."

"Only priests may walk in the sanctuary."

"I and my sisters are consecrated to God. Your predecessors were pleased to have our presence."

"I know some believe virgins through their sacrifice 'give birth to God', but this is an error. Women give birth to Satan! Women are the daughters of Eve, through whom sin came into this world. They cannot step foot in the most holy of holies in the Church. Augusta, be gone, or I will have my monks remove you and your women."

Stunned and humiliated, Pulcheria turned on her heel and left, her women trailing behind. *Theo will hear of this disrespect!* she fumed.

Over the next several months, the situation worsened.

*Imperial Palace, June 428*

"Brother, you must rein in your bishop!" Pulcheria paced back and forth in Theo's private audience chamber. "He is riling the populace with his suppression of their entertainments."

"You've frequently bemoaned the people's love of the circus, mimes, and dancers, wishing they spent more time in church. Nestorius is doing what you could not."

"Because I could not and keep their love! Not all are suited to our life of prayer and duty. The common people need entertainments or they become dangerous. God put you on the throne, but the people keep you there. Don't antagonize them by taking away their theater and games!"

"The populace will soon settle into amity with their bishop. He is persuasive."

Theo's jaw firmed. "That was one of his gifts you most admired, if I remember right."

Pulcheria backed off that tack, fearing he might become even more stubborn. "And the monks? Nestorius tells them to forgo their good work among the people. He orders them back to the monasteries to live a life of prayer and excommunicates any who fail to follow through. He had the holy man Basel beaten and exiled for protesting these actions. The people rescued him and took him to the safety of a suburban church. You cannot condone such behavior by the bishop!"

"The monks frequently lead the people in protest against my officials. The city will be more peaceful with them back in their cells."

*That sounds like the arguments of corrupt Hellenes who don't want to give up their lucrative honors when the monks call them out!* Pulcheria struggled to keep her tone reasonable. "The monks protest *corrupt* officials. If your appointees do their jobs, the people will praise them. With the monks behind walls, who will minister to the sick and poor?"

"Maybe their relatives, now that they no longer are absent at the games?"

Pulcheria stopped pacing, fists clenched, anger stopping her mouth.

"I jest, Sister."

She let out a breath. "Good. I thought for a moment you had lost your wits."

"Are you sure your displeasure is with his closing theaters and sending the monks back to their cells?" Theo asked. "Your outrage has nothing to do with his banning women from evening prayers or watches for the dead?"

"It is all of one piece. Nestorius alienates the people, the monks, and the women of Constantinople. He says women are so weak that being out at night leads to promiscuity! He even denies I am a virgin!" Her teeth ground in frustration.

"Now we get to the heart of the matter. I heard his comment that you and Paulinus are lovers. He truly is unaware of your likes and dislikes." Theo laughed.

Pulcheria took a deep breath to calm herself. "This slander against an Augusta blackens your reputation as well. I am your sister. What I do, for good or ill, reflects on you, Brother."

Her icy tones removed the smile from his face. "I have taken steps to restore your reputation. I assured Nestorius you have never shown the weakness typical of young women and conducted adulterous affairs. He will apologize to you."

"I will forgive him as the Good Lord requires. That won't be enough to prevent the turmoil that is coming." She ceased her pacing and stood, shaking with rage. *Why can't I get through to him?* "Nestorius preaches heresy in denying Mary is the Mother of God—long-settled doctrine."

"Dearest Sister." Theo took her arm. "Ever my champion and advisor. But on this you are wrong. Nestorius is a godly man and I approve his positions. Just yesterday, he said, 'Give me the world free of heretics and I'll give you heaven on earth.' I'll publish a list of heresies and penalties shortly. Constantinople will be a pure place."

"And who are these heretics?"

"The Novatians, Manicheans, Arians, and other Christians that deviate from orthodoxy."

"Oh, God." Pulcheria put a hand to her mouth. "You take away the people's entertainments and direct them to persecute their Christian neighbors? The city will riot and despair."

Theo dropped her arm, frowning. "I thought you, of all people, would be pleased. You taught me to love God. We turn the people toward the orthodox religion. We rid them of the erroneous beliefs that threaten their immortal souls."

Pulcheria shivered at the implications for Theo's reign. "This goes beyond religion and belief. This threatens your rule. Most of your generals are Arian. What if they abandon you?" She dropped to her knees. "I'm begging you, Brother. Give up your support for Nestorius. He will bring you to ruin."

"I'm sure Nestorius will not be so foolish." Theo raised Pulcheria from her knees and kissed her on the forehead. "Go in peace, with my blessings."

Dismissed, Pulcheria left, mourning. *This is what I wrought! Without me by his side, Theo alienates his people and strays from the true path into heresy. I must save my brother from this disastrous bishop, not only for his reign, but for his soul's sake. But how?*

# Chapter 25



*Imperial Palace, July 428*

GENERAL, THERE'S A COMMOTION OUTSIDE."
Ardaburius looked up from the worktable in his palace office. His guard stood in the door. "What's the problem?"

"A man who says he's from your church claims the new bishop is trying to confiscate it. He calls on you for help in repelling the attack."

"Let him in."

A young priest, breathing heavily, pushed past the guard. "Thank you, General. Please. We need your help."

"Stephen, isn't it?" The young man nodded. "Have some water and tell me what happened."

He handed the priest a cup of water, which he gulped. "Nestorius is at the door of our church. He demands we vacate the building and hand it over to him. Father Andrew has barred the door to him and his followers, but I don't know how long he can hold out."

"Christ on the cross! Doesn't that idiot bishop know who we are?"

"He says Arians are heretics. We should convert or leave the city."

"I'll settle this." The General grabbed his helmet and called for his escort and mounts to meet them at the Chalke Gate.

They rode to the German district of the city, where most of the army's dependents lived and several officers had substantial homes. Streets grew crowded the closer he got to the church. Most people recognized him, calling for his help in saving their church and trailing behind his squad of soldiers.

Ardaburius broke through the crowd into a small square. A modest brick and timber church, shops, and apartment buildings faced a central fountain. He reined his horse to a stop at the church steps. Nestorius stood at the topmost, shouting through the door. Several of his priests pounded on the brass-bound barrier with thick chunks of wood.

"Bishop! Stop!" the General shouted in his best parade ground voice. Quiet descended in the near vicinity, but the vague roar of a crowd thundered on the next block.

Nestorius turned. "I am on the emperor's business! This church preaches the heresy of Arianism. It must be closed."

"Do you know who I am, Bishop?"

"It matters not."

"I am *magister militum* for the Emperor's Armies in His Presence. I and my men protect the emperor and the city against our enemies. This is *my* church!"

"Then you are a heretic and should have no place in the emperor's presence, much less be a general in his army!"

"We Arians won the right to worship in our own *Christian* churches through our service to Emperor and Empire. We've had that right for ten years!" Ardaburius sharply reined his horse, which pranced and shied in response to his agitation. "You, Bishop, take your people and go before I drag you from the steps."

"The emperor will hear of this." Nestorius shook his fist at the general.

"I'll make sure of it!" Ardaburius shouted back.

"Fire! The church is on fire!" Shouts went up from the crowd.

The general looked up to see flames licking the wooden roof. Smoke curled from narrow windows. He rode up the steps, sweeping Nestorius and his men aside, and pounded on the door with his sword hilt, shouting, "Father Andrew, bring your people out! It's Ardaburius. I'll protect you!"

The door gave way. Several men in multiple layers of vestments, carrying altar cloths, chalices, and other church treasures, stumbled through the entrance, coughing. The last one through halted in front of Nestorius. "You'll never set foot inside our church, Bishop!"

Nestorius, red-faced, retreated from the flames.

Ardaburius guided his mount, snorting and wild-eyed from the smoke and heat, back down the steps.

"It's spreading!" the crowd cried.

Ardaburius looked up. Sparks lit on roofs of nearby buildings. Cursing roundly, the General dismounted. "You men, get buckets and start a line at the fountain. Call out the local vigiles! Let's get this under control before the whole city goes up."

"God cleanses by fire!" Nestorius shouted

The general turned to the errant bishop. "Leave now, or I'll toss you into the flames myself!"

Nestorius and his followers fled to shouts of "firebrand" as the local fire patrol arrived with ladders, pickaxes, and additional buckets.

Ardaburius accosted the captain of the fire brigade. "Can you save the church?"

The stocky freedman, arms scarred by past burns, shook his head. "The church is gone. We'll concentrate on saving the buildings next to it."

"I have soldiers. What can we do?" Ardaburius wiped soot from his face.

"Make sure people are out of those apartments. Join the bucket lines dousing the buildings. My men will knock down the church and try to contain the fire." The captain gazed into the still morning sky. "Luckily, we have no wind. Where's a good dousing rain when you need it?"

Ardaburius deployed his men, then ran into the four-story apartment building next to the church, shouting, "Fire! Everyone out!" The smell of smoke pervaded the first floor. *From the outside, or was the roof going on this building?* A trickle of people raced downstairs clutching odd-shaped bundles of clothes and small chests. One old man carried a cage with a blanket thrown over it, which failed to keep the frantic bird inside from squawking. Luckily, few were home at this time of day.

"Help!" A frantic female voice called from the top floor. "Help, please!"

The general sprinted up three flights, choking and gasping for air. *I'm getting too old for this!*

A young woman, with a baby strapped to her chest and a toddler clutching her skirts, carried a gray-haired woman on her back. "Thank the Good Lord! I don't think I can carry my mother down the steps. She can't walk!"

"I'll get her out." Ardaburius took a steadying breath. "Any others on this floor?"

The young woman shook her head.

Ardaburius took her frail mother in his arms. She weighed little more than a child!

"Good! Now go. I'll be right behind you."

The old woman cackled in his ear. "The Good Lord bless you, Sir! I begged Mariana to leave me, but she refused. You've saved more than my life today."

"Glad to be of service, Grandmother."

Back in the square, Ardaburius deposited his charges with a group of holy women attached to his church. They had set up an aid station: giving water, treating burns, and comforting victims. He surveyed the scene. The vigiles demolished the church with battering rams, pulled apart burning timbers with pickaxes, and spread sand on the embers. Bucket brigades on ladders doused roofs and walls of nearby buildings. Unless the wind picked up, it looked like they could confine the damage to this square.

"Water, General?" A heavily pregnant woman, with a round face and curly blonde hair, handed him a clay cup.

"Thanks!" He gulped the water. "How do you know me?"

"My husband, Flavius Marcian, is your tribune." Dimples appeared in her cheeks as she patted her stomach. "We're to name him Ardaburius, if he's a boy."

"Quite an honor." He grinned through soot and returned the cup. "Thanks for the water."

He ran to the fountain to join a bucket brigade. *What a mess! Will we be able to rebuild our church? Does the emperor turn against us or does the bishop overstep his bounds? In either case, I must consult with Pulcheria!*

*Episcopal Palace, Alexandria, Egypt, September 428*

"Wretched man!" Bishop Cyril of Alexandria muttered as he read over reports from his agents in Constantinople. He reached for a cooling draught of melon juice. The sultry summer lingered in the Nile delta, turning his saturnine face red with heat and sweat. His anger only grew with the reading.

"Which man?" Paul, his arch deacon and scribe, looked up from his own stack of papers.

"The Bishop of Constantinople. Nestorius. Those traitorous clerics brought our dispute over that church in the Rhokatis quarter to the Constantinople Bishop—as if he had any rule over us!—and *he* brought it to the emperor. I might be charged in an ecclesiastical court with that Antiochene as judge!" Cyril stood to look out the window, hoping for an errant breeze from the sea. "Why take such a trivial matter to the emperor, if not to embarrass me? First

Nestorius declines to send me the traditional gifts due my office when he took his See. Now he hopes to bring me up on charges."

Paul leaned back and fanned himself with a report. "I heard he convinced the emperor to introduce an annual memorial to that other Antiochene Chrysostom at the imperial court."

Cyril turned, back stiff, jaw set. "Is he trying to assert the primacy of the Antioch See over Alexandria's? That will never happen." He sat, taking up a reed pen. "I'll direct my agents to send me copies of his sermons, speeches, and prayers. If he mumbles when he shits, I'll hear of it. My agents say he is extreme in his beliefs, and close to preaching heresy. Nestorius will learn it does not pay to dispute with the Bishop of Alexandria."

*Constantinople, December 428*

The Feast of Mary. Pulcheria surveyed the Great Church crowded with women—highborn noblewomen in their finest silks, lowly washerwomen in their cleanest woolens, holy women in their somber colors, and, of course, the Virgin Princesses and their following. Men attended as well, but women far outnumbered them. They came to be celebrated as well as to celebrate the Mother of God. Pulcheria settled in her seat with a sigh.

One year earlier, the gentle Sisinnius held the See, and peace reigned. Now all was in turmoil over that wretched Nestorius and his fanaticism. He sat on his throne behind the pulpit in full episcopal raiment—gold pectoral cross and ring, casula embroidered with gold and silver crosses, and crozier in the shape of a gold-headed shepherd's crook. The mere sight of him made blood pound in Pulcheria's temple. What a difference a year makes!

After opening rituals, Father Proclus took the pulpit to deliver the traditional sermon on the Virgin Mary. Proclus was an ambitious man, a stout supporter of Mary Theotokos, and a good friend. After months of controversy and recriminations from the bishop, Pulcheria looked forward to hearing something pleasing.

"Our present gathering, in honor of the Most Holy Virgin, inspires me, brethren, to offer Her a word of praise, of benefit also for those who have come to this holy celebration. It is in praise of women, a glorification of their gender, a celebration of She Who is both Mother and Virgin at the same time. O desired and wondrous gathering! O nature, celebrate that whereby honor is rendered to

Woman; rejoice, O human race, that in which the Virgin is glorified."

*An auspicious start.* Pulcheria sat back, hands folded, smiling. Nestorius looked calm. He shortly wouldn't be.

"The Holy Mother of God, the Virgin Mary, has gathered us here."

Nestorius sat up straighter. He regularly upbraided people for using the term "Mother of God" and suggested they use the title Christotokos—Mother of Christ—instead. As planned, Proclus baited him, goading Nestorius into publicly expressing his heresy.

"She is the pure treasure of virginity," Proclus continued, "the intended paradise of Second Adam, the place where the union of natures—divine and human—was accomplished. The Lover of Mankind did not disdain to be born of woman, since She gave Him life in His human nature. If this Mother had not remained a Virgin, the Child born of Her might be a mere man, and the birth would not be miraculous in any way. Since She remained a Virgin after giving birth, how is He Who is born not God?"

Pulcheria smiled. *The heart of the matter.* If someone denied Mary the title Mother of God, they denied Christ's divinity.

Proclus continued supporting his argument with quote after quote from scripture. He concluded, "Through these words, the Holy Virgin and Mother of God is clearly indicated. Let all contention cease, and let the Holy Scripture enlighten our reason, so that we too may receive the Heavenly Kingdom unto all eternity. Amen."

The congregation thundered back, "Amen!"

Nestorius rose from his episcopal throne and took the pulpit. "It is not surprising that you who love Christ should applaud those who preach in honor of the blessed Mary, for the fact that she became the temple of our Lord's flesh exceeds everything else worthy of praise."

Pulcheria's eyebrows rose. *Did the Good Bishop concede the point?*

"But whoever claims—without qualification—that *God* was born of Mary prostitutes the reputation of the faith. Has God a mother? If so, we may excuse paganism for giving mothers to its deities. Mary was not Theotokos. For that which is born of flesh is flesh. A creature did not bring forth Him who is uncreated; the Father did not beget by the Virgin a new God."

"Heresy!" A man stood in the nave, shaking his clenched fist at the bishop.

"Who is that man?" Arcadia whispered to Pulcheria.

"I believe that's Eusebius, a high official in our brother's government."

"Not a holy man?"

"No, but a godly one. I spoke with him frequently when we resided in the palace. I believe his faith will bring him to service in the church. Now he speaks for the people. If Nestorius were wise, he'd listen closely. I expect he will not."

"Bishop, recant your words!" Eusebuis demanded. "The nature of Christ was settled over a hundred years ago. The Divine Word underwent a second birth in the flesh of a woman. Christ is God. Mary is His mother. Mary is the Mother of God."

"It's not that simple…"

The restless crowd shouted "Heresy!" "Blessed is Mary Theotokos!" and, most pleasing to Pulcheria: "Blessed are the Virgin Princesses! All grace to the Most Pious Ones!"

Nestorius tried to regain control with his golden voice and rhetorical style but went unheard by the thundering crowd. He gathered his robes and left the pulpit, back rigid, face stormy. Just as Pulcheria hoped.

As they exited the Great Church, Proclus approached the princesses and bowed. "May I have a word, Your Serenity?"

Pulcheria took the man's arm, leading him a few steps away from her women. "Nicely done, Proclus. I believe we have our bishop on the run."

"Thank you, Augusta. Nestorius made his own mistakes, and they were many. It is up to us to capitalize on them." He watched the jubilant crowd of women streaming past. "I don't understand his antipathy to Mary Theotokos. It's been settled doctrine for years. Why does he bring this trouble down on himself?"

"Some few men hate women and cannot abide their presence or influence in any sphere. If these men have no power except over their wives and daughters, it is bad enough. I've seen women in my hospitals bruised and battered for no reason other than men believe they have the right to beat their women. I believe Nestorius is such a man.

"Unfortunately, his position gives him the power to do great harm. He seeks to strip women of all dignity and worth and uses his position to do so. To him, every woman, no matter how holy or selfless, is a vile daughter of Eve, a vessel for sin and temptress to men. I do not deny such women exist, but most women do not deserve such approbation. He also slandered and tried to humiliate me. I will not stand by and let my virtue be maligned."

Proclus nodded. "The people know of your goodness and piety. They do not believe his lies."

"I know." She suppressed a wolfish grin. "It is time the bishop knows it, as well. I want you to preach on Mary Theotokos in my church in the Pulcheria quarter. If the bishop remains recalcitrant and orders you to stop, we women will abandon his churches and hold services in private residences. Let him preach to empty pews."

She continued to plot as they walked to her wagon. "I will make sure Nestorius' words against Mary Theotokos reach the other Sees. We have the support of the suburban bishops, the archimandrites, and the monks. Even that snake Cyril of Alexandria backs us, though I suspect it has more to do with his own animus than the holiness of the cause." She patted Proclus' arm. "What do you know of this Eusebius, who called out our Good Bishop? I believe we can enlist him in our plans to rid the city of this wretched man."

# Chapter 26



*Hebdomon Palace, January 431*

Have you seen this?" Arcadia and Marina showed their sister the codex.

"Address to the Most Pious Princesses, From the Bishop of Alexandria," Pulcheria read. "I have. He sent the same, addressed to Theo and Athenais. With Cyril entering the fray, our two-year battle against Nestorius is coming to a head. Have you read it?"

Her sisters nodded.

"Your thoughts?"

"He is most persuasive in his support of Mary as Mother of God. He shows how, historically, bishops have referred to Mary as Theotokos," Arcadia said.

"I counted over two hundred New Testament references to prove Nestorius wrong. Bishop Cyril suggests we share our thoughts with our brother." Marina giggled. "The man is very thorough."

"And flattering to us." Arcadia pointed to a passage. "He begins with praise for 'the sacred and wholly pure brides of Christ, famous for their virginity, which glorifies the court and keeps our image brilliant throughout the world.'" She looked up, a twinkle in her eye. "It's good you taught us humility, Sister, or this might feed our vanity."

"Cyril is a subtle thinker and dangerous enemy. I've had dealings with him in the past. When I was but a year into my regency, he stirred up the populace of Alexandria in his bid for supremacy. They nearly murdered our prefect, and did murder a learned woman, Hypatia, a philosopher and teacher. I still regret not investigating that incident more thoroughly, but she was a pagan and I was new to my rule. The city was purged of dissent. It seemed best to let the situation rest." Pulcheria shook her head. "Nestorius opened a hornet's nest when he threatened to bring the Bishop of Alexandria to an ecclesiastic court. This goes beyond a simple doctrinal dispute and is now personal between them. Cyril seeks our support. We can use him in our campaign to rid ourselves of this heretical bishop."

"Should we visit our brother?" Arcadia asked.

"Yes, but I think not to overwhelm him. We go one at a time."

"Poor Theo." Arcadia gave her a mock sorrowful look. "Three holy sisters. Three lectures."

### Imperial Palace, February 431

"How goes the Code, Brother?" Pulcheria took her brother's arm as they walked through a room of lawyers and scribes busily sorting through stacks of papers and making notes. "This is quite an undertaking."

"I'm proud of the progress we've made. Within a few years we will compile all the laws of the empire and can set about simplifying and expunging the out-of-date ones. We'll restore order to our magistrates and courts."

"I'm proud of you, too, Theo." She kissed him on the cheek. "You're a great emperor, just like your grandfather."

He rubbed a hand through his thinning hair. "In all ways but one, I suppose?"

"I always say what I mean, Brother."

"You're not here to castigate me about Nestorius?" He smiled ruefully. "Arcadia and Marina visited earlier in the week, fortified with the writing of Cyril of Alexandria."

"If your two holy sisters, the Good Bishop of Alexandria, your Generals, the monks, and people of Constantinople can't convince you to abandon Nestorius, why should I believe my influence will prevail? I am here only to support you, if I can."

They left the scriptorium, with its smell of vellum and ink behind.

"The gardens?" she asked. "You look as if you could use some sunshine."

As they passed from shadow into light, Theo's shoulders loosened. He turned his face to the winter sun, like a flower seeking sustenance. "I have missed our strolls, Sister. I can always count on you to counsel me wisely."

"I would be at your side every day, if you wish it." Pulcheria pulled her wool cloak tighter as a brisk February breeze wafted in from the sea, bringing the scent of salt and dead fish.

"I know." He patted her arm. "This Nestorius business is a hornet's nest. I don't like the divisions and contentions it causes—between us, and within the empire. Bishop Celestine of Rome has now demanded Nestorius recant his so-called heresies or face ex-communication. The metropolitans preach to empty churches, since the women withdrew to worship in private residences. Can't you do something?"

Pulcheria shrugged. "What would you have me do? Nestorius has made enemies of the monks and women with his heresies and disrespect. They do not wish to honor Nestorius with their presence. The earliest Christians met to worship in private homes. We are following a long tradition."

"They were persecuted!" Theo said, exasperated. "You can attend Church without fear."

"Women are told to stay in their homes, and monks in their cells. Bishop Nestorius is clear that we have no say in the Church or any part in Christ's directive to alleviate the plight of the poor and dispossessed." Pulcheria raised an eyebrow. "Beyond that, he denies Christ's divinity when he preaches Mary is not the Mother of God. We don't have to participate in the bishop's heresies at the peril of our souls."

Theo seemed to understand she would not budge on this issue. He tried a more personal appeal. "About these letters from Cyril. They circulate widely and tell one and all we are at odds. Ria, it's…embarrassing!"

"Cyril knows nothing of our love for one another. We can disagree on Nestorius, but that does not diminish my loyalty to you. That said, you cannot let this situation continue. The people grow riotous." She sat on a marble bench, closed her eyes, and lifted her face to the sun. "What do you intend to do?" she murmured, enjoying the meager warmth. She sensed Theo taking a seat to her right and opened her eyes.

"This is a doctrinal issue. The bishops should decide. I'm calling an Ecumenical Council for the next Pentecost in June. All the bishops will convene to resolve these difficulties."

"Where will this Council be held?"

"I haven't decided. Chalcedon, perhaps. Or Ephesus?"

"Chalcedon is just across the water. People might think you controlled the

Council if it were that close. Ephesus would be better. It's central and on the coast, so the bishops can easily reach it by land or sea."

"We can also easily provision a large gathering from ships, if the Council goes beyond a week or two. Ephesus, it is." Theo sighed. "Thank you, Sister." His hand took hers.

Pulcheria smiled. *And so it begins.*

*Episcopal Palace, Alexandria, Egypt, March 431*

"The Council will be in Ephesus!" Cyril cried to Archdeacon Paul. "Only Alexandria would have been better, and we could not hope for that. I see the Augusta's hand in this. The See of Ephesus is a rival of Constantinople's and a natural ally of mine. Bishop Memnon is a firm Mariologist. We can work with him. The Council will take place in a Theotokos Church. Nestorius cannot prevail in a church dedicated to the Virgin." He chuckled. "We have won before the Council begins!"

Cyril opened a second imperial letter. His face darkened, and hands shook with anger as he tossed it to his desk.

"Bishop?" Paul looked concerned. "Bad news?"

"The emperor chides me as if I were a child. He accuses me of sowing discord between him and his sister, as if he had no hand in the matter." Cyril took the letter up, read it again, and smiled. "On the other hand, the emperor says he and his sister are of one accord. I believe Pulcheria Augusta has made her move. We will soon see our most holy and Virgin Empress back in power." He looked up. "In the meantime, we have a war to prepare for."

"War?" Paul's voice squeaked in alarm.

"Ephesus. We will seize and occupy it. Nestorius will have no support whatsoever, and these scurrilous attacks on me will cease!"

*Episcopal Palace, Ephesus, June 431*

"Do something, Memnon!" Nestorius shook with anger. "The Egyptians riot in your streets. Those so-called monks attack me and my supporters. Last night, they broke into the house where one of my deacons stayed, pulled him out of bed, and beat him senseless."

"I believe they are not monks, but the bishop's hospital attendants." The Bishop of Ephesus pointedly corrected the Bishop of Constantinople. "They are called parabalans."

"I don't care what they're called. They are murderous bullies intent on making this council a farce!" Nestorius' eyes flashed with indignation.

"Not all the rioters are from Alexandria. Quite a few come from your own See to protest against you." Memnon had put his own contingent of rowdies at Cyril's disposal, but Nestorius didn't have to know that. He stood, putting a hand on his colleague's shoulder, urging him toward the door. "The Council convenes tomorrow. Go home. Prepare your position."

"I am not without my own resources." Nestorius blocked the door. "Count Candidian, the emperor's agent, has his soldiers, and I bring my own monks and supporters."

"Fine." Memnon gave the Bishop a little push out the door. "They will provide you protection from the Egyptians."

Nestorius shrugged off his hand, glared, and left.

*Good!* Memnon smiled. *Tomorrow we restore Mary to her proper place and rid our church of this heresy.*

The next morning Memnon presided over the opening proceedings in the Theotokos Church, which abutted his episcopal palace. A large fresco of Mary with the infant Jesus loomed behind the altar. Images of the apostles trooped down one wall, while the other showed scenes from Christ's life. Oil chandeliers lit the dark interior; sweet incense struggled to mask the scent of hundreds of male bodies sweating in the June heat.

Cyril's and Memnon's supporters packed the nave behind sitting rows of bishops from throughout the empire. Memnon had met with each delegate and knew their preferences. A couple wavered, but Cyril's men convinced them to take his side. Memnon wasn't completely happy with the Bishop of Alexandria's methods, but they were effective in achieving the result the Augusta wished.

After prayers, a small group of imperial officers, led by Count Candidian approached the episcopal throne. He bowed. "Bishop Memnon. I have come from the emperor to open the Council."

"Read your charge." Memnon waved a ringed hand at the young officer.

Candidian unrolled a scroll. "The Most Honorable and Pious Emperor of Rome, Theodosius, Second of that Name, charges this Ecumenical Council to resolve the confusion arising from disagreements over doctrinal issues according to the canons, correct the failures of the past, and provide firm guidance toward piety before God and the good of the state. Do your duty."

Memnon rapped his staff on the floor. "Who brings charges before this Council?"

Nestorius jumped to his feet. "We're not here to discuss charges! We're here to discuss doctrine."

"Heretic! Drive him out!" rose from the crowd behind the bishops. "Death to the heretic Nestorius!"

More people took up the chant. A few bishops started to shove Nestorius and his supporters. They shoved back. Some monks brought out short sticks to beat the protestors. One struck an elderly bishop on the head; blood gushed down the old man's shocked face.

"Murder! Nestorius commits murder!" several protestors cried. The crowd surged forward.

Memnon rapped his staff on the floor. "Order! Order! Return to your seats."

To no effect. This was not supposed to happen! He had planned an orderly reading of charges and votes on ex-communication.

"Count! Help!" the frightened Nestorius called.

Candidian and his lightly armed soldiers formed a protective wedge around the beleaguered Bishop. "Which way?" the Count shouted at Memnon.

"Out the back!" He pointed towards a corridor to the left.

Candidian and his soldiers escorted Nestorius out of the nave.

Cheers erupted as they left. Memnon rapped his staff on the floor for quiet. "Take your seats. Evacuate the injured."

The injured elderly bishop, along with a couple of others with bumps and bruises, left the church for aid. The rest returned to their seats. Memnon stood, intoning, "Again, who brings charges before this Council?"

"I do." Cyril of Alexandria rose. "As I've demonstrated in these texts, Nestorius is in error in his denial of Mary as Mother of God. He should be deposed from his See and excommunicated. Bishop Celestine of Rome agrees, and asked me to act on his behalf in this matter."

The Church shook with acclamations.

At the end of the day, as the crowd left the church, people lined the streets and cheered. A huge crowd of women, bearing lighted candles and incense censers, escorted Memnon, Cyril, and their supporters through the streets.

Mary was still Queen of Heaven and Mother of God.

*As she should be.* Memnon beamed.

*Hebdomon Palace, July 431*

"How goes Ephesus, Sister?" Arcadia looked up from sewing a small wool tunic for a poor child. Pulcheria perused a dispatch. Their assembled coterie of women worked at their usual tasks of spinning, sewing and embroidery.

"Not as I had hoped." Pulcheria frowned. "Bishop Cyril, as usual, overreached himself. He incited violence in the streets and the Council. That man!" She put down the paper to rub her temples. "I had hoped he would leave his army of unruly monks in Egypt. We had the bishops to overrule Nestorius on doctrine. Because of the threats and rioting, several bishops switched sides. Our holy cause is compromised because of human pride and privilege!"

Arcadia motioned a servant to attend to her sister. The young woman brought a soothing drink of willow bark and honey.

Pulcheria took a sip, smiling at her sister. "Thank you, Arcadia. I don't know how I'd fare if you didn't look after me."

"You'd starve at your desk or die of apoplexy and exasperation," Arcadia teased.

Pulcheria picked up the missive to examine it again. "Bishop John of Antioch arrived late and immediately set about winning a result more to our brother's liking. He has convened a smaller counter synod, claiming the one Memnon convened illegal because not all the bishops had arrived. John's synod excommunicated and deposed both Memnon and Cyril. Memnon's synod excommunicated and deposed the Nestorians."

Pulcheria stood and began pacing, to stimulate thought.

"This is why the Church should not be left to its own affairs! The bishops mire themselves in charges and countercharges, arguing the smallest minutia, flinging excommunication at each other as if they were pagan curses. And is it for the greater glory of God or to benefit the souls of the people?"

The assembled women shook their heads, muttering, "No!" to the rhetorical question.

"It is not! These bishops live in luxury in their episcopal palaces, dressed in rich robes, attended by scribes and servants. Most are petty tyrants, ruling over their narrow kingdoms, squabbling with their neighbors over who is most

201

powerful and enjoys the most influence over the mind of the emperor and souls of his people. It is the rare bishop these days who is truly a holy man."

Pulcheria sat at her worktable. "I must send a note to Theo. The bishops failed in their task. He must decide which finding he will accept, and what will be the law of the land and practice of the Church. Theo seeks a reconciliation with us, if only to counter rumors of our discord. It's time we present a united front."

"You will accept Nestorius?" Arcadia asked, eyes round with disbelief.

Pulcheria smiled. "I didn't say that, Sister."

# Chapter 27

*Imperial Palace, July 431*

PULCHERIA SAT TO THE RIGHT OF HER BROTHER IN THE DAPHNE audience room. It felt good to be back in the seat of power. The ancient archimandrite, Dalmatius, stood before them in rough brown robes, his gray hair and beard long and matted. The revered holy man hobbled forward with the help of a staff. Pulcheria caught a whiff of sweat, urine, and incense.

Theo stepped down from his throne and personally sat the ancient on a stool. Dalmatius looked at Theo with blazing eyes. "Emperor, I have broken my vow. I left my cell and life of perpetual prayer for the first time in forty-eight years because this cause is most important to the souls of your people."

Pulcheria nodded. The holy archimandrite's sacrifice, to confront her brother, must surely shake Theo to his core. He had wanted Dalmatius as bishop and had high regard for the holy man.

"I am most humbled by your presence, Father, and understand the issue must be very grave to bring you from your holy house into our presence." Theo bowed briefly. "In what way may I serve you?"

"Agents and agitators block communication with you from your most humble and holy servants in Ephesus. Bishop Cyril sent me a message concealed in this beggar's staff, as the only way his words might come to your ears. He begs you to receive his emissaries." The old man unscrewed the steel tip from his staff, pulled out the rolled-up message, and handed it to Theo.

Her brother read the missive, then shot an angry glance around the receiving room. "I had no notion messages and emissaries were blocked from my presence. I vowed to hear both sides, if the bishops could come to no conclusion."

Pulcheria was pleased he had given no such orders. It meant Theo was open to persuasion—from the outside, if not from her.

Dalmatius continued. "Your own man, Count Candidian, set spies and guards on all the gates of Ephesus and Constantinople, to stop any word from Bishop Memnon and Bishop Cyril reaching you."

Theo reddened under the holy man's scrutiny. "I will replace Count Candidian and order the way clear at once. Both delegations shall provide their findings, and I will decide."

"That is all I ask." The holy man rose. "Blessings on the house of Theodosius. God give wisdom to the Pious Emperor and long life to the Virgin Augusta."

"Thank you, Father, for your wisdom and blessings." Pulcheria rose to escort the old man to the door. "Our guards will provide a litter to your monastery."

"That is not necessary, Daughter. The people escort me and offer a shoulder when I falter." She knelt before him. He put a dirty hand on her head. "The people love you, Augusta. You are their voice with the emperor. God bless you and give you strength to guide your brother onto the right path. Amen."

"Amen." Pulcheria rose.

The old man hobbled out to a cheering crowd. Dalmatius' command rang in her ears. She was the voice of the people. They needed to be heard.


THE NEXT WEEK, AFTER HEARING BOTH DELEGATIONS, THEO RETIRED TO THE Saint Stephen chapel to pray on his decision. Pulcheria silently prayed in the audience room that he would make the right one and disavow Nestorius and his heresies. She took the opportunity to circulate among the courtiers to see how the court reacted to the emissaries. As she suspected, most were cautious, awaiting Theo's decision before taking a stand. About to leave in disgust, she spied Arcadia entering the audience room, face screwed in a worried frown. She and Marina were supposed to be ministering in the hospital attached to the Great Church. What could have brought her to the court?

Pulcheria hurried over. "Arcadia, what's wrong? Where's Marina and our ladies?"

"Marina's fine. She and the ladies stayed to work at the hospital." Arcadia wiped sweat from her flushed face. "I came to warn Theo. The people gather in the Great Church and demand his presence. They want Nestorius gone. They threaten riot if he does not answer their call."

"It's as I feared." Pulcheria reviewed Theo's options, and could come up with only a single satisfactory one. She escorted Arcadia out. "Take an extra contingent of guards to the hospital. Escort Marina and the ladies back to our palace in Hebdomon. I'll fetch Theo. We will confront the people."

Arcadia nodded. "Be careful, Ria. I've never seen such a restless mob. God be with you."

"And with you." Pulcheria kissed her sister on the cheek. "Now go."

Pulcheria hurried through corridors, past dawdling servants and alert guards, to the chapel. She entered to find her brother prostrate before the shrine. The carved ivory triptych, covering the small vault where the saint's bones resided, showed the adventus from ten years ago in exquisite detail. The sight brought back memories of her triumph. She waited, head bowed, sending her own prayers to the Protomartyr for success in this next battle.

Theo must have heard her rustling. He slowly came to his feet. A beatific smile graced his face to tug at her heart. "Ria! Did you come to join me in prayer?"

"No." This was the Theo she loved, the gentle man who shared her devotion to God. Pulcheria was genuinely sorry she had to spoil his peace. "Brother, the people have occupied the Great Church. They demand your presence."

"What for?" Theo stood gape mouthed.

"They recognize your responsibility to govern both Empire and Church. They tire of turmoil in the streets. Riot and dissension are not good for trade or family. The people have rejected Nestorius. They wish his ouster. Some even demand his death. You must take control, make a decision. Be aware, siding with Nestorius will mean the end of your rule."

"I know." He turned his back on her to look up at the bejeweled cross above the marble altar. "But Nestorius is a friend and loyal supporter. How can I give him up?" His shoulders shook with the violence of his emotions.

"Theo." She put an arm around him. "His time is done. All stand against him and his heresies. Your continued support brings discord to your people, confusion to their minds, danger to their souls. Their love for you is slipping away. Go to them. Show your people you are their Father and Emperor. You love them and care for them. You protect them from their enemies, both external and spiritual. They need you."

"Husband."

Pulcheria looked over her shoulder. A visibly distraught Athenais stood in the door.

Theo turned around. "What's wrong?"

"Flacilla." Athenais wrung her hands, eyes darting from place to place. "The doctors say you should come."

"I didn't know she was ill. How serious is it?" Pulcheria took her sister-in-law's hand in hers, looking into her anguished eyes. She barely knew her six-year old niece, since she left the palace.

"The doctors are with her. She runs a high fever." Athenais reached out to her husband. "Theo, will you come? I need you."

"Yes, My Love." Theo took Athenais from Pulcheria's grasp, escorting her from the room, an arm about her waist. He looked back over his shoulder. "Ria, will you go to the Great Church? Hear what the people have to say?"

"Of course." She bowed slightly. "I'll say prayers for Flacilla while I'm there."

FOR ONCE, PULCHERIA WAS GRATEFUL FOR HER ESCORT OF GUARDS. THE SQUARE outside the Chalke Gate and the Great Church teemed with people: monks, holy women, shopkeepers, tradesmen, dock workers, all manner of people mixed and cheered. Monks led choruses in praise of Cyril "the gift of God" and in condemnation of Nestorius "the heretic." They demanded Nestorius and his supporters be thrown from the episcopal palace and delivered to flames as "sorcerers and shameful creatures."

She entered the Great Church, head high with confidence her people would listen to her. Despite the press, they parted before her, crying "Make way for the Virgin Augusta! Make way for the Pious One!" She reached the front of the crowd and mounted the steps to stand before the altar, flanked by her guards. Sweat trickled down her back and ribs. The Great Church, normally a pleasant place in late July, reflected a fierce heat from the crowd, as well as a sense of violence. Pulcheria looked left to make sure there was an avenue of escape into the priests' quarters if needed. *Please God, give me strength and keep my voice steady!*

"Peace, my good people." The crowd quieted. "I have come among you with armed guards in the sanctity of the Church because there is riot and danger in the streets."

"No danger to you, Augusta!" several people shouted. "The Holy Virgin protects you!"

"Why have you assembled in this holy place?" Pulcheria cried.

"The emperor must listen!"

"Nestorius must die!"

"Cyril must be restored!"

Again, Pulcheria signaled for silence. "I have heard your voices, and the emperor will hear them through me. He would come, but his daughter, the Princess Flacilla is ill and he will not leave her side."

Murmurs of sympathy and concern spread through the crowd. The feelings of anger and menace subsided.

"You must do your part, as well. Go home in peace. Leave this holy place for prayers and joy, not riot and despair. Be assured, I am on the side of our most holy and revered Mary Theotokos, as is my brother, your emperor! He will hear your words. Do the Holy Virgin honor and moderate your behavior."

The crowd erupted in a chorus of "Many years to Pulcheria! She who strengthens the faith! Many years to the Virgin Augusta. Blessings on the orthodox one!"

The cries spread to the people outside as she left the Great Church. Voices boomed through the square, lifting her soul. Her people! With them at her back, she knew she had won. Nestorius was defeated. *Blessings on you, Mary Theotokos. Thank you, Saint Stephen, for answering my prayer.*

Now she had to convince Theo to do the right thing.

TEARS TRACKED HER FACE AS PULCHERIA RAN A HAND OVER THE SMALL MARBLE coffin. She had forgotten to say a prayer for her niece in the Great Church a week ago but made up for it now. After her speech to the people, they had dispersed. As word of the little princess' illness spread, people brought wooden crosses, dolls, and flowers to the palace gates. Pulcheria knew this was a temporary truce. The people would mourn their loss, but come back all the stronger, probably blaming Nestorius for bringing God's wrath down on the child.

As dawn lightened the sky, she said her last prayer and rose stiffly to greet the morning. She had spent the night on her knees in vigil with her sisters in the palace chapel. Candles burned nearly to their stubs at both ends of the bier.

The doctors had put the grieving Athenais to bed long ago, with a tincture of poppy to help her sleep.

Pulcheria touched Arcadia and Marina lightly on the shoulders. "We have done all we can, sisters. Go, break your fast. I will see to Theo."

Arcadia lifted a tear-stained face, sniffing. "Are you sure we shouldn't accompany you? He is our brother, as well."

"Later, sisters. I have something important to discuss with Theo."

They left.

"Where is my brother?" she asked the guard on the door to the chapel.

"He retired to his quarters late last night, Augusta."

Pulcheria made her way down familiar halls to her brother's suite of rooms. She found him kneeling at a private altar.

She thought her entrance silent, but he looked up before resuming his quiet prayers. Finally, he said, "Amen," and rose.

Pulcheria enveloped him in a fierce hug. "Flacilla is with God now, and beyond all pain."

"I know, but it still hurts, Ria." He sobbed, turning away, shoulders shaking. "She was only six, with so much life to live!"

"Come sit." Pulcheria led her brother to a padded bench and fetched him a cup of water. She settled next to him to watch the sun come up through the narrow windows as he mastered his grief.

After several minutes, Theo grasped her hand in a painful grip. "My son Arcadius dead. My daughter Flacilla dead. My empire in turmoil. I am cursed."

"You are not cursed, Theo." Pulcheria freed her hand to put an arm around his shoulders. "You have Eudoxia. She's a fine girl. You are still young. Athenais is only twenty-eight. You can have more children."

"I believe God is punishing me for my sins. I enjoy the pleasures of the flesh too much and have neglected my duties to God and Empire. Athenais' womb has not quickened since Flacilla's birth." Theo leaned into her embrace. "You tried to warn me, but I would not listen."

"We cannot know God's reasons. All we can do is obey his commandments." She hesitated. "I would not bring this up in this time of sorrow, but you have already touched upon it. After this week of mourning, the people will return to their riotous ways and the bishops will take up their squabbles. If this tragedy has changed your mind or strengthened your resolve, you need to let the Church and people know. End this turmoil, Brother."

"And your advice?"

"Is already known to you. Pray on what God demands and make your decision."

"I have already prayed. Nestorius must go. I cannot stand against the will of the people and God's judgment." He sighed. "Sister, your support and unfailing advice during this trying time reminded me of your value. Please do me the honor of returning to court as my chief advisor. I realize you will have to curtail some of your charity work, but surely Arcadia and Marina can take up your causes?"

"Oh, Theo." She stroked his hair. "You know you have only to ask and I will obey. Your wife will need you during this time of mourning. I will take some of the burden from your shoulders, and gladly."

# Part IV

## Empress in Exile

## October 437 - April 450

# Chapter 28



*Hebdomon, October 437*

SWEAT TRICKLED DOWN PULCHERIA'S BACK AND GATHERED UNDER HER breasts. Tomorrow, the imperial family celebrated the long-awaited marriage of Eudoxia and Valentinian III, co-ruler of the Roman Empire. Today, they braved a rare fall heat wave with a picnic and archery outside the walls of the city on her Hebdomon estate.

"Well done, Val!" Eudoxia cried as her betrothed sent an arrow straight to the heart of a stuffed target shaped like a deer. Pulcheria looked up from her conversation with her sisters. In the week since Val arrived for his wedding, her niece had become quite enamored. "Can you top him, Papa?"

Pulcheria had to admit the eighteen-year-old emperor from Ravenna created a dashing figure: tall, regular featured, well-muscled. Her brother, although only thirty-six, suffered in comparison. Riding and fasting kept him from corpulence, but he had the weak eyes and stooped shoulders of a scholar.

Theo squinted at the target. "I'm afraid that's too far for my old eyes, Precious. I'll try something closer." He sent an arrow at the nearest round target, puncturing the outermost ring. He laughed, pounding Val on the back. "I concede, young Cousin."

Theo handed his bow and arrows to a servant and joined the women on the bench at the edge of the course. Eudoxia jumped up to take his arm. Athenais turned to watch Val's superior prowess.

"You did fine, Papa. Val has much more experience than you."

"Luckily, I'll never have to keep barbarians from our gates. If I did, we would be overrun." Theo laughed.

"Martial abilities are not required in an emperor, if he picks good and loyal generals," Pulcheria said. "And you, Brother, have provided your empire with the best."

Val, no longer the focus of his intended's attention, walked over, wiping sweat from his brow with a cotton cloth which he then tucked into his leather belt. He grabbed a goblet of chilled wine and sat at Eudoxia's feet.

"Cousin, have you had much martial training?" Pulcheria asked.

"Private instruction in archery and the sword." Val frowned. "Mother felt soldiering too risky for me, in these unsettled times."

"It is no longer necessary to rule from the back of a horse, as our grandfather did. Your mother is wise not to risk her only son."

"Perhaps." Val stared into his cup, frowning.

Athenais stroked her daughter's hair. "You look warm, Sweet. We should go back to the palace for a cool bath before the evening meal."

Val looked at his intended bride and winked. Eudoxia blushed furiously.

Arcadia exchanged a weary glance with Marina. "We will stay here in Hebdomon, Sister, and join the family for the wedding ceremonies tomorrow."

Pulcheria gave each sister the kiss of peace and murmured, "God's grace on you."

Servants gathered their things. Pulcheria took Val's arm on the way to their wagons. "Join me for the ride back, Cousin. I would have a word."

"My pleasure." He masked his disappointment, pulling his gaze from Eudoxia's golden curls and graciously helping Pulcheria into the wagon. He took the padded seat opposite her forward-facing one.

They sat in silence for several minutes as the wagon swayed and creaked along the cobbled road. Soon Val started babbling about the weather and the food.

Pulcheria hid a smile behind her hand. This was an old trick for gaining the upper hand; she almost regretted using it on her young cousin, but he had to learn. When he nearly stuttered to a stop, she looked him in the eyes and said. "I have heard disturbing rumors about you and your court."

"Rumors by their nature are scurrilous. Don't put any stock in them." His eyes darted away.

"I consider my sources quite reliable."

A blush crept up his neck.

Pulcheria pierced him with her stare. "I'm told you sleep with many women, wives and daughters of men in your court."

He briefly squirmed, then stilled, "Lies. I do no such thing."

"Yet these same men receive honors, offices, and favors from your hands." She stared at him in silence. When he made no reply, she continued. "You should realize, these women don't favor you for yourself. They—and their men—seek power over you. It is an age-old stratagem."

"As I said, Cousin, you are in error."

"I love my niece and wish her—and you—all happiness in your marriage. If you are tempted, in the future, do not dishonor her or yourself with this unworthy behavior." This time, as he looked Pulcheria in the eyes, his jaw set in a mulish line. *He is a stubborn, spoiled boy. I'll get no more from him on this subject.* "Now, tell me about General Aetius. Is he really the Great Savior of the West?"

Val's face relaxed a little but did not lose its guarded look for the rest of the ride.

AT A FORMAL COURT RECEPTION THAT EVENING, PULCHERIA NODDED APPROVAL as her Aunt Placidia and Cousin Honoria joined the family in the Daphne audience room. They wore full imperial regalia, heads held high, meeting their relatives as equals. Twelve years had touched her aunt lightly. Honoria, at twenty, had grown into a handsome woman, with her mother's curly brown hair and a long, graceful neck. She also had more womanly curves than her mother, who tended to unfashionable slenderness.

"Placidia!" Athenais enveloped the Western Augusta in a warm embrace after she had been announced. "Welcome."

"My dear." Placidia held Athenais at arm's length. "You are still as beautiful as your patron goddess."

Pulcheria agreed. Athenais looked little older than she had at twenty-three. Still, sadness in her eyes told of her losses: her infant son, her young daughter, and something more. Pulcheria knew her brother shunned his wife's bed; whether in penance for his lustful feelings or guilt over the loss of their children as God's punishment for Nestorius, she had no idea. Athenais' failure to give her husband a male heir reduced her influence at court and with the people. As Theo became more and more ascetic, he also neglected his imperial duties.

Except for his beloved Law Code project, he left most of the running of the empire in Pulcheria's capable hands.

Athenais didn't blush as readily as in her youth but did dimple with a smile. "You will think me a kitchen drudge when you see Eudoxia."

"My wife, a kitchen drudge? Hardly!" Theodosius embraced his aunt and turned to his cousin. "And Honoria! You've grown into a beauty yourself."

Pulcheria, growing restive with the excessive compliments, nodded a greeting. "Aunt, I am glad to see the Lord brought you safely to our shores."

"The Lord and my best horses." Placidia smiled.

Before Pulcheria could retort, Val stepped forward. "Mother, may I present my bride, Licinia Eudoxia?"

Athenais' daughter lived up to her early promise of beauty. At fifteen, the girl was luminous, with porcelain skin, golden curls, and her mother's startling violet eyes. As to her character, Pulcheria could only attest to her frequency at prayers and church. The young woman was shy with her.

Eudoxia cast her eyes modestly down as she approached Placidia, extending her hand and executing a brief curtsy. "Welcome, Mother."

Placidia took her hand in both of hers. "Thank you, my child."

"Is she not exquisite?" Val's eyes gleamed. "I shall have the most beautiful woman in the empire for a bride."

"Maybe then you won't dip your stick in other men's honey pots," Honoria muttered, just loud enough for Pulcheria to catch. She threw the girl a sharp glance. If his sister knew of Val's affairs, what kind of court did Placidia allow?

Pulcheria waved over a trusted older slave, one who had been in her service sixteen years. "You shall attend Princess Eudoxia for the rest of the reception and accompany her to her quarters when finished." Pulcheria noted Val's disappointed look and silently thanked God for the princess' constant chaperonage. He would have a lifetime with his bride; he could wait a few more hours.

Theo indicated a door leading to a smaller audience room. "Let's retire. We have much to discuss, Aunt."

"May I come with you, Mother?" Honoria asked.

"No, dear, stay with your brother and enjoy the reception." Placidia smiled.

"But—"

"No." Placidia firmly cut off Honoria's protest with a raised hand. Her smile disappeared. "Stay with Val and Eudoxia." The two vertical lines marking her forehead deepened. Honoria stalked off; her face marked with lines identical to her mother's.

"Honoria grew into a handsome woman." Athenais took Placidia's arm. "But I sense some tension between you two."

"She has always been a difficult child. Willful and argumentative." Placidia glanced wistfully over her shoulder at her daughter's retreating back.

"You mean she shows spirit and intelligence?" Theo laughed. "I have much experience with women who exhibit those traits."

"Lately she has been asking to sit in council meetings." Placidia sighed.

"The urge to rule runs strong in Theodosius' female line." Pulcheria gave her aunt a significant look. "She sees you ruling for her brother, and my—our…" Pulcheria nodded at Athenais, "influence with Theo. Why should she not want a similar role for herself?"

"I see the truth of your words, but I have experience Honoria does not. Val is of age and rules for himself. I only advise."

Athenais patted Placidia's arm. "Maybe it is time to think of a husband for her. Give her a domain of her own to rule."

"I could never see Honoria's future clearly, as I could Val's." Placidia's face softened. "I only knew what I didn't want for her—an unhappy marriage for the sole purpose of producing heirs. Let's pray your Eudoxia will have many healthy children and make that fate unnecessary."

Athenais' full lips trembled; her eyes brightened with unshed tears. "The palace will seem empty without my only child. But she will be well loved with you." She glanced at her husband through lowered lashes. "I've been thinking I might make a pilgrimage to Jerusalem. It will be good for the people of the Holy Land to see a member of the imperial family and might ease my lonely… uh…soul."

"An admirable ambition, Sister," Pulcheria agreed. "Perhaps time in the Holy Land will have a moderating effect on you."

Athenais' mouth tightened. Her eyes flashed with resentment.

Pulcheria suppressed a sigh. Why did her sister-in-law always twist her meaning and take offence? Obviously, Athenais took her comment as a slight when she meant the Holy Land might give her some peace from her relentless sadness. Pulcheria longed to go to the Holy Land herself and visit the shrines but could not tear herself from her duties.

They came to a sitting room, much more lavishly appointed than the last time Placidia visited. Servants provided a repast of shellfish, cheese, black olives, cold fowl with a pungent fish sauce, and a selection of fruit tarts. Pulcheria admitted Athenais had made her presence felt—at least in the palace—with rich furnishings and regular literary salons. She much preferred her own ascetic residences, especially Hebdomon. The imperial palace was Athenais' domain, and Pulcheria held her tongue for many years, even when Theo complained of his wife's excesses.

Pulcheria removed a cushion from a chair to sit on the bare wood. When they had all settled with wine and food, she said, "I've had opportunity to speak on several occasions with young Valentinian. Your son seems to know little of the state of his empire, for one who rules."

Placidia colored at the bald criticism. "Val is an active boy and grows impatient with administration. Age and marriage will settle him into his duties." She gave Pulcheria a level stare. "And I will be there to guide him."

Pulcheria started to reply, but Theo interrupted. "How fare your borders? The Huns have been raiding our provinces again."

"The Patrician Aetius assures me the Huns are under his control. He recently used them to put down the Burgundian rebellion in Gaul." Placidia pursed her mouth. "As much as I detest the man, he is a cunning general. Aetius guards the western provinces with the fierceness of a mother lion protecting her cubs."

"But he leaves your African provinces orphaned and prey for the Vandals." Theo frowned.

"Will Aetius stay in Gaul during your absence?" Pulcheria asked. She had been surprised when the dispatches announced Placidia's intention to attend her son's wedding. The West seemed unsettled and in need of a firm hand in Ravenna.

"General Sigisvult holds the passes to Italy. I will return to Ravenna shortly after the wedding and represent my son, while Val escorts his lovely bride in a progress back to our home. There will not be enough time for the General to make mischief."

"To our children." Athenais raised her cup high. "May God grant they live long and happily."

Pulcheria sipped her watered wine, silently wishing the young couple well and very fruitful.

# Chapter 29



*Imperial Palace, October 437*

AFTER THE FORMAL CEREMONIES THE NEXT DAY, THEY SENT THE BRIDAL couple off to the marriage bed with fanfare, flowers, and good wishes. The entire empire celebrated the Imperial nuptials with feasts and games. Statues were sent to every major city, and new coins minted with Valentinian and Eudoxia's profiles. In Constantinople, the festivities would continue for a full week.

Pulcheria had alternate plans. She hadn't forgotten Placidia's anguish when she previously took refuge in their court. Now that her son was coming into his own, perhaps she was ready to embrace a more ascetic life to ease her soul. Honoria could also use something to occupy her mind and hands, or that girl would be trouble. An emperor's marriageable sister could be prey to all sorts of plots—as Pulcheria knew. Honoria should be safely married or dedicated to the Church, and soon!

She approached Placidia and Honoria after the wedding feast. "Aunt, I will celebrate the next week by doing good works. I hope you and Honoria will join me."

Seemingly surprised by the offer, Placidia stammered, "Wh-Why, yes. We will be honored."

"We leave right after morning prayers." She looked at Placidia's regal attire. "I recommend you wear something plain you do not mind getting stained."

Placidia gave a crooked smile. "I'll see what I can find among the servants."

The next morning, Pulcheria took them to a hospital run by the Great Church. A plump woman with pox-scarred cheeks bobbed her head in greeting. "Welcome, Augusta."

"Sister Helena." Pulcheria nodded. "This is my aunt, Placidia Augusta, and her daughter, Honoria Augusta. They will be helping in the hospital today."

"We are grateful for your kindness, Most Gracious Ladies." More head bobbing, and a low bow. "And your sisters, the Virgin Princesses? Are they well?"

"Quite. They feed the hungry at Hagia Irene today." Pulcheria envied her sisters. It had been too long since she personally ministered to the poor. As she took on more of Theo's administrative duties, her sisters had taken on more of her charitable activities. Arcadia had turned into an excellent manager of their households and resources. Pulcheria wanted for nothing when she returned home from the palace tired and vexed. Marina eased both her sisters' burdens with a light and gentle spirit.

"What should we do?" Honoria asked.

"Whatever needs doing." Pulcheria shrugged. "Feed them, bathe them, clean their beds, pray with them."

"Bathe them and clean their beds!" Honoria's mouth pulled into a grim line. "But I'm an Augusta. Why should I dirty my hands on the poor and destitute? I can buy slaves to minister to them or pay others to work here in my stead."

"Because God chose you for your high office. How do you know the will of the people you wish to rule, what is right, what is good, if you do not go among them?" Pulcheria gave Honoria a chilly smile. "I understand you wish to take part in your brother's government. You could do worse than follow my example."

Honoria gave her a calculating look.

Placidia hid a smile. "Come, Honoria. I nursed many during the siege of Rome, and again among the Goths. I will show you what to do."

"There is no need, Mother. I am sure I can master a spoon and wash cloth."

Pulcheria raised an eyebrow. "Do not neglect their souls. Our prayers do as much good as our hands."

"This way." Sister Helena showed them into a long hall filled almost to bursting with women, some with infants, on straw pallets. "We had a bad outbreak of fever last week. These are the survivors, but they are weak. Soup and hot water are through there." She pointed to a door that led into a courtyard. The scent of woodsmoke and barley soup wafted through.

They spent the rest of the day tending sick women. Pulcheria noted Honoria did not shirk any task. *So the girl has capacity for hard work. Good.*

Placidia, likewise, worked with a will. She spoke to the women in low, soothing tones, tended their physical needs, listened to their stories. She obviously had spent some time among the destitute and abandoned. Pulcheria quietly observed one incident that confirmed her confidence in her aunt.

A woman in a fine wool robe held a baby to her chest, mumbling in delirium. She convulsed, clutching the child in a bone-crushing grip.

"No!" Placidia rushed to save the child.

Sister Helena intervened. "The babe's been dead since midnight. Poor soul wouldn't let me take him. She'll be gone soon herself."

"You can't have him!" the sick woman shrieked. She turned away, hiding the child from Placidia's gaze.

Her aunt stayed with the woman, stroking her hair, bathing her forehead with cool water, until she lapsed into the coma that augured death. Placidia knelt in prayer a few moments, then moved on to someone who could use her services in this life.

At the end of the day, strain showed on both mother and daughter's faces. Placidia dropped onto the seat of the royal wagon opposite Pulcheria with a sigh, blinking tears from her eyes. "Thank you for that opportunity."

"Are you tired?"

"Yes, but with physical exhaustion, not the weariness of spirit that plagues me in the dark of night." Placidia leaned back and closed her eyes.

"And you, young Cousin?" Pulcheria turned to Honoria.

"A revelation. I see why the people love you so."

Pulcheria raised an eyebrow, but it didn't seem to affect the younger woman as it did her servants. Honoria gave her an enigmatic smile.

The week filled with such activities: they delivered food and clothing to the poor, visited the sick and abandoned, prayed with the holy sisters, donated altar cloths and plate to churches. Everywhere they went, people crowded around Pulcheria, touching her robe, talking to her in hushed, reverent tones. The poor of the city truly loved her. It was good to be among them again.

Pulcheria hesitated before entering Placidia's residence. She had arranged to dine privately with her Aunt this evening shortly before Placidia left for Ravenna. She remembered the disastrous meal she and Placidia had shared before her aunt went to war to regain her son's *imperium* and wanted to present her concerns in the best light. Composing her thoughts, she entered the residence and dismissed her guards.

"This way, Augusta." A liveried servant bowed. "My mistress awaits you." The servant showed her to a small private dining room, attractively decorated with frescoes of fruiting vines.

"Niece, welcome." Placidia rose as Pulcheria entered. "I'm glad we have this last opportunity to talk before I leave for Ravenna. Who knows when we will meet again?"

"As you say and God wills." Pulcheria took a chair at the intimate table.

After prayers and throughout the meal, the two women discussed strategies for keeping the barbarians at bay. Pulcheria was pleased her aunt honored her preferences for plain fare, serving boiled beef with a variety of cold salads. After the servants offered mulled wine with fruit and cheese, Placidia dismissed them, leaving only the mute body servant Lucilla to serve.

Her aunt took up a grape, inspected it, and put it down. "I have the feeling you didn't come to discuss the Huns, Niece. You have been guarded all evening. You rarely withhold your opinions. Why do you hesitate now?"

Pulcheria's eyes widened. "Why would I not offer my opinions and advice, if it provides guidance and instruction?" She waved her hand in dismissal. "I do have a delicate matter to discuss."

"The state of my soul? I know that concerned you greatly during my last visit." Placidia sipped wine. Her gaze turned inward. "Twelve years ago. It was a dark time. I've done even more dark deeds, but I do see the light. This past week brought back memories of a more innocent time, when I thought I was on another path."

"No. I believe you make your peace with God." Pulcheria hesitated. "It's… your children."

"What about them?" Placidia sat up straighter, frown lines deepening from nose to mouth.

"I believe you have been lax in control of your court. Val is lazy and licentious, his sister sly and ambitious. I know I can have no influence with the boy, but I might take the girl in hand, if you give permission for her to stay."

"How dare you!" Placidia's voice trembled with anger. "You are with them for one week and criticize me for their upbringing?"

"I fear they will be trouble for you and weaken the empire, if you do not take pains to correct the faults in their characters."

"Weaken the empire? Like you haven't already doomed the East?"

"What?" Pulcheria's jaw firmed under this unwarranted attack.

"I would not be so quick to cast stones, Niece. All is not so Eden-like in Constantinople. I spent time with Athenais this week, despite your attempts to keep us apart."

"I didn't—"

"You deprive Theo of an heir!" Placidia interrupted. "Athenais told me you convinced Theo to give up the marriage bed after Flacilla's' death."

"That was Theo's idea. He felt God punished him for the sins of the flesh by taking his daughter."

"And you encouraged that belief?" Placidia accused.

"I supported my brother." She put down her goblet, striving to hold onto her dignity. "As is my duty."

"Convenient for you that the emperor abandons his wife and cleaves to his sister. By encouraging his celibacy, you have no rivals for his affections."

"I want only what is best for Theo and the empire." Blood drained from Pulcheria's face. "I have no base motive."

"Whether your motives are pure or base, the result is the same. You've not only deprived your brother of the affections of his wife, you have taken his unborn children. I thought better of you, Pulcheria, at least where the empire is concerned. What do you think will happen when Theo dies?"

"God's will," Pulcheria whispered.

"Civil war!" Placidia rose and paced. "God is good, but men are not. They crave power and will rush to fill the vacuum left by his lack of legacy. My son— who you feel is incapable!—will have to go to war to hold this empire together. I've seen war, Pulcheria. It is bloody, murderous, hell on earth. All those people you minister to will be victims. All your good work will be for nothing." She stood before Pulcheria, trembling. "As to my children? At least I have a son and a capable daughter; the prospect of grandchildren. What do you have, Niece, but your prayers?"

*Prayers? God give me peace, grace, and the wisdom to do right.* Pulcheria bowed. She saw how her actions might be misconstrued, particularly regarding her brother. She worked hard to hide his weaknesses from the world; she would not expose them to her aunt.

"I'm sorry, Aunt, that my words have brought such discord between us. It was not my intention." She looked Placidia in the eye. "My duty compelled me to bring up my reservations. They are still valid. But I leave you to deal with them as you see fit in the West. I will carry on as I feel is right in the East. If you should change your mind, I would welcome Honoria into my household."

A shadow passed across Placidia's face. "I believe you should go now."

Pulcheria nodded. "God's blessings on you and safe journeys."

### Church of the Holy Apostles, Constantinople, January 438

Pulcheria glowed with pride as Bishop Proclus preached on Jesus' commandments to care for the poor. Her good friend had finally been confirmed as Patriarch of the Constantinople Church. *If Theo had only followed my advice and installed him after Atticus' death, we could have avoided that Nestorius disaster.* Pulcheria shook her head. *What's done is done. Better to concentrate on the now than regret the past.*

Proclus had discussed his sermon with Pulcheria. She approved his message on this auspicious day, when the bones of former Patriarch John Chrysostom were returned to Constantinople. Proclus had requested, and she and Theo had agreed, to atone for their parents' sin in sending the holy man into exile by providing a fitting final resting place thirty-one years after his death. Interring his sainted bones in the Church of the Holy Apostles, where the Eastern Emperors were buried, would bring even more holiness to the site.

"These are the words of our sainted John Chrysostom," Proclus intoned. "'Do you wish to honor the body of Christ? Do not ignore him when he is naked. Do not pay him homage in the temple clad in silk, only then to neglect him outside where he is cold and ill-clad.'"

The reference to silk soured her mood. Pulcheria glanced at the empty seat reserved for Athenais. *Insufferable woman! There is no excuse for missing this important adventus. The people note her absence and begin to gossip. After seventeen years in the palace, you'd think Athenais would know her duty. Theo should take her in hand, or I will!*

The bishop's sonorous voice brought her back to the ceremony. "He who said: 'This is my body' is the same who said: 'You saw me hungry and you gave me no food,' and 'Whatever you did to the least of my brothers you did also to me.'"

Proclus looked around the crowded nave, then thundered, "What good if the Eucharistic table is overloaded with golden chalices, when your brother is dying of hunger? Start by satisfying his hunger; then, with what is left, you may adorn the altar!"

The masses of ordinary people cheered.

"Heed the words of Saint John Chrysostom!"

"Blessings on those who care for the poor!"

"Blessings on our Most Pious Virgin Princesses!"

Shouts echoed through the long nave, shaking the gallery where Pulcheria and her sisters sat above and to the side of the altar in their holy women's robes, heads bowed. She reached out on both sides to grasp Arcadia's and Marina's hands. It was only right she share the people's love with her sisters. They had worked diligently with the poor these last several years, taking up the slack as she served their brother.

Proclus raised his hands. The congregants settled. Pulcheria suppressed a smile at the consternation on the faces of the nobles in the closest rows. *Good! They should be preached to more often on this topic. Maybe they will loosen their purse strings and do what is right for the people and for their own souls!*

"The people, the Church, and the emperor welcome Saint John of the Golden Mouth home to Constantinople. May his sainted presence bring blessings on us all!"

Pulcheria watched Theo lead the procession in full regalia, holding a tall candle of pure beeswax. A contingent of the most important men in Theo's government followed, shouldering the plain white marble sarcophagus containing the bones of the new saint. Monks followed the coffin up the middle aisle, chanting blessings and holding censers that wafted the sweet woody smell of frankincense throughout the church.

Contentment settled in Pulcheria's soul. *Theo and Val are secure on their thrones. Our borders are quiet. The bones of Saint John Chrysostom protect our city. Other than that consistent thorn in my thumb, Athenais, all is as it should be. With God's help, I've done well.*

# Chapter 30



*Imperial Palace, April 439*

PULCHERIA PUT ASIDE HER AUGUSTAL REGALIA AND SLUMPED INTO A CHAIR in her spartan work room. Whereas church ritual soothed her soul, court ritual irritated her more each year. At forty, she began to feel her age and see her end time. She still had so much to do and resented anything that took her from that purpose. Today, a month after Athenais' triumphant return from her year in the Holy Land, her sister-in-law had celebrated with an adventus for additional relics of Saint Stephen. Pulcheria had to stand with her brother and smile as Athenais processed in mock humility through the streets of Constantinople to an acclaiming crowd.

Her clever sister-in-law and her Hellenic faction finally figured out that, if they could not control Theo through his loins, they could influence him through his faith. Athenais obviously felt one year of association with the holy woman Melania, kneeling at a few sites in Jerusalem, and the gift of bones to Constantinople, equaled Pulcheria's own decades of piety. The relics were an obvious bribe for her pious husband and the faithful of Constantinople. *Saint Stephen! At least Athenais could have obtained the bones of a saint they didn't already possess.*

A cramp knifed through her groin. She groaned. On top of the aggravation of watching Athenais lauded for fake piety, her courses had started today. Throughout her adult life, her courses had been sporadic, and always painful. The midwives said she needed to put on more flesh, that fasting interrupted the natural cycles of a woman's body, but she refused to give up any holy observance. She had not bled for several months and had hoped she was done with this curse of Eve.

"God give me patience." She waved over one of the ever-present servants. "Willow-bark tea and call for my scribe." Work took her mind off physical discomfort. At least, she could review border troop distributions before the grand reception tonight.

SEVERAL HOURS LATER, PULCHERIA ARRIVED AT THE PALACE WITH HER SISTERS. The audience hall glittered with lights bouncing off multi-colored marble walls and gilt furnishings, not to mention the brilliant silks and flashing jewels adorning the courtiers and their wives. The excess of color and mixing of scents from food and perfumes made Pulcheria's gorge rise. She took a deep breath to calm her queasy stomach.

"Are you feeling ill, Ria?" Arcadia put a hand on her arm. "You look pale."

Pulcheria blotted at her sweaty forehead with the sleeve of her plain dark robe. "I'm fine. It's just my courses."

Arcadia and Marina exchanged a significant look. Neither suffered with their monthly bleeding as Pulcheria had, but they did their best to make her comfortable during the more painful episodes.

"Come sit for moment, Sister." Arcadia led her to a padded bench behind a column while Marina commandeered a servant.

"I've ordered you some warm red wine, spiced with ginger," her youngest sister announced. "That should fix you up."

The three sisters sat quietly in the shadows until a bevy of servants arrived with all manner of food and drink. Well-trained slaves whisked food, drink, plates, goblets, napkins, and washing bowls into their hands, and effortlessly made the detritus of their meal disappear.

Pulcheria drank her spiced wine from an exquisite ruby red goblet chased with silver. She extracted the ginger slices to chew on them. The spicy root settled her stomach. Her sisters enjoyed crispy roasted squab dipped in honey and crushed almonds, sharp cheese on fresh bread, and a flakey fruit tart. Pulcheria hid her smile when she saw Marina pocket a pistachio, sesame seed, and honey confection. Her youngest sister had a penchant for sweets but didn't over-indulge.

Stomach settled and pain subsiding, Pulcheria decided it was time to get to work. "Sisters, there are people I need to talk to. Please enjoy the feast and the company of anyone you find congenial." At their startled looks, Pulcheria smiled. "You both work hard at your calling and deserve some earthly reward as well as a heavenly one." She turned to the servants. "See that the emperor's sisters lack nothing during the evening." The servants bowed, murmuring concurrence.

She scanned the shifting crowd for her brother. He most likely presided at the far end, close to his dais. Pulcheria knifed through the assembly. She wanted to congratulate Theo on the success of his consolidated law code and was disappointed to find Athenais already glued to his side. Her sister-in-law wore blue silk covered with embroidered silver birds. She glowed in the light of the oil lamps, chatting happily. Theo held her hand in his, laughing at some remark.

"Brother. Sister." Pulcheria approached, noting the guarded look that came over Athenais' face. "I have yet to congratulate you on the baptism of your granddaughter."

Genuine delight brightened Athenais' features. "I am so pleased they named the baby after me. If a girl, I was sure they would do Placidia the honor."

Val and Eudoxia had named the child Eudocia, the Christian name Athenais took at her baptism but only used in public. She clung to her pagan name among family and friends.

"I'm sure, when they have another daughter, Placidia will receive her due." Theo beamed at his wife.

"I wish I could have been there when Eudoxia was brought to childbed. A daughter needs her mother at such times. Only the Good Lord knows when I will see her again." Unshed tears sparkled in her eyes as she squeezed her husband's hand. "I do so envy Placidia, that she gets to hold our precious grandchild. The palace feels so empty without children."

Theo's smile tightened; the light left his eyes. Evidently, he was abiding by his vow to live in a chaste marriage. Pulcheria wondered if he might give in to his wife's wishes and seek her bed after her return from the Holy Land. Athenais was thirty-six, still within child-bearing age. They could yet produce a male heir, but her brother seemed set on his course.

"You could plan a visit to Ravenna," Pulcheria suggested. Things had been much more peaceful with Athenais absent from the palace.

"After a year away?" Athenais laughed. "No. My place is at my husband's side." She linked his arm in hers. "We have been too much apart for too long a time."

Pulcheria thought she meant more than their physical separation this past year. She suspected Athenais' recent taste of power had renewed her lust for it.

"Athenais." Theo patted his wife's arm. "Come meet my sword-bearer. I'm thinking of promoting him to chief eunuch of the household. With your return, you should have some say in the decision. Sister, would you care to join us?"

"No, Brother, that appointment is for you and your wife. I have other business to conduct."

"My serious sister." He smiled. "Don't forget to enjoy the assembly while you are here. This is a celebration in honor of Saint Stephen. You *are* allowed to enjoy it!"

"I will try, Theo." She nodded. "For your sake."

The imperial couple strolled over to Chrysaphius, a martial-looking eunuch dressed in white scholae uniform. He sported a long purple cloak decorated with encircled red birds on a gold background. Unlike many eunuchs, he was tall and well-muscled. Pulcheria speculated he was cut after attaining his adult height. A gold medallion on a chain around his neck marked his office, and a silver band held his straight black chin-length hair in place. Chrysaphius carried the emperor's ceremonial sword—the *spatha*—in a gold sheath.

Pulcheria knew little about him except he was baptized and schooled in religious matters by the famous holy man Eutyches. *No doubt that is what appeals to Theo.* Pulcheria shrugged. There were far worse candidates for the influential post. No eunuch had rivaled her influence over Theo since she had dismissed Antiochus. She saw nothing in Chrysaphius to fear.

A pleasant voice caught her attention. She turned to see Flavius Cyrus, better known as Cyrus of Panopolis, the new praetorian prefect of the East, reciting one of his poems to a small crowd. A poet as prefect! Athenais was again making her presence felt with this appointment to the second most powerful title in the land. He seemed a likable fellow, medium height, dark coloring, with an animated face. He already had several novel proposals to light the streets of the city after dark and improve the university. It remained to be seen if he was another civic-minded man in the mold of Anthemius or held more ambition, like the unlamented Isidorus.

"Prefect." Pulcheria approached the group. Cyrus turned to her with a wary smile.

"Your Sovereignty." He bowed. "How may I be of assistance?"

"I understand you studied with the philosopher Hypatia of Alexandria."

"A couple of years in my youth, Augusta." Sadness clouded his eyes. "She was a great lady and scholar."

She guided him by an arm to a more private nook, where they could sit and be served by the swarming attendants. "I would like to know more about her."

*Imperial Palace, October 439*

"Augusta."

Pulcheria looked up from her stack of papers to find General Aspar bowing, a frown on his handsome face. Ardaburius' son had stepped nimbly into his dead father's boots as general of one of the standing armies in the east. She missed Ardaburius but found his son an eager and willing ally.

"General. Grave news?"

"The Vandals broke out of their African territories, took Carthage and the fleet. They now threaten Rome."

"They have the Carthaginian fleet?" Blood drained from Pulcheria's face. "They will control the Mediterranean and can strike at will...even here! I knew it was a mistake for Placidia to cede them territory in Africa."

"Placidia Augusta had little choice, with the Burgundians in rebellion and Count Boniface dead. She didn't have the troops to spare."

Pulcheria gave him an appraising look. Aspar had had a soft spot for her aunt ever since he accompanied her West to recover the throne for her son. Had it been fourteen years ago? The admiration seemed mutual; Placidia requested Aspar be honored as Western Consul three years ago—an unusual move. Given rumors from that licentious court, Pulcheria hoped nothing untoward had happened.

"Do we have troops to spare? Can we send aid to Valentinian?" Pulcheria tapped the desk with her fingernail.

"Yes, Augusta. I can lead the army myself." Aspar had fought the Vandals with Count Boniface and General Sigisvult ten years ago—and failed. No doubt he smarted from the defeat.

*And he should be ashamed, letting that ragtag army of Gaiseric's defeat the combined forces of the West and the East.* Pulcheria pushed those complaints away. They had a new problem to deal with. "Get me a full report of your proposals tomorrow. I'll consult with my brother on our actions."

"As you command, Augusta." Aspar bowed and exited the room.

*Huns raiding the Danube, Vandals taking Carthage, and Athenais back in Constantinople. What next?*

*Imperial Palace, March 440*

"What is the situation in the West?" Pulcheria's brother looked calm as he discussed strategy with his council and officers.

"The Ravenna court reports General Aetius and his army are summoned from Gaul. General Sigisvult guards the coasts of Italy from raids. King Gaiseric and his Vandals threaten Sicily." General Aspar hesitated and shot Pulcheria a glance. "Reports are that he persecutes the orthodox in all territory he takes, as he did in Carthage."

"Our preparations? How soon can we send relief?" Pulcheria's hands tightened on the arms of her chair.

"We gather our troops and ships, Augusta, but it will be some months before we can act."

"Months? While those of the true faith are tortured and killed?" She narrowed her gaze at Aspar, who shared the cursed Arian heresy with his fellow barbarians. Did he hesitate to act against his co-religionists? She had been the Arian generals' staunch supporter in the council ever since the Persian War of her youth. Surely, he would not desert her now?

He met her gaze, a slow flush rising into his cheeks. He turned to Theo. "My Emperor, my family has served Rome with distinction for three generations as Generals and Consuls. I have served you faithfully for many years. I fought the Vandals before." A quick glance at Pulcheria. "I will do my utmost to expel Gaiseric from Sicily and Carthage. I will drive them into the sea."

Theo nodded approval. "I'll prepare a statement to be read in Constantinople, Ravenna, and Rome detailing our preparations and support. The people will know we are there to protect them." He turned to Cyrus. "Prefect, how goes our own defense?"

She stifled a snort. *A poet in charge of the defense of their city!* She found the prefect a learned and literary man, but he had yet to exhibit that martial spirit they would need in this crisis.

"The land walls of Constantinople are impregnable, Your Serenity, but we are vulnerable from the seaward side, now that the Vandals have the Carthage fleet. I have drawn up plans to strengthen and expand the sea wall." He unrolled a map showing the proposed extensions. "Once these are in place, the city will stand for a thousand years."

"God willing." Pulcheria raised an eyebrow, surprised at the prefect's preparations. Perhaps she had been in error dismissing him so quickly. "I have no doubt God favors the pious—and the prepared."

# Chapter 31



*Sicily, March 441*

IT TOOK A YEAR, BUT WE MADE IT!" ASPAR INSPECTED HIS CAMP WITH DEEP satisfaction. The tents stood in orderly rows, protected by a ditch and a wooden wall encircling the camp. He felt a slight ground tremor and looked warily north at the smoking mountain of Etna. Locals claimed these signs from the volcano did not indicate an immediate eruption. He hoped he could drive Gaiseric into the sea before he tested the Sicilians' predictions. The Vandal general had invaded months ago, ravaged the western part of the island, and now camped in one of Placidia Augusta's estates—a deliberate insult to that most noble lady that Aspar meant to avenge.

Theodosius sent ten thousand troops to stop the carnage. They had arrived safely in the ancient port of Syracuse on the southeastern tip of Sicily only days ago. At the thought of the sea voyage, Aspar crossed himself and thanked God. He had a dread of transporting armies by sea ever since his father's disastrous invasion of Italy to support Placidia sixteen years ago. They had lost most of the land forces in terrible storms. Only the empress's cunning had won the day in that campaign. The thought of the Western Augusta, traveling on horseback, eating with his cavalry, and commanding the bloodless coup in Ravenna brought warmth to his heart. The martial Placidia was a worthy leader and ruler! If not for his deep roots in Constantinople, he might have asked permission to leave his Eastern Augusti to serve in the West.

He shook his head. Theodosius and particularly Pulcheria had been generous to him and his family. He had wealth, fame, and influence with the imperial court. What more did he want?

"General!" Marcian, his father's former tribune and now his own top staff officer, approached with an Arian priest in tow. Marcian was overdue a promotion to general. The man was approaching fifty and might have stayed behind in an administrative post but couldn't pass up a field assignment. "Gaiseric sends an envoy."

Aspar cursed under his breath. He came to finish the Vandals and wipe the stain of his previous defeat from his reputation, not talk.

"General Aspar?" The little priest bobbed a quick bow.

"Yes."

"My name is Geilar. I come with a good faith offer from King Gaiseric. One that will save many lives, God willing."

"In my tent." Aspar motioned toward his command tent in the center of the camp. "Marcian, with me."

"Yes, General." Marcian followed them into the dim spartan interior, lit oil lamps. and took a seat to the side of the general's worktable. He readied parchment, ink, and quill to memorialize the meeting.

Aspar seated the priest. "Wine, Father Geilar?" He indicated a rude clay pitcher and two dented metal cups.

"Thanks. I've traveled steadily for three days." The priest shivered. "There is still snow in the mountain passes."

Aspar and Marcian waited patiently while the little man emptied his cup in a few gulps. He wiped his mouth on his sleeve and set the cup aside with a loud belch.

"Good wine. Local vintage?" Geilar asked.

"What does Gaiseric propose?" Aspar got right to the point.

Geilar frowned at the bluntness and glanced around the tent—perhaps looking for food to go with the drink? "*King* Gaiseric of the Vandals proposes both forces withdraw from Sicily and he will forego any further attacks on Rome—East or West—for some…uh…considerations."

"You mean bribes?" Aspar leaned back and stared pointedly at the little priest. "I outnumber his forces five to one. Why should I not cross the mountains and smash his army?"

"King Gaiseric has only an expeditionary force on Sicily. He can board his ships and be on his way to Carthage well before you can flog your men through the frozen passes."

"Then I'll follow the coward back to Carthage!" Aspar pounded the table with his fist.

Unblinking, Geilar saluted Aspar with his empty tin cup. "Another draught, General?"

Marcian jumped up to refill the priest's cup.

Geilar kept a neutral face while countering Aspar's outburst. "We outnumber you on the water, General. Our fleet would send your army to the bottom of the sea before you got anywhere close to Carthage."

*God's eyes blast the little man!* He was right. Gaiseric could escape easily and continue raiding the coastal cities of the empire. If the coward refused to fight on land, there was no way Aspar could force him. He narrowed his eyes and asked the obvious question. "What guarantees do we have that Gaiseric will retreat to Carthage and stop his raiding?"

"The King has already sent envoys to negotiate with the Ravenna court. I imagine they will work out the terms of hostages, payments, and so forth." The little priest waved a hand, as if making all those details disappear. "I am here to propose you return to your Eastern master while the weather holds. What message do you have for King Gaiseric?"

"I'll take counsel and tell you in the morning." Aspar turned to Marcian. "Have one of the guards find a tent for our guest and see to his needs. He is confined to his tent except for latrine trips and will be accompanied at all times."

"General, I protest! You treat me like a prisoner."

"More like a spy, Father Geilar. You have my word you will be released tomorrow."

"Your word is good with me." The Arian priest bowed stiffly. "If you have additional questions…you'll know where to find me." One corner of his mouth quirked up in a smile.

When Marcian returned, Aspar asked him to sit, serving both cups of wine. "Thoughts?"

Marcian shook his head. "I believe we are put in a corner, General. The priest is right on all counts. We might try to divide our forces: send half by sea to cut Gaiseric off while attacking over the mountains with the rest, but we have no intelligence on his sea forces. He is likely capable of blockading the eastern ports and keeping us bottled up until he can escape."

"You spent some time with him as a hostage, after that fiasco with Boniface. Can we trust the Vandal dog to keep his promises not to raid?" Aspar watched Marcian for any sign of resentment. He had personally ransomed him from the Vandal king twelve years ago. He saw no sign in the last years that Marcian held him responsible for the circumstances of his capture.

"Gaiseric is a shrewd man and cunning general. I believe we can trust him in the short run. That will allow us to regroup and prepare for any future attacks. In the long run…?" Marcian shrugged his shoulders. "Gaiseric competes with the Goths. He hates them with a passion because they fought the Vandals in Hispania at the behest of Rome and reduced the tribe to a ragtag army. The Goths took Rome—and an imperial princess—thirty years ago. Gaiseric's pride will not be content until he brings that city to heel and—possibly—scores an imperial marriage as well."

Aspar stared into his wine cup. He truly wanted to smash that upstart barbarian king…but with the imperial armies fractured and fighting on so many fronts? He wasn't sure he could marshal the might of Rome on land, much less at sea.

Marcian chuckled softly, interrupting his reverie.

"What's so funny?" Aspar huffed.

"Nothing!" Marcian laughed again. "I was just thinking about the first time I met Gaiseric. He paraded down our line of hostages covered in so much gold he could barely walk. He recognized different insignia, stopped to ask officers their names. He mocked us for being captured. His entourage laughed and humiliated us. When he came to me, Gaiseric didn't laugh or joke. He stood briefly trembling, then passed a hand over his eyes. When I told him my name and rank, he asked me to repeat it. 'You will be an emperor and I want to remember your name,' he said. Strange!" Marcian shook his head. "Me! An aging soldier from Thrace, emperor? I do believe Gaiseric had a fit!"

"Let's hope he has another and it kills him…soon!" Aspar saluted Marcian with his cup.

"I can drink to that!" Marcian drained his cup and rose, reaching for his writing materials. "I'll write up that report for you, General."

"Tomorrow will be early enough. We'll send Geilar on his way, and dispatches to Constantinople and Ravenna. Sleep well." Aspar rose and clapped his friend on the shoulder. "I'm sorry we'll see no action, after all this preparation."

"Preparation never goes to waste. I wouldn't be surprised if we're sent to the

Danube next. The Huns are getting restless again." Marcian frowned. "If I were emperor, I wouldn't be paying off those bloody savages. It makes us look weak and drains the treasury until we *are* weak."

"I agree! I'll argue that point with the Augustus next time we meet." *And little good it will do me.*

*Imperial Palace, June 442*

"How could Val do such a thing!" Athenais wailed.

Theo patted her back as she sobbed. "He had little choice, once we withdrew our troops to fight the Huns."

"Our baby granddaughter betrothed to that…that…bloody barbarian!"

"Huneric is the Vandal king's son and was a hostage at the Ravenna court for years. He is quite civilized."

"You heard what his father did to that poor Goth girl, Huneric's previous wife." Athenais pushed her husband away. "He cut off her nose and ears! What's to stop him from doing something similar to our granddaughter?"

"Gaiseric claims the woman tried to poison him."

She dashed the tears from her eyes and glared.

He had the decency to blush. "As to what will stop him? We will. That girl was the daughter of another barbarian king. He would not dare touch a princess of the Theodosian House."

"Why should he respect us? We honor him by promising one of our own." Her hands curled into fists. "He beat us! The greatest empire the world has ever known couldn't muster the army to defeat a single barbarian tribe." Her face crumpled and she started sobbing again.

He folded her into his arms, stroking her hair. "But it isn't a single tribe, my dear. It's the Huns along the Danube; the Goths, Burgundians and Franks in Gaul; the Alans in Hispania; the Saxons in Britain; as well as the Vandals in Africa. We could fight any one or two, maybe even three, but not all at once."

"What is to become of us?" she mumbled into his chest.

"We will survive." He tightened his arms around her. He had forgotten how good it felt to hold his wife close. "Chrysaphius has a plan to deal with the Huns. We negotiate with the others and fight when we must. The walls of the city are impregnable. We are safe."

"Our poor daughter. Eudoxia must be heartbroken!" Athenais sobbed.

"She has little Placidia for solace. Eudocia is but four. There are many years

237

before a marriage can take place. We may yet defeat the Vandals, or something might befall Huneric." He smelled the lemon Athenais used to brighten her golden hair; his manhood stirred. Ashamed of his growing lust, he tried to quell it. "God will shield us. Let us pray for his good grace."

Athenais pushed away from his arms. The fury on her face stunned him. "Pray, Husband? As if that is all it takes to keep our granddaughter safe. I'll put my faith in a strong army."

Athenais stormed out of the room, back stiff and head high.

Theo shook his head. He had hoped his wife's year in the Holy Land would bring her closer to God. Her faith never ran as deep as his, but he had thought Athenais more content with God's plan. She'd ceased reproaching him for abandoning their marriage bed and often joined his sisters in their charity work. He tried to bring back the feelings of love and promise from the early days of their marriage, but twenty-one years had dulled those feelings to mere echoes, drowned by more recent sorrow and disappointment.

Tears prickled his eyes. "Oh, my love. What happened to us?"

*Imperial Palace, March 443*

Overcome with melancholy, Athenais put aside her favorite book of poems by Olympiodorus—another friend gone these many years. She rarely heard from Placidia or her beloved daughter in the Western court. She sometimes wondered if someone intercepted their letters to her or hers to them. She shook her head. No! No one would be so bold as to interfere with her correspondence.

A musician played an eight-stringed kithara in the background. She felt the kitharode's talent was wasted on this unappreciative audience. This wasn't the literary salon she had wanted, but it was much friendlier than Pulcheria's ascetic court. Her attention wandered to the chatter of her women as they read to one another or gossiped in small groups. Unfortunately, she was forced to maintain a proper distance with the young matrons who made up her retinue. She could trust none of them as friends or confidants.

Her eyes itched with tears as she thought of her dear Aunt Doria, who died of a fever before Athenais left for the Holy Land. They had seen little of each other after Asclepiodotus was dismissed from service. Her face screwed up in an unattractive scowl. Another mark against Pulcheria!

Athenais had felt quietly content these four years since returning from Jerusalem. Her fights with Theo over his choice to remain chaste in their marriage were done. She thought she had regained his friendship and trust. She was reconciled to her life and found pleasure in it where she could. Except for these brief episodes of sadness—more frequent now that she had attained the mature age of forty—her only source of discontent continued to be her sister-in-law. Pulcheria constantly flaunted her power over Theo. Her husband was a good and wise ruler. Why did he need to defer to his interfering sister?

"Count Paulinus to see the Augusta," a servant announced.

Athenais looked up in anticipation. Paulinus dropped by frequently to tell her the latest gossip or introduce her to a new author or philosopher. In a court dominated by church rules and routines, he reminded her of a past life with gayer possibilities. Before she met Theo, she had hoped for more than friendship with Paulinus. Now, she cherished their time together. She had tried bringing culture to the court but failed. Instead of transforming the court, she found herself changed, and sometimes regretted it. Her year in Jerusalem had given her an insight into another life she might lead, but she was unwilling to wholly embrace it…yet.

"Augusta! You look beautiful today." Paulinus gave her a slight bow and a big grin.

"You say that every day, my friend." She patted the seat next to her on the divan; he sat.

"Every day it's true." He picked up her hand to kiss the palm.

Athenais pulled her hand away. "Stop that! We're too old for such foolishness. I'm a married woman."

"And well-guarded from any lascivious attacks. What fool would offend you in a room full of your women and servants?"

She looked around the room. His playful antics seemed to draw no special notice. She relaxed. Her guest was still quite handsome in his maturity, a full head of dark hair just starting to gray at the temples, his body fit, face beginning to weather in a pleasant way, but there were dark rings under his eyes and a slight pouchiness to his jowls. "You look tired, Paulinus. Has Theo been working you too hard? Or perhaps a woman keeps you up late?"

A shadow crossed his eyes but he replied brightly, "What woman could compete with a goddess like you, Athenais? Since you are my best friend's wife, I must settle for mere mortals, and they do not satisfy."

"I worry about you, Paulinus. You should have married long ago and started a family." She patted his hand. "It's not too late. I'm sure I could arrange a suitable match with a rich widow."

"No, my dear. We've had this chat before. I'm content with my life as it is." He smiled. "As long as I can see you often."

"Whenever you wish." A pleasant unexpected warmth radiated from her womb. She dug her nails into her palms. She had thought herself above such temptations, but occasionally her body betrayed her with lustful feelings. She tamped them down. "Now, tell me the latest about Cyrus. I was shocked when he resigned his posts and withdrew from the court. Theo is furious with him over something but doesn't confide in me about government business."

"I'm afraid it isn't good news." Paulinus lowered his voice. "Theo is confiscating Cyrus' property and forcing him to become a bishop in Phrygia."

"No! Why? Cyrus has never shown an inclination for the church." Athenais put a hand to her throat. "This smacks of punishment, not reward for all the good Cyrus did for the city."

"It's worse than punishment. The people of that bishopric murdered the last four Episcopal appointees. I fear Theo has sent our friend to his death."

"This has to be Pulcheria's doing!" Anger brought hectic red spots to her cheeks. "She is ever against any in the government who urge moderation or champion culture. Cyrus supported expanding the University and decreed that wills and judicial decisions be written and read in Greek—the people's language. She is jealous of the people's esteem. She also knows I support him, and therefore she automatically becomes his enemy."

Paulinus rubbed his jaw. "I don't think Pulcheria is behind this. There is another rising power at the court: Chrysaphius. As Chief Eunuch and head of the household, he is constantly in Theo's presence. Even I, as Master of Offices, have difficulty getting an audience lately. Have you been much in your husband's company?"

"Now that you bring it up, I haven't. But surely that is because of Theo's duties. He doesn't have time for idle chatter. What does this have to do with Cyrus? Theo raised him to Patrician and honored him with the consulship. There's been no hint of scandal or corruption."

"I believe Chrysaphius saw Cyrus as a threat to his influence for those very reasons. You heard what happened at the hippodrome?"

Athenais frowned, shaking her head.

"When Theo held races in Cyrus' honor, the crowd shouted, 'Constantine built the city, Cyrus renewed it!' Theo was not happy. I think Chrysaphius inflamed that jealousy."

"Oh, Paulinus!" Athenais laughed. "The people were happy Cyrus lit the city streets and extended the sea walls against the threatened Vandal attacks. So he is acclaimed in the hippodrome one day. Theo is not so little a man that he would hold that against a loyal servant." She sobered. "No, there is only one person who wields that kind of power over Theo—Pulcheria."

"Perhaps you are right, my goddess." Paulinus retrieved her hand, tracing her lifeline with his thumb.

Tingling waves of desire coursed through her hand, spread throughout her body. This time Athenais did not pull her hand back.

# Chapter 32



*Imperial Palace, April 443*

WHAT ARE YOUR WISHES, AUGUSTA?" CHRYSAPHIUS BOWED TO ATHENAIS. The woman sat before a large silver mirror—as usual—a slave brushing her long golden hair. He thought the Augusta became vainer as she aged. Although he had to admit she looked much younger than her forty years. It was typical she demanded his presence during the middle of the morning when he was most busy. Athenais treated him as an ordinary servant rather than the right hand of the emperor, and he resented it. His face in the mirror didn't betray his annoyance as he put up with her whims—for now. The wife was a small nuisance, next to the formidable obstacle of the sister, in the eunuch's plans to dominate the emperor for his own gain.

"I want an intimate banquet in honor of the emperor's thirty-five years on the throne on the ides of next month." Athenais gave him an imperious look in the mirror.

"In addition to the week-long celebrations in the city?" Chrysaphius frowned. His staff had already planned the celebrations and arranged the Emperor's presence at various churches, games, and gatherings. He could easily handle the Augusta's wishes, but didn't want her to know that.

"There will be free food, drink, and special races at the hippodrome for the people, but my husband should have a more appropriate celebration with his closest friends and advisors. I wish to honor him by having the city's nobles and holy men as guests."

"I will have a menu, guest list, and suggested entertainment prepared for you in three days." He enjoyed these affairs. They gave him opportunity to include people who sought his favor. They met the emperor and, depending on their means, gave Chrysaphius a generous gift or owed him a big favor. The more intimate the gathering, the larger the gift.

"Three days?" Athenais frowned, marking her forehead with unattractive lines. "Why not this afternoon?"

"Most Noble Lady." He bowed again. "I regret the delay, but my staff is busy with the emperor's business. Three days is the earliest we could do."

"That's not good enough!" She glared into the mirror. "I require this done immediately."

"Augusta, I humbly regret the inconvenience." He pulled a sorrowful face. "You could make the request for my immediate services directly to the emperor, but…" He hesitated. "May I make suggestion?"

She waved her hand which he took for assent.

"Pulcheria Augusta has a full imperial staff. Is it not appropriate that you have one as well? Then you would have no need to call on me."

"My husband has made it clear he feels I have no need of staff beyond those assigned to him. He and I are one in the sight of God…or so he thinks." She mumbled the last bit.

"It seems wrong to me that the emperor's sister enjoys such a privilege, but the emperor's wife does not. You are equal in rank." Chrysaphius enjoyed the myriad opportunities to sow discord between the sisters-in-law. If they fought each other, they wouldn't notice him usurping their influence. Once he pushed the women out of his way, he would have complete control of that weak fool of an emperor. "I'm afraid the emperor does not appreciate your needs and slights your dignity. As he says, what you do reflects on him."

"You are right, but my husband is stubborn on the matter. He refuses to give me staff in my own right and Pulcheria won't share hers with me."

"How unfortunate! I would not have thought the Augusta so selfish, given her modest needs."

"That woman has ever usurped my place. No matter how hard I try, Theo always turns to her first. A wife should come before a sister!" Athenais scowled into the mirror.

That was the heart of the matter: the wife was jealous of the sister and the sister of the wife. For four years, he had fanned those embers of discord. His heart raced with eagerness and he took a calming breath. His plans were near to fruition; he had only to be patient.

"I agree, Augusta! The emperor should honor you above all others." He cupped his chin, drawing down his brows in mock concentration. Athenais responded well to flattery, unlike the sharp Pulcheria. After a moment, his face brightened. "Sometimes a strength can be a weakness."

"What do you mean?" Her brow furrowed again.

"Your husband has great regard for his sister. He wants her happiness above all else."

"Yes," she replied bitterly. "And she is happy ruling the empire."

"I suspect she does not tell her brother that." He offered a sly smile. "She likely tells him it is her duty to serve him. She would not openly usurp his role. What does she profess to love most…after her brother?"

"The Church." Athenais looked puzzled. "How does that help me?"

He suppressed a sigh. Would he have to spell everything out? "If the emperor believes his sister serves only out of duty, that her real calling is the Church, he could order her to take holy orders out of love for her. In his eyes, he gives her a precious gift—possibly even one the Augustus would covet for himself—while ridding you of a rival for his affections."

"What a clever idea!" Athenais clapped her hands together, then gave him a sharp look. "You have given this some prior thought. How does it benefit you?"

Maybe she wasn't as naïve as he believed. He bowed again to give himself a moment's reflection. "I have long thought you were poorly treated, Augusta, and the ways of the court too strict. Church hours and chastity are for monasteries, not a palace." A telltale blush crept into her cheeks. "This is Pulcheria's work, not your husband's. With her gone, you will have a more moderating influence on the Augustus."

"You still haven't told me how this benefits you." She raised an eyebrow in unconscious imitation of Pulcheria.

"Your sister-in-law is not my friend. She whispers against me as often as she whispers against you." He grinned at the blatant lie. "And with her gone, you get her imperial staff and I have less work to do."

"We make common cause?" Worry lines reappeared on her forehead. "This scheme to take Pulcheria off the playing board might not work."

He shrugged. "If not this, something else will present itself. We need only be patient and work together for our mutual benefit."

"I'll give it some thought." Athenais turned back to her mirror, dismissing Chrysaphius.

She didn't see the triumphant look that crossed his face as he exited her rooms.

*Thirty-five years I've been Emperor!* Theo reviewed the guest list for his banquet with his wife. It contained not only the most prominent families, but the most important bishops and holy men in and around the city, which might make it tolerable. In many ways, he still felt like that boy, more content with prayers than parties. He didn't particularly want a banquet, but Athenais had put considerable planning into the affair and he wanted to make her happy. Since returning from Jerusalem, she was much more attentive to her prayers and the rituals of the church. Her behavior had gone a long way toward healing the rift between them.

"My sisters are not on the list." Theo frowned.

"Because they are family and assumed to be present." Athenais took the list back. "I'll seat Pulcheria next to Bishop Proclus. They are great friends and will have much to discuss."

"I leave the details to you and Chrysaphius." The eunuch had proved most intelligent and capable. Theo relied more and more on his advice and action, freeing himself for contemplative activities—and the occasional ride outside the city. Pulcheria chided him for his laxness, but he found details of troop movements, grain storage, and petty land disputes…lacking. She of all people should understand his need for the soothing rituals of the church. Their shared love of God bonded them more deeply than any of his other relationships.

"Speaking of Chrysaphius, have you given any more thought to my request for a court of my own? Or perhaps you could reassign Pulcheria's to me?" Athenais pursed her lips in a slight pout. "Given her preference for a simple life, she has no need for a chief eunuch, guards, and the trappings of a separate court at her own palace. I could put them to much better use. You would then have Chrysaphius to serve you alone."

"Don't trouble yourself over this." Theo sighed. "Pulcheria governs beside me with wit and piety. She deserves her own court. I will not deprive her of it. You share in my dignity and have no need for your own court."

"But…"

"I've spoken my last word on the subject." Annoyance crept into his voice. This was an old complaint from his wife. He was tired of it.

"I understand, Husband. I will not trouble you with the issue again." Athenais bowed in humility. "However…"

He looked at her with a weary smile. "Yes, my dear?"

"You make an interesting point. Pulcheria is a most pious woman. Many call her the modern Olympias, that most holy of all women who ministered with Bishop John Chrysostom of just a generation past."

"There are many parallels." Theo had only the highest esteem for his sister's piety and wished he could attain the same regard from her and his people. He sometimes felt Pulcheria saw him as lacking—especially when it came to the finer points of religious doctrine. After that fiasco with Nestorius, she kept an iron grip on any decisions that touched on the Church.

"I met many holy women in Jerusalem and was struck with their resemblance to Pulcheria in their dedication to the Church. Melania the Younger, particularly, comes to mind. Both women have followers pledged to chastity, take meals with bishops, communion with the priests and, above all, command the love and respect of the people for their charity and compassion."

His wife gazed at a flickering candle. A shadow briefly crossed her face. Envy? Regret? She twirled a curl by her cheek, deep in thought. "I think Pulcheria longs to fully commit herself to the Church and take holy orders, but does not, out of love and loyalty to you."

"Do you really think so?" Theo paused. Pulcheria had frequently of late urged him to take on more than the ceremonial aspects of governing. Did she find the work wearying? Just yesterday, she mentioned, with a sense of longing, all the charity work their sisters Arcadia and Marina did in her name.

"How often has she told you she lives to serve you?" Athenais put a light hand on his arm. Her eyes glistened with unshed tears. "It is obvious your sister yearns for a quiet life dedicated to Christ. She stays in the government only out of love for you. But you no longer need her counsel. Chrysaphius has proved more than capable in helping you govern. And Paulinus never fails to give you good advice. Do you keep her with you out of love? If so, you do her no service."

"I had not thought of it that way." Realization struck Theo like a bolt. He had been extremely selfish in keeping Pulcheria from her true calling. Chrysaphius had hinted at something similar just the other day. If his wife and trusted servant gave him the same advice, he should carefully consider it. As he aged, he found governing a burden. Surely his sister did, as well.

"Your love and respect for Pulcheria are as great as hers for you," Athenais said. "You are not to blame for wanting your sister at your side, but it is selfish to keep her there, when her heart lies elsewhere. She has provided you with nearly thirty years of honorable service. Does she not deserve some reward, some life of her own choosing? She lives as a holy woman. Why not free her to take holy orders? Think how happy it would make her to become a deaconess."

"You are right, Athenais." Theo's heart filled with love for his sister and his considerate wife. If he could give up this burden of ruling and take holy orders, he would. He longed to devote his life to Christ, but that was impossible. At least he could give this gift to his beloved sister. He took his wife's hands in his, brought them to his lips for a chaste kiss. "Thank you, my dear. I will contact Bishop Proclus and make it so."

Her brilliant smile lightened his world. "Thank you, Husband. I'm sure Pulcheria will be delighted with this decision. You are a truly loving brother."

*Hebdomon Palace, April 443*

Servants helped Pulcheria and her sisters put on their traveling cloaks before the trip into the city to attend Sunday services at the Great Church. She smiled at the thought of soothing prayers, contemplation, and the peace of holy communion to come. The trip through the city also afforded the people an opportunity to gather and honor the Virgin Princesses with their acclamations. It was one of her favorite activities of the week.

"Augusta, a messenger from the bishop," her chamberlain announced.

Pulcheria pinned her dark robe with a gold fibula in the shape of the letters *chi rho*, the first two letters of Christ, then turned to the voice. A messenger in episcopal livery clutched a packet with a dusty hand. Most of the messengers from the bishop were little more than boys, employed in various mundane tasks before taking orders. Pulcheria recognized this man as an intimate of Proclus—someone to whom the bishop entrusted more delicate tasks.

"Basil, we are about to leave for Sunday services. What conversation cannot wait until we meet Bishop Proclus in person?" Pulcheria's voice rang steady, despite her rising alarm.

"Your Serenity, please read this immediately." The messenger held out the missive. "The bishop particularly charged me with finding you before you came into his presence."

Pulcheria took the letter and broke the seal. Scanning, she first turned pale, then flushed with anger. "Do you know the contents?"

"I do, Augusta. Bishop Proclus strongly urges you to avoid his presence at all costs, while he works on your behalf to have this reversed. He promises to keep you apprised of the situation."

"Thank you for your service. My chamberlain will see you well compensated." As Basil left, she turned to her sisters. "We will not attend services today."

"Sister, what is it?" Arcadia asked, frowning at this departure from routine.

"Bishop Proclus sends word that our brother intends me to take holy orders and become a deaconess. Theo has ordered Proclus to make this happen…" She took the letter and read: "…'so as to provide the greatest happiness for my beloved sister.' Proclus advises me to stay out of his presence, if I wish to retain my freedom and avoid a confrontation with Theo."

"We already perform the duties. Why not take the next step in the sight of God, and confirm our devotion?" Marina asked. "Is our brother wrong? Would that not make you happy?"

Would it? Pulcheria hesitated. A life in the Church. Comforting ritual. Daily ministering in Christ's name. The life that called to her soul.

"Yes, sister, it would make me happy." She shook her head. "But I cannot take that step. I have ruled for and with Theo for almost thirty years—since I was fifteen! I know his mind, heart, and soul. He cannot see malice in any who are close, and they manipulate him for their own purposes. I hoped he would grow more aware but, if anything, this flaw has grown bigger. If I take holy orders, I come under the supervision of the bishop and owe him alone my obedience. I give up my freedom of thought and action. Proclus is a friend and would never abuse that privilege, but any who come after…? You remember Nestorius." She shrugged. "I must remain free to help our brother and our empire."

"Why do you think Theo did this? Does he want you gone from his government?" Arcadia asked.

"I don't think so." Pulcheria blinked away tears. "I suspect it is not his idea. When we look at who most benefits from my absence, it is clear: Athenais and the Hellenes."

"What will you do, Ria?" Marina, ever the more tender one, offered a kerchief so she could blot her eyes.

"For now?" She looked at her sisters. "We withdraw to fight another day. I will dismiss the court Theo provides. We stay here in the suburbs in Hebdomon. We will avoid our brother and Bishop Proclus, until we can sort this out." *And I pray to God that will be soon.*

# Chapter 33

*Imperial Palace, January 444*

"Most Noble Augustus." Chrysaphius bowed low.

Theo, in his specially built scriptorium, looked up from his calligraphy. He enjoyed these quiet moments with his hobby, copying holy texts in his flowing script. Today, he copied one of his favorites, *The Life of Anthony*, about the third century Egyptian saint who founded the monastic movement. Reluctantly he put down his quill. "You know you needn't be so formal in my presence when we are alone."

The eunuch dropped to his knees, bowing again. "I bring you grave news, my emperor."

"Are we under attack?" Theo rose, looking out on the bleak winter garden with alarm.

"Not the city, Sire, but your own person. I have uncovered a treasonous plot hatched right here in the palace."

"What? Who?" Theo threw anxious glances at the doors and windows.

"Your wife conspires with your Master of Offices, Paulinus. They have conducted an adulterous affair for months, possibly years. They now plan to assassinate you and put him on the throne."

"My wife and best friend?" Blood drained from Theo's face. His vision grayed. He dropped to his chair.

"Drink this." Chrysaphius held a cup to his lips. "It will revive you."

Theo took a sip of strong red wine—unwatered—and coughed. He feebly pushed the cup away. "I've had enough." He straightened as the initial shock wore off. Disbelief set in. "This can't be true. What proof do you have?"

"I've observed the Augusta and Paulinus many times in intimate conversation."

"They are great friends. Paulinus introduced us. It is not unusual for them to speak or spend time together."

"I've observed behavior that speaks of more than friendship: intimate touches and kisses. I would not trouble you with only disturbing rumors, Augustus, or just my observations." The eunuch pulled sheets of parchment from his tunic. "Here is sworn testimony from one of the Augusta's servants that Paulinus frequently comes to your wife's rooms and stays the night. One of his men swears the same."

"How was this testimony obtained?" The missives shook in Theo's hands.

"The servants are slaves, Augustus. Their testimony was got by torture, as prescribed by law."

"I still do not believe it." Theo put the papers face down on the table, his heart rejecting what his eyes just read: the slaves' testimony that his wife and best friend plotted his death. "Athenais and Paulinus would not betray me. She is a pious, God-fearing woman, and he my best friend."

"May I bring up a delicate point?" Chrysaphius bowed again.

"Of course."

"The Augusta is a most beautiful and desirable woman. You had three children together. Are her…needs…satisfied?" He extended his hands, palms up. "Everyone knows women are the font of evil, and carnal lust is one of the devil's most potent weapons. To have an affair with the Augusta is punishable by death. Paulinus doubtless plans your assassination to protect himself and the Augusta. Your death has the added advantage that he can take your place both as emperor and in your wife's bed."

Theo sat back. Athenais, earlier in their marriage, startled him with her sexual desires. He had complied and enjoyed their intimacy until God punished him for his lust by taking two of his children. His wife pleaded with him to return to her bed, heaping recriminations on his head, until her return from Jerusalem. He had thought her reconciled to a chaste marriage dedicated to God. Was he wrong? Had she fallen back into her old lustful ways? If so, did she really seek his death? He wanted to deny the accusations, but doubt crept in.

"I know this is difficult for you to believe, Augustus. Perhaps if you observe them yourself for a day or two you will be convinced." The eunuch glanced over his shoulder. "For your own sake, do not take too long. I will double your guard and taste your food myself. Do not be alone with either of them."

"Go!" Theo cried, desperate to sort through this bewildering situation in solitude.

The eunuch bowed out the door. Theo clutched his chest in pain. If true? No. His wife and best friend would never…His thoughts whirled and his breath came in ragged gasps. *Why did God constantly test me with such betrayal? First Cyrus, then Pulcheria, now Athenais and Paulinus. Who can I trust?*

His shoulders shook with unexpressed sobs.


OVER THE NEXT TWO DAYS, THEO STUDIED HIS WIFE AND FRIEND. THEY DID seem much in each other's company. If there were an explosion of laughter in the quiet court, it came from them. They shared glances over meals and smiles across the room. Still, Theo could not find it in his heart to believe them capable of betrayal. Affection? Yes. But not murderous plots.

He took his doubts to Chrysaphius. "The Augusta and Paulinus share some levity, and perhaps their conduct in public is not as circumspect as it should be. But treason? Murder?"

"It grieves me beyond measure, Your Serenity, to be the one to bring this to you." The eunuch wrung his hands. "I have had the Augusta watched night and day. There are rooms which are observable." Chrysaphius coughed delicately.

"I've known of the secret passageways and spy holes since I was a child." Theo waved his hand. "Continue."

"When the Augusta feels safe, she meets Paulinus and they…couple." The eunuch blushed. "I saw them myself just this afternoon and overheard their plans. Paulinus proposes he poison you slowly, so it looks like a natural sickness and death. After a suitable time of mourning, the Augusta will marry Paulinus and declare him Augustus."

"And Athenais agreed to this?" He clutched the eunuch's arm. "No. You must be mistaken!"

"I understand this is a blow." Chrysaphius shook his head. "The Augusta is probably under your groomsman's thrall. He seems to be the instigator. Master, I would never suggest you lower yourself to spy on your wife personally, but I've devised a test that, with my testimony and that of her own servants, should convince you. After…uh…being together, the Augusta likes to give Paulinus small gifts. He is currently in residence, having injured his foot, but the Augusta is unaware. I have a plan…"

"GOOD DAY, MY DEAR." THEO FELT THE SMILE ON HIS FACE START TO CRUMBLE. He pinched his thigh to focus his attention. How could he go through with this charade?

Athenais looked up from her reading. "Theo, what a wonderful surprise. I thought you held audience all morning."

As he approached, she offered her cheek for a kiss.

"I have a present for you." His voice cracked.

She met his eyes and her smile died on her lips. "Are you ill, my love? You look pale."

"No! No!" He felt chill sweat drip down this back. "I have trouble sleeping, that is all."

The smile returned. "That is easily remedied. I can speak to the physicians and have a draught made up. Paulinus recommends warm red wine, with a drop or two of poppy juice."

A draught? That would be convenient! "No need, my dear." Was it concern or disappointment that shone in her eyes?

"Sit, Husband, and talk to me. We see so little of each other these days." She patted the blue silk divan.

His mouth dried. He needed to get this done and leave before he broke down.

"I-I can't stay." Theo clapped. A servant by the door glided to his side to present a prodigious golden yellow apple on a silver tray. "An embassy from Phyrgia gave me this, in celebration of Epiphany." He handed the apple to his wife with trembling hands. She needed both hands to hold it.

"This is wondrous!" She examined the fruit. "It's huge! Its skin has no blemish. How did they grow such a marvelous, perfect apple?"

"The man said a local priest blessed the tree with holy water and promised a bumper crop. This is the result."

"Thank you, Husband, for such a miraculous gift. I'll treasure it."

Theo dipped his head to his wife and her ladies. "I'll leave you to enjoy the rest of the morning. I'm practicing swords in the armory later. Care to watch?"

"You know I have no interest in the martial arts, my dear. But go!" Athenais made shooing motions with her hands. "Go get sweaty. I'll stay here comfortable with my book."

He fled her apartments, heart pounding. *Eve has her apple. What will she do with it?*

"Master of Offices Paulinus sends his regrets, Augusta." Chrysaphius bowed to Athenais. "He cannot visit you as promised. He injured his foot."

"Oh, the poor man!" Athenais turned a worried gaze on the eunuch. Paulinus must be in considerable pain to miss their afternoon visit. She couldn't remember the last time he failed to attend her when he was in the palace. "How did this happen? Is he at his home in the city?"

"He stumbled in loose gravel. It is a bad sprain, but not broken. The Augustus insisted he stay in the guest apartments in the Daphne."

"I must see he is being properly attended to." Athenais rose, then hesitated with a vague sense of disquiet. "Why bring this message yourself, Chrysaphius? A messenger page could have done as well."

"The emperor knows of your fondness for Master Paulinus. He sent me personally to reassure you." He pointed to the giant apple on its silver platter by divan. "That's a remarkable piece of fruit."

"And just the thing to cheer up my friend." She commanded, "Show me to his quarters. Bring the apple with you."

They hurried down halls and through courtyards of two complexes to reach the oldest part of the palace, just off the audience chamber, where foreign embassies resided. It was far more luxurious than the emperor's own spartan quarters, sporting gilded furniture, intricate mosaics and frescoes of classic themes, paintings and statues by Greek masters. It was too early in the year for flowers from the garden, but a faint scent of sandalwood incense pervaded the rooms.

Athenais entered one of the guest suites to find Paulinus on a padded divan, right leg elevated on a silk cushion and wrapped tightly. The physician nearly ran into her on his way out.

"My apologies, Augusta." The doctor ducked his head.

"Is the Master of Offices well?" Athenais looked past the physician, noting lines of pain pinching her friend's face.

"It is a bad sprain, but he should be on his feet in a few days. Until then, I recommend he rest, and use a crutch when he must move."

"Is he in much pain? What have you given him for ease?"

"It throbs but a little, Augusta." Paulinus answered for himself. "Let the poor man go. He can do no more for me."

The physician bowed out.

Athenais flew to his side and placed a hand on his forehead. Anxiety fluttered in her chest. What would she do without her most intimate confidant?

"I don't have a fever. It's just a sprain." His eyes flicked over her shoulder. She remembered Chrysaphius.

She motioned to the eunuch. "I brought you a present to take your mind off your injury."

"Thank you." Paulinus took the fruit from the tray and turned it round. "I don't think I've ever seen such an apple before. Remarkable, and welcome." He set it aside. "Though not as welcome as you."

She blushed. "Chrysaphius, you may go. Send in this apartment's servants. I have specific instructions for the master's care."

"As you wish, Augusta." The eunuch bowed out.

"I don't trust that eunuch." Paulinus said after Chrysaphius left.

"I know you have doubts, but he's been a good friend to me." She settled on a chair by his side. "It was his idea I suggest to Theo that Pulcheria take holy orders."

"That's just what I mean. Why not make the suggestion to Theo himself? He is constantly in the emperor's presence."

"Perhaps he thought Theo wouldn't take his advice when it pertained to family."

"Pulcheria refused the trap," Paulinus grumbled.

"And got caught in another. Theo was hurt and furious when she refused. After all he did to bring about her happiness, she threw his gift back in his face. It finally proved to him Pulcheria wanted power only for herself. She's no better than those sycophants she constantly decries. I'm glad he finally sees her for what she is. And…" she giggled, "…Theo gave me her staff! I'm happy. Chrysaphius is happy. All ended as planned."

"I still don't trust that eunuch. I feel like I have a target on my back in his presence. He waits only for me to turn so he can throw a knife into it."

"Don't fret so!" She pushed hair back from his forehead. "You are Theo's oldest and dearest friend. He values you above all other men. If I were a courtier, I should be envious of his love for you."

"Then I'm extremely lucky you are a beautiful woman and not a courtier."

"Silly man!" She leaned in to give him a light kiss on the forehead, starting back guiltily as the requested servants trooped in. Athenais gave them their orders and left with a renewed sense of calm. Paulinus was in no danger. She could visit his quarters as easily as he could visit hers.

# Chapter 34



*Imperial Palace, January 444*

Theo went to see Athenais with Chrysaphius after morning prayers. He stalked into the room, quivering with rage and pain. For once, he didn't suppress his feelings. He would ask God to forgive his lack of control later.

"Leave us," he ordered.

His wife's retinue and servants scurried from the room with anxious glances.

"Husband? What—" Athenais looked up, eyes wide.

"Silence!"

She instinctively covered her mouth with her hands.

After the room emptied, he pulled her from her chair by the arm. "The apple I gave you yesterday. What did you do with it?"

"I…I…I ate it." She struggled in his grasp. "Please, Theo you're hurting me."

He let go her arm. She rubbed where his fingers dug into her flesh. There would be bruises later. He didn't care.

"Are you sure?" He thrust his face close to hers. She backed away.

"I should know what I ate or didn't," Athenais replied sharply.

"Chysaphius." Theo nodded.

The eunuch produced the silver platter with the huge yellow apple sitting in the middle.

"Paulinus gave me this just now, saying he had received it as a gift from a friend and thought I might enjoy it."

257

Her cheeks paled. "I'm sorry, Husband. I gave it to Paulinus yesterday when I checked to see he was properly cared for after his accident. A small token, to cheer him up."

"Why did you lie?" Theo's gaze wavered as pain clinched his chest.

"You took me by surprise. I thought you wanted the miraculous apple back. I was embarrassed that I gave away your gift." She hung her head in shame. "Forgive me, Husband. It was a small mistake."

"Do you," he choked on the words, "betray me with Paulinus?"

"What?" Her eyes went wide. "No! What put that notion in your head? This silly apple? I told you, your question surprised me and I told a clumsy lie."

"If you lie about one thing, you'll lie about another."

She looked him directly in his eyes. "On my honor, as your wife and the mother of your child. I have been faithful to you throughout our marriage, and chaste—as was your wish—these past thirteen years."

"Chrysaphius says otherwise. He saw you fornicating with Paulinus." He pulled the slave testimony from his belt and tossed it in her face. "Others swear, as well. You have disgraced me and committed treason."

"Treason?" She picked up the papers, read them quickly. "You would take the word of slaves and eunuchs over that of your wife of twenty-three years?" She tossed the papers back at him. "These are lies. I'll swear before Bishop Proclus and God, on saints' bones, whatever oath you prescribe. I did not sleep with Paulinus. We do not plot your death. I have not disgraced you."

"I wish I could believe you." Doubt pushed at his heart. Could she be telling the truth?

She clasped her hands as if in prayer. "You can, Theo."

His doubt grew. How could his lovely wife betray him? His gaze slid to rest on the cursed apple—the symbol of Eve's sin and Athenais' betrayal. His anger returned three-fold. "Chrysaphius, the Augusta is confined to her rooms. I don't wish to see her deceiving face ever again."

"Theo!" She dropped to her knees. "Please, don't do this! I am innocent. The eunuch lies!"

He turned his back, leaving his sobbing wife to contemplate her sins. As he strode down the hall, his rage drained, leaving only pain at this ultimate betrayal. He staggered, putting a hand to the wall to hold himself up. Whom could he trust now? Even Bishop Proclus plotted with Pulcheria to thwart his wishes.

"Augustus." Chrysaphius came up beside him. "I know how hard this is for you. Let us go to your chapel, where you can pray. God will soothe your soul."

"Yes. I can trust in God." Theo put a hand to his suddenly throbbing head. "Please, my friend, don't leave me alone. Pray with me?"

"Of course."

The eunuch gave him such a warm and beatific smile, his pain lightened —a little.

### Holding Cells, Imperial Palace

PAULINUS SCREAMED UNTIL HIS THROAT ACHED WITH AS MUCH FIRE AS HIS mangled hand. The screws turned again, crushing his fingers. His eyes were bound. A calm, persistent voice commanded from the darkness "Tell me how you seduced the Augusta and planned the emperor's death."

"I did no such things!" They wanted him to implicate Athenais. He would die first. "Water," he whispered, "please?" He hated the pleading in his voice.

"Tell me how you seduced the Augusta and planned the emperor's death, and you can have water."

"I cannot confess what I have not done!"

A low chuckle came from a corner. "I misjudged this one. I thought him soft. His very intransigence shows his guilt. He loves the woman. He'll never confess."

"Chrysaphius?" Paulinus turned toward the voice. "You son of a whore! You did this! You suggested I give the apple to Theo."

"And you and the Augusta made it so easy." The eunuch laughed. "Say what you want. I write your confession, and you and that Athenian whore are guilty."

*Of course. There will be no justice. There are probably no witnesses other than those the bloody eunuch has bribed. I'm lost, but I will not bring down Athenais.*

Paulinus heard footsteps approaching. A hard hand gripped his jaw. "You and your soft rotten kind always think you can have it your way. You look down on such as me, if you see us at all." Chrysaphius spat in his face. "Not this time." The eunuch let go to address the torturer. "Do what you want with this one, but don't kill him. The Augustus must sign his death warrant."

Paulinus heard the door creak shut. The torturer chuckled. "No more questions then."

Pain shrieked from his hand through his arm to his throat. Paulinus screamed until he fainted into the flickering darkness that must be hell.

He came to, wet and shivering, on a filthy mat of rotten straw, in total darkness. From the stench, either he soiled himself or a previous occupant left their shit behind. He sat and took stock. Each finger of his left hand was crushed and bleeding, the pain almost unbearable. If he didn't get the wounds tended, they would turn gangrenous and kill him.

Cradling his hand against his chest, he stood, limping two paces before bumping into a damp stone wall—the cell barely four by four paces. "Let me talk to the emperor!" He husked through the brass-bound door into the silent dark. "Tell Theo I'm innocent!"

No sounds—not even the rustling of rats—came back. He slumped, back to the door, and laughed hysterically. *What is worse, rotting in this cell or a clean sword stroke? My life is over. It was over the minute I fell in love with an empress— my best friend's wife.*

"Athenais!" Paulinus sobbed. "What is to become of you?"

*Hebdomon Palace, January 444*

Pulcheria paced her workroom in a rare frenzy that prayers could not soothe. Something was desperately wrong with Theo. She feared for him. For the past week, the city roiled with rumors. Dismissed noblewomen from Athenais' court spread throughout the city and suburbs with a dozen different stories, with no way to tell who spoke truth. Theo didn't answer her notes. The discreet servants she sent to talk with the staff at the palace returned empty-handed. General Aspar seemed as much in the dark as she.

"Oh, Theo! What have you done?" she muttered, struggling to bring her scattered feelings under control.

On top of those issues, she worried about her sister. Arcadia seemed pale and listless lately, troubled by a cough and poor sleep. That settled her somewhat. She could do something about Arcadia's health: consult a physician, provide a posset, feed her bracing broth. All she could do for her brother was pray—and that seemed inadequate at the moment.

Before she could grow more agitated, Arcadia knocked softly on the door. "Ria, Basil is here from Bishop Proclus."

Pulcheria whirled toward the door, then took a deep breath. It wouldn't do for the bishop's envoy to see her in such a state. She smoothed her sweaty palms along the sides of her dark blue gown and sat on a padded leather divan. With a final pat to her head covering, she said, "Come in."

Arcadia accompanied Basil into the room. Yes, her sister seemed short of breath. Pulcheria made a mental note to consult a doctor as soon as the envoy left.

Pulcheria did not rise to greet her visitor but indicated a couple of serviceable chairs. "Basil, it is good see you again. I hope the bishop has good news for me."

"Augusta." The Bishop's middle-aged envoy bowed and took a chair. "I'm afraid the palace is in turmoil."

Arcadia poured three goblets of lemon water at a sideboard, served them on a black-lacquered tray, and a took a seat next to Pulcheria. Her sister's quiet attendance and support steadied Pulcheria.

"Tell me what you know."

"The emperor seems to think that his wife and the Master of Offices plotted his murder in order to take the throne for Paulinus."

"I've heard those rumors—among many others. Is there any evidence?" Pulcheria reached for a goblet to sip its sour contents. The taste matched her mood.

"The usual testimony from slaves, gotten by torture. There's a strange story about a miraculous apple that makes no sense."

"Have Athenais and Paulinus been examined by the council?"

"No. Theo forbids it. Both protest their innocence. The Augusta is confined to her rooms with a minimum of servants. It is said she pleads her case most eloquently, citing law and demanding an examination of the evidence against her. The Master of Offices was tortured and supposedly confessed, but when confronted with the document by the emperor's chief legal advisor, he refused to sign, claiming he made no confession. He said the chief eunuch manufactured the evidence and forged the confession."

"Paulinus accuses Chrysaphius?" Pulcheria's gazed turned inward. She tapped her glass goblet with her index finger, pulling together pieces of a puzzle. "I think I see a pattern from the last three years, and the eunuch is at the center."

"Bishop Proclus agrees. He went to the palace to consult with the emperor. The Augustus met with him but was cold and distant in his manner. He informed the bishop he was making the Archimandrite Eutyches his personal spiritual advisor."

Arcadia startled Pulcheria by speaking. She usually kept a silent presence. "Eutyches is a most holy man. Most consider him a worthy successor to our late beloved Dalmatius."

"He also schooled Chrysaphius and personally baptized him." Pulcheria gave her sister a significant look.

Arcadia looked puzzled. "Is this a problem?"

"Not of itself, but it's obvious Chrysaphius is purging Theo's most intimate relationships and replacing them with creatures of his own. First Cyrus of Panopolis, then me, now Athenais, Paulinus, and Proclus." Pulcheria turned back to Basil with a grim frown. "I had thought the Hellenes behind my brother's estrangement. I was wrong. Do we know what's to become of Athenais and Paulinus?"

Basil shook his head. "The Hellene faction has fractured. Some of the oldest families back the Augusta and Paulinus. Others see a shift in power and flock to Chrysaphius for favors and offices." The envoy's face crinkled in a worried frown. "Bishop Proclus asks what you intend to do?"

"Nothing, for now. I have no contact with my brother. It is best to stay out of his way until Chrysaphius feels secure. The eunuch will overreach. My enemies always do. When he falls, I'll be there to pick up the pieces. I just hope they will not be too small to put back together. In the meantime, I and my sisters will continue our charity work. I have built good relationships with the suburban bishops and city holy men. When it is time, they will back me, as will the people of Constantinople."

Basil rose and bowed. "May God be with you and your sisters, Augusta. The bishop will keep you informed."

"Thank Proclus for me. He has been a good friend. I miss his companionship."

After Basil left, Arcadia rose to tidy the room. Bending to clear the goblets, she started coughing.

"Sister, sit!" Pulcheria rose and forced Arcadia back onto the divan. Once the coughing subsided, she offered a drink. "Take this."

Arcadia sipped obediently, then put the goblet aside. "It is nothing, Ria. I'll be fine once I catch my breath."

"You will go to your bed and rest. I'll send for the physician." Pulcheria opened the door and called to a servant. "Take the princess to her bed. See that she drinks a cup of honey and lemon. Oh, and put a warm brick at her feet."

"Ria, there is no need for such fuss!"

"I pray to God you are right, but a little extra rest never hurt anyone. Go sleep, Sister. I'll visit later."

Pulcheria watched the servant assist Arcadia from the room with an increasing concern. Surely it was just a cold coming on? Her sister was only forty-four, just a year younger than she. Pulcheria sighed and returned to her desk to write a note. *I must warn General Aspar. He is the most likely next target of that infernal eunuch!*


*Hebdomon Palace, April 444*

"How is she?" Theo paced in the chamber outside Arcadia's bedroom.

"Sleeping. Marina is with her." Pulcheria washed her hands in a bowl of rose water outside the door. "The doctor says it won't be long. She grows weaker each day, can hardly take a breath." She had not seen Theo since he "gifted" her with the demand she take holy orders. Had it been a whole year?

She searched his face for signs of change. Theo looked no older. In fact, his face exhibited an inner peace. He seemed calm, in control, which only agitated her. She had been dealing with unaccustomed feelings of anger and incipient grief since Arcadia's confinement to her bed. Pulcheria's voice came out colder than intended. "I only left her side because the servant said you were here."

"I couldn't let my sister die without seeing her one last time and giving her my prayers."

His genuine concern softened her. Maybe she could get through about his dangerous eunuch. Chrysaphius was rarely out of Theo's company since Athenais left for permanent residence in Jerusalem and Paulinus retired—under guard—to remote Cappadocia.

Pulcheria had to admit Athenais fought shrewdly during the scandal. Theo reluctantly agreed executing Paulinus would be as much as admitting he believed his wife and best friend had had an affair—something both fiercely denied. She argued the testimony of tortured slaves was insufficient. Her brother did not want to appear the cuckold in front of his court or his people. The clever Hellene even managed to hold onto her rank as Augusta and the trappings of an imperial household while sojourning in Jerusalem. Athenais' minor success didn't change the fact that Theo's intimate circle had fallen one-by-one, as the wily eunuch consolidated power over her brother.

She looked past her brother's shoulder. "Where's Chrysaphius?"

"Dealing with a delegation from the Huns. Attila killed his brother Bleda and now unites the Huns under his banner. We negotiate a new treaty."

"You mean bribe? We already pay seven hundred pounds of gold annually to the extortionists and return all their deserters freely while we pay ten gold solidi a head for our own. They suck the life blood from the empire and will attack when we are weak." Pulcheria regretted her sharp words the minute they left her mouth.

"It is still cheaper than war," Theo snapped; then, in a gentler tone, "Now is not the time, Ria. Our sister is dying."

"You are right, Brother." She slumped into a chair and rubbed her tired eyes. "I've had little sleep these last few days. Please forgive my harsh tone."

He sat beside her, taking her hand. "Will you pray with me for the soul of our sister?"

They dropped to their knees and prayed for several minutes. Her heart calmed. Pulcheria moved another step toward peace with God's plan to take her beloved sister. Arcadia would soon be in the land of grace and the bosom of their Blessed Mary. It was selfish to want to keep her sister at her side, suffering. Theo helped Pulcheria to her feet.

"I'm getting stiff in my old age." She saw the tears in her brother's eyes and clasped him close. "Oh, Theo, I have missed you so!"

They stood, supporting each other in their shared sadness.

Eventually, Theo pushed free of her arms. "What happened, Ria? Why did you disobey me? I wanted only your happiness and thought to free you from your burden of governing."

"I could not take holy orders and leave you to the machinations of your enemies."

"Your old excuse!" Theo stamped his foot. "I cannot think or care for myself!"

Anger flashing so readily in his voice startled Pulcheria. When had her brother become so mercurial?

"Brother," she replied wearily. "Think. I have often said you are too tenderhearted. Time after time, that has proven true. Chrysaphius is a snake in your bosom. He has driven off all who love you. It was he who convinced Athenais to suggest I take holy orders. It was he who arranged the so-called proof of her infidelity with Paulinus, conveniently getting rid of two rivals at once. Who else from your inner circle remain?" She shook her head. "He will attack General Aspar next."

"You wrong him! He serves me loyally and piously." Theo paced, hands behind his back.

"And I did not for thirty years?" Pulcheria stood, fists clenched at her side, the peace she harbored fled in an instant.

"You disobeyed me! Shamed me before the court! How can I expect my subjects to obey if my own sister flouts my authority?"

The physician, a small rotund man with a bristling white beard and bald head, appeared at the sickroom door. "Please, Your Sovereignties. The Lady Arcadia is agitated by your discord. I would not normally presume, but…"

"Of course." Her brother nodded. "May I see her now?"

The doctor stepped aside, opening the door for Theo, leaving Pulcheria with her renewed grief.

"So that was what the snake whispered in his ears," she mumbled. "Like the devil playing on Adam's pride and weakness. When I rebuffed his 'gift', I wounded his heart. When I gave my reasons, I wounded his pride. The wily eunuch fanned the flames of his vanity." Pulcheria shook her head wearily. "Dearest Brother, you said you wanted only my happiness, but didn't consult me. Did it ever occur to you I might be happier serving you and the empire?"

Shadows inched across the room as the sun went down, touching the walls with a rosy hue. Pulcheria's heart felt heavy with the double loss of her sister and her brother. *How will I ever win him back?*

# Chapter 35



*Hebdomon Palace, January 447*

PULCHERIA MOANED IN HER SLEEP, DREAMING OF HER DEAD SISTER. Arcadia grabbed her by the shoulders and shook her, screaming, "Run, Ria! Run!" In the way of dreams, she sensed terrible menace lurking behind her, but her legs wouldn't move. Her heart pounded with fright; her breathing quickened. She woke in the dark of early morning, confused. Nearly three years had passed since she buried her sister. Why did Arcadia haunt her dreams now?

With a start, Pulcheria sat up in bed. Screams and crashes came from other rooms. "Good God, are we under attack?" The Huns had been raiding across the Danube again. Attila threatened to besiege Constantinople if Theo didn't meet his price. Could the barbarians have reached this far without some warning?

As her muzzy thoughts cleared, she realized her bed shook.

*Earthquake!*

She tossed her coverings aside and leapt from bed, only to lose her footing and fall to her knees. The floor shook and rolled like a ship at sea. The water pitcher on the stand next to her bed shuddered, danced to the edge, and plummeted to the floor, breaking into sharp shards, flooding the marble. She crawled away from the puddle; her nightdress soaked from the knees down.

The tremors slowed. She pulled herself erect using the bedstead. The last quake, nine years ago, badly damaged this stone palace. She needed to get herself and the household out of the residence to open land.

"Augusta! Where are you?" A shadowy figure appeared at her door. The voice of her chamberlain quavered with panic.

"I'm here." She stumbled to the open door. The eunuch grabbed her arm. "Marina? The other women?"

"Everyone is fleeing." He threw a wool cloak over her shoulders and pulled her along the hallway. "This way, Mistress!"

Another strong tremor threw them against shivering walls. Pulcheria shouted the prayer to ward off earthquakes, "Holy God, Holy Mighty One, Holy Immortal One, have mercy on us," as they were showered with plaster from the ceiling.

Wails of frightened people rose around her in the dusty dark. She heard her sister's voice joining her prayer. "Holy God, Holy Mighty One, Holy Immortal One, have mercy on us!" Soon the household chanted in unison.

The tremor subsided.

"Everyone out! To the garden!" She coughed as she breathed plaster dust.

Someone lit an oil lamp and waved it in the corridor ahead. "This way!" Its dim light provided a beacon in the murk.

Pulcheria covered her nose and mouth with the hem of her wet nightdress to ease her breathing and stumbled toward the light, her chamberlain at her elbow. She sensed, rather than saw, others crowding the hallway ahead and behind, moving with deliberate haste, but not panic.

She stumbled over a broken vase inside the door, cutting her bare feet. The eunuch pulled her into the fresh air of the garden. She took a deep breath. January cold hit her like a fist in the chest. She shivered—a bone-deep shudder that nearly paralyzed her. Her breath puffed white before her.

"Ria, are you injured?"

Faint starlight revealed her sister. The moon had set hours ago; dawn was still to come. Marina took one elbow while her chamberlain took the other. They sat Pulcheria on a frigid stone bench. The pain in her bleeding feet subsided as cold took away the feeling. Her damp shift lay freezing against thin legs.

"You're wet and chilled!" Marina unwrapped a blanket from her shoulders and tried to put it over Pulcheria's lap. "Take this, Sister."

"No!" Hot shame warmed her cold flesh. Who was this old woman shivering with fright in a cold winter garden? *You are Aelia Pulcheria Augusta! Act like the ruler you are!* She pulled herself together and rose. "I'll warm myself when I know everyone is safe. Chamberlain, light the garden torches. Build fires with wooden benches if you must. Take a census. I want to know that every soul got out of the palace. We'll make a place for the injured around the fountain. Tell the captain to set the watch outside the walls of the palace to guard against looting."

"Yes, Augusta!" The eunuch bustled off with a sense of purpose, armed with directions.

"Sister," she said to Marina, "tear the hem from this cloak and wrap my feet. Then we will tend to our women."

They spent the next hour comforting the frightened household and praying. Most had escaped with only their nightclothes. A few grabbed a cloak or blanket or wore knitted socks against the winter cold. Those with coverings shared with the less fortunate, sometimes huddling two or three together for warmth. Pulcheria sighed with relief when she learned all her court women and servants escaped. Injuries were limited to cuts and bruises. When the tremors subsided, a few brave servants recovered additional blankets, cloaks, and more oil lamps from the palace. Marina and a servant cut blankets into strips to provide rough coverings for the barefoot and stave off frostbite.

As Pulcheria finished binding a young servant's feet, she heard chanting from the direction of the city. It was too far away to make out the words, but the rhythm was familiar. A smile crossed her face. As dawn broke, the people of Constantinople streamed from the city, raising their voices in prayer. "Holy God, Holy Mighty One, Holy Immortal One, have mercy on us."

"Augusta?" The captain of her guards sought her attention. His normally impassive face was streaked with plaster dust. His brows knit in a frown.

"Problems, Captain?"

"Th-the walls, Augusta," he stammered.

Her gaze flickered past his shoulder. "The palace still stands. Are the walls too weak for us to return when the tremors cease?"

"Not your palace, Augusta." He swallowed hard. "The city walls. They are destroyed. Over half the defensive towers are down."

"Good Lord Jesus save us!" Pulcheria reflexively put her hand to her heart. "When Attila gets word, the Huns will attack! Our city will be defenseless."


*Imperial Palace, February 447*

Chrysaphius hurried down the short hall to the emperor's private receiving room, rapidly coming up with recommendations for dealing with his dire news and how he could make the most of this situation. Entering, he was displeased to see Theo and Constantinus, the prefect of the East, huddled over a map of the city. Irritation rippled across his normally impassive features. He would have to have a word with the new Master of Offices about allowing high placed officials to attend the Augustus without his presence.

"Augustus. Prefect." He approached the two and bowed. "I bring grave news."

The two men looked up. Theo looked pale and drawn. "What is it?"

"As we feared, Augustus, the Huns have crossed the Danube and are riding south through Moesia. They are heading for Constantinople."

"Good Lord Protect us!" Theo gasped. "I had not thought Attila would move so quickly. It's been only two weeks since the earthquake."

"Our spies report he had word within days and immediately mustered his troops. His horsemen can move swiftly with no baggage train. Because our walls are down, he leaves his new siege engines behind." Chrysaphius looked grim. "They can be here within weeks."

Theo looked stunned. He indicated the map spread before him, marked with red lines where wall repairs were needed—over seventy percent of its length. "We have barely begun repairs."

"Your Serenity." Constantinus jabbed his finger at the heart of the city. "The people of Constantinople will rally to their own defense. I have a plan I believe will repair the walls in record time."

"An impossible task." Chrysaphius tried to keep the sneer from his voice. "Augustus, we should make plans to move the court, possibly across the channel to Chalcedon. Attila has yet to master ships."

"Sovereignty, I believe that would be a grave mistake." The prefect dropped to his knees, bowing. "The people need to see their leaders in times of peril. You led the populace in prayer and stopped the earthquake. You should not abandon them as this new threat approaches. Let me tell you how this can be averted."

"Rise, Prefect. Show me your plan." Theo offered a hand to help Constantinus off his knees.

The prefect turned back to his map. "This is too big a project to leave to imperial slaves. Three decades ago, it took Anthemius years to build these walls. We need to rebuild in less than three months—two if Attila bypasses other cities to strike at us first. I plan to enlist the help of the hippodrome factions. The free men of the Greens and the Blues are fierce competitors. They will literally move earth to win the honor of being known as the saviors of their city. Between them, I can muster sixteen thousand men to work on the walls."

"What a clever plan!" Theo clapped Constantinus on the back. "Do you think it will work, Chrysaphius?"

The eunuch rubbed his jaw. "It might." His tight smile covered bitter thoughts. *This is what comes of letting high placed officials talk to the emperor without going through him. He could have brought this plan to Theo and claimed it as his own rather than proposing an embarrassing retreat. Blast that Master of Offices!*

"Excellent!" Theo rolled up the map and handed it to Constantinus. "Keep me personally apprised of the progress. Any additional resources you need, ask Chrysaphius."

Dismissed, the prefect bowed low and left the room, offering the eunuch a bland smile as he passed. *Chrysaphius would keep a sharp eye on that man. If Constantinus was in danger of becoming a hero to the city, like his predecessor Cyrus, he would need to start a whispering campaign to undermine him. He was lucky the emperor's pride was so prickly and easily ignited. He had the bitch sister's earlier domination to thank for that. Maybe the Huns would raid the suburbs and take the dried-up old harpy as hostage. That would knock her down a peg or two.*

"Chrys? Have you further news?"

Theo's voice brought him back to the matter at hand. "Augustus, I've come to discuss troop deployments. We need to stop Attila before he reaches our walls." He unrolled his own map, this one of the western provinces. "This is the most likely route Attila will take." He traced a small river flowing north to the Danube, turned east over a mountain pass which led through forests and onto the plains west of Constantinople. "I believe our best option is to combine our forces. The Army of the Emperor's Presence, the field army in Illyricum and the infantry and cavalry based in Marcianopolis, all under General Arnegisclus."

"Not General Aspar?" Theo frowned.

Chrysaphius needed to be subtle. *Aspar was much beloved by the citizens of Constantinople and trusted by the emperor. He still had headquarters in the palace and access to the emperor on demand. This was his opportunity to reduce the general's influence, if not eliminate it.*

"I hesitate to say anything against the general who has served you so faithfully for so many years..." Chrysaphius left the sentence hanging.

"You are not a sycophant, my friend. That is why I value your advice." Theo tapped his foot impatiently. "I depend on you to tell me the truth, even when it is not pleasant."

"Of course, Augustus." He looked at his emperor directly. "I heard rumors recently that Aspar is unhappy about being passed over for consul or appointed Patrician. His pride is such he is turning away from you."

"He is unhappy after all the honors I have heaped on him?" Theo huffed. "The ungrateful wretch!"

"I have heard of no specific plots, but I believe you cannot put your trust in him with an army at his back. Of course, Augustus, you know him best. How has he acted toward you recently?"

"Aspar has been cool. He is only a year older but implies I should listen to him because he has much more experience."

"I believe Pulcheria Augusta was his most vocal champion at court. It is not inconceivable he shares her contempt for your abilities to govern." Chrysaphius let that last statement sink in. "This is an opportunity for you to show your leadership in taking control of this war. Put General Arnegisclus in charge of Aspar's army. Retire the Arian General from the court."

"Who will protect the city if the Huns defeat the combined armies?" Theo's voice trembled.

"I want to bring General Zeno and his army into the city to guard the walls— if Constantinus can finish them in time."

Theo frowned. "Isn't General Zeno a pagan? His band of Isaurians are half-wild, nearly as barbaric as the Huns! Won't they cause havoc in the city?"

"Their deserved reputation for barbarism is for actions against their enemies. They will be formidable foes to the Huns. Zeno will keep them in line while barracked in the city."

"I will think on it." Theo waved his hand. "You are dismissed."

"Of course, Augustus." Chrysaphius took a deep bow. "I will send the orders to General Arnegisclus and consult with you again tomorrow about General Zeno." He left the private audience chamber pleased. The pliant emperor always hesitated a day or two, then took his advice, issuing orders as if they were his own ideas. General Zeno would owe him a considerable fortune for this promotion!

# Chapter 36



*Hebdomon Palace, April 447*

LADIES, HURRY! THE HUNS ARE BUT TWO DAYS' RIDE FROM THE WALLS," Pulcheria urged her retinue. Prefect Constantinus had performed a miracle with the Greens and Blues over the two months since the earthquake. They not only repaired the old walls but added a lower outer wall with defense towers and dug a moat. Constantinople was the best defended city in the empire. The suburbs and hinterlands were not.

At least Theo saw fit to send wagons and horses to bring her people inside the newly repaired city walls. Most wagons had been sent to the front to evacuate the sick and wounded from the disastrous battle of Utus. General Arnegisclus and thousands of Roman soldiers dead. The armies protecting their frontier shattered, leaving the western provinces ripe for ravishing. The only saving grace was the news that the Huns had also taken heavy losses and now suffered with a plague. It had slowed them down, but not defeated them. Word came yesterday Attila was on the march again. Pulcheria and her retinue joined the steady stream of people on the roads heading for safety in the city.

Her women and servants trooped obediently to the wagons and, as each filled, took off for the capital along the Via Egnatia. Pulcheria and Marina were last to leave, with a contingent of guards. Her chamberlain stowed a heavy money chest under the wagon seat and sat beside the driver. The sisters took their places in the enclosed carriage—not as fancy as their former imperial one, but it served them well. Pulcheria pushed back the curtains to see out.

Marina looked back at the stately Hebdomon palace, their home for the past several years, and sighed. "We just finished the repairs from the earthquake. Will the Huns burn it?"

"Probably not. They may loot it, if they get this far. In any case, it is but an earthly abode. We have other palaces in the city." She turned toward the formidable city walls, horizontally striped with white stone and red brick. Her chest swelled with pride for her city and its people. "Prefect Constantinus did well. Attila will not enter Constantinople."

They joined the spate of humanity taking shelter from the barbarians: people carrying bundles on their backs, wagons and carts piled high with worldly possessions. Normally they would use every other gate, as the military had priority for alternate gates and roads. Today, all were thrown open to civilians.

A piercing cry caught Pulcheria's attention. A child sat along the road, clutching a ragged doll, tears streaming down its face. The hustling crowd ignored its piteous cries.

"Stop!" Pulcheria shouted to the wagon driver. She ordered a guard, "Bring the child to me."

"Yes, Augusta." The wagon pulled to the side of the road as best it could. A steady stream of people cursed the stalled wagon for blocking their way. The guard pushed against the surging crowd and eventually came to the child, lifted it to his shoulder, and made his way back. He passed the burden into Pulcheria's waiting hands.

"Thank you. Driver, continue." She settled the child in her lap, doing a quick check to make sure it wasn't injured. The child was a girl, three, maybe four years of age, with dark curly hair and a rough tunic.

"Poor thing." Marina cooed. "She must have fallen off a cart or been left behind accidentally."

"What's your name, child?" Pulcheria asked.

"Ria." The girl stuffed her middle two fingers in her mouth, eyes growing round as sucked on them.

"Why, that's my name!" Pulcheria smiled. "And your mother's?"

She removed her fingers to whisper, "Mama," then promptly popped them back in.

Pulcheria glanced at her sister. "Well, we'll do our best to find your Mama. For now, you're safe with us."

Tears trembled in the child's eyes. She clutched the doll tighter. Her mouth opened for another piercing shriek.

"Do you like sweets?" Marina asked.

The girl nodded.

"I think I have something here." Marina rummaged in her personal bag, shooting a guilty look at her sister. "Here it is." She unwrapped a grape leaf to reveal a sticky date, stuffed with honey and walnuts, and handed it to the child. "I sometimes feel faint when I don't have a little something to eat every couple of hours."

Pulcheria knew the comment was for her benefit, not the child's, and smiled. "I've known of your fondness for sweets since you were little, Sister. No need for embarrassment."

Just then another commotion caught her attention. The crowd milled complaining as a man leading a donkey cart and a frantic woman, pulling two children by the hands, pushed against the flow.

"Ria!" the woman shouted. "Ria! Where are you?" She stopped an older woman hauling a bundle on her back. "My child! Have you seen a child in the road? A little girl, black hair, carrying a doll?"

The old woman shook her head, mumbling something Pulcheria couldn't hear.

"We have her!" the driver shouted, waving at the family.

The woman left her other children with her husband and made her way to the wagon.

"Is she yours?" Pulcheria propped the girl up in the wagon door.

"Mama!" The child wriggled, putting out her arms.

"Oh, thank the Good Lord you found her!" Tears tracked the woman's dusty cheeks. Pulcheria surrendered the child. "I can't thank you enough. Her brother let go of her hand and…and…I didn't know what to do. I feared her trampled." The woman wiped her cheeks, leaving a muddy streak.

"We are glad to be of service and happy you found us." Pulcheria smiled. "Little Ria seems none the worse for her adventure."

The woman looked closely at Pulcheria and the guards in their imperial uniforms. Her eyes grew round. She dropped to her knees, hugging her child to her breast. "Augusta, please forgive me. I didn't recognize you."

"Rise and go with my blessings. Be safe." She handed the woman a couple of coins. "If you have need of more money or shelter, come to my palace and tell the chamberlain you are Ria's mother. I can't let my namesake go hungry, can I?"

"God bless you, Augusta!" The woman bowed and hustled her child back to her family.

Marina watched the family trudging back up the road toward the city with a look of longing.

"Do you regret not having a family, Marina?" Pulcheria asked quietly.

"Yes…and no." Her sister sighed. "If I could have had a normal life, yes, I would have liked a husband and children." She looked directly at Pulcheria. "Imperial princesses are not normal women. I do not regret my vow. I've lived a good life, full of love and service." Marina's gaze shifted back to the teeming crowds headed for the gates. "I've helped thousands of children and will help thousands more."

Pulcheria patted her sister's knee. "I'm glad you are content. You and Arcadia have been my pillars during these years. I couldn't have helped Theo rule without your steadfast support, but often wondered if I did you a disservice in leading you this direction."

"I miss our sister terribly." Tears trembled in Marina's eyes. "When you were busy with the court or the church, she was my main companion."

"I miss her, too." Pulcheria quietly mourned all those she had lost in recent years. "Arcadia, then Bishop Proclus the next year. Bishop Flavian is a fine and holy man, but Proclus was a friend for nearly two decades. So many of my friends are gone. My only consolation is we will all be joined in Heaven when our time on this earthly plain is done."

The hollow sound of hooves on wood told Pulcheria they were on the temporary bridge that crossed the new moat. A shadow from the outer wall gate briefly darkened the windows as they entered the area between the two walls. Pulcheria looked out between the driver and the chamberlain to see the magnificent Golden Gate—a former triumphal arch commemorating her grandfather's victory over the Visigoths—incorporated into the walls. The brass doors fitted in the triple arches glittered like gold. A quadriga of four gilded bronze elephants, flanked by two statues of winged victory, graced the top. Two projecting towers offered defenders ample opportunity to fight off invaders with arrows, rocks, or hot oil.

They passed through the tallest central arch, pulled to the side, and came to a halt. Pulcheria frowned. "Why are we detained?"

"Maybe the streets are too clogged?" Marina peeked out of the window and squeaked, "Oh!" when a man's face appeared.

"My apologies, Princess. I did not mean to give you a fright." The captain of the guards bowed to Marina, then addressed Pulcheria. "Augusta, Constantinus, prefect of the East wishes to offer his regards."

A tall, fair-haired man with a slightly crooked nose and shrewd gray eyes approached the carriage and bowed. "Augusta. My highest regards and good wishes. I am pleased you and your good ladies are safe within our walls."

Pulcheria nodded. "You have done a miraculous job in repairing and augmenting the walls, Prefect. You have my gratitude and esteem."

"Thank you, Augusta."

She caught a satisfied gleam in his eyes before he ducked his head. Pulcheria had an impulse. "Prefect. I wish to see the top of the walls and inspect the preparations for defense."

The smile on the prefect's face changed to surprise, but he made a smooth transition. "Of course, Augusta, I am at your disposal."

Her captain frowned but knew better than to counsel caution. He opened the door and offered a hand. She turned to her sister. "Marina?"

"There is much to do to open our palace and prepare for the coming days. I will continue on with the chamberlain and send the carriage back for you."

"Of course." Pulcheria gave her sister a proud smile. Marina had stepped into Arcadia's place as manager of their households with grace and competence. Her younger sister would see that their empty palace was transformed into a comfortable home for her and their retinue. "I will return for our evening meal and prayers."

"This way, Augusta." Constantinus showed her to the bottom of a steep set of stairs leading to the top of the inner wall. He turned to a well-groomed young man overseeing several workers. "You there! Get a chair for the Augusta, and slaves to carry her to the top!"

"No need, Prefect." Pulcheria put a restraining hand on his arm. "I am perfectly capable of climbing stairs."

"B-But…"

"I will accept a steadying hand, since these stairs have no railing on the outside." She smiled. The prefect took her elbow.

As she ascended, she heard the crowd of workers murmuring below. Soon they started shouting, "Look! It's the Holy One, the Virgin Augusta! She comes to bless the walls and turn back the Huns!" The shouts coalesced into acclamations.

"Bless the Holy One, the Virgin Augusta!"

"The Holy Virgin will save us!"

At the top, Pulcheria took time to catch her breath. She turned to the workers and soldiers below and spread her arms until the crowd quieted. Love and certainty flowed through her. In her strongest voice, she shouted, "May the Good Lord bless these stout walls and the good men who built and defend them. Hold them fast against our enemies. Save our city from the pagan Huns. In the name of God, the Father, His Son Jesus Christ, and the Holy Ghost, Amen."

The men erupted in ecstatic cheers.

"Thank you, Augusta." The prefect shouted in her ear to be heard above the roar of the crowd. "You are a true inspiration to the people."

THE NEXT MORNING, PULCHERIA BUSIED HERSELF AT THE HOSPITAL ATTACHED to the Great Church, preparing for the onslaught of wounded from a battle. She worked in the storeroom, inventorying medicines and bandages. She closed her eyes and sniffed. Lavender, feverfew, and poppy, she identified the herbs by their scents. Shouts and cheers outside startled her.

Marina rushed in to grab Pulcheria in a hug. "Remarkable news, Sister! The Huns have turned aside!"

"What?" Pulcheria pushed Marina back and grabbed her sister's shoulders to look directly into her eyes. "Is this a jape?"

"I swear, it's true, Ria!" Marina's smile nearly cracked her face. "Word arrived just minutes ago. Criers are in the streets. Attila's forces are weakened by a plague sent from God. They turn away from the strong walls of Constantinople and go West."

"Thank the Good Lord!"

"There's more." Marina's eyes twinkled with laughter. "It seems the Holy Virgin Mary herself blessed the walls and protects the city. She was seen walking the ramparts near the Golden Gate."

"The Virgin—?" Pulcheria broke off as her sister doubled over with laughter. "What's so funny about the Holy Virgin protecting us?"

"Oh, Ria. Don't you see?" Marina struggled to get herself under control. "Forgive me. I am a bit mad with relief." She took deep breaths while Pulcheria tapped her foot impatiently. "Did you not walk the ramparts by the Golden

Gate yesterday? Did you not bless the walls? You told me the crowd acclaimed you."

"Yes, but how could they confuse me with the Holy Virgin?"

"You are an impressive woman, Ria." Marina turned sober. "I can easily understand how people at a distance see a commanding, compassionate figure giving blessings and hearing cries of 'Holy Virgin' might make a mistake. It's not the first time you were mistaken for the Holy Mother. Remember when you saved Theo from that assassin?"

"How do you remember? You were little more than a baby!"

"Theo told that story to us so many times, I almost came to believe you *were* the Holy Virgin!"

"Well, I'm not, and it's blasphemous to say so!"

"Sister." Marina sat her down. "I know, and you know, that you are not *the* Holy Virgin. But it does no harm, and may do considerable good, that the people feel they are protected. Let them have their sense of peace." She arched an eyebrow. "You can't say the Holy Mother didn't guide your actions yesterday."

Pulcheria gave a skeptical snort, then thought, *Maybe Marina was right. Perhaps Mary Theotokos did inspire my actions. In any case, I should leave the people with their hopes.*

A sense of relief flooded her. The city was safe—for now.

"Augusta?" Sister Helena stuck her head in the storeroom. "I'm sorry to interrupt. We have a problem."

"What is it?" Pulcheria took her arms from around her sister.

"The plague." Helena's usual calm face was pale and drawn. "A family just came in for help. They all show symptoms: fever, vomiting, and a rash. The father is covered with pus-filled boils."

Pulcheria handed her inventory to Marina. "We'll need more ginger, garlic, and honey."

"I'll see to it, Sister."

# Chapter 37

*Hospital, Constantinople, April 448*

BASIL, WHAT NEWS FROM BISHOP FLAVIAN?" PULCHERIA DRIED HER hands on a cloth. It had been a difficult year, with famine and plague stalking the land. The Huns devastated the provinces south and west of Constantinople, having taken and destroyed over one hundred cities before being turned back at Thermopylae. Dealing with the immense number of sick and homeless strained her physical as well as her financial resources.

Basil looked around the hospital overflowing with refugees and city dwellers alike. "We should talk in private."

She nodded, calling to Sister Helena, "I must consult with the bishop's envoy. May we use your cell?" She led the way to the tiny room Sister Helena used as an office and sleeping place.

Pulcheria sat on the hard, narrow bed. Basil took the wooden chair. "Chrysaphius is stumbling. He now has enemies in the church, the government, and the army."

"I know he alienated Aspar with his elevation of the pagan General Zeno. A clever move to keep Aspar in check, but little good against the Huns." She snorted. "Now we're paying triple the bribe we paid before."

"Zeno is feeling his power after being named Consul. He realizes your brother needs his armies more than he needs Chrysaphius. But it is the eunuch's dealings with the Huns that roils the landowners. He sent an embassy to Attila's court: Maximin and his friend Priscus."

"I know them. Maximin served as tribune in the Persian War." She looked back on that conflict almost with nostalgia. At least the Persians were a civilized enemy.

"Included in that embassy was an envoy from Attila returning home. Our sly eunuch paid the envoy to assassinate his master Attila, but the envoy kept the money and promptly told Attila of the plot. Only because Maximin and Priscus knew nothing did they escape with their lives. Attila demands six thousand pounds of gold in "missed payments" for the insult, in addition to the annual tribute of twenty-one hundred pounds of gold. The people are groaning under increased taxes in a time when their lands are unproductive and trade disrupted. Even the nobles that previously sided with Chrysaphius are not happy." Basil sat back; hands clasped over his small protruding stomach.

"So, the army and the people turn against Chrysaphius. I have heard no whispering against the emperor as a result of his eunuch's schemes. Have you?" Theo would be in danger if the army and the people blamed her brother for the eunuch's actions.

"No, Augusta, but the emperor is causing consternation and confusion in the Church."

"My brother is a most pious man. What could he have possibly done to offend the Church?" Given her estrangement from the court, Pulcheria had little influence with the nobles or the army. The Church was a different matter; she had considerable ability to support her brother or hinder her enemies.

Basil frowned. "Bishop Diascorus of Alexandria—"

"A thoroughly despicable man, even more prone to violence than his predecessor Cyril," Pulcheria interrupted with some heat. She still resented Bishop Cyril's disruption of the Council of Ephesus. If he had left his murderers and bully boys at home, they could have resolved the Nestorian mess in short order. "What does Diascorus have to do with the emperor?"

Basil stifled a sigh and continued, "Bishop Diascorus has renewed his doctrinal feud with the Bishop of Antioch. The emperor seems to be inserting himself—at Chrysaphius' behest—into the controversy. He's taking the side of the Alexandrines that the Incarnate Christ possessed a single nature and that nature was divine. He sent General Zeno to enforce his orders in Antioch, where they preach Christ had a single nature and it was human."

"Good Lord!" Pulcheria jumped up and started to pace. "The dual nature of Christ as both man and God has been settled canon for a century!"

Basil rose.

"Sit! Sit!" She impatiently waved her hands at the envoy, while assessing the implications of her brother's actions. "Did he learn nothing from the Nestorian controversy? He needs to bring both bishops to heel and impose a compromise. Taking one side or the other only contributes to chaos and confusion." She stopped before Basil, fists on hips. "How deeply is my brother committed to this heresy?"

"It seems Eutyches is behind it. A most holy man, much admired by your brother."

"And the man who baptized Chrysaphius." Pulcheria retook her seat on the bed. "The eunuch's godfather would have influence even without being the preeminent archimandrite of Constantinople."

"For now, this conflict is confined to Alexandria and Antioch, but Bishop Flavian fears Eutyches may take to preaching his heresy in Constantinople. Then he would be forced to act against him." Basil clasped his hands, leaning forward. "The divine nature of Christ is quite appealing to the masses: Jesus as God who looks out for you, protects you from demons, and answers prayers. Jesus as the perfect man and a model for all men to follow is less appealing because it requires change in human behavior. It's a doctrinal dilemma that was only papered over by past ecumenical summits."

"I understand the underlying arguments, Basil," Pulcheria answered tartly. She liked the Archbishop's envoy, but occasionally he acted as if she had not studied these conundrums nearly her entire life. Few had her experience in meshing the religious with the political. "Combining the two doctrines with Christ as perfect man and perfect God is the only way to impose order and avoid schisms. Why on earth would the emperor take sides after imposing the compromise in Ephesus?"

She put up a hand to forestall the answer. "I know. Chrysaphius. I suppose our good Bishop Flavian did not shower the greedy eunuch with 'golden eulogies' to buy his favor?"

"Not a *solidus*."

"To think Theo replaced me with that corrupt son of a sewer rat…" Pulcheria sighed. "I swear, my brother becomes more feeble-willed each year."

"Bishop Flavian feels we have a crisis coming. Constantinople has always imposed its will on the other Sees and kept them in check. If the emperor publicly supports Eutyches' heresy, Flavian will have to denounce him. Your brother's actions could fracture the local Church." Basil gave Pulcheria a sharp look. "Flavian wishes to rally the city orthodox. Can he count on your support, Augusta? Even against your brother?"

"Of course. In this, my brother is in error—both doctrinally and politically." Pulcheria gave a tight smile. "I'll work with the Bishop, and anyone else, to bring down the infernal eunuch who leads my brother astray. The suburban bishops and holy men and women will support the orthodox. They will follow where I lead. When the time comes, I'll be ready."

*Church in suburbs of Constantinople, October 449*

PULCHERIA ADMIRED THE BEAUTY OF THE SMALL THEOTOKOS CHURCH ON THE outskirts of Constantinople's suburbs. Carved lotus leaves graced interior pillars. Realistic wall frescoes of the Virgin's life shone under the glow of dozens of candles and lamps. A blue silk robe graced the gilded altar, flanked by elaborate candlesticks.

But she wasn't here to worship.

It had been a fraught two years, trying to oust that infernal eunuch. This meeting should be the beginning of the end. Her women and guards took their places in the nave and prayed, while she accompanied the local bishop to a private room. Two cloaked figures waited there.

Both pushed back their hoods and bowed. The taller one spoke. "Augusta. We are honored you agreed to meet with us. Especially since your sister is so ill."

"General Aspar." She nodded. "Marina suffers from a wasting disease. There is little we can do except pray."

"Be assured, my prayers are with you and the emperor in this time of sorrow." Aspar indicated his companion. "My second-in-command, General Marcian of Thrace. A most capable and discreet man."

"General." Pulcheria acknowledged. Marcian showed the hallmarks of a field military man—deeply tanned face with lines crinkling at the corners of his eyes, straight bearing, and a lean frame used to hard riding and indifferent food.

"Augusta, please sit." Aspar pulled forward a padded chair, then indicated a second. "May I?"

"General, we are old friends. I have always championed your family, despite your unfortunate beliefs. There is no need for formality when we meet in private."

Aspar sat, leaning forward, clasping his hands as if in appeal. "We need you back at the court, Augusta. Your brother needs your steady guiding hand. Several in my acquaintance wish to make that happen. The eunuch has reigned disastrously for ten years. He must fall."

"I agree. I've watched Chrysaphius with ever-mounting alarm. General Zeno revolts and demands the eunuch's dismissal. The Church rips itself apart. Bishops unseated and restored, councils summoned and discredited. Anathemas streak between Rome and Constantinople, Ephesus, and Alexandria. It is more than time, but my brother stands stubbornly behind his choices."

"I was greatly saddened by Bishop Flavian's death."

"A most holy and noble man, and a dear friend." Pulcheria's face hardened. "I heard reports he was abused on his way to exile and died of the poor treatment. That will not stand. His replacement, Bishop Anatolius, espouses the Eutychian heresy. He was ordained by that wretched Bishop Cyril and represented Dioscorus at the Council that deposed Flavian."

"My understanding is that you rally the faithful of Constantinople and its environs?"

"Yes, with the backing of Pope Leo of Rome. He told me he enlisted our relatives in the Ravenna court to appeal to Theo to give up his heresies. Our aunt Placidia and cousin Valentinian—even Theo's daughter Eudoxia— appealed to my brother, pointing out his errors in belief. The effort seems to have come to naught. According to them, the responses they received sounded more like Chrysaphius than my brother. At least they received replies. I have heard nothing from the Augustus." Pulcheria struggled to conceal her pain at the silence. "As he ages, my brother becomes more intolerant of anything resembling disobedience. Chrysaphius feeds his vanity and frames any contrary view as rebellion against the emperor's will."

"All the more reason to bring you back. You were always able to get the best from your brother. I believe the time is ripe, Augusta." A crafty smile spread across Aspar's face. "Zeno and his troops are not popular. They threaten revolt. He espouses the return of paganism! Yet Chrysaphius refuses to recall me to defend the realm."

"You have allies? A plan in place?"

"The nobles will put pressure on your brother to dismiss the eunuch and bring me back. The people of Constantinople and the Church are unhappy over the treatment of their bishop and blame Chrysaphius. You are beloved by the people and respected by the Church. Ask and they will follow you, demanding the eunuch's dismissal and your restoration. We can both be back in power within the year."

"Agreed." Pulcheria had turned fifty the year before and was feeling her age. If she did not move soon, she would never be able to rescue her brother from his follies. She raised an eyebrow. "Now to specifics. Exactly who among the nobles will support this plan?"

It was late in the afternoon before her women were off their knees.

# Chapter 38



*Constantinople, November 449*

THE CHURCH OF THE APOSTLES SHONE WITH IMPERIAL SPLENDOR FOR Marina's funeral. People thronged the streets to mourn the passing of the Virgin Princess, calling blessings on the gentle woman who ministered to the less fortunate, and praising her older sister. Pulcheria stood, shoulders shaking with suppressed sobs, in front of the beautiful porphyry sarcophagus installed in the imperial mausoleum of the church, where nearly all the Eastern imperial family rested. Myriad candles threw flickering shadows across the multi-colored marble floor. The woody-lemony smell of frankincense lingered in the air.

"Dearest Sister!" Pulcheria murmured as she placed a hand on the cold stone. "What will I do without you to brighten my days with a laugh or joke? Times are already too dark, and now your light is gone."

She heard footsteps and turned, startled anyone dared intrude on her mourning. Her brother stood in the doorway, shuffling his feet like a guilty little boy. Pulcheria glared. His face went pale. She turned her back to him, listening as his hesitant steps approached.

"Sister." Theo put a comforting arm around her shoulders. "I'm sorry I couldn't be there at the end."

"She called for you, Theo!" Pulcheria shrugged off his arm. "She wanted to say good-bye and have your blessing. I sent word. Why didn't you come?"

"I didn't receive your message."

"Messages! Three times I wrote. One message going awry I could understand, but three?"

"I swear to you, Ria, I received no word." Grief made his voice hoarse.

"And who do you think responsible for that? Chrysaphius!" She turned back to the sarcophagus. "Your best friend and closest advisor keeps you in seclusion and tells you only what he wants you to hear. What do your other advisors say? Your generals? The bishops and holy men you consult?"

"They all wish me to dismiss Chrysaphius." Theo sighed. "But he has done so much for me, taken my burdens, given me time for prayer and reflection. He opened my heart to the errors in my belief about the nature of Christ and helped me bring the truth to the people."

"Chrysaphius opened your heart?" She grabbed him by the shoulders. "Open your *eyes*, Brother. He does you great harm. Open your *ears*. Don't you hear the people in the streets?" A dull roar lapped at the quiet inside the church. "They denounce Chrysaphius, but still love you. Who has sown discord between us, time and again? The eunuch has stolen your family—kept my correspondence from you and dictated responses to Eudoxia. Your daughter, Theo! How dare he intrude in these sacred relationships?"

"I have been having many doubts lately. General Zeno's revolt frightened me. I regret heartily Bishop Flavian's treatment and death. I pray for forgiveness daily." Her brother stroked the coffin. "I am most angry over this. You must believe me. I would have come."

"I know, Theo. You wouldn't abandon me in this time of sorrow, nor I you." She stood quiet, letting her anger ebb, to be replaced with her abiding love for her brother. She took his hand in both of hers. "It is not your fault. It is his, and only his. You must show the people you are in charge, not Chrysaphius. Rid yourself of this tumor. Cut it from your flesh! Save yourself! If you don't, your people will cut it from you and leave you bleeding."

"How do I do that, Ria, without looking a fool and a lack-wit? I cannot abandon my beliefs. They are rooted in my soul. I truly believe Eutyches is right."

"I don't ask you to abandon your beliefs about Christ and his divinity." She folded him in her arms. "I ask that you dismiss that snake sent from the devil to separate you from your loving family and loyal people. Be the emperor I know you to be. Dismiss Chrysaphius."

"I will." He pulled back, tears sparkling in his eyes. "But I need your help. I don't know who to turn to, who to trust. Please come back to the palace."

"Dearest brother, of course I'll come back." They stood shoulder to shoulder, holding hands, by their sister's coffin. "As always, my life is yours and the empire's."

Imperial Palace, April 450

"Done!" Theo signed the paper with a flourish, grinning at Pulcheria, who sat beside him in the court receiving room. "I've confiscated the last of Chrysaphius' holdings and distributed them to his victims." The courtiers and petitioners clapped their approval of this final act regarding the hated eunuch.

He handed the paper to a scribe, who would send the requisite copies to various government officials to execute. Pulcheria was pleased Theo came back to governing with a will. She had feared the eunuch had neutered her brother by taking over so many of his duties. She feared to find him lazy and uninformed, but Theo proved her wrong—much to her pleasure.

"Good." Pulcheria added, in a tone meant for his ears only, "I still believe you should have signed his death warrant instead of banishing him to that tiny island. He is a traitor who usurped your imperium." Theo's frown gave her pause. She was back in his good graces after ten years of estrangement, but needed to be more diplomatic with her brother, however difficult. Time to change topics. "Have you given any more thought to—"

"Constantius, Envoy from King Attila of the Huns, seeks an audience," the herald announced from the door.

Pulcheria and Theo exchanged glances. Constantius, although Roman, served in Attila's court as his secretary. What could the Hunnish king want? He practically bled the East dry. Another thing Pulcheria wanted to talk to Theo about. It was past time to stop the extortionate payments to that pagan barbarian.

Theo nodded. "Send him in."

A tall Roman entered, dressed in his best court robes, dripping with gold and gems, as required by Attila to affirm the Hun's wealth and status. Pulcheria thought he struck a vulgar figure in contrast to their own more austere dress.

"My Most Noble Lord and Emperor. Augusta." He prostrated himself before the seated siblings.

"Rise and state your business," Theo commanded.

"I have a message from my master, for your eyes only." The envoy handed a sealed packet to Theo.

Theo broke the seal, scanned the message, and handed it to Pulcheria with a grim look.

Pulcheria read the missive with increasing anger and incredulity. She glared at Constantius. "Do you know the contents of this letter?"

"Yes, Augusta."

Pulcheria leaned toward Theo. "I believe this is better discussed privately. There is no need to involve the court in our family business."

"I agree." Theo rose. "Envoy Constantius, follow us."

They left, followed by a wave of whispers and speculative glances, retiring to Pulcheria's favorite room for receiving unwanted guests—an austere space with two tall chairs for Theo and herself but no other furniture. The unadorned marble floor offered no comfort to tired feet or bent knees.

Once seated, Pulcheria hissed at Constantius. "How dare your master demand the Princess Honoria in marriage and half the western realm as dowry. She's to marry Flavius Bassus Herculanus, a Senator and man of impeccable reputation." She threw the paper to the floor. "Attila must be mad."

Theo asked. "What precipitated this extraordinary request?"

"Just before the New Year, My Lord Attila, King of the Huns, received a letter from Honoria Augusta, sister to your co-ruler Valentinian." The envoy's eyes lowered. He extended his hands as if beseeching forgiveness for his unwelcome news. "She asked Attila to intercede on her behalf with her brother to forestall the planned wedding. Evidently, she objects to his choice of a husband and wishes to choose her own. She settled on Attila as the man most likely to deliver her from her brother's tyranny."

"Ridiculous. It must have been a forgery designed to sow discord between your King and the Empire." Theo sneered.

"The message came with the Augusta's signet ring. My Lord Attila believes it is a promise to wed and demands his bride and dowry."

"Why come to me? Attila's business is with my cousin Valentinian."

Constantius bowed to Theo. "You are the senior Emperor. My Lord follows protocol in contacting you first for your permission."

"Plus, we are closer to his lands, and richer," Pulcheria added. "He seeks to squeeze more gold from us, knowing the West has emptied its coffers fighting him and the other barbarians."

"I would not say so, Your Serenity." The Roman kept his face neutral. "I believe he is sincere in his championship of Honoria Augusta."

Pulcheria snorted. "Leave us to our counsel. We will have an answer tomorrow."

Constantius backed out of the room, bowing low.

"I knew that girl was trouble!" Pulcheria flung herself from her chair and started pacing. "Smart, ambitious, and with nothing to occupy her. Placidia should have sent her to me years ago. I would have kept her busy!"

"I heard disturbing rumors last summer that Honoria had an affair with her chamberlain. Placidia and Val issued no statements, but the man was executed. That would account for the sudden engagement, after all these years. Honoria is, what? Thirty-two?"

"Yes. But what are we to do about this ridiculous demand from Attila?" She nudged the letter with her toe.

Theo brooded, chin in hand. "It's Val's mess to clean up. I'll write to Attila and tell him to treat with my cousin. In the meantime, I'll send word to Val, warning him of the demand."

"You should tell our cousin to turn Honoria over to the barbarian. Serves her right for the chaos she's causing. Let her go live in a hut with Attila's other wives."

"I agree, but you know Val can't do that! He and my daughter have no sons. Just as he succeeded his uncle, a boy from Honoria might claim the diadem with the Hunnish armies at his back."

"I know! It's frustrating!" Pulcheria returned to her chair. "Val should execute her for such treason, but that would ensure Attila's invasion. Honoria has put her brother between the devil and the sea. The West has been crumbling for decades. Placidia held it together for a moment, but her children are disasters. I warned her at the wedding, but she would hear nothing against them." Pulcheria slumped in her chair. "We must see to our own defenses. Attila knows where the treasure lies. That's why he approached you first, looking for another bribe. I recommend we deny him any more payments, shore up our own defenses, and deflect Attila to the West. General Aetius and his barbarian troops will hold him off, if anyone can."

"Should we recall General Aspar?"

"Immediately. I was about to talk to you about the good General just as that turncoat Constantius was announced. Send General Zeno and his Isaurians to the front. Bring General Aspar and his troops back to protect the city." At least this latest crisis allowed her to repay Aspar for his steadfast support during her exile.

There was much to be done to repair the damage of the last ten years. Pulcheria looked forward to it.

# PART V

# EMPRESS AT WAR REDUX

# JULY 450 – JULY 453

# Chapter 39



*Imperial Palace, July 450*

PULCHERIA WIPED SWEAT FROM HER BROW AS SHE WALKED IN THE GARDENS. Shady olive trees and cool sea breezes offered some respite from the humid July heat. Theo rode out this morning for a hunt; his first in months, in celebration of good news from General Aspar. Attila and his Huns migrated West, avoiding the Eastern Empire during this raiding season. They were safe, for now. She said a short prayer for her Aunt Placidia and her cousins in Ravenna, hoping their defenses held. Val had stripped his sister Honoria of her rank and held her in close confinement—some said prison—while he negotiated with the Hun.

"Augusta!" A fat eunuch ran across the garden, face red, jowls wobbling.

Pulcheria sighed. She wanted a few moments alone for reflection, but that—it seemed—was not to be.

The servant threw himself at her feet. "The Emperor!" he wheezed.

"What about the Emperor?" Fear sent her heart racing.

"He...he fell from his horse, Augusta. They just brought him back to the palace."

"How serious a fall?" She pulled the man to his feet, grunting. "Speak up! How bad is it?"

"I don't know, Augusta!" he wailed.

She raised her skirts and ran inside. Word spread fast. Servants, courtiers, and guards packed the corridors. All gave way as she rushed to her brother's rooms.

Pulcheria pushed past the crowd inside his door to reach his bed. She whirled and shouted, with a wheezing breath, "Out! All of you!"

The guards used their spears to push the mob back into the corridor, leaving only the doctors, a body servant, and Pulcheria by her brother's bed.

"Stay at the door. Let no one in without my permission." Pulcheria panted from the unaccustomed exercise. She took a deep breath, turned to her brother, and took his hand in hers. "Theo! Brother, it's me."

He didn't look injured: a little pale, with a few scratches on his cheeks and hands. She calmed somewhat, continuing to call softly to her brother. He moaned and opened his eyes. They wandered, fixed on nothing, closed again. Sweat covered his pale face. He breathed rapidly.

She turned to the doctors. "How bad is it? Will he recover?"

The two court physicians cleared their throats, exchanging glances. The elder finally spoke. "He injured his spine in the fall, Augusta."

"Will he walk again?"

"Unlikely."

Pulcheria said, "I've known other injured people from my time working in the hospitals. They can lead productive lives in a chair."

The doctors coughed, shuffling their feet.

Pulcheria felt like a band constrict her chest. "Out with it. Tell me all." She steeled herself.

"He hit his head. We fear other, more extensive, internal injuries."

Her heart missed a beat and her breath caught. She whispered, "Will he live?"

"His injuries are quite severe, Augusta. We fear he bleeds inside, where we cannot help."

"*Will he live?*" she shouted.

"We don't wish you to give up all hope, Augusta, but it is very unlikely."

"What can we do?" She fought back tears. This was not the time to mourn. This was the time to act.

"We have medicines to ease the pain, but they cloud the mind. We've already administered a dose of poppy juice. That's why he doesn't know you. Do you wish us to continue with that treatment?"

"How long does he have?"

They shrugged. "Two days. Maybe more. It depends on how fast he bleeds."

"No more poppy until I've talked with him." She stroked her brother's hand, then turned to the body servant. "Send in priests to pray for his recovery. God does, sometimes, grant miracles."

Pulcheria pushed Theo's thin hair back from his pale forehead, murmuring, "Please God, don't take my brother. His people need him." She choked back a sob. "*I* need him!"

Pulcheria spent that first night and the following day tending her brother, praying for a miracle. The second night, she sat at her brother's bed, raging at her God.

"Good Lord, what have I done that you punish me so? I've dedicated my life to your service and praise your name many times daily. Why take my brother when we have just reconciled?" Her anger burned hot and fast as she struggled with her faith. She believed in a loving God. A God who redeemed mankind after their fall from grace. "Lord, how can you be so cruel?"

The anger burned out, leaving Pulcheria cold and numb; her only feeling a sharp pain in her chest, blocking breath and words. She had never felt such a bone-deep, primal sense of abandonment and loss. Her body convulsed. Arcadia, Marina, and now Theo! Not just her siblings, but her children. She had raised and loved them as if she had given them life.

Pulcheria left Theo's bedside to collapse at his personal altar. "Mary, Mother of God, Holy Virgin, help me!" She curled into a ball, crying, "It hurts!"

Once her sobs subsided, she looked up at the calm face of the Virgin. Her body stopped shaking. The soft brown eyes of the painting seemed to look deep into her own with love and sympathy. Of course, the Holy Mother had experienced wrenching loss and survived. The pain receded to a throbbing wound in Pulcheria's heart. With Mother Mary's help, she could see a path forward. Pulcheria knelt before the cross. The familiar ritual calmed her. The pain did not lessen, but she could put it aside. She prayed.

"Mary, Mother of God, give me the strength to let my brother go to his just reward in heaven. Forgive me for doubting God's will in this and all things. Bless me with the wisdom to carry on his rule."

Pulcheria knelt for hours, offering her pain to the Blessed Virgin, receiving peace and a renewed purpose.

*****

"Augusta."

Pulcheria raised her head from Theo's bed. A priest gently shook her shoulder.

"Augusta, you should go to your rooms and rest. You've had little sleep for two days. We will send word if there are any changes."

"No." She shook the shadows from her tired brain. "I will not leave him."

She waved over a servant. "Bring me the arnica paste and a pail of hot water." Her nose wrinkled at the smell of urine. "And clean bed linen."

With a servant's help, Pulcheria gently rolled her brother to his side so she could change the soiled bed. Yesterday, the doctors objected to her nursing, pointing out she had servants and skilled nurses at her disposal. She replied, "I've tended the bodies of the sick and poor. It is the least I can do for my own brother."

Pulcheria pushed her pain to a dark place to be examined later, as she washed her brother's battered body. He looked so vulnerable naked—a slight, middle-aged man with small pot belly and stringy arms and legs. What happened to the rambunctious boy and athletic youth she had raised with such love? A large purple bruise covered his lower back. Smaller ones, turning green and yellow, dotted his arms and legs. The arnica paste helped the bruising but couldn't mend his broken spine. She checked the lump on the back of his head. It seemed smaller. She massaged Theo's hands and feet. They were so cold nothing seemed to warm them.

"Oh Lord!" she cried as mottled red streaks, crept up his legs—a sign of encroaching death. Her breath came in short gasps as she struggled to maintain her calm demeanor.

"Please God, let him wake. Let him know me, so we can make our peace." She knew many people, shortly before dying, had a brief lucid period and showed some recovery, before succumbing. She prayed that would be so. Pulcheria needed to talk to her brother. After that, she only wanted his suffering to stop.

After tucking blankets around his body and placing a hot brick at his feet, she sat holding her brother's hand, softly singing a nursery song from their childhood.

Theo moaned. His eyes flickered open. "Ria?"

"I'm here." Pulcheria clutched his hand.

"It hurts!" His face convulsed in a grimace. "What happened?"

"You fell from your horse. You're safe now. I'll take care of you."

"My legs!" His eyes flew wide. "I can't feel my legs."

"You injured your back in the fall. There's some swelling and…" her voice caught in her throat. Pulcheria saw fear in his eyes and wished it away. She wanted to lie; tell him he would recover…but she couldn't. "I'm sorry about the pain, but you needed to be awake. Only for a little while. I've brought Bishop Anatolius to comfort you and bear witness to your last wishes."

"L-last wishes?" Theo's grip on her hand strengthened. "I'm going to die?"

"We all die in our time. This is yours, dearest brother."

"I'm not afraid of death, Ria. I go to our Maker." Theo stopped to draw a breath. "But…the pain… I know our Lord Christ suffered greatly…" His eyes pleaded.

"I will take care of it, Theo." She stroked his forehead. "The Bishop is here. I'll be right back."

She waved Anatolius over to pray with Theo.

Pulcheria took the opportunity to use the chamber pot in an anteroom, gulp a goblet of water, and run a comb through her hair. She then conferred with the doctors. "Make me a draught with the poppy juice. I'll give it to the Augustus after the Bishop leaves. I want my brother to die in peace, with no pain."

She returned to Theo's bed with the medicine. "Thank you, Bishop. Please stay a moment." He stationed himself on the other side of the bed. "Theo, what are your wishes for the succession?"

"You, Ria. You must convince the council to let you rule. They will never accept Val…" Theo's eyes wavered, then screwed shut as a spasm of pain racked his body. "I'm…so tired."

"Only a little longer." She grasped his hand and kissed it. Turning to the bishop she pointed to the door. He nodded and retired to the anteroom "Theo, I ask your forgiveness."

"For what, Ria?"

"All my trespasses against you. For doubting your abilities, for causing you pain."

"There is nothing to forgive, Sister. Without you I never would have been emperor. You have been and always will be my rock." Theo grimaced; eyes clouded with pain. "It hurts, Ria."

"The doctors have something for you." Pulcheria held his head up and put a cup to his lips. "Drink what you can."

He took a gulp and choked. "Bitter…"

"It will ease your pain. More?"

He took a few more sips, then shook his head. "I'm sorry…"

"Shhhh." She put a finger to his lips.

"No." He clutched her hand. "Sorry for last ten years…leaving you…now… to rule alone."

"You have nothing to apologize for. You are the Augustus, God's Viceroy on Earth, and my beloved brother." She leaned over, kissed his cheek, and whispered in his ear. "I'll take care of everything. Go in peace."

He looked up at her and smiled. "Know you will." His eyes fluttered shut and breathing slowed.

Early next morning, his breathing stopped.

# Chapter 40



*Imperial Palace, August 450*

PULCHERIA FACED THE FULL COUNCIL IN HER AUGUSTAL REGALIA, TRYING to suppress her towering rage. This Consistory had been the site of so many of her victories: when she took over the council from Anthemius at age fifteen, concluded the Persian War at twenty-two, ordered the heretic Bishop Nestorius banished to barren Petra at thirty-six... She tasted gall at this defeat, in such familiar surroundings. At least she managed to have the scoundrel Chrysaphius executed before the council brought her their odious proposal.

Marriage! They wanted her to subject her body and rule to a man! She shuddered to think of it.

The faces around the ebony table reflected her relationship with them. Her friends blushed with guilt, her enemies hid smirks, those on the fence exhibited neutral looks. She steeled her own roiled emotions behind a chilly mask.

"I'll carefully consider your proposal, gentlemen. You are dismissed." She rose. The men bowed as she exited. At the door she turned, as if in afterthought. "General Aspar. Attend me. I have some questions about Attila's movements."

She led the general to her favorite sitting room, dismissed her women and all but one servant to provide food and drink.

Taking a goblet of wine, Aspar raised an eyebrow. "You have a report of Attila's movements. I can add nothing to it."

"Whose idea is it that I marry?" Pulcheria nearly spat. "My brother is barely cold in his grave. His mourning weeks are not done, and the council 'requires' my marriage. I am a pledged virgin. That is the font of my power with the people and the Church."

"Augusta, you know a woman cannot rule Rome." Aspar spoke with quiet authority.

"I ruled Rome for all but ten of thirty-five years."

"In your brother's name. Women cannot hold magisterial powers, and the emperor is the chief magistrate of the land. The council and the generals reject your nephew Valentinian as sole ruler. They want *you*…with a husband."

"A husband they think they can control, unlike me!" Pulcheria slumped in her chair, feeling every one of her fifty-one years. Did she really want to continue this everlasting battle? Fighting for her place? Theo was dead. She was tired. She rubbed throbbing temples. "I thought, in this perilous time…? For an interim…? Later, I could adopt a suitable male successor, as did the early emperors."

"Augusta, I am one of your oldest friends and allies. If it were possible, I would back you with my armies. It's not. The council, the Church, the people will not follow a woman alone."

"Ungrateful wretches!" Pulcheria brooded. "After all I've done for them. I'd retire to Hebdomon and leave the council to rip this country apart, but I know how much horror the people would suffer. The poor always pay for the follies of the rich and powerful. I cannot abandon them."

"Augusta, we all want you to govern. Choose a husband and do so."

"And who do I choose?" She flung herself out of her chair and paced. "One of the council? It would tear itself apart in jealousy. A rich noble? I have plenty of money. More than I can count, with the legacies of my sisters and brother. I've observed that a taste of power goes to a noble's head. I'd be pushed aside, if not dead within a year. A military man is too used to command and will seek to subjugate me and his fellow generals, which would cause jealousy among the ranks."

"The right military man might not."

"Are you putting yourself forward, General?" Pulcheria smiled. "I might consider you, except you are already married."

"No, Augusta. I would not presume." Aspar laughed. "But I do have a candidate in mind. You've met him. General Marcian."

"Your second in command from Thrace?" She leaned forward. "What recommends him?"

"He has no family but a daughter, and no sponsors at court, so he brings no blood ties or patronage obligations to complicate the marriage. His loyalty is to me, and mine is to you."

"There will be no children. Even if I were capable of bearing, I will not violate my vow of chastity. Any husband must honor that vow."

"This will be a chaste marriage of convenience. You continue to govern… in both your names, satisfying Roman law. He continues in the military. The marriage allows you to settle the succession in the next few years to your satisfaction and avoid a civil war."

"What of General Zeno?" The Isaurian had accumulated much influence since being promoted by Chrysaphius, especially among those who resented being by ruled by a woman.

"I believe he will back Marcian in exchange for some honor or promotion. Consul, perhaps? Or Patrician?"

Pulcheria eyed Aspar speculatively. "You've given a good deal of thought to this, General. Could you not have warned me of the council's plans?"

"I suspected something like this might come up, but not so soon. I thought the council would wait at least until the mourning period was over before making any proposals." Aspar bowed. "I'm sorry, Augusta. My plans are in early stages. I wanted to have something more concrete for you—if the need arose. There will still have be considerable negotiation if you approve of Marcian."

"I will consider it." Her stomach soured, but Pulcheria was a practical woman. The council and the generals would never coalesce behind a rival candidate. She would take advantage of their weakness. If she had to have a husband, at least she would choose for herself. First, she would have to know this man better.


*Hebdomon, September 450*

THE FOLLOWING WEEK, PULCHERIA TRAVELLED TO HER SUBURBAN PALACE IN Hebdomon, supposedly to escape the late summer heat in the city. In reality, she came to secretly meet her prospective husband. If she approved the general, she would negotiate with Zeno and the council. If not? Maybe she could convince the council to let her adopt rather than marry, though she still had no candidate.

Pulcheria waited for Marcian in the apple orchard outside the palace. She rejected the cool white linen robes suggested by her wardrobe servant for the day. White was the color of virgin youth. Instead she chose her favorite dark blue—the color of the Holy Virgin—for the interview.

Guards ringed the orchard. One of her oldest, deafest ladies occupied a nearby chair, dozing in the sun, providing token chaperone duties. Pulcheria plucked a red apple from the branch and bit into the ripe fruit. Sweetness filled her mouth. The heavy scent of fallen ripe apples filled the air, accompanied by the buzzing of bees and wasps feasting on rotting fruit. Pulcheria made a note to reprimand her gardener for not gathering the harvest in time.

"Augusta?"

A male voice startled her. She had heard no steps on the path. Pulcheria turned to greet General Marcian in civilian dress—a simple tunic and traditional toga, edged with gold embroidery. His erect carriage and slightly bowed legs signaled his martial profession. Seven years her senior, with gray-shot light brown hair and hooded green eyes, he seemed in robust health.

She tossed the half-eaten apple aside and wiped her hand on her dark robes. "General." Pulcheria eyed her prospective husband. "Do you know why I asked you here?"

"General Aspar told me." A slow smile stole across Marcian's weathered face. "I did not believe him."

"I understand." She indicated a bench under a further tree. "Come sit, General. It is cooler in the shade."

They settled on the bench. Pulcheria waved over a hovering servant. "Cucumber water? Or do you prefer wine?"

"Water is fine for me, Augusta."

The slave served them, then retreated to a respectful distance.

"Do you not believe Aspar is your friend?" Pulcheria looked at Marcian over her goblet. "Do you believe he would lie to you about such an important matter?"

"Apologies, Augusta. I cast no aspersions on my friend and superior." A slow flush crept up his neck. "My point was, I did not comprehend what could possibly recommend me to you as a husband and emperor."

"It was my brother's deathbed wish. He named you his successor." Pulcheria wanted to see how the man would respond to such a claim.

"Forgive me, Augusta, if I think you misheard, or the emperor was not in his right mind. He barely knew me."

A blunt and honest answer. Pulcheria tried another test. "You may think as you like, as long as you support my words in public."

The smile disappeared from his face. "I am a plain-spoken man and pride myself on my honesty. I value honesty in others. May I speak freely, Augusta?"

She nodded.

"I understand your need, since a woman cannot rule Rome. Nothing about me, or my past, recommends me for this honor. I come from no great family; bring no wealth, prestige or connections. I have no head for statecraft. My heart is with the military. My one great ambition is to serve the empire faithfully."

"All you say perfectly suits my needs," Pulcheria explained. "No one will object. The nobles will be glad I did not choose from one of their opponents' factions. The military has one of their own and will approve, again, because I did not elevate one *magister militum* over the others. Since you have no ambition or inclination to govern, the Church and people keep me as their champion. The empire avoids a civil war of succession."

"I do not feel court life would suit me—the ritual and ceremony." Marcian shuddered.

"All the more reason for you to escape to the troops. An absent martial husband suits me very well." Pulcheria had not thought she would have to persuade the man to marriage. His very reluctance told her Aspar did, indeed, provide the perfect candidate. "Come see the design from the mint for our marriage coin. It's quite ingenious, with Christ between you and me, giving his blessing to our chaste marriage." She pulled a piece of folded parchment from her belt.

"I have no choice in the matter?" Marcian rose and took a soldier's stance, as if receiving orders.

"Not if you truly want to serve the empire. General." She dropped the paper on her lap. "Marcian. I could threaten you with exile and ruin, but I won't. If you truly don't want to serve in this way, I will let you go with my blessings. But I implore you to accept the diadem from my hands. This is the greatest sacrifice you could make for the empire."

Marcian dropped to his knees, bowing. "If it is truly your wish, Augusta, I will serve."

"I have some conditions." She hesitated.

"I would never ask that you break your vow of chastity. I understand this marriage is for reasons of state, not dynasty."

"There's one more."

Marcian looked up, curious.

"It was my legal right, as an unmarried woman, to leave all my wealth and worldly possessions to the poor. As my husband, my estate should go to you. I ask that you honor my current will. As emperor, you will have a private income from imperial lands and factories. You and your daughter will not be left destitute, if I should die before you."

"I will do as you wish." Marcian stood. "I have a condition of my own."

"Yes?" What did he want? Lands? A prestigious marriage for his daughter? All doable…to a degree.

"You have suffered many personal losses over the last few years. I know I cannot take the place of your brother or sisters, but, to the extent you can, I hope you regard me as a friend. I have always admired you, your piety and steadfastness, your cleverness and kindness. I would know the woman behind the Augusta and serve her as well as serve Rome. Do not dismiss me as a figurehead only. Use me as a confidant. I vow to keep your counsel."

Tears prickled the back of her eyes. Since Marina's death, she had no one to confide her most intimate thoughts to. Even during her reconciliation with Theo, she kept many things to herself, fearing to open the newly healed wound in their love.

"I will think on it." Pulcheria hoped she could trust this man. It remained to be seen.

"That is all I ask." Marcian swept her a deep bow. "May I see the mint's design?"

She handed him the drawing.

He frowned. "Doesn't look a thing like you or me!"

Pulcheria laughed at the familiar complaint. Yes, this marriage might work.

# Chapter 41

*Field of Mars, Hebdomon, November 450*

PULCHERIA STOOD, STIFF AND UNCOMFORTABLE, ON THE REVIEWING stand, in her purple silk robes and fur-lined paludamentum. She had vivid memories of the warm summer's day when seven-year-old Theo had been acclaimed Emperor on this very spot. They were seared into her soul, along with the fear of those perilous times when she had no power to protect her brother from his enemies. *Oh, Theo, why did God take you from me so soon? We could have ruled for ten or twenty more years and spared me this humiliation.*

Aspar's army arrayed themselves before her and the council, chanting acclamations for Marcian as their next Augustus. Marcian took the field on a white stallion, followed by a full unit of cavalry. He rode past the triumphal pillar with its equestrian statue of Theo dedicated to their victories over the Persians. For twenty-five years that statue had looked out over the armies of the East.

*Twenty-five years! What happened to us, Theo? I had hoped to die before you, so I would never know another Augustus. Now I'm here to anoint Marcian. Please know, brother, no one can replace you in my heart.*

Pulcheria had no tears on this auspicious day, but little to celebrate, either. General Zeno was named Patrician, and key council members got additional titles and privileges. She had negotiated hard and won all that she asked for, except the most important thing—she was still to marry shortly after she elevated Marcian to the purple.

Her prospective groom rode up to the reviewing stand and saluted her with his sword. The army broke into raucous shouts before settling into prepared chants of "Marcian for Augustus" and "We want only Marcian." He saluted them, letting the thunder of their voices pour over him.

He dismounted to ascend the steps to the reviewing stand. Marcian approached, saying, in a voice loud enough to reach the back of the crowd, "The people, armies, and the Senate of Constantinople acclaim me Augustus."

She came forward, followed by General Aspar, General Zeno, and Bishop Anatolius. "I, Aelia Pulcheria Augusta, do proclaim you Augustus, and accept you as my husband in a chaste marriage blessed by God. With these hands and tokens, I name you Flavius Marcian Augustus." A few people—unaware she would introduce this innovation—gasped but were quickly shushed. No Augusta had ever elevated an Augustus before. In an emergency, the Great Constantine's daughter had elevated an aging soldier to Caesar, but Pulcheria was the first to imbue an emperor with her own imperium.

Zeno stepped forward with the magisterial belt. Pulcheria wrapped it around Marcian's waist, a sour taste in the back of her throat. This belt symbolized the one power the laws of Rome forbade her. Marcian was now chief magistrate in the land. She could not overrule any of his decisions.

Aspar handed her the gold-embroidered paludamentum which she put over Marcian's shoulders, closing the purple cloak with a brilliant amethyst fibula. Pulcheria had to admit, the imperial symbol looked good on his tall spare frame.

Bishop Anatolius came forward with the diadem—the last symbol of Marcian's ascension—on a purple cushion. She lifted the gold band, encrusted with amethysts and pearls, and presented it to the council, then the armies, to shouts and stomping feet. To her surprise, Marcian knelt on one knee and bowed, acknowledging her role in this transfer of power and making it easier for her carry out her duty. Pulcheria tied the band around his graying hair and pulled the tasseled strings forward over his shoulders.

She offered her hand to help Marcian rise, then held his hand aloft, proclaiming, "I present Flavius Marcian Augustus to his people. Blessed be his reign and merciful be his rule."

The armies and the council took up the chants. Soldiers beat their shields. Civilians stomped their feet in time. Pulcheria, remembering the earthquake, wondered if the vibrations would jitter them both off the edge of the stand. They kept their feet.

She shouted in Marcian's ear: "Before we leave for celebrations in the city, we will sign the wedding contract with Aspar and Anatolius as witnesses. Then all will be done."

Marcian nodded. "Thank you, Augusta. I will renew my vow, in front of the Holy Bishop, to respect your chastity and take your advice in all matters."

Pulcheria faced the future with reservations, but renewed hope.

*The Great Church, December 450*

PULCHERIA KNELT BESIDE HER NEW HUSBAND DURING THE SERVICE FOR THE soul of her Aunt Placidia. The Western Augusta had suffered a stroke earlier in the summer and they just received word she had died in late November. Another of her family gone. She had never been close to her aunt, but they shared the bond of governing. She prayed for Placidia's soul. "I hope you found peace, Aunt."

As she and Marcian left the secluded imperial balcony, they accosted General Aspar. "Augusta, Augustus." He bowed.

Pulcheria recognized the grief marking the general's face: dark shadows under eyes red from weeping, a hoarse tone to his voice. She put a comforting hand on his arm. "Aspar, my friend. I had forgotten that you and my aunt were close. Theo and I feared you might wish to move to the Ravenna court after your successful installation of Placidia and her son."

"Your aunt was a great lady. Placidia Augusta inspired many men to her cause. That is how she managed to hold the West together with so many enemies both outside and inside her realm. My only hope for Ravenna is that her son learned from his mother." Aspar's voice dropped as he added, "Placidia Augusta's example is forever cemented in my heart and mind, that a woman could be an able ruler. You benefited from that belief, Augusta. I knew, in your youth, you would succeed, just as your aunt did, and vowed to support you. The Theodosian women rule wisely and fairly. It is only when their men interfere that things go wrong." He looked pointedly at Marcian. "Remember that, Tribune."

"I will, General." Marcian seemed to take no offense at Aspar's use of his former title.

Pulcheria, irritated at the informality, thought she would have to give her new husband some lessons in imperial comportment, as she did her brother when he was young. "I have always valued your friendship and support, General. I did not know I had my aunt to thank for it." Pulcheria allowed a trace of sharpness in her reply.

"Do not mistake me, Augusta." Aspar made a deep bow. "You've earned my respect and support many times over. I am proud of my service to you and your brother. I expect to give similar service to you and the Augustus."

Pulcheria put her hand on Marcian's arm. Their guard surrounded them, and they left the Great Church for their imperial wagon. As they stepped into the weak winter sunlight, the people cried their acclamations.

"I'm not sure I'll ever get used to this." Marcian nodded at people shouting their names and blessings.

Gradually the shouting took on a different tone. From "Blessings and many years to the Augustus and Augusta" it shifted to "Down with the heretic Eutyches!" and "Justice for Bishop Flavian!"

Marcian helped Pulcheria into the carriage for the short trip to the palace and took his place opposite her. "Your doing?" Marcian raised an eyebrow. "I know you've been meeting with Anatolius and some of the suburban bishops this week."

"The people are genuinely angry over Bishop Flavian's death. I spoke with Anatolius about the people's dissatisfaction over the violent means by which he was installed after Theo called that disastrous second Council of Ephesus. I merely pointed out the best way to obtain the people's love and trust was to denounce Eutyches' heresy and embrace orthodoxy."

"And gain your support as well?" Marcian smiled. "I'm just a soldier, my dear, and do not understand the minutiae of these controversies. They seem abstract and of little consequence, but I'm sure you will set me straight."

"These matters of 'little consequence,' as you say, are the root of much unrest in all the cities of the East. The people in the street argue over Christ's nature. They divide into factions as strong and violent as the rivalry between the Blues and the Greens."

"It's that bad?" Marcian sat back in contemplation. "In the army, we have more tolerance. If a man can wield a sword or shoot an arrow, no one asks how or who he worships."

"I know. As much as it has chafed me over the years, I long ago realized how dangerous it would be to purge the armies. I leave them to your care. I will reform the Church. The clergy want an end to the violence and controversy.

Pope Leo of Rome fully supports my positions and urges us both to bring the heretics back to orthodoxy."

She leaned forward, placing a hand on his knee. "I know you will be busy preparing for the Hun invasion massing on our borders, but I face a similar war. It is more than time this controversy over the nature of Christ is settled. I'll have some proclamations for you to sign this week."

"As you wish, Ria."

Pulcheria again praised God and Aspar for finding her such a compliant husband.

# Chapter 42



*Rome, March 451*

Bishop Leo opened his letter from the Eastern Augusta:

*To Our Most Holy Father Leo, Bishop of Rome,*

*We received your epistle with the reverence owed to every bishop. I and my lord, the Most Tranquil Emperor, my Consort, always have and do remain in the same faith, spurning all depravity, all pollution, and all evil. I am pleased to report that Anatolius, the Bishop of Constantinople, installed by violence to replace our Beloved Flavian, has willingly given up his heresies and subscribed to the orthodox Formula of Union you stated in your Tome. By orders of the Emperor, the remains of Flavian are returned to Constantinople and deposited in their rightful place in the Apostles Church. All bishops exiled for supporting Flavian are to return by force of an imperial pragmatic to await judgment of a new general council restoring them to their Sees.*

*The Emperor intends to convene this council in Nicaea on September 1 of this year to complete the work begun there by the venerable council of the Great Constantine. I beg you to instruct the Oriental bishops to gather for that council so that we may bring peace to our people and understanding to the bishops.*

*Your Most Loving and Obedient Daughter*
*Aelia Pulcheria Augusta*

"Ha! I knew Pulcheria could bring those unruly bishops to heel!" Leo's smile faded as he read of the council. "There is no need for another council. Father Joseph—" His clerk looked up from recording expenses from his bishop's last progress. "Come take a letter."

"Of course, Your Holiness." The stoop-shouldered priest brought over his lap desk and writing supplies.

Leo put Pulcheria's letter aside and dictated:

*To my Most Holy Daughter, Aelia Pulcheria Augusta,*

*I give thanks to God when I see how you commit yourself to every concern of the Universal Church, so that whatever I think might contribute to justice and goodwill I confidently suggest to you, expecting that with Christ's help what has been accomplished faultlessly thus far through the zeal of Your Piety might be brought more swiftly to a welcome conclusion, most glorious Augusta.*

*To that point, I believe another council would be difficult to arrange, owing to the invasion of the Huns. The trouble lies principally with Dioscorus of Alexandria and Juvenal of Jerusalem and can easily be settled without a council. The orthodox position is clearly written in my Tome, copies of which have been distributed throughout the realm. It remains only to enforce that position among the bishops in the East. I trust that Your Piety will labor, as is habitual for you, so that the heretical doctrine of Eutyches will be suppressed, and all bishops, like Anatolius, will be returned to the right path of the orthodox church.*

*Your Friend and Father in the Church*
*Leo, Bishop of Rome*

"That should put the problem to rest." Leo dismissed his clerk and turned back to his own untidy worktable. "Now, where did I put that report on the Huns?"

*Imperial Palace, April 451*

PULCHERIA FROWNED AS SHE READ LEO'S LETTER. SHE COULDN'T BLAME THE Pope for his position. All of Italy and Gaul braced for the Hunnic invasion, not knowing which path the barbarians would take. Attila still insisted the western emperor "prepare a palace to receive him" after he claimed Princess Honoria as his bride. Drat the girl! She caused as much death and turmoil as the legendary Helen of Troy. Although, if pressed, Pulcheria would admit Honoria's letter was just an excuse for Attila to do what he planned anyway. She and Marcian had stopped payments to Attila and braced for the onslaught if he turned East rather than West.

She looked across the room to where Marcian studied his maps. She would miss him when he joined his troops to make sure Attila did not turn his attention their way. Little good it would do the pagan king if he invaded the East! He still could not breach their walls, and the lands west and south lay devasted from his last sortie. Attila's most logical move was toward Italy or Gaul, where General Aetius awaited him, but her husband wanted to be in the field, just in case.

Husband! Still such a strange word for her. Over the past five months, Marcian proved as good as his word. He took her lead in all things dealing with the Church and governance, and she took his in all things military. They made good partners. Of course, her enemies started nasty rumors that she gave up her chastity in the marriage—to undermine the power she received from being a pledged virgin. Her agents spread throughout the city, painting over obscene graffiti and countering any scurrilous talk with logic or threats, as the case called for.

"Bad news, Ria?" Marcian looked up from his maps and noticed her frown.

Her husband had proved attuned to her moods and attentive to her needs, whether that be for quiet thought or a receptive ear. His question brought her back to the issue at hand. "Leo feels his position on the dual nature of Christ, as put forward in his Tome, is enough to restore the bishops to their sees, and no council is needed."

"Isn't he right?"

"In a way." Pulcheria put the letter down. "We could declare our support for his position and send generals to enforce it as my brother did in Antioch, but that will not end the matter—even if we had generals to spare. It didn't work then and won't work now. Putting a bandage over an infected wound does not heal it. The infection spreads; eventually you lose the limb, if not the whole body. We must bring the bishops together and cauterize this wound in the church."

"Over the Pope's objections?"

"He does not know the Eastern Church. I do. I've done what I can to persuade Bishop Leo of this necessity. He will not listen. We must act without him. I will encourage him to send legates. After all, we are doing his work."

"What if the bishops decide differently than what you want?"

"That is what Bishop Leo fears, but there will be no repeat of Ephesus. I'll see to that." Pulcheria felt her pulse elevate at the challenge. "God will give me the strength to bring these bishops back to orthodoxy. I'll have the letter commanding the council for you to sign tomorrow."

*Imperial Palace, July 451*

Pulcheria surveyed her troops for the upcoming battle: Aspar, the praetorian prefect of the East, the city prefect, her master of offices, and fifteen more of the most prominent men in eastern Roman society. She gave them their marching orders.

"My imperial husband and consort is called to the front to deal with the cursed Huns. He labors to protect our lands, goods, and bodies from the ravishing barbarians. He leaves us with the sacred duty to protect our souls and that of our people. For three years now, the church is divided, our people confused. Councils summoned and discredited, bishops unseated and restored, violence committed against holy men. This must stop!"

She stood, pounding a fist on the table to emphasize her point, eyes moving from man to man, looking for weakness. They nodded, responding with solemn gazes. Satisfied, she again sat.

"Emperor Marcian has called a council of bishops to review these actions and produce a definitive statement on the nature of Christ. You all know the imperial position. Christ possessed two natures, one human and one divine. As God, he suffered for our sins; as man, he shows us the way to perfectibility. Pope Leo of Rome lays out these arguments in his Tome. You all have copies and will study them before the council."

A scribe passed out copies of the Pope's missive. They riffled through the pages.

The prefect of Bithynia spoke. "Augusta, I'm sorry to report that Bishop Dioscorus of Alexandria plans to disrupt the council at Nicaea and has already begun agitation."

"That is why you are all here, Prefect." Pulcheria had learned much from the disaster at Ephesus and planned every detail of this council. "We are moving the date and place of the council so the emperor may attend the closing ceremonies. We'll now convene in early October in the city of Chalcedon. This location, directly across the strait from our city, has an additional advantage. We will have access to the General's troops and the city prefect's guards to keep order." She turned to the city prefect. "You will eject from the meeting and city all clerics, monks, and lay persons who have no reason to be at the council. Be sure no other troublemakers show up before, during, or after I and the Augustus arrive to conclude the gathering."

She gave him a particularly hard stare. "If anything disrupts this council or impedes its business, you will be held personally responsible by me. Is that understood?"

"Quite, Your Serenity." The prefect looked slightly pale, but calm.

"The rest of you will preside over the council, present the order of business as I have outlined, and call the questions."

"Where will the new council meet in Chalcedon?" Aspar asked.

"In the Basilica of St. Euphemia. It has space to hold six hundred." Pulcheria did not add that she trusted the spirit of the beloved and powerful female saint—a victim of Emperor Diocletian's persecution—to protect the council and guide it to the desired result.

"Any other questions?" She looked around the table. "Good. I expect you all to be in attendance for as long as it takes to achieve the outcomes we've discussed . You'll receive further instructions as needed."

Pulcheria stood. They rose and bowed in unison.


During October, Pulcheria read the daily reports of the council proceedings with more and more satisfaction. The council confirmed and wrote into canon the Chalcedonian Definition that "Christ was established as the possessor of one person with two natures, united unconfusedly, unchangeably, indivisibly and inseparable: perfect God and perfect man."

They deposed the heretics and restored the orthodox to their positions. Bishop Anatolius even went so far as to elevate the See of Constantinople to the first rank of episcopacy, putting it on a par with Rome—over the objections of Pope Leo's legates. A bold move on his part, but Pulcheria felt it warranted. Rome fell once, when she was a child, and the barbarians took her Aunt Placidia hostage. General Aetius had barely fought Attila to a draw in Gaul, with huge losses on both sides. Attila retreated, but for how long? Rome could fall again, leaving the East the sole bastion of Christianity.

The most gratifying part of the reports came in the recording of the bishops' acclamations throughout the proceedings. On two occasions they broke tradition and praised her before Marcian: "The Augusta cast out Nestorius! Many years to the orthodox one! The Augusta believes thus! Thus we all believe!"

*I've spent my life breaking traditions,* she thought, *and I have one more to break.*


*Chalcedon, October 25, 451*

PULCHERIA TOOK A MOMENT TO SAVOR HER VICTORY. SHE STOOD, HAND LIGHTLY touching the arm of her consort, both attired in imperial splendor, before the entrance to St. Euphemia's basilica. Acclamations had already started inside, echoing down the street. No other Augusta had come before such a deliberative body as this ecumenical council, but she would not be denied her due. The healing of the Church was her doing and the people recognized it.

"Many years to the Augusta!" they cried. "There will be peace everywhere! Lord protect those who bring the light of peace, those who lighten the world!"

Marcian smiled at her. "General Aetius may have stopped the Huns, but you have done more for your people than any mere general. You give them peace and hope."

They stepped into the church to shouts: "Marcian is the New Constantine. Pulcheria the New Helena. Her life is the security of all. Her faith is the glory of the church!"

Her people loved her. The nobles did her bidding. The church was restored to orthodoxy. Her heart warred between pride and humility at this, her greatest achievement.

*This I have wrought.*
*With God's help.*

# Epilog

*Constantinople, July 453*

THE SKY MIRRORED THE MOOD OF THE PEOPLE, GRAY AND DREARY, WITH frequent showers. A sturdy woman with graying hair stood along the route to Constantine's mausoleum, clutching the hand of a nine-year-old girl.

"The angels weep for our dear lady." The woman wiped away the tears and rain mixing on her face, then pulled her daughter closer, under a cloak.

Troops of soldiers cleared the way down the wide avenue, pressing the grieving people back under the stoa.

The little girl wriggled out from under the cloak. "I can't see anything, Mama!"

"Stay close, Ria. I don't want to lose you. When she comes, I'll lift you up on my shoulders."

The woman watched a seemingly endless stream of holy men and women process, carrying censers and chanting prayers. She couldn't see them directly over the heads of the crowd, but she heard their voices. The sweet scent of incense warred with the smell of wet wool and unwashed bodies.

"Why is everyone so sad, Mama?" The little girl looked around her with wide eyes at the adults crying.

"The Augusta was a great lady, child. She fed the poor and tended the sick, when she could have stayed in a warm palace and eaten her fill. She didn't have to get her hands dirty, but she did, because she loved her people and gave her life for them." The woman clasped her child closer. "I named you after her. She saved your life, Ria, and helped our family start the shop."

The little girl eyed her fingers. Bored by a story told frequently in her home, she wanted to put the middle two in her mouth but knew her mother would slap them out. She sighed, cuddling closer. There was little to do but bear the tedium and try to stay dry.

Anticipation rippled through the crowd.

"I see it!" someone shouted. Chants started to coalesce. "God's peace for the soul of the most pious Aelia Pulcheria Augusta, most beloved by her people."

As the cortege got closer, the woman made out the wagon carrying the plain porphyry sarcophagus, pulled by a matched team of four black horses, caparisoned in purple and gold. The coffin rested on purple silk, protected from the rain by a gold tasseled awning.

"Now, Ria!" She struggled to lift her daughter to her shoulders. "Can you see now?"

"Yes!"

The rain let up briefly. A stray ray of sun shone through, lingering only long enough to accompany the cortege past the woman and girl, before disappearing in a light drizzle.

"The emperor follows, Mama!"

The woman trembled. "You'll have to come down now. I can't hold you longer." She leaned over. Her daughter jumped off her shoulders.

Flavius Marcian Augustus, in his purple cloak and gold diadem, followed his wife's sarcophagus on a black stallion, looking grim and sad. Almoners followed, throwing coins into the crowd. The little girl scrambled to pick up a few brass coins. Her mother stood straight, watching the wagon until it was gone from view, an ache in her heart, tears streaming down her face at the loss of her beloved empress.

# Enjoyed this book?

I'd love a review of *Dawn Empress*. Please leave your feedback at your favorite book review sharing site. No need for a literary critique—just a couple of sentences on what you liked/didn't like and why. Reviews can be tough to come by these days and having them (or not) can make or break a book. So, I hope you share your opinion with others. If you review at Amazon, scan the QR code to go directly to the review page.

## Thank you!

# Author's Note

I FELL IN LOVE WITH THE THEODOSIAN WOMEN—PULCHERIA, ATHENAIS, AND Placidia—many years ago, when writing my first book, *Selene of Alexandria*, which featured a fictional student of the historical Hypatia, Lady Philosopher of Alexandria. While researching the life and times of Hypatia, I kept running across these great women who ruled the failing Western Roman Empire and set the stage for the rise of the Byzantine Empire in the East.

It wasn't just the dry fact of their power; they each had compelling human stories. Pulcheria outwitted the Constantinople court worthies to claim sole regency over her brother and the empire at the tender age of fifteen. Athenais, the beautiful but impoverished daughter of a pagan Athenian scholar, captured the heart of a Most Christian Emperor. Placidia, held the crumbling Western Roman Empire together for her under-aged son. Why hadn't I heard of these women before?

I originally planned a single book, telling their intertwining stories, but soon found I had far too much material. Each woman deserved her own story. This is the second in a set of three books about the Theodosian women. *Twilight Empress* (Book One), about Placidia, came out in 2017. *Rebel Empress* (Book Three), featuring Athenais is out in 2024. They can be read as stand alone novels.

Throughout the series I attempt to stay close to known historical facts. Dates for wars, births, deaths, Church convocations, etc. are generally known. Quoted letters and sermons are shortened and the language somewhat modernized, but they come from primary sources. However, the fifth century was a notoriously chaotic time, as the Roman Empire reeled under repeated attacks by barbarians and failed leadership over the course of several decades. Primary sources are scant, lean heavily toward Church documents rather than secular historians, and are sometimes contradictory. Primary historians discussed Theodosius II's paternity settling on a mysterious "Count John" as their favorite candidate for baby daddy. Did Arcadius know or believe his wife unfaithful? Was she? We have no way of knowing. Modern scholars occasionally interpret the primary sources differently. Where there is disagreement, I chose the interpretation that best suited my story.

Most of the fun personal incidents used to color this story are attested to and accepted by most people as true. Pulcheria most likely tricked Theodosius into selling his wife to her as a slave. The army probably discovered three protective silver statues at the Hunnish border and demanded their return. Honoria did send a ring to Attila the Hun and ask for his "protection."

But did King Gaeseric of the Vandals tell Marcian he would be Emperor? Did the Virgin Mary save young Theodosius from assassination and protect the walls of Constantinople prior to Attila's invasion? Those stories, along with "the Golden Apple of Discord" that brought about Athenais' downfall, are likely apocryphal. Where the Virgin Mary appeared, I created less miraculous source material for the story, substituting Pulcheria for the Virgin Mary in a way that the legend could grow from the facts. There is no historical basis for that substitution—just artistic license.

I left the "Golden Apple of Discord" pretty much as told, because it tickled me. Most historians consider the story apocryphal because variations exist in several histories about other people. There was even one in which Theodosius presented the apple to Pulcheria and she sent it to her lover Marcian, whom she would shortly marry and raise to be Emperor. That version shows up as one of the "vicious rumors and graffiti" Pulcheria fought against after her marriage to Marcian.

A popular story—sometimes repeated as history—is a sweet romance telling how Athenais met Theodosius. Supposedly, when her father died, he left his money to his sons and told the beautiful Athenais her face would be her fortune. She sued her brothers for her share of the inheritance taking her complaint to the imperial court, where Pulcheria heard her argue so eloquently she thought the girl a fit consort for her brother. Pulcheria introduced Athenais to Theodosius; they fell in love and married shortly after. Given the politics of the times and the animosity between the two women, most historians believe this story is a fable circulated for the masses. This is another case where I took literary license to fill in the unknown with a more likely political motivation and outcome. How close I came to truth is unknowable.

Because I covered nearly fifty years in the book, I necessarily limited the number of historical characters. Anthemius and his son Isidorus stand in for a multitude of courtiers of the "Hellene" faction in the ever-changing world of politics. Likewise, General Ardaburius and his son General Aspar represent the military. They were both at all the battles where I placed them and earned all the honors I gave them but their personal and political relationships with the imperial family are unknown.

My biggest challenge was simplifying the early Church battles over doctrine. What was to become the Catholic Church (and later the Eastern Orthodox Church in Byzantium) was in its infancy but gaining enormous political power. Six different archbishops served in Constantinople during Placidia's political life with hundreds of others in sees across the Eastern empire. Philosophical differences over the meaning of a single word from much copied/translated early gospels sprouted into internecine religious warfare, resulting in accusations of heresy, ecumenical trials, excommunications, and frequently violence and riots among the faithful. I sympathized with a ruler's impatience with such turmoil and the need to impose their will on the Church to have peace in the land. Both Constantine the Great and Pulcheria Augusta influenced the early direction of Christianity in profound ways. But those struggles don't always make for fun reading, so please forgive me for losing the nuance in very complicated religious controversies.

History has generally treated Pulcheria more kindly than her Aunt Placidia (*Twilight Empress*), who ruled in the failing West. Primary sources (mostly churchmen) admired Pulcheria's asceticism and good works. They considered Pulcheria an excellent role model of a Christian woman and ruler and found Placidia's more conventional secular rule less satisfactory. They particularly lauded Pulcheria for her efforts to enforce orthodoxy and rout out heresies at the Councils of Ephesus and Chalcedon. Aelia Pulcheria Augusta is recognized as a saint by both the Catholic and Eastern Orthodox Churches.

It's the novelist's job to create interesting characters that would plausibly do the things that history says they did. I wanted to go beyond the halo awarded Pulcheria. Even saints have flaws and make mistakes. Her religiosity—

considered extreme in our modern Western world, where religious fanaticism is usually feared—makes it difficult for some people to sympathize with Pulcheria. After much study, I saw a fierce and brilliant woman, scarred by a lonely, frightening childhood, who used the levers of power available to her in a time when women—even imperial women—had little power over their lives.

Pulcheria secured her brother's reign, insured her own and her sister's independence, and cared for her people with her own sweat and riches. She put her stamp on the early Christian Church, influencing its direction more than any other woman (and most men) for centuries before and after. Her fusion of government and Church signaled the dawn of the Byzantine Empire, which continued for a thousand years after the "fall" of Western Rome. I hope I humanized Aelia Pulcheria Augusta: a fascinating woman, empress, saint, and worthy member of the formidable Theodosian Women.

Finally, if you'd like my free eBook *Angel of the Marshes*, (set in the Theodosian Women series) please join my monthly newsletter by scanning the QR code below. I generally talk about history, my writing progress, rescue cats, and garden...as well as provide links to free and discounted books by authors I think you might enjoy. Of course, you can unsubscribe at any time. *Angel* tells the backstory of the character that helped Placidia take back Ravenna in a bloodless coup featured in *Twilight Empress*. Primary writers of the time said, "The Lord sent an angel to guide her armies through the marshes." Was he an angel? Or more of a scamp?

## Thank you for reading *Dawn Empress.*

*Faith L. Justice*

# Glossary

*adventus*—originally a ceremony in which an emperor was formally welcomed into a city either during a progress or after a military campaign; adapted as a ceremony to formally welcome religious relics such as saints' bones to a new city/resting place

*agentes in rebus*—imperial spy and messenger network controlled by the Master of Offices

**Alans**—an Iranian nomadic pastoral people; when the Huns invaded their ancestral lands, north of the Black Sea, many of the Alans migrated westwards, along with various Germanic tribes; they settled in the Iberian Peninsula and helped the Vandals invade North Africa in AD 428

*Amores*—Ovid's first completed book of poetry; written in elegiac couplets (first used by the Greeks for funeral epigrams), it set the standard for erotic poetry; first published in 16 BC

**Arian Heresy**—a non-trinitarian Christian sect that believed Jesus Christ to be the Son of God, created by God the Father, distinct from the Father and therefore subordinate to the Father; named after Arius (c. AD 250–336), a Christian presbyter in Alexandria, Egypt; many of the barbarian tribes were converted to Christianity by Arian missionaries under the Arian Emperors Constantius II (337–361) and Valens (364–378); the Council of Nicaea of 325 declared Arius a heretic, but he was exonerated, then denounced again at the Ecumenical First Council of Constantinople of 381

**archimandrite**—a title of honor, with no connection to any actual monastery, bestowed on clergy as a mark of respect or gratitude for service to the Church

*bigae*—two-horse chariots

*casula*—a priest's large poncho-like garment covering ordinary clothing at mass; developed from the ordinary Roman attire of a farmer, who wore the large poncho as protection from the elements; associated with Christians starting in the 3rd century

*comes rerum privatarum*—person who administered the estates and managed the private revenues of the emperor; similar to Minister of the Privy Purse in later monarchies

*comes sacrarum largitionum*—head of the office that collected taxes and duties, supervised the mints and other imperial workshops and paid out salaries and donatives to civil servants and troops

**consistory**—the anglicized form of *sacrum consistorium* (sacred assembly), a council of the closest advisors of the Roman emperors from the time of Constantine the Great; also, the room where the council meets

**constitution**—formal law or commandment signed and approved by the Roman Emperor

**diadem**—"band" or "fillet"; originally, in Greece, an embroidered white silk ribbon, ending in a knot and two fringed strips often draped over the shoulders, that surrounded the head of the king to denote his authority; later made of precious metals and decorated with gems; evolved into the modern crown

*fibula* (singular), *fibulae* (plural)—an ornamental clasp designed to hold clothing together; usually made of silver or gold, sometimes bronze or some other material; used by Greeks, Romans, and Celts

*forum* (singular), *fora* (plural)—a rectangular plaza surrounded by important government buildings at the center of the city; the site of triumphal processions and elections; the venue for public speeches, criminal trials, and gladiatorial matches; the nucleus of commercial affairs

*garum*—a fermented fish sauce used as a condiment in the cuisines of ancient Greece, Rome, Carthage and, later, Byzantium

**Gaul**—a region of Western Europe inhabited by Celtic tribes, encompassing present day France, Luxembourg, Belgium, most of Switzerland, parts of Northern Italy, as well as those parts of the Netherlands and Germany on the west bank of the Rhine; Rome divided it into three parts: Gallia Celtica, Belgica and Aquitania

**Hagia Sophia, Church of**—the second church on that site, next to the imperial palace; ordered by Theodosius II, who inaugurated it in 415; a basilica with a wooden roof, built by architect Rufinus; a fire burned it to the ground in 532

**hippodrome**—an arena for chariot races and other entertainment; the U-shaped Hippodrome of Constantine was about 450 m (1,476 ft) long and 130 m (427 ft) wide; its stands could hold 100,000 spectators

**Goths**—an early Germanic people, possibly originating in southern Sweden; mentioned by Roman authors as living in northern Poland in the 1st century AD; in later centuries they expanded towards the Black Sea, where they replaced the Sarmatians as the dominant power on the Pontic Steppe and launched a series expeditions against the Roman Empire

**Hebdomon**—a seaside retreat outside Constantinople where emperors built palaces and two churches; emperors were acclaimed by the army on the Field of Mars there; the imperial court came often to attend military parades and welcome the emperor returning from campaigns

**Huns**—a nomadic group of people who lived in Eastern Europe, the Caucasus, and Central Asia between the 1st and 7th centuries AD; may have stimulated the Great Migration, a contributing factor in the collapse of the Western Roman Empire; they formed a unified empire under Attila the Hun, who died in 453; their empire broke up the following year

***imperium***—"power to command"; a man with imperium, in principle, had absolute authority to apply the law within the scope of his magistracy; he could be vetoed or overruled by a colleague with equal power (e.g., a fellow consul) or by one whose imperium outranked his

***kithara***—seven-stringed instrument of the lyre family; ***kitharode***—kithara player

***latrones (a.k.a. ludus latrunculorum or latrunculin)***—"the game of brigands", a two-player strategy board game played throughout the Roman Empire resembling chess or draughts; generally accepted to be a game of military tactics

***magister militum***—"Master of the Soldiers"; a top-level military command used in the late Roman Empire, referring to a senior military officer, equivalent to a modern war theater commander

*magister utriusque militia*—"Master of both branches of the soldiery"; the highest rank a general can achieve

**Mary** *Theotokos*—Mary, Mother of God

*nobilissima puella, nobilissimus puer*—"Most Noble Girl/Boy"; title conferred on imperial children by a sitting Augustus, before given a higher title

*paludamentum*—the purple military cloak used only by Emperors and Empresses, who were often portrayed wearing it in their statues and on their coinage; originally a cloak or cape fastened at one shoulder, worn by military commanders

*parabalans*—"persons who risk their lives as nurses"; members of a brotherhood who, in early Christianity, voluntarily undertook care of the sick and burial of the dead, knowing they too could die; generally drawn from the lower strata of society, they also functioned as attendants to local bishops; sometimes used by them as bodyguards and in violent clashes with their opponents

*pater familias* (singular), *patres familias* (plural)—"father of the family" or the "owner of the family estate"; traditionally the oldest living male in a family; he held legal rights over family property, and varying levels of authority over his dependents: wife, children, certain other relatives through blood or adoption, clients, freedmen, and slaves. In theory, he held powers of life and death over every member of his extended family, but in practice, this right was limited by law

**Patrician**—a personal title which conferred on the person to whom it was granted a very high rank and certain privileges; it was given to such men as had for a long time distinguished themselves by good and faithful services to the empire or the emperor

**porphyry**—from Ancient Greek, means "purple," the color of royalty; "imperial porphyry" was a deep purple igneous rock

**praetorian prefect**—the chief minister of territories (city, province, etc.), equivalent to mayors in cities and governors in provinces

*quadriga* (singular), *quadrigae* (plural)—four-horse chariot

**sarcophagus**—a box-like funeral receptacle for a corpse, most carved in stone, and usually displayed above ground, though it may also be buried

*scholae*—an elite troop of soldiers in the Roman army created by Emperor Constantine the Great to provide personal protection of the emperor and his immediate family

*siliqua* (singular), *siliquae* (plural)—the modern name given to small, thin, Roman silver coins produced in the 4th century A.D. and later; a term of convenience, as no name for these coins is indicated by contemporary sources; when the coins were in circulation, the Latin word *siliqua* was a unit of weight defined by one late Roman writer as one twenty-fourth of the weight of a Roman *solidus*

*Solidus* (singular), *solidi* (plural)—a gold coin introduced by Emperor Diocletian in 301 as a replacement for the *aureus*; entered widespread circulation under Constantine I after 312

*spatha*—a type of straight long sword, measuring between 0.75 and 1 m (29.5 and 39.4 in), with a handle length between 18 and 20 cm (7.1 and 7.9 in), in use in the Roman Empire during the 1st to 6th centuries AD

*spina*—a row of obelisks, statues and art decorating the middle of the hippodrome, around which charioteers raced

*stola*—a long, pleated dress, worn over a tunic, generally sleeveless, fastened by clasps at the shoulder called *fibulae,* usually made of fabrics like silk, linen or wool, worn as a symbol representing a Roman woman's marital status

**stylite**—a type of Christian ascetic who lived on pillars, preaching, fasting and praying; they believed mortification of their bodies would help ensure salvation of their souls

**tisane**—herbal teas; beverages made from the infusion or decoction of herbs, spices, or other plant material in hot water.

**Vandals**—an East Germanic tribe, or group of tribes, believed to have migrated from southern Scandinavia to the area between the lower Oder and Vistula rivers during the 2nd century BC; pushed westwards by the Huns, they crossed the Rhine into Gaul along with other tribes in AD 406; in 409, the Vandals crossed the Pyrenees into the Iberian Peninsula; in 429, under King Gaiseric, the Vandals entered North Africa; by 439 they had established a kingdom which included the Roman province of Africa as well as Sicily, Corsica, Sardinia, Malta and the Balearic Islands; they fended off several Roman attempts to recapture the African province and sacked the city of Rome in 455

*vigiles* or *vigiles urbani*—"watchmen of the city"; firefighters and police of Roman cities; usually made up of freemen and paid by the city

# Acknowledgments

It has been my pleasure to write this story and bring these characters and this time to life. Among the many people who helped and encouraged me, I want to particularly thank my beta readers for providing insightful feedback: Loretta Goldberg, Gordon Linzner, Roy Post, Mary Ann Trail, Susan Wands, Hanson Wong, and Lisa Yarde. They spent a significant amount of time and effort to make this a better book, and I can't thank them enough for their help. Special and loving thanks go to my husband Gordon for supporting me in countless ways, and to my daughter Hannah, who grew up sharing me with my writing career and showing no sibling rivalry whatsoever.

No historical fiction acknowledgment would be complete without thanks to the many librarians and collections that tirelessly answer questions and find obscure documents. My special thanks go to the New York Public Library—a world class institution. I consulted dozens of books and hundreds of articles but relied most heavily on the research of Kenneth G. Holum from his *Theodosian Empresses: Women and Imperial Dominion in Late Antiquity* and Ada B. Teetgen's *The Life and Times of Empress Pulcheria AD 399 to AD 452*. A bibliography of the most useful works can be found on my website (faithljustice.com).

Although I tried to get it right, no one is perfect. If the gentle reader should find errors in the book, please know they are my own and not those of my sources.

Again, thanks to all who helped make this book possible, with special thanks to those of you who read it and share it in the future.

# About the Author

FAITH L. JUSTICE WRITES AWARD-WINNING FICTION AND ARTICLES IN Brooklyn, New York. Her work appears in such publications as *Salon.com*, *Writer's Digest*, and *The Copperfield Review*. She is past Chair of the New York City Chapter of the Historical Novel Society and is an Associate Editor for *Space and Time Magazine*. She co-founded a writers' workshop many more years ago than she cares to admit to. For fun, Faith likes to dig in the dirt—both her garden and various archaeological sites. Sample her work, check out her blog, or ask her a question at her website (scan the QR code below). She loves to hear from readers.

Connect with Faith online:

Website/Blog: www.faithljustice.com
Twitter: https://twitter.com/faithljustice
Facebook: https://www.facebook.com/faithljusticeauthor/
Instagram: https://www.instagram.com/fljusticeauthor

## Book 1:

### *Twilight Empress: A Novel of Imperial Rome*

**She lives in the shadows of incapable men. With a sharp mind and ambitious drive, can she direct the destiny of millions?**

Rome, AD 410. Princess Placidia knows her duty. Well-loved and respected, the stalwart woman fights to protect her people from invaders despite her brother's inept rule. When conspirators open the gates to the barbarians, the courageous royal refuses to quail as she's taken captive.

Abandoned to her captor's mercies when her sibling declines to negotiate, the determined survivor slowly grows close to the enemy general and his motherless children. And though she weds the rugged Visigoth for love, Placidia fears a jealous rival and the emperor's incompetence may bring her happiness crashing to earth.

With central authority crumbling and loyalties splintering across the West, can one woman hold together an empire?

In this sweeping epic of fifth-century politics, author Faith L. Justice tells the compelling story of one of the Classical world's most influential women. From her capture during the Sack of Rome through her rise to power as regent for her son, last of the Theodosian emperors, readers will thrill to Placidia's tenacious drive to protect those she loves and shape the course of history.

*Twilight Empress* is the enthralling first book in the Theodosian Women historical fiction series. If you like real-world heroines, impeccable research, and gripping glimpses into the past, then you'll love Faith L. Justice's war-torn saga.

Available wherever books are sold or inquire at your local library. Scan the QR code to buy direct from the publisher:

Raggedy Moon Books

raggedymoonbooks.com